PRAISE FOR THE NOVELS OF

kayla perrin

"[A] writer that everyone should read."
—Eric Jerome Dickey

"…[a] fun diversion."
—*Publishers Weekly* on *Gimme an O!*

"This is not just a story of female bonding
and friendship but a skillfully written combination
of romance and mystery."
—*Booklist* on *The Sisters of Theta Phi Kappa*

"…a delicious cocktail with a lot of zing…
secrets, lies and alibis."
—*Essence* on *The Sisters of Theta Phi Kappa*

"…start this book early in the day—this one
won't rest on your nightstand until it is finished!"
—*Romantic Times BOOKclub* on *If You Want Me*

"Kayla Perrin has her finger on the pulse
of male/female relationships and she does
an excellent job of examining it."
—*Literary Times* on *Again, My Love*

"This is a story you will read in one sitting. Superb!!"
—*Rendezvous* on *Everlasting Love*

"The character development is stellar…[it]
enthralls to the last page."
—*Romantic Times BOOKclub* on *The Delta Sisters*

Getting Even

kayla perrin

Spice

Spice

GETTING EVEN

ISBN 0-373-60507-2

Copyright © 2006 by Kayla Perrin.

www.Spice-Books.com

Printed in U.S.A.

This one's for my single friends—some divorced, some never married. Mary and Marissa in Atlanta, Nicole in Hamilton and Allette in Toronto—to name a few. Keep standing proud and never settle for less than you deserve!

And it's also for you—my loyal readers. In particular, this is for my readers who have given their hearts in love, and had them trampled on in a serious way. I know how much that hurts, that the pain can be overwhelming.

Sometimes the only thing that makes you feel better is the thought of revenge. Often tricky to execute in real life, but in fiction everything's game. So if you've had your heart broken (especially in a low-down, dirty way), here's a little vicarious revenge to help ease the pain—to make you laugh, and perhaps cry, but most of all to help you realize that life without the jerk is oh, so much better.

Trust me, I know.

Now, enjoy!

FOOL FOR LOVE

Chapter One

Claudia

They say the way to a man's heart is through his stomach, but if you ask me, that's a load of bull. Hands down, that gold-lined path travels through his libido.

I should know. Right now, I'm practically dying of embarrassment as I sit in a north Atlanta restaurant with the man of my dreams, Adam Hart. I'm trying to look nonchalant beside him in our booth, sipping a margarita through a straw, while Adam has his hand between my legs. His fingers tickle my skin as they inch farther up my thighs.

"Adam," I admonish playfully as his fingers skirt my panties. "I'm trying to have a serious conversation."

"Don't I look serious to you?"

He *does* look serious—which is exactly the problem.

He is entirely too serious about this naughty bit of foreplay. "Sweetheart, you know how much I love this, but—"

"What, this?"

My eyelids flutter as he strokes my nub.

"Mmm," I moan softly. Then look up in horror as the waiter appears at our table. My face flames, and I wonder if my pale brown skin registers any blush of my embarrassment. I squeeze my legs together, but that does nothing to stop Adam's fingers.

"Have you decided what you'd like?" the waiter asks. I'm not sure if there's a knowing glint in his eye. If not, he must think Adam and I are so in love that we can't bear to be physically apart from each other. Why else would we be sharing the same side of a booth, practically glued at the hip?

"Um," I begin. I haven't even looked at the menu. "I think we need a few more minutes."

"I know what I want," Adam says. He's looking at me though, not at the waiter, and I want to smack him. No, that's a lie. I want to take him outside and get busy with him in the back seat of his Mercedes SUV. I really do enjoy Adam's obvious lust for me. I'm just not comfortable with how much he likes to display it in public.

"New York steak," Adam continues. "Rare. I like it red."

"I'll have the same," I say, hoping to hell that I'm not blushing. "Medium well."

"Rice or baked potato?"

"Rice," both Adam and I respond.

The waiter scribbles notes on a pad. "That comes with soup or salad—"

"Two house salads to start," I interject, cutting off the waiter. "And an order of garlic bread. Also, a half liter of Chardonnay."

"Make it a bottle," Adam says.

My eyes meet his in surprise. His gaze is smoky, and as he bites down on his bottom lip, I feel an excited shiver dance across my shoulders. I know what he wants. To get me drunk so I'm more likely to be less inhibited.

I wonder what he wants me to try *this* time.

"That's everything?" the waiter asks.

I have all but forgotten about the waiter. I look up at the college kid and grin. "That's plenty."

Thank the Lord, the waiter turns and walks away. He doesn't know me, but still I let out a relieved breath. The reason I like to come here is that it's far from the Buckhead neighborhood where Adam and I live. If I get caught doing something scandalous here, at least no one will know who I am. And because it's a Monday night, this place isn't as busy as it would be on the weekend.

"Now." Adam smiles at me as his fingers explore my nether region. "Where were we?"

I push his hand away, feeling slightly annoyed at his one-track mind, considering everything we need to discuss. "Adam, seriously. We need to talk."

He pouts a little but finally relents. "All right." He sits back against the booth. "Let's talk."

Now I smile from ear to ear. I am absolutely crazy about Adam, but it's possible, if only slightly, that I'm even more crazy about our upcoming wedding.

You see, I'm almost thirty, and for a while I wasn't sure

if I'd ever get married or die a spinster. What self-respecting woman still uses the term *spinster,* you ask? You haven't met my high-society, Black-American Princess friends. Not to mention my mother, who has been dreaming of my wedding since the time I was in her womb. In most respects I have a fairly cushy life, but if I don't get married, I'll never live that one down.

But I *am* getting married. In six weeks, I will become Mrs. Adam Hart. For the past year, I've been busy planning every detail of our lavish wedding. As far as I'm concerned, it's going to be the most spectacular wedding Atlanta society has ever seen.

Notice I didn't say "Adam and I" have been planning the wedding. Unfortunately, Adam is a man—which is to say that he's not the least bit interested in the intricate details that go into pulling off a wedding as elaborate as ours will be. He thinks the big day is more of a fairy tale for the bride, and I can't say he's wrong.

But I have to tell you, there's nothing remotely fun about planning the fairy-tale wedding. It's a lot of headaches and hard work. And there are things I need to know now, considering our big day is fast approaching.

I take my planner out of my Gucci tote and open it. "Diana needs to meet with us this weekend to go over all the wedding details. I made a tentative appointment for 10:00 a.m. on Saturday. Will that work for you?"

"Sure."

"I know we had all the colors pretty much picked out, but I'm going back and forth over the bridesmaid dresses. I found out Rebecca Morrison's bridesmaids will be wearing buttercup yellow, and considering our weddings are two weeks apart—" I stop when Adam begins stroking the inside of my wrist. "Are you listening to me?"

"You want to change the colors?"

"I'm considering it, yes."

"Go ahead."

"But I know you and the groomsmen have already picked out your tuxes." Not to mention that the dresses have already been made and it will be a great expense for the designer to make new ones.

"So we'll change the color of the flower we wear on our lapel." He shrugs nonchalantly, as if to say I'm making a big deal out of nothing.

Maybe I am, but this wedding business is stressful. I decide to leave the subject of colors alone until our meeting with the wedding planner. But, there is another pressing matter. "You know how in the reply cards we gave people the chance to say whether they wanted red snapper or duck?"

"Uh-huh."

"Well, the phone calls have started. People are wondering why there isn't a beef option. It's like they expect this to be some sort of backyard buffet instead of a five-star wedding. They're driving me and my mother nuts, but now I'm wondering if we shouldn't have a beef entrée as an option, as well." Rolling my eyes, I groan.

"How hard will it be to have beef?"

"I don't know. I guess not that hard. As long as we get the count a couple weeks before the wedding." Diana has arranged a fantastic lineup of chefs for our big day—straight from Commander's Palace in New Orleans. "But maybe we should put our foot down. There'll be eight courses. No one's gonna starve."

"If it's no big deal," Adam begins, covering my hands with his, "then we'll have a beef entrée."

"Are you sure, honey? What if it's more complicated?"

"But we want everyone happy. Let's have the variety. It'll cost more, but that's not a concern."

"No. No, you're right." I relax in my seat. My father's not worried about the cost, so why am I? "I do want everyone to be happy." *So happy that they'll talk about our wedding for months after the grand event....*

"I don't know why you're getting so stressed. Seems like everything's in order."

"That's easy for you to say. You haven't been doing the planning."

I give Adam a look of reproof, and in response he plants a soft kiss on my lips. "You know I love you for it."

"You'd better."

"I promise you, our honeymoon will be the perfect reward for all your hard work."

Right now, the honeymoon seems like some mythical fantasy that will never come to pass. "When will you tell me where we're going?"

"When we get there."

I should be excited, but I'm not. I think the idea of the honeymoon will really excite me once I know that all the kinks in our wedding plans are ironed out.

Adam releases my hands to reach for my margarita. He samples it and as I watch him, I can't help thinking how truly hot he is. He's six foot two, has closely cropped hair and perfect golden-brown skin. Adam is the kind of guy who commands attention whenever he walks into a room. Even here, at this eatery, I've seen the surreptitious and even brazen glances some of the other women have thrown his way.

But I'm not worried. They can look all they like. Adam isn't going anywhere. He has no need to. I more than please my man in the bedroom.

As an attractive sister gives Adam a lingering look, I place a hand on his leg under the table.

"Mmm," is his soft response.

"I love you, Adam Hart," I whisper.

"I love you, Claudia Fisher."

"I know." I blow out a huff of air. "That's why it's been killing me to keep this from you." Adam looks at me in alarm, and I realize how he has construed my words. "It's not bad news," I quickly assure him. "In fact, it's the *best* news."

"You've got my attention."

Excitement bubbles up inside me. What I'm about to tell Adam is absolutely *the* most thrilling news. The perfect touch to make our wedding forever memorable—*and* the talk of Atlanta.

"Remember I told you I had a surprise for you?"

"Yes," Adam replies.

"I wasn't planning to tell you about this until the rehearsal dinner, but I'm so excited, I can't wait that long."

"What is it, baby?"

"You're never going to believe who'll be singing at our wedding. I'm so blown away by this, I could just *die!*"

Adam's eyes are on fire with curiosity. "Tell me."

"Babyface! Can you believe it?"

Adam plants a serious lip-lock on me, tongue and all, and I don't even care. When we finally break for air, he asks, "How? When?"

"My cousin came through for me." Morgan Fisher, one of my many cousins, is an executive at Palm Records in Los Angeles. He knows Babyface personally, but that wasn't a guarantee that he'd be available to sing at the wedding.

"Oh, man." Adam smiles from ear to ear. "*The* Baby-face?"

"The one and only. Isn't it fabulous?"

"*You're* fabulous." Adam's tone changes, grows deeper. I can read what he's thinking in his eyes. He wants to get me naked.

The waiter appears with our wine. He opens the bottle, pours some wine into a glass, and Adam samples it. "Very good," Adam tells the waiter.

When we are alone again, Adam raises his wineglass. "To us," he says. "And a very bright future."

"I'll drink to that," I say, then clink my glass against my fiancé's, knowing that I am the luckiest girl in the world.

Again, Adam slips a hand between my legs and says, "Come on, baby. Let me make you come."

"Adam…" I protest weakly.

But he's already stroking me, with much more determination, and against my own resolve, I am getting very wet.

"Do you know how much I love it when you're wet like this?" he asks hotly against my ear. He slips a finger inside me and wiggles it around. "Let me taste you. Please, baby…"

I moan softly. "Right here?"

"God, yes."

He pulls his hand away from me and lifts it to his face. He inhales the scent of my essence, groaning his delight, then slowly puts the finger in his mouth. It's enough to almost make me orgasm.

"Damn, I love you," he utters, then slips his hand between my legs once more. Now he goes in for the kill, putting two fingers inside me while stroking my nub with his thumb.

"How do you always do this to me?" I ask. "Make me so fucking horny?"

His movements are faster, and I'm sure people know what's going on. How could they not?

Oh, damn. I'm so close…

I close my legs around his hand and bury my face against his shoulder. "That's it, baby. You know I own you."

And then I come. And come. And come.

I bite down on Adam's shoulder. It's an effort to keep any sound from escaping my mouth. I pray anyone within earshot only thinks I'm laughing.

"You two must be celebrating something."

I whip my gaze up to see the waiter standing at our table. Adam keeps a firm hand wrapped around my waist so I can't move apart from him. His other hand is still in my panties.

"Um, yes," I answer shakily. I'm still light-headed from the aftermath of my orgasm. "We're getting married."

"Ah," the waiter coos and places the garlic bread on the table. "Congratulations."

Only when the waiter disappears do I dare move away from Adam. He grins at me, victorious, knowing he has conquered me sexually once again.

And I can't help it. I grin back at him.

I love this man.

A little over an hour later—at least I think it's an hour later (I can't be sure, since I had the lion's share of the wine)—I am holding on tight to Adam's arm as he's driving along the 285 perimeter around Atlanta. It seems we've been going around and around for ages, but I could be wrong, considering my head's in a fog. I can barely keep my eyes open, but when Adam veers suddenly to the right, I perk up. I see that he is taking an exit several miles from my home.

"Hey," I say.

He squeezes my hand. "Don't worry, babe."

"Where are we going?"

He glances at me and flashes a playful grin. "You had a surprise for me. Now it's my turn to surprise you."

I eye Adam warily. He's not big on romantic surprises. Besides, what on earth can he be surprising me with in the middle of nowhere? Unless he's going to…

As the answer hits me, I am almost sobered with the excitement.

"Adam," I squeal, "you didn't!" Of course, I'm hoping he did. I look around expectantly, hoping to see large suburban houses with sprawling lawns and aged oaks any second now. I thought for sure we'd stay in Buckhead, but maybe he's decided that we'll live in Duluth.

But as we continue to drive, the industrial landscape doesn't change, and I'm a bit confused. This area isn't only industrial, it's fairly run-down. Not exactly the neighborhood where Adam would buy a house.

Growing nervous, I grip Adam's hand.

"Relax, sweetheart," he tells me. "You'll see what it is when we get there."

I am more than surprised when Adam turns into the driveway of a large, one-story gray building. At least a hundred yards long, it's got to be some sort of ware-house. I can't imagine why he'd be bringing me here, un-less he wants an isolated place to make out. Which irritates me, since I already gave him a blow job in the restaurant parking lot. At least, I think I did. The mem-ory is kind of blurry. In any case, I'm not in the mood to get kinky out here.

"Adam, I think you should take me home."

"Don't worry."

He travels the length of the building, then turns left around the corner. Suddenly a row of cars comes into view. Lexuses, Jaguars, BMWs. What is this place? Some kind of club?

I ask him.

"Yeah, it's a club."

"But I thought..." I snuggle against my man. "I thought we were heading back to your place before you take me home."

Adam pulls up next to a Ford Explorer and parks the car. "I think you'll like this."

I frown slightly as Adam disentangles himself from me and exits the vehicle. Moments later, he opens my door and offers me his hand. I'm not convinced I'm going to like whatever's inside, but Adam is grinning at me like a fool.

Shaking my head at him, I let him help me out of the SUV. We walk hand in hand to a door at the back of the building. This is not the kind of club I normally go to. I'm partial to the classy joints in my Buckhead neighborhood. Clubs with a piano bar, a live jazz band. This one is…well, *secretive* is the only word that comes to mind.

I cling to Adam as we step into the entrance. This place is weird, all right. Barely lit, the foyer area is completely blocked off from the rest of the place. I can hear soulful, seductive music coming through the walls—the only real indication that something's going on here. I feel the way people must have felt during the days of prohibition, sneaking into speakeasies after dark—like I'm doing something illegal.

There's a big-breasted cashier in a very small cubicle, and Adam hands her two crisp one-hundred-dollar bills. She doesn't give him any change back. That's more money than we've ever paid to get into any club. I wonder again just what kind of surprise this is.

The bouncer opens a heavy metal door for us, and the light is almost blinding as it streaks into the foyer. Adam steps forward and I walk with him into the club—and then I stop dead in my tracks.

I am so stunned, I'm not sure what to think. I close my eyes in case I'm hallucinating. But when I open them, I see the same shocking images, and I know that what's going on is very real.

Everywhere—and I mean *everywhere*—there are people engaged in sex acts. Immediately before me on a mattress on the floor, a woman is sandwiched between two men. To the right of that trio, a woman is on her knees giving a man a blow job. And beyond them, a man has a woman braced against a wall and he's ramming her hard from behind.

My God. This is sick. It's like I'm in a room with animals that are gorging on sex.

I feel a surge of panic. I'm light-headed, yes, but not so drunk that I don't wonder why Adam has brought me here. This is no ordinary club. I'm not even sure it's legal. The absurd icing on the cake is the group of partially dressed people dancing on the dance floor, as if they're completely oblivious to the acts of illicit sex surrounding them.

"Adam—"

"We can just watch if that makes you feel better."

My mouth nearly hits the floor as I look up at him. I expected him to say many things, but not the words I just heard. Surely he has to be as shocked as I am, as disgusted that we are in some kind of sex club.

Instead, he's staring at me with a hopeful look in his eyes, and his palm is sweaty.

God help me, he's excited.

But I am not. "You knew what this place was before you brought me here?" I ask him, outraged.

"Someone told me about it, and I wanted to check it out."

My head is spinning, and I'm not sure what to think. "Great," I say. "You've seen it. Can we go now?"

Adam pulls me close and slides his hands over my butt. "Come on, Claudia. Doesn't this turn you on?"

"Turn me on?"

"Yeah." He pauses. "All these people—having hot, wild sex."

"You've got to be kidding me."

"Sex is natural, babe. Beautiful. Why shouldn't people openly express how they feel about one another?"

If my mother could see me now, she'd drop dead on the spot. Forget my mother, *I'm* about to drop dead. If anyone I know ever saw me in this place, I would never live it down. Besides, I'm not into watching other people having sex.

"I want to leave," I tell Adam.

With a finger, he guides my head to the left. "Look at that woman right there," he says softly. "Look at the expression on her face as that guy is going down on her." The woman is biting on her finger and her eyes are rolling backward. "She's given herself over completely to the experience."

I watch the woman, listen to her—then I swallow. Disgusted with myself for even looking, I jerk my gaze away. "And she probably doesn't even know the guy." I've only heard about swingers, never seen them up close and personal like I am now. "Adam, honestly—I'm not comfortable here."

Adam all but ignores me as he takes my hand and guides it to his erection. My God, he's rock hard. I'm not sure if I should be appalled or accept the reality that getting a hard-on in this environment is only natural.

A man and a woman, nicely dressed like Adam and I

are, saunter in our direction. Alarm shoots through me when the woman, an older white lady, checks me out from head to toe. I lean against Adam, hoping he'll protect me. From exactly what, I'm not sure.

"Hello," the woman says.

"Not interested," I reply quickly, wrapping my arms around Adam's torso. I step to my right, dragging Adam with me. Adam shrugs as the couple continues to walk by us.

"I know you're apprehensive," Adam begins.

"That doesn't even begin to describe what I'm feeling."

"Let's find a corner."

"What?" I shake my head. "Adam, no."

"Just for a little while."

My heart takes a nosedive into the pit of despair. I have done so many things to please Adam sexually, it's like a slap in the face that he wants to get off while watching others.

He gives me a soft peck on the lips. "I know this is crazy. But we'll be married soon. And I just want to...try something really different...just one time. Before we say 'I do' and commit to each other forever."

I'm not exactly sure what Adam means. Worse, I'm afraid to ask. Does he want us to get freaky with some other couple and in the morning pretend it didn't happen?

Because of Adam's insatiable appetite for sex, I have done a lot of things that I otherwise wouldn't have. Things I am embarrassed to admit. From exhibitionist-type sex to sex so kinky it would make my grandmother roll over in her grave, I have done my part to make my man happy. I'm a woman of the new millennium and I'm hardly a prude. But swapping partners—that's a whole other story.

"We'll have a drink, watch a little."

"I'm not screwing some other guy. And I sure as hell don't want to watch you screw some other woman."

Adam squeezes my hand. "No, no. That's not what this is about, sweetheart. This is about us. You and me. About the two of us experiencing all that's out there before we settle down in marriage."

"Are you unhappy with me?" I ask, dreading the reality that despite everything I try, I somehow fail to please him.

"No, of course not. You have my heart, and you always will. But we won't be young forever. I don't want us to have any regrets."

"Regret that we never swapped couples?" I ask incredulously.

"I don't want the day to come when we wish we'd tried something and regret having held back. This is about being open to new experiences."

I really don't know what to say to Adam. I'm getting that uneasy feeling, though, the one I get when I think I might lose him.

"I don't want to be with anyone else," he assures me. "I just want to watch...then I want to go down on you...."

Brazenly—or perhaps not so brazenly given the environment—Adam slips a hand up my skirt. He strokes me with his thumb, and despite my reservations, I feel a zap of excitement.

"I want to eat you with everyone watching," he adds

in a husky voice. "And then, I want to make love to you."

I'm not sure about this, not sure at all. No, that's a lie— I *am* sure. Sure that I don't want to do this. But I think about my sister, whose husband left her because he said she was a prude, and I wonder if Adam would leave me over something like this. And if he did leave me because of my aversion to swingers' clubs, then he's not really the guy I think he is. But still, we're engaged. I've got a lot invested in my wedding day and I'll be damned if it doesn't happen as planned.

"Just one time?" I ask.

His smile is like a neon sign, it's so friggin' bright. "One time, baby."

I sigh softly as I let Adam lead me to a dark corner. And then I rationalize the fact that I'm going along with this: It's just a crazy fantasy. Once he's made it a reality, he'll move on and we won't have to deal with this again.

Chapter Two

Annelise

I am in the zone.

"Yes! Oh God, *yes!*" A rush of excitement flows through me and my breathing picks up speed. I love this part—the moment when we are completely in tune with each other. There is a comfort level now, and neither of us is holding anything back. The flow and rhythm is steady, and I am moving rapidly toward the moment of total satisfaction.

I press my finger on the camera's trigger and snap a round of shots. "Wonderful. Now, get a little closer. That's right. You love this woman. Let it shine from your soul. Angle your head, Mark." I glide toward him and guide his head in the direction I want. "Oh, that's it." I actually moan my pleasure. "Now hold that pose, and smile."

I am holding the camera; I prefer this to mounting it

on a tripod. I am much freer this way, free to explore different angles. I step backward, then move from left to right until I am satisfied. I look through the viewfinder, adjust the focus and voilà: perfection. The camera loves this couple.

I click off a few more shots of Mark and Robin in yet another perfect pose. I've gotten several photos, but I am not quite finished. The next shot will be *the* moment, the thrilling denouement.

"Turn slightly, both of you. Look at each other. Less of a smile, more of a romantic gaze." God, there is so much honesty between them. "Yes, that's absolutely perfect."

I hold down the trigger and don't let go until I've finished the roll. I was *so* born to do this. Photography is in my blood.

I lower the camera from my face. "That was great," I tell Mark and Robin, feeling the high that comes from a great session. "The pictures will be fabulous."

Robin grins from ear to ear. "You think so?"

"Absolutely. The camera loved you."

"I can't wait to see them." Robin turns to Mark and nuzzles her nose with his.

I watch them for a moment, their happiness giving me a warm feeling in my chest. There's nothing quite like capturing two people in love on film. I love the way their eyes convey everything that's in their souls.

This particular couple has recently gotten engaged. That's why they're here at my studio—to take pictures they'll use for an engagement announcement.

That's also why they're so openly affectionate. There's hardly a moment when one isn't touching the other. Even as they get up from the sofa, their hands are linked. As much as I enjoy seeing happy couples together, a feeling of longing stirs in my gut.

"Can we see the proofs now?"

I shake my head as I place the camera on a table near the set. "Call me old-fashioned, but I'm not a fan of digital photography. When you see physical proofs, you get a much better idea of what your prints will look like."

Robin nods, but she looks a little disappointed. "How soon will they be ready?"

It has been a busy week at the studio. "Oh, probably around nine or ten days."

"That long?" She looks from me to Mark in alarm. She is clearly eager to announce her engagement.

"I do offer two rush options. Three days or five."

"Three," Robin tells me without hesitation. "We'd like to get the announcement out right away."

Ah, young love. I try to remember a time my husband and I were so in love. When each hour apart from each other seemed like an excruciating eternity.

The memory is fuzzy, but it's there. Ten years ago, when we were both in college, before Charles went to law school. There was an easiness between us then. We laughed a lot, joked a lot.

Had a lot of sex.

Forget Charles, I tell myself. I do *not* want to think about him right now, not when I'm feeling such a high.

So I throw myself back into work, giving Robin and Mark an array of times when they can come back and view the proofs. They decide, pay me a deposit and I see them to the door. Arm in arm, the two descend the studio's steps. I watch them climb into a BMW, and even give a little wave. It's the personal touches that keep people coming back.

Once they drive away, I sigh softly and step back into the studio. Despite my desire to cling to my high, now that I am alone, my mood plummets.

It's so easy to forget about my troubles when I'm in that perfect zone. But I remember them now. Seeing love in its purest form always makes me ponder my own love life. I think of the contrasts: Mark and Robin so happy, so affectionate. Charles and I so miserable, so distant.

I've been married to Charles for five years now, and most of it has been happy. But lately, over the last fourteen months, there has been a drastic change in our relationship. You see, Charles went from being loving and affectionate to cold and remote. He hasn't touched me in over a year.

Oh we kiss, we hug. With about as much passion as a brother and sister. If I try to get closer to him, take our interaction beyond the platonic, Charles pulls away.

He tells me it's stress, which I do understand. My husband is a civil-litigation attorney and has a lot on his plate. I'm not at all insensitive to that. But fourteen months? I thought sex was supposed to be a great stress reliever.

I get so frustrated that at times I simply want to give up. But then I think, how can I give up? This is the man I love more than anything. I'll be married to him forever. And forever is a long time to go without getting any sex.

When I pressure him, he immediately shuts down, so I have tried to do subtle things to get his interest. Like give him a back rub, or reach for his hand as we sit on the couch together. But even that doesn't work. Because just when I think he's sufficiently relaxed and I might hit a home run, he'll give me a chaste kiss and tell me he's going to bed.

This happened last night.

The night before that, Charles went to bed after I did. He didn't curl up next to me. He never does. It's like there's a line down the middle of our bed and he doesn't want to cross it.

I cried this morning as I asked him if he still wants to be married to me. He assured me that he does—then kissed me on the forehead before heading out the door.

Truly, I am at my wit's end. I don't know what to do. But I can't throw in the towel. I have to find a way to help us reconnect as a couple.

Today, I am more determined than ever to get some love from my husband. I was thinking about ways to make that happen as I drove to the studio, and came up with the conclusion that I have to do something different. Something drastically different.

I'm thinking scented candles and wine and a completely relaxing environment. You're probably thinking no big deal. And you're right. But I'm going to up the ante by wearing something scandalous. The kind of outfit my husband won't be able to resist me in.

We used to do this sort of thing in the early days of our marriage, but somewhere along the way I guess we got stale. Boring.

Great sex is on my mind as I lock up the studio. It's a small space, one room and an office area in a strip mall-type building. It's all I can afford in order to make a marginal profit doing the job I love. But the landscape out back is lush and beautiful and free—I use it often when taking photos.

This month has been a good one for me, with more weddings than I expected. Thankfully, I have a few extra dollars to spend. And I am going to spend them on spicing up my marriage.

There is one person who can probably help me in my quest. My sister. As I get behind the wheel of my Jetta, I'm already dialing her number on my cell phone. My sister and I don't talk very often. We don't exactly see eye to eye. But this is an emergency. I need her expertise.

I've always been the good girl. Samera's always been the whore.

I love her in spite of it, and I can hardly blame her for her choices. My mother is a religious nut—if I haven't said so before. Sent my sister right into the sex trade, while for a long time I thought that even feeling sexual desire would send me straight to hell.

For the past six years, Samera has worked as a stripper. She prefers "exotic dancer" but I like to call a spade a spade.

Samera's phone rings and I wait. "Hello," she says cheerfully when she answers after three rings.

"Hey, Sam. It's me."

She pauses for a moment, then says, "Annie. Wow, this is a surprise."

"I know. Sorry I've been out of touch. I've been busy with work."

"I hear you. I've been busy, too. Are you finally making decent money?"

What she really wants to know is if I'm making enough money to be self-sufficient. Samera hates the idea that if Charles and I were to split, I wouldn't be able to support myself.

"Things are looking up," I tell her. I don't add, "Just barely."

"Because if things aren't going well, you know I can always get you work at the club."

I chuckle sarcastically, like I always do. This is a running joke between us—though I don't particularly find it funny. It's Samera's way of saying she thinks I'm a prude. Of course, she doesn't think she's loose. She says she's sexually liberated.

"How about we settle on lunch instead?" I suggest. "Sometime soon. It's been way too long."

"You're on, sis."

It remains to be seen if this will happen. "Listen," I say. "The reason I'm calling. I need to ask a favor."

"Sure."

"This is going to sound weird, but where can I find an adult store?"

"An adult store? You mean like JCPenney?"

She knows exactly what I mean. "No, a store that sells...stuff. You know."

"You mean a sex shop?"

"Yeah, whatever."

Samera laughs. "I swear, Annie, I can see you turning

red. I don't know why you get so embarrassed. This *is* the new millennium. Women are allowed to say *sex* without fear of being persecuted."

"I don't need a lecture. Just directions."

"What do you want exactly? Videos? Toys?"

"I was thinking more along the lines of sexy lingerie. I want to spice things up with Charles." As I say this, I envision a laughing devil with a pitchfork. Believe me, it's hard to undo eighteen years of my mother's conditioning.

"Why not come by the club? That'll get you both in the mood."

"No thanks." I wouldn't be caught dead in a strip joint with Charles. That's not the drastically different I had in mind. "I just want to find a place where I can buy some naughty stuff. Lace and feathers. Maybe even crotchless underwear."

"Oh, my. You *are* serious."

"You can stop your snickering. I haven't been living under a rock."

"Okay, okay." Samera settles down. "Crotchless is great, by the way. Always gets a guy in the mood. So are edible undies. There was one time when I bought them for this guy I was seeing and let me tell—"

"Too much information," I announce, cutting my sister off. Samera often gets carried away, telling me details I don't want to know. "I just want to know where I can find a place to buy some stuff."

"Where are you? Coming from the studio?"

"Yep."

"There's a place in Sugarloaf that I highly recommend.

It's on your way home. I get a ton of my stuff there. It's called A Little Naughty. Corner of John and Hibiscus."

Now that Samera's said this, I get a mental image of this shop. I've driven by it but haven't consciously noticed it. "I think I know the place," I say.

"It's got everything you could possibly dream of. Ask for Suzie. Tell her I sent you and she'll give you a discount."

I wonder how much stuff my sister buys there. Actually, I don't want to know. "Thanks a bunch, sis. Listen, I'll talk to you later, okay?"

"You don't have to stay with Charles if he doesn't appreciate you. And if this doesn't get him aroused, I'd seriously start wondering if he's not screwing around."

"Bye." I roll my eyes as I end the call, remembering exactly why we don't talk that often. Between her implying that I'm a docile wife who's far too sexually inexperienced and her often brazen suggestion that I dump my husband, I can only take so much of her. I love Samera, but our lives are as different as night and day. She's single and doesn't believe in marriage, much less monogamy. She's more into what men can give her, since she says she's been burned too many times. I, on the other hand, would never think of being with a man for his money. Samera thinks I'm setting myself up for failure, especially since she knows that Charles isn't giving me any love these days.

Thirty minutes later, I'm pulling into the strip mall at the corner of John and Hibiscus Streets. Right away I see the neon-pink lights and naughtily dressed mannequin in the window. The sun is already disappearing on the horizon, but nonetheless, I slip my sunglasses on as I exit my car. I don't want to chance being recognized.

I enter the store and for what seems like minutes, I just stand there, checking it all out. I'm experiencing sensory overload. There's lots of skimpy lingerie to my left, but nothing I haven't seen before. It's the stuff to my right that makes me blush.

There's a wall with dildos on display—some so large I can't imagine any woman ever buying one. And apparently they come in all the colors of the rainbow, which makes me wonder if they're flavored like Life Savers.

"Hi!" A petite brunette bounces toward me. She has a piercing in her eyebrow and is into dark makeup. "Can I help you?"

"I'm…just looking."

Her eyes narrow, as if she's trying to decide if she knows me. "You look really familiar. Have you been here before?"

"Me? God, no." Then it hits me. "You're probably confusing me with my sister. Samera Peyton."

"Yes, of course."

"Are you Suzie?"

"Uh-huh. Are you sure there's nothing I can help you find?"

I know this is a sex shop, but I don't want this cute little thing getting a visual image of what I might be doing later. I shake my head. "Not right now, anyway. But I'll let you know."

I turn and wander to the left, heading toward the safe-looking lingerie I have no intention of buying. Not that that really makes much sense when I think about it. Suzie will see what I purchase soon enough.

"Relax," I whisper to myself as I finger a lacy black teddy. "You're a grown woman. You're allowed to have good sex."

Hell, I'd take mediocre sex right now. That sad reality has me forgetting about my reservations and I forge ahead to find the raunchiest piece of lingerie here. I find panties with no crotch, bras with feathers at the nipple. I hang on to both like they're the answers to all my problems.

When I see a maid's outfit on a mannequin, I can't help but laugh. But once I stop chuckling, I take a closer look. This maid's outfit is barely there. Talk about stepping out of your comfort zone to do something different. In this uniform, I can role-play. I can be a lousy cook, or suck at dusting.

And Charles can spank me, then punish me with his piercing shaft....

I bite down on my lip to keep from laughing out loud. I've been reading way too many historical romances.

I continue to browse. There's also a mannequin in leather, wearing a dog collar and holding a whip. That's an idea. I could always whip Charles for being a bad boy. But I can't quite imagine him on all fours with his butt in the air. I pick up a package with the maid's uniform and stuff it under my arm. I even choose a black wig. If I'm going to role-play, I may as well go all out.

Fifteen minutes in this place and I'm feeling like a different woman. So much so that when I stroll toward the cash register—passing through an aisle full of vibrators—I stop and take a gander. I more than take a gander, actually, but hey, I'm curious. The shaft that gets my attention is long, thick and blue (an odd color given its lifelike dimensions but I'm not about to ask why). I pick it up and examine it through the packaging.

"Oooh, I *love* that one."

I jump with fright, dropping the blue penis and my crotchless underwear to the floor. Cute little Suzie doesn't miss a beat. She quickly scoops my items up.

Knowing that my face is flaming, I accept the items but don't meet her eyes.

"There's also this," Suzie says. She picks up a display penis that's extremely huge. "This one feels so real. Touch it."

God forgive me, I say to myself. Then I touch the proffered penis and am surprised at just how soft it is. "Nice," I mumble, for lack of something more appropriate to say.

"The balls even move on this one, giving added stimulation. And it has three speed levels, depending on what you prefer."

I know I'm as red as a beet. "Um…I think I'll stick with this stuff." I lift the lingerie items. There's no way I can bring another penis into my house, even if I could use it. What would my husband say?

Suzie leads the way to the register and I follow her. I know this is the new millennium, but this place is so…sinful. I can hardly believe I'm really here. I feel a rush of guilt and consider going to confession.

"You might want to try some of these." Suzie points to a bin with small tubes. "Flavored lubricant," she announces proudly. "Personally, I like the raspberry best."

Good Lord, she looks way too young to have tried all this stuff. I'm about to tell her I'm not interested, but I suddenly change my mind. How much have I missed out on? Too much, clearly. I want to catch up, and that's exactly what I'm going to do.

I pick up a handful of the tubes. "Can't get too much of these."

"I know exactly what you mean."

I'm actually chuckling, enjoying this moment, when I sense someone to my right. Turning, I nearly die of horror when I see a total hottie standing a few feet away from me. How long has he been here, and how did I not see him before?

Worse, how much of my conversation has he heard?

He grins as he meets my gaze.

God help me, he thinks I'm a freak. I quickly pay for my items and rush out of the store.

Nine o'clock and still no Charles.

What seemed like a good idea three hours ago seems utterly foolish right now. I'm lying on the sofa wearing that ridiculous maid's uniform and the even more ridiculous wig, only half paying attention to some pathetic reality dating show. The meat loaf I prepared is lukewarm in the oven.

Not even so much as a phone call to tell me he'd be late.

I could have changed—in fact I almost did—but I want Charles to see what I've done to try to seduce him. And if I'm entirely honest, I guess a part of me still hopes that he'll walk through the door, see me half-naked and perk right up—then ravish me until I can't even blink.

Like that's gonna happen. Why the hell do I bother? Maybe my sister's right. Maybe Charles *is* having some torrid affair.

The cordless phone is at the foot of the sofa, nice and close to me, because I'd hoped Charles would call. Now I lift it and punch in the digits to one of my girlfriend's. I desperately need to hear a friendly voice right now.

"Hello?"

Thank God, Lishelle is home. She's a newscaster and sometimes works through the evening. I met her at Spelman, the same place I met my other best friend, Claudia Fisher. I think they took pity on me—one of the few white girls who had the guts to go to a predominantly black school. I didn't care about any of that, of course. I wanted to experience life at an all-girl college, probably to please my mother who was worried about all the temptation I'd face on a regular college campus.

"Hey, Lishelle," I say, pulling the wig off. "It's Annelise."

"What's up, girl?"

I sigh softly. "Nothing much. Just sitting here watching some TV and I thought I'd call." I don't want to talk about Charles. I'm depressed enough as it is. "Did you get a message from Claudia today?"

"Mmm-hmm."

"So there *is* another fitting on Saturday?"

"You know that girl's tripping. The way she's going through dresses and designers, I'm not sure anything will be good enough for her."

"She's got to make up her mind soon. The wedding's

on May twenty-seventh." I lift my head when I hear the doorknob turning. Charles. My heart slams against my chest. "Lishelle, I have to go."

"What?"

"I'll call you tomorrow," I tell her, then disconnect the call.

My whole seduction scene has been ruined, and I'm now confused about what to do. Simply stand up and greet my husband, or lie provocatively on the sofa?

The decision is made for me. I don't have time to get up. I toss the wig across the room, then fluff my blond hair. Drawing in a deep breath, I bend one leg at the knee and ease up onto my elbows. As Charles comes into view, I whisper, "Hi."

Charles stops dead in his tracks, as though he is surprised to see me. I guess he is, because he's got the stack of mail from the hall table in his hands and he must have been looking at that.

"Hi," I say again, this time adding a smile.

"Hey."

Charles glances to the left, at the row of candles burning on the table. I wait for his reaction…

He goes back to sifting through the mail.

The mail! I'm dressed like a French slut and he's concerned with the mail!

I sit up, not sure if I should scream or cry. Really, I want to pummel him.

"Charles," I say, noting the hint of exasperation in my voice.

He makes his way around the sofa and sits beside me. My heart lifts. Maybe there's hope after all.

I lean into him and kiss his cheek. "I missed you, sweetheart."

"It's been a long day." His eyes roam over me. "What are you wearing?"

Yes! I think. He's noticing me. He's getting turned on. We're going to have wild, passionate sex right here on the sofa.

"Just a little something I picked up today." Now I press my mouth to his. I open my lips and move them over his lips. Instantly I'm getting hot...until I realize I may as well be kissing a dead fish.

My shoulders slump in defeat. "Charles..."

"God, I'm sorry. But honestly, Ann, I've had a long day. My head is pounding."

I tune out the rest of his spiel. I can probably recite it by heart if I have to.

I don't want to give up, but how can I fight this? Before Charles even walks through the door he's thinking of ways to reject me. What happened to the man who used to write me poetry, sing to me off-key? I miss that man.

"There's meat loaf in the oven."

Charles makes a sound of derision. "Meat loaf? You know I'm not big on red meat."

The nerve of this man! I embarrass myself at a sex shop, come home and slave over a meal for him, and he doesn't even care? I want to smother him to death with the sofa cushion.

"Sorry," I say. "It was..." My voice trails off. I don't want to tell him I made an easy meal because I was hoping he'd come home early and ravish me.

"I already ate, anyway," he tells me.

Then, to add insult to injury, Charles reaches for the remote and starts channel surfing. This is poor, over-worked Charles, so friggin' tired that he can't even give me a decent kiss, yet he's up for watching TV. Why isn't he taking two aspirin and heading straight to bed?

Charles finds a soccer game. Since when does he like soccer?

I can't help wondering if it's me he doesn't like.

It hurts being rejected. Like you've reached inside yourself and given your very soul to someone and they spit on it. That's how I feel. And it sucks.

Tears well up in my eyes, but my dear husband doesn't notice. I've seen talk of this on *Oprah,* read about it in magazines, women wondering *What happened to the passion?* Never once in my wildest dreams would I have thought I would be one of those women.

"Oh, you moron!" Charles shouts, as if he even knows what's going on in the game. But at least with soccer, he's willing to pick a team and play.

Me—I'm left standing on the sidelines.

Silently, I rise from the sofa and disappear from the room.

Chapter Three

Lishelle

I am not in the mood for this.

I pop the lid on my bottle of Motrin and drop two capsules into my mouth. I down the pills with water, then lean forward on my desk and groan.

Believe me, I've had a stressful enough day at the television station. I certainly didn't need a call from him.

Him being my ex-husband. I have just gotten off the phone with the jerk, and I swear, he must be on a mission to make my life miserable. There's a reason I divorced him, although he doesn't seem to get it. And he should, considering his girlfriend showed up on our doorstep two and a half years ago carrying *their* child.

Do you believe that my ex actually wants a second chance with me?

But then, maybe I shouldn't be surprised. David literally believes he's God's gift to women. I'm sure he's deluded himself into thinking that without him, I've been utterly unhappy. Which is so far from reality, let me make that perfectly clear. There was the obvious sadness when we split, but mostly, I felt free.

You see, I always sensed something was wrong in our relationship, even if I wasn't sure what. And when I learned that he was screwing around on me, everything suddenly made sense. If he was ever faithful to me after our wedding, it was probably for about three minutes. It's amazing the stuff people are willing to tell you once the divorce papers have been signed. I only wish these friends and family members had seen it wise to give me this information before I married the man.

Somewhere along the way, though, it seems I've gotten some poetic justice. As I always knew he would, David has come to his senses and realized that I am the best thing that ever happened to him. Though the divorce became final over a year ago, he wants me back in a bad way.

I can't tell you how much pleasure it gives me to be able to reject him.

That thought makes me smile, and I sit up straight. I eye my phone warily though, hoping it won't ring again. I am getting tired of David's phone calls. I've changed my home number and my cell number, but the bad thing is he knows where I work. I can't quite escape that one. I'm a prominent newscaster at Channel Four news.

In the last couple years, I've advanced from field reporter to news anchor. I can't help but wonder if this is why David wants me back. I have a more prestigious role at the news station, one that's giving me fame and more money. Funny that this might interest David now, because he never liked me pursuing my dream before. In fact, he once told me that he was tired of hearing his police colleagues tell him they had seen me on the news.

Karen—the woman he'd cheated with—is a teacher. Nice and safe for David; i.e., noncompetitive in terms of his job.

I have to give Karen credit, though. Apparently even she has a limit to what she will put up with. Guess she finally realized that my ex is a worthless cheater and worthless cheaters aren't even faithful to their mistresses. Bet she now wishes she'd found an unattached man to get involved with. I do take some pleasure in this. And why shouldn't I? I've never understood how some women get off on being home wreckers.

David will never admit it, but I heard through the grapevine that Karen left with their child while he was at work. Oh, to have been a fly on the wall when David returned home.

Anyway, enough about my ex. Despite my long-winded rant, I really don't think about him. He called to say that he has changed, that if I give him another chance I will see, but I am so not going there again. He thinks it's because there's someone else in my life. This time, I let him believe that.

The truth is, there's no one special in my life. I hate to say it, but the men I meet these days are losers with a capital L. If they're not starstruck because of who I am, then they're just plain weirdos. For the most part, if the man is someone a self-respecting woman wouldn't be caught dead with, then you can bet he'll hit on me. Trust me, it never fails.

There's something about being on television that makes people think they know you. And when guys think they know you, they're much more forward. For example, a few weeks ago at a fund-raising event, a well-dressed black man approached me and passed me a note. It read, "You and me, outside in the gazebo in five minutes."

Needless to say, I didn't make that date.

I have such shitty luck with men that I have sworn off dating. I really have. What's the point? There's not one decent single guy out there.

But Rhonda, a camerawoman at the station, tells me I'm wrong. She swears that she's got the perfect man for me—her cousin.

I'm not particularly interested in seeing this guy, but Rhonda has been on my case about it for months. So, despite my obvious bad luck with men, I have decided I am a glutton for punishment and have accepted a date with Rhonda's cousin for this evening. I put off meeting Trevor for months—until I realized that Rhonda wasn't going to drop the issue.

There is a knock on my dressing-room door. "Come in," I call.

Rhonda pokes her head through the door. "Hey, Lishelle."

"Hey."

"I love your hair like that."

I tuck some locks behind my ear. I'm still a bit self-conscious about it. When it comes to hair, I'm pretty con-

servative. I keep it nape length, and never color it anything other than black. At least I hadn't. All that changed
last weekend when my stylist urged me to do something
different. I caved under pressure and allowed her to add
some auburn highlights. Believe me, I started having a
panic attack once I'd passed the point of no return. But
Jenny, my stylist, promised me it would complement my
skin tone. And she was right.

"Thanks," I say to Rhonda.

"Trevor will be impressed." She winks.

But will I be impressed with Trevor? For Rhonda's
sake, I hope so. She's been trying for so long to get us together.

"What time are you meeting him?" she asks.

"Eight o'clock." That will give me a little time to
freshen up after the newscast is over. I plan to meet
Trevor at a restaurant downtown. He offered to pick me
up, but I politely declined. If I have my own car and
things don't go well, I can leave.

I'm jaded, can you tell?

"You'll have a good time," Rhonda assures me. "Trevor
really is a sweetheart."

"I hope so."

Rhonda gives me a smile then disappears. Knowing
I have work to do, I force myself out of my chair. I still
have to get my hair and makeup done, and after that,
it's showtime.

Two hours later, my head is still pounding. I'm at the
restaurant now, sitting in my car in the parking lot, dreading the thought of going inside. I just don't know if I

should do this. Knowing my luck, this date will cap off a stressful day with even more stress. I should probably just go home and go to bed.

But I am here already, resigned to my fate. I may as well try to enjoy myself. There are worse ways to spend a Thursday night than meeting a potential new boyfriend.

I apply more lipstick before getting out of the car. Then, as I walk up to the restaurant door, my stomach flutters with nerves. I hope I'm not making a mistake. Really, it's not like I need a man, although I admit that having one might be nice.

"Hello," I say to the male host once I'm inside. "I'm meeting someone. Crenshaw. Trevor."

The host peruses his open schedule book. "Ah, yes. Right this way."

My hands sweat on my Louis Vuitton clutch as I follow the host through the Macaroni Grill. This was Trevor's choice, and a good one. It's casual but upscale and has great food.

"Here you go."

"Thank—" The rest of the word dies on my lips as I see a man rise. For a moment, I am stunned. Pleasantly stunned.

So *this* is Trevor. Wow. He is tall, very well groomed. A gorgeous dark-skinned brother. I am definitely impressed.

"Lishelle, hello."

God, that smile must have broken countless hearts.

"You found the place okay?"

I force myself to speak. "Yes, yes, I did." I smile awkwardly. "Hi."

I extend my hand, but Trevor steps toward me and gives me a hug instead. "It's so good to meet you. Believe me, I'm a fan."

I smile bashfully and wave off his compliment. (I really did smile bashfully. Sheesh, what's come over me?)

Without missing a beat, Trevor pulls out my chair for me. As I sit, I can't help thinking that his mama must have raised him right.

"I've taken the liberty of ordering some wine," he tells me, and gestures to the chilled carafe. "It's white, Riesling."

"Lovely," I practically sing. *Lovely?* Lord, when was the last time I used that word? Really, I need to tamp down on my overexcitement. Trevor is going to think I've been dating men from Mars.

Which isn't exactly a stretch.

Trevor pours me a glass, then lifts his own glass in a toast. He touches it to mine and says, "To new friendships."

"To new friendships," I echo, thinking that maybe, just maybe, I have finally hit pay dirt.

Two glasses of wine later, I'm feeling very relaxed. And headache free. Accepting this date with Trevor is probably the best thing I've done in a long, long time. I'm even thinking of inviting him home, depending on how things progress. This isn't like me, but you have to understand, I haven't had sex in ages, and the fact that I'm sitting across from an eligible man has sent my libido into overdrive.

Trevor has been telling me about what it's like to work

as a lawyer. (Did I tell you I'm intrigued by the legal profession? Especially when it comes to fine-looking brothers who do their best to keep creeps off the streets?) I'm sipping wine and grinning like a fool, hanging on to his every word.

"I couldn't believe this guy. It was like, every single one of his neighbors testified to the fact that they saw him chasing the guy with a knife, heard him uttering death threats, and he totally denied it. No defense, just a straight denial. And when he fired his lawyer and proceeded to defend himself… Even the jury could hardly keep their laughter under control."

Trevor laughs, and I do, too. It might be interesting to see Trevor in action—in court. And I'm definitely thinking that it would be *very* interesting to see him in action in the bedroom.

"Ah, well." Trevor's laughter subsides. "Enough about me. I want to hear all about you."

"Me?" I point to myself, as if there's any question as to whom he's referring. "Oh, there's not much to tell. Certainly nothing as interesting as what you've told me."

Trevor tilts his head ever so slightly and says, "I seriously doubt that."

I draw in a deep breath to keep my erratic heart under control. "I…I guess I do have some interesting stories. Mostly from earlier in my career, when I was a field reporter." The truth is, I have a lot of interesting stories. But I'd rather talk about me and Trevor and whether he's doing anything later. It's not exactly the time to bring up this suggestion, though. "What do you want to hear about? The streakers or the death threats?"

"Death threats?"

"Oh, yeah. I was covering a story about a feud between two business owners. One guy had a cleaning business in town for twenty years. The new guy set up shop and was stealing his customers. When I asked the new guy about his business practices, he shoved my cameraman to the ground and vowed to slit my throat."

"Whoa."

"Nothing came of it. But there have been other instances like that, and I've been worried more than a few times. There are some crazy people out there."

"What else?"

"More stories?"

Trevor shakes his head. "No, tell me about you. Your life."

My heart flutters. Okay, so he likes me. That's good to know, because I really like him. "Well," I begin, "I'm from Idaho."

"Idaho?" Trevor looks at me like I'm nuts.

"Yep."

"Wow," he says. "I didn't know there were black folks in Idaho." There are laugh lines around his eyes as he smiles.

"That's the first thing people always say, but yes, there definitely are."

"Atlanta's a far way from Idaho. Why'd you move here?"

"Because I always knew there was something bigger and better out there. Not to knock Boise, but I craved big-city life. I also wanted to go to a black college, and there aren't any there. I applied to Spelman, got accepted, and the rest is history."

"Any regrets?"

I wonder if he's talking about my moving to Atlanta or about us. "No. No regrets."

"Good," Trevor says.

Maybe it's the wine, but my tongue is suddenly feeling loose. I lean across the table and say, "You know, I'm really glad that Rhonda matched us up. Before this, I was pretty jaded about dating. Seems I kept meeting the same type of man—the wrong one."

"Same here," Trevor says. "The wrong woman, I mean."

Trevor and I share a chuckle. As our laughter dies, I glance away, wondering if I should invite him home now. No, not yet. There's no need to rush.

So instead I ask, "When was your last relationship?" Depending on what he says, I'll get an idea of where his head is at. If he's hung up on someone else. As much as I want to have sex, I don't want a one-night stand.

"It's been a while for me," he answers. "Four months."

"That's not so long," I comment. I hope he's over this woman. "Were you in love?"

Trevor shrugs. "I thought I was, but in the end I realized I wasn't."

He's being a bit evasive. I wonder if I should be concerned. Then again, he might not want to talk about it because it was a bad breakup.

"Ever been married?" I ask.

"Nope. What about you?"

"Oh yeah. But thankfully, I came to my senses." I force a grin. I don't want him thinking I'm bitter. "He was the wrong man, but hey, it happens."

I notice that Trevor's eyes have shifted to beyond my shoulder. He seems to have tuned me out. Oh, shit. I sounded like a moron and now he's turned off.

But his eyes linger, and I realize he's not avoiding me but looking at something else. Or someone else.

I quickly glance over my shoulder and peruse the restaurant. I see a family of four, two young couples, a table with two men.

Damn, I'm obviously being paranoid, but it's easy to be paranoid when you've dated the men I have.

When I turn back to Trevor, he is grinning at me. I have his undivided attention again.

He reaches for the bottle of wine and pours the dregs into my glass. "I don't know you very well, but I feel confident in saying that it's your husband's loss."

"You don't have to convince me," I agree.

I see the waitress coming toward us and I finish off my wine. The evening is going better than planned and I'm not ready for it to end. I'm thinking that maybe I'll throw caution to the wind and have a specialty coffee. I can always stay at Trevor's place, or he at mine, and get my car in the morning.

"Have you had a chance to check out the dessert menu?" the waitress asks.

"I'll have a Baileys coffee," I tell her.

"Nothing for me," Trevor says, but he's not looking at the waitress. He's looking past her.

Now I *know* I'm missing something. Trevor is definitely preoccupied. Either he's suddenly not digging me, or there's someone here that he knows.

"Trevor," I begin slowly. "Is everything okay?"

"Sure," he answers quickly, but his body language says he is lying. His jawline is tense, and he suddenly looks irritated.

I'm confused. "Trevor, did I say something wrong?"

"Why would you ask that?"

"You seem...upset."

Trevor shakes his head, but his eyes wander. This time, I follow his line of sight. It lands on a well-dressed white man sitting at a table with an Asian man. The white man is staring at Trevor.

I turn back to Trevor. "Do you know that guy? Oh, God. Don't tell me you prosecuted him in court."

"I think we should go." Trevor is already rising and reaching into his jacket pocket. "Where's that waitress?"

My stomach tightens painfully. God help me, I'm in a restaurant with a madman who was charming enough to convince a jury to acquit him. I can see why—the guy who is eyeing Trevor doesn't look as if he could hurt a fly.

But I know better than that. There is no specific look for the criminal. If only they boasted fangs and bulging eyes.

Trevor drags a hand over his face, and as I watch him, I'm really starting to freak out. Just what is this madman going to do? I envision the broadcast on the eleven o'clock news. *Local prosecutor gunned down in revenge killing.*

There is relief on Trevor's face when he spots the waitress. Without waiting a second, he marches toward her. As he does so, I slowly stand. I don't know if this matters to killers, but I'm guessing that no sudden movement is a good plan of action.

The seconds that pass seem like hours. I want to take off, but I can't just leave Trevor. If the situation were reversed, I wouldn't want him leaving me.

When Trevor returns to me, I'm ready to hustle. We start for the door, heading to safety. But God help us, it's too late. The madman jumps to his feet as we near his table. My entire body freezes as I'm seized with fright.

I do the first thing I can think of—take cover behind Trevor. What can I say? He's not my man. I'm not ready to die for him.

"Trevor," the white man says.

"Not now," Trevor replies, moving past the other man.

The guy grabs Trevor's arm, stopping him. "Look, I know what I said. But I've had time to think—"

"I said *not now*," Trevor hisses.

Trevor starts walking again, and I'm right beside him.

"Please don't walk away from me."

Those words make me halt. The guy almost sounds… I shake my head, dismissing the thought. Clearly, this man is not some deranged criminal. He obviously knows Trevor, but I have no clue how.

Trevor breezes into the lobby. The white man follows him. I lag behind a little, observing this confusing situation.

The man reaches for Trevor's hand. Trevor hesitates a moment before yanking his hand away.

Whoa, wait a minute. Did that just happen?

Oh, shit. *Shit!*

"We'll talk later, Brian," Trevor says.

"When?" Brian demands. "You've already been avoiding me."

Trevor meets my eyes, and I can tell he's mortified that I'm witnessing this. Brian looks at me, too. But it's not so much a look as it is a leer, the kind another woman gives you when she's possessive over her man.

I snort my disgust and make my way around them.

"Lishelle, wait," Trevor says.

"I don't think so," I reply.

And then I all but run out of the restaurant.

By the time I get to Claudia's place, I'm exhausted. Winded, like I've run a friggin' marathon. My heart hasn't stopped beating since I hightailed it out of the restaurant.

I'm about to knock on her door, but it opens before I can. Although Claudia shares a place in Buckhead with Adam, she's living with her parents until her wedding. (Don't ask why. Something about appearances.) She has her own apartment within their mammoth house, where she used to live before things got serious with Adam. Thank God that apartment has a separate entrance. I don't want anyone else witnessing me in my frazzled state.

Claudia swings the door open and eyes me with concern. "Sweetie, what is it?"

I feel a little foolish for having called her in such a panic, but damn, I needed someone to talk to after what happened.

I walk past her into the house. "Do me a favor. If you ever hear me say that I'm going on another date, shoot me."

"That bad?"

I drop my clutch onto the hall table. "Fuck, yeah."

The reality of tonight hits me anew and I want to

scream. Instead, I growl a little and move farther into the house. I stop short when I see Annelise sitting on the couch. "Oh. Hi."

"Annelise was here when you called," Claudia explains. "She decided to stay, figuring you might need both of us."

Despite my shaky nerves, my spirits lift a little. These two women ground me. I love them to death, and I know that they love me. They'd drop everything for me if I needed them to.

"I appreciate it," I say.

Annelise makes her way toward me and snakes an arm around my waist. "What happened?"

"Let's just say, I thought my date was going to make the eleven o'clock news."

"Whoa." This from Claudia. "Why?"

We all sit on the sofa and I spend the next few minutes telling them everything, and by the time I'm done, Annelise is snickering and Claudia is roaring with laughter.

"It's not funny," I tell them. "You don't know how afraid I was."

"Oh, shit." Claudia's eyes are tearing. "Too much drama for me."

"For you? I'm the one who was caught in the middle of this guy's sexual identity drama. Hell, the brother didn't even know if he was straight or not. I should have known. He was much too pretty. And the Kenneth Cole shoes. They should have been a dead giveaway."

"God, how scary," Annelise says. "Dating a guy who goes both ways." She shudders.

"Thank God I didn't sleep with him." Now *I* shudder. "This had to be a sign. Obviously, I'm supposed to stop dating."

"Don't say that," Annelise tells me. "There's a great guy out there for you. I know you'll find him."

"Ha!" Both Claudia and Annelise shoot me looks of concern. "Don't look at me like that. You both don't know what it's like. You have men. Trying to find the right one—my God, it's so hard."

"I know," Annelise says. "But you can't give up."

"Why not? Dating these days is like Russian roulette. I think I'd rather put a gun to my head and be done with it."

"I think you need a glass of wine." Annelise dashes off in the direction of the kitchen.

"Make it a scotch, honey."

With Annelise out of view, I turn to Claudia. I'm feeling much better and want to think about something positive. "So. Saturday night? You sure you've made a decision about the dresses this time?"

"No, but I can't straddle the fence much longer. The wedding is only five weeks away."

"For what it's worth, I love the pastel mauve fabric you showed me. I think it's much better than the yellow."

"Really?" Claudia's eyes light up.

"Of course. I look better in the mauve."

Now her smile fizzles. She absolutely hates the idea that if she commits to one color, it will be the wrong one.

I reach for her hand and squeeze it. "Relax. The mauve is the right color. It'll look great on everyone."

"You're sure?"

God, she is such a typical Gemini. Unable to make a

decision. I still can't believe she planned a wedding for two days after her thirtieth birthday. But according to her, it's the best way to celebrate this milestone.

"Yes, I'm sure," I tell her. I don't bother to mention that I liked the first color as much, or that will send her world into a tizzy.

"What I want to know," I continue, "is if you're ready for this wedding? You left me a message saying you wanted to talk about Adam."

Claudia motions for me to drop the subject as Annelise reappears. I eye her suspiciously, but she's now reaching for her drink from the coffee table. Her demeanor gives nothing away.

"Here you go." Annelise passes me the scotch. For herself, she has a glass full of wine.

"What do you say that for tonight we forget about men and concentrate on us?" Annelise suggests.

"Sounds like a plan," Claudia agrees.

"I'll drink to that," I say. And then I down my scotch.

Chapter Four

Claudia

Nearly a full week has passed since I went to that sex club with Adam, and I have to say, he's been *really* sweet to me. On Tuesday, the very next day, he surprised me with a diamond tennis bracelet, set in platinum. On Wednesday, he gave me this Dior purse I told him I was dying to have—the Vintage Flowers Bag. Yesterday evening, he took me to this park near his brownstone where we had a totally romantic dinner. I swear, I fell in love with him all over again as he fed me chocolate-covered strawberries. He specifically thanked me for working so hard on our wedding, and promised me that it was all worth it because we're going to have such a wonderful life together.

I couldn't have had a better week with him. So I'm really surprised tonight, as I'm lying naked on top of him in his bed, when he guides my body off of his, reaches under the bed and produces a fairly large, gift-wrapped box.

Another gift. I can get used to this treatment.

A smile breaks out on my face. "Adam, what *is* this?"

"Open it."

Taking the box from him, I sit up. I pull at the ribbon, then the gold wrapping, giggling the entire time. But when I lift the lid and pull out all the tissue paper, my smile fizzles. In fact, my stomach tightens with immense disappointment.

"It's my gift to you," he says while gently stroking my arm.

It's a huge dildo. And I mean huge. It's got straps on it, as well, so there's no doubt that this is a strap-on.

But Adam already has a penis. One I'm very happy with.

"I don't get it," I admit.

"You remember what we saw last week—at that club?"

How can I forget? My eyes are still burning. "I saw lots of stuff."

"Remember that woman in the cage, and the guy she was with?"

The visual hits me in the face. Yes, I remember. The woman was wearing the strap-on and screwing the guy from behind.

"Adam…" I laugh nervously as I look at him. "Come on, you don't want me to do that…do you?"

He sucks on the tip of my finger. "If you want to try it, I'm up for it."

I stare at him in total disbelief. "Are you gay?" It's the

only thing I can think of to ask. Especially after Lishelle's disastrous date.

He throws his head back and roars with laughter. "Gay? Me? Come on, you know better than that."

"Then why…" My voice trails off and I shake my head.

"There's a whole sexual world out there that we have yet to discover. I want to discover it all with you."

"Are you unhappy with me?" I can't help blurting.

Adam's smile is full of love as he gazes at me, and he frames my face with his hands. "Of course not. I have so much love for you, so much passion, that I want to try everything with you. That's what this is about."

"You're sure?"

"Of course I'm sure. I want us to have the kind of re-lationship where we can try anything, knowing it will bring us closer together. And I never want you to be timid about suggesting anything to me, because whatever you want to try, I'll be game."

"Anything?"

"Anything."

I swallow as I gaze into the box. "I'm not so sure I'm comfortable—" I lift the strap-on "—with this."

"It's not a world we've experienced before. Who knows? Changing roles…it might be fun."

I really don't know what's gotten into Adam. It's like he's become a freak.

Or is it me who's a complete prude? But how can I be a prude? Adam and I have tried every position. We've had sex in public places, tried a myriad of sex toys and watched sex videos together. He even convinced me to try anal sex—something I haven't dared to tell a soul. I thought I would hate every second of it, but I liked it. It was taboo and dirty and turned me on more than I expected.

But this?

I drop the strap-on back into the box and move it behind us. Then I stretch my body out on Adam's. "Sweetie," I purr in his ear. "I *like* being the girl."

"And I like being the guy. Nothing's gonna change that. But I saw how much that woman in the cage enjoyed the way she was doing that guy…and I thought…I want that for you. A different kind of sexual pleasure."

I make a sound of derision.

"Hold on to it until you become comfortable," Adam tells me. "Maybe you never will, but you never know."

I don't see that happening. The truth is, the things I've tried with Adam I would never have suggested. And quite frankly, while we don't do it often, I don't care if we never watch another porn video. And I certainly don't want to go to another sex club. Adam turns me on. Him alone. Everything about him.

"I'll tell you right now, I'm not bringing that thing to my parents' place. We'll keep it here. I can just imagine what would happen if the cleaner stumbled upon it, or worse—my mother!"

I laugh, and to my relief, Adam does, too. But Lord, I hope he forgets about this strap-on thing. I can't help wondering if he's going through some sort of sexual crisis with all the weird and different stuff he's wanted us to try in the past few months. I pray this phase passes soon, and we can start our lives in the wedded bliss I've dreamed of since I was a child.

* * *

Is Diana staring at me weirdly? I can't help wondering the next morning as we sit across from her in my parents' backyard. We're getting together with the wedding planner this morning to go over the final menu. It's decision day. The week before the wedding, we fly the chefs up from New Orleans to prepare all the items on the menu for us to sample. If there's anything we don't like, we can change our minds then, but we need a pretty solid idea of what we're going with today.

Diana, a graying woman in her late fifties who looks a lot like Diane Keaton, slips her glasses on and opens her planner. "So for appetizers you're going with the five tomato mozzarella salad, the gumbo and the petite couchon baton. What about the main course? Were you still hoping for beef?"

I look at Adam. He's wearing dark glasses so no one can see his eyes. But I already know what they look like. Red. He got high this morning before we came to meet Diana.

It's one other change in him I don't like. In the past year, Adam's weed smoking has gotten excessive. He says he needs to relax because he's so stressed with all the planning for the wedding, as well as his aspirations to run for mayor. I understand that, but there's a limit for everything.

I ask, "What do you think, Adam?"

"I told you what I think. Let's have beef."

I face Diana. "My mother and I have been getting calls. People are wondering why there isn't a beef option."

"Those people aren't planning a wedding for six hundred guests."

"I know, but—"

"Can I make a suggestion?" she asks.

"Of course," I answer.

"You've got onion-crusted American red snapper and pecan smoked Muscovy duck breast. That's an excellent menu, certainly satisfactory for even the most discriminating eater. If you want to add anything else, I'd suggest another appetizer. The truffled soft-shell crab bisque. There's plenty of choice for everyone."

"You're probably right."

"I am right," Diana assures me. "If anyone wants to complain, tell them to come to me." She smiles sweetly, a smile that says she's been planning weddings for over thirty years and knows her stuff.

"Can we make a decision on this, Adam?"

"Whatever you suggest is fine."

I roll my eyes slightly. I swear, I wish he'd get more involved.

"What about the dessert?" Diana asks.

"The best part," I say. "I think I'll gain ten pounds before my honeymoon."

Diana lifts the sheet with the dessert items and their descriptions. Adam and I have a copy of the same sheet to peruse. "Lemon flan," Diana reads. "Chocolate-fudge Sheba, crème brûlée, Commander's pecan pie à la mode, praline parfait, Creole bread pudding soufflé and Creole cream-cheese cheesecake." She lowers the sheet. "You're choosing two."

I glance at Adam, but he's not even looking our way. His gaze is off in the direction of the woods behind my parents' house.

I reach for his leg under the table.

"Honey?"

"Yeah, sure. Sounds great."

Great, he's not even paying attention! I hide my embarrassment by quickly saying, "We'll do the Creole bread pudding soufflé and crème brûlée." I nod. "Yeah, that's good."

Diana scribbles some notes.

Is that the right choice? I wonder. "Wait. You know what—if they're preparing a sampling menu for us, why don't you add the lemon flan and praline parfait to the list. That way, we can see what we like best before the wedding."

"No problem." Diana makes more notes. "You're paying big bucks for perfection, and I assure you you'll have perfection."

At the price she's charging, we most certainly should have perfection.

"Now for the fun part."

"Oh?" I say.

"I have a surprise for you."

I squeeze Adam's hand. "A surprise. Isn't that exciting, Adam?"

"Oh, yeah. It's great."

Diana removes her glasses, pushes her chair back and stands. "Let's head to the pool-area bar, because you two lovebirds are going to create your own drink."

"Our own drink?" I can't help smiling.

"I brought in a mixologist today and he'll work with you to concoct a cocktail specifically for you and your guests that they'll enjoy as they arrive at the reception."

"That sounds amazing." I look to Adam, who's got a cheesy smile on his face. "I had no clue."

"I like to add some personal touches of my own," Diana tells us.

Adam and I get up. We follow Diana to the pool area in my parents' vast backyard. They have a full bar there housed in a Caribbean-style hut. Behind the bar's counter, I see a white man with shoulder-length blond hair. He's tanned and looks as if he just stepped off a beach. He's the type I associate with surfers and a carefree lifestyle.

"I'm gonna like this," Adam proclaims.

At least he's interested again. No surprise there. With the amount of drinks we'll sample, I'm sure we'll have a nice buzz before noon.

"I'll leave you two to Jason," Diana announces, "and I'll head back into the house, as I have some things to go over with your parents."

Adam and I slip onto bar stools. Jason extends his hand and we take turns shaking it as we introduce ourselves.

"Jason, you look like you flew in from Hawaii last night," I can't help commenting.

Jason chuckles. "Nope, I'm from Atlanta. I work at a bar in Buckhead."

"Adam and I live in Buckhead."

"Have you been to Apple?"

"No. That's the piano bar, right? We keep meaning to check it out. Don't we, Adam?"

"Yeah," he responds, and I'm sure Jason must realize he's high.

"Why don't you?" Jason asks. "That's where I am almost every day of the week."

Jason's eyes linger on mine, and I wonder if he's just hit on me.

Adam, however, is oblivious. He reaches for my hand. I can't help gazing at him with affection. I like when he's amorous with me.

But Adam doesn't just link fingers with me, he pulls my hand toward him, stopping only when it's on his crotch.

Oh my God. He's hard.

My face flushing, I quickly glance away. "Jason, what do you have for us?"

"Yes, what indeed?" Adam asks.

Jason shrugs. "What are you in the mood for?"

"Oh, we're pretty risqué. Like to live life on the edge. I'm sure whatever you suggest will excite us."

OhmyGodtellmeheisn'tpropositioningthebartender!

"I was thinking something fruity," I quickly tell Jason. "Maybe with vodka, or rum. Something that will make me think of lazy days on an island beach."

"Got ya."

Jason spins around and grabs some bottles. If he thought there was anything strange about Adam's words, he's chosen to ignore it.

Thank the Lord.

I lift my sunglasses and glare at Adam. He flashes me a devilish smile, one that confirms my worst fear.

What's happened to you, Adam? I wonder.

What's happened to the man I love?

On Monday, I'm still feeling very weird about what happened on the weekend with the bartender. I could

stay home and ruminate by myself, but instead I call Annelise and see if she wants to get together for dinner.
Nothing fancy, just dinner at my place. Lishelle's working, or I would have invited her, too.

But maybe it's good that it's just me and Annelise. Not
only do we have to discuss the wedding photography, I've
decided to confide in her about my concerns over Adam.
Originally, I figured I might broach the subject of Adam's
bizarre sexual appetite with Lishelle, but considering
Annelise is in a relationship, she might be the better one
to discuss this with. Because I have to talk to someone,
or I'm gonna go out of my mind.

I swallow my bite of Caesar salad, then put down my
fork. "Annelise," I say cautiously.

She looks up from her salad. "Yeah?"

I think of how best to phrase what I want to ask, but
there's only one way to say it. I've got to say it straight.
"Does Charles ever want…really kinky sex?"

Annelise's eyes widen in surprise. "Why do you ask
that?"

"I just…" I lean forward and whisper, as though there's
a fly on the wall that could hear us. "Adam is into all
kinds of weird stuff lately. I'm hoping it's a phase. But I'm
also wondering…is it me? Am I uncomfortable with it
because I'm a prude or something? I know times have
changed drastically even in ten years, so maybe it is me.
Then again…" I blow out a breath. "I know it's a personal
question, but has Charles ever been into…weird stuff?
And if so, did he get over it? I guess I want to hear that
it won't last forever."

Annelise clears her throat. "Wow. That was—"

"A mouthful, I know. And probably too much information. But I need to know if I'm obsessing over this, or if perhaps I need to be more sexually liberated."

Annelise's fork clinks against her plate as she lowers it. "I'm afraid I can't help you. I have no experience in that department."

"Damn," I mutter. "So Adam *is* a freak—that's what you think?"

"You haven't said enough for me to form an opinion. Just how 'kinky' are we talking?"

I can't meet her inquiring gaze. "Anal sex," I admit shamefully. "Having sex in public places. Not that anyone would see us," I quickly point out, "but there's the threat of getting caught. That threat really turns him on. Then on Friday night…" I let out a heavy sigh. "He bought me a *strap-on*. As a present for *me*."

Annelise's eyes bulge. "What?"

"I know. It's horrible, isn't it?"

"But I don't get—"

"He said he wants *me* to do *him*." Now I meet Annelise's blue-eyed gaze. "Can you believe it?"

Annelise shakes her head. "I'm sorry. Not really."

I groan my dissatisfaction. "I knew it. I knew this was over the top." I push my salad away, no longer hungry. "And please, don't mention this to Lishelle. I'm embarrassed enough as it is."

"Honey, I only wish I had your problem."

Now my eyes widen. "What?"

"Maybe a strap-on is a little freaky, but at least Adam wants to have sex with you. Experience it all with you. I'd love it if I had that in my life."

"Okay, I'm a little lost. No, a lot lost."

Annelise sighs softly. "I haven't said anything before because…well, because it's been too painful. But Charles hasn't slept with me in over fourteen months."

I'm so stunned, I can't even speak.

"Yeah, it's true. My husband doesn't even want to touch me. It's a real boost to my self-esteem, let me tell you."

"Oh my God." I reach across the table to cover Annelise's hand. "Honey."

"It's driving me *nuts*. I'm at my wit's end. I'm trying so hard, but he's always so tired, so stressed. And when I touch him, it's like he's a block of stone."

"I had no clue."

"I didn't want to say anything, but since we're talking about sex. I welcome any suggestions you might have."

"You could always borrow my strap-on."

That gets a smile from Annelise. We both laugh.

Then I ask, "What have you tried?"

"Candles, nice dinners, wine. All that. Stuff to relax him and get him in the mood. But nothing's been working. So, last week, I went to a…a sex shop. I picked up this slutty French maid's outfit. It was raunchy, let me tell you."

"That didn't work?" I ask in surprise. I don't know a man alive who doesn't get turned on by the French maid fantasy.

Annelise shakes her head in disappointment. "He completely ignored me. Turned on a soccer game, and I don't think he even likes soccer."

"Wow. This calls for drastic measures."

"I know, but what?"

Going to a swingers' club.… But I don't dare suggest that because I can't admit to anyone that I went there with Adam, albeit unwillingly.

"I don't know," I say after a moment. "Let me think about it. In the meantime, I hope his stress level lessens. He *is* working on that big case."

"I know, I know. Believe me, I know. And I feel for all those people who got sick from Kitler's Cookies. I support all the hard work he's doing. But isn't sex supposed to be a great stress reliever?"

"I thought so. For Adam it definitely is."

Annelise sighs softly, and she looks so disheartened that I can't help but feel bad for her.

"Well," I begin, "if this is work related, then it won't go on forever. I know that's not much comfort now, but tomorrow's another day. Don't give up hope."

"I'm hanging in there," she says. But she sounds as if she could burst into tears any moment.

Here I was, thinking I had it bad because Adam's sexual appetite is endless. But maybe I don't have it bad at all.

Sure, he wants to try everything, but like Annelise said, at least he's trying it with me. He obviously trusts me with his fantasies, and that says a lot.

Yeah, I guess I've been a bit of a prude. Nothing is shameless between committed partners—between two people who love each other with their whole hearts and souls.

Chapter Five

Annelise

All that talk about sex with Claudia over dinner has me totally hot and bothered and completely frustrated. So the first thing I do when I head back home and find that Charles is still at work is lock myself in the bedroom and masturbate.

I imagine that I'm with the Charles from the early days of our relationship. The Charles who was always passionate for me, even when I woke up next to him with morning breath. The Charles who would slip his hand down my pants on a ride at an amusement park, or undo my blouse and fondle my breasts in a movie theatre. The Charles who would know with just a look that I was ready to make love.

"Charles, Charles, Charles," I mutter as I touch myself, imagining it's his fingers on me, his tongue tracing circles around my nipple.

I cry out as I climax, happily riding the sensuous wave— but only for a moment. Because immediately afterward I feel cold and empty. So cold and empty I could cry.

I have a husband, damn it. Why do I have to pleasure myself, when I have a man who's young and should be wild about me?

"Forget Charles," I tell myself and climb off the bed. I head to the bathroom and start the shower. Maybe cool water will help put out the fire inside me.

Ten minutes later, I step out of the shower and towel off. I try to forget about sex, but even as I apply scented lotion to my legs, I can't help but think of the way Charles used to do this for me, his hands moving over my body with aching slowness.

Surely Oprah will help get my mind off sex. For an hour I can feel better about myself by observing others' miserable lives. I quickly dress in a T-shirt and shorts, then head to the living room to queue up the VCR. I tape *Oprah* daily.

I rewind the tape for several seconds, then stop and hit play. When the show comes on, Oprah is looking thoughtfully at a teary-eyed woman.

"So what do you think happened?" Oprah asks the dark-haired woman. "Why did the passion in your marriage die?"

The woman looks downright confused. "I don't know."

"You have to know," Oprah insists. "When you think about your marriage, your life—and I'm sure you have— you have to have at least an idea of what went wrong."

That's not fair, Oprah, I think. *Maybe she doesn't know. I'm living proof that things can go sour and a person has no clue why.*

"The children," the woman finally answers. "I suppose once the children came along, that's when the spark started to fizzle."

"I've said this once," Oprah begins, "I'll say it again. Women often put themselves last when the children come along. They get so caught up in mothering, they forget their own needs as women."

"Not all the time," I say to the TV. I know without a doubt that if Charles and I were to have children, I'd still make room for an active sex life. As it is, we have no kids, so what's Charles's damn excuse?

Stretched out on the sofa, I continue to watch the show, though I'm not sure why. This isn't exactly making me forget about my dismal situation with my husband. But on the bright side, as I watch a series of women talk about their passionless marriages, I know I'm not alone.

I sit up when Oprah announces that she has a surprise for her guests. She does the best surprises.

"I know you're all here today because you want help," Oprah says. "And I want to help you regain the passion your marriages are missing. That's why I'm sending you and your spouses on a four-day getaway to the romantic Canyon Ranch Spa in Tucson, Arizona!"

The couples burst into full-blown smiles and the audience rowdily applauds.

"This spa has everything you can possibly think of for couples. Classes on kissing. How to create exceptional sex." The audience hoots and hollers. "If you can't re-connect sexually with your partner after this four-day weekend, then I don't think you ever will."

Oh my God. This is it. The answer I've been waiting for.

Of course! How could I have been so narrow-minded?

When was the last time Charles and I took a trip to-gether? About a year and a half ago, and we had really great sex then. I have to get Charles away from work, take him on a romantic trip to this place designed for lovers, and there's no way we won't recapture what's missing in our relationship.

I jump off the sofa and head toward the home office. I intend to find out everything there is to know about the Canyon Ranch Spa. I don't care what it costs. I'd pay any amount to get Charles alone somewhere where the en-tire object of the place is to have sex.

If nothing else, I'll be able to figure out once and for all if my husband is attracted to me. If we're alone to-gether in a sexual paradise and he still can't get it up, then I'll have to…

Truthfully, I don't want to think about what I'll have to do. I don't want to be in a loveless marriage, and I *do* want to have children.

All of which I'm sure will happen, just as soon as Charles and I recharge our marriage. And I'm rearing to go. But I can hear Charles's protests that work will keep him at home. He puts in more hours than one would think humanly possible.

I know it's going to be hard to get him away from work, but I'm going to try. One weekend is all we need.

I type in the words *Canyon Ranch Spa*.

As the page loads, I'm instantly impressed. This place is stunning. Outdoor Jacuzzi tubs, palm trees... This is romantic at its best.

I look heavenward and utter, "Thank you, God."

Hours later, I can't sleep.

Beside me, Charles is lightly snoring. He hasn't touched me, of course, despite the red negligee I'm wearing. I know priests who couldn't resist me in this outfit, yet Charles is painfully oblivious.

I stroke his arm. "Charles."

He doesn't move, so this time I shake his shoulder. I don't care that it's two in the morning. I want to make love, or at least talk to him.

"Charles."

"Hmm?" he finally mutters.

"Sorry to wake you up," I tell him. But I'm not. I need to talk to him about this, and it has to be now.

"What is it?" he asks in a sleep-filled voice.

"I was wondering...wondering if you might be able to take some time off work soon."

"What?"

"There's this place I found out about, and I'd like us to go. It's in Arizona."

Charles groans. "Can't we talk about this in the morning?"

"I guess so... But I'm excited. Do you know when you will have some time?"

"I don't know."

"Can you check tomorrow?"

"What's this about?"

Now I hesitate. "It's about us reconnecting. Going away together so we get out of the routine we're in."

"Oh." He pauses. "Can I go back to sleep now?"

My heart is beating hard as I edge my body closer to his. It shouldn't be, damn it. This is my husband. I should feel one hundred percent comfortable holding him in the night, comfortable slipping my body onto his, comfortable taking his penis into my hands... But I don't, because I'm afraid he'll reject me.

Slowly, I slip an arm around him, settling my hand on his warm stomach. My fingers tease the hairs around his navel.

I don't realize that I'm holding my breath until Charles does something that he hasn't done in a long time.

He places a hand over mine.

A surge of warmth rushes through my body. I release the breath I was holding on a low moan. The ache inside me is so intense as I trail a finger down past his belly button, straight toward his groin. I feel the mass of hair and already I'm getting wet.

Finally, Charles and I are going to make love.

I cover him with my hand and as soon as I do, he covers my hand again. I press my lips against his shoulder. "Oh, Charles..."

He pries my fingers off of him.

"Ann, it's two in the morning. I'm tired."

I stifle my moan of disappointment as I roll over, but I can't stop the tears filling my eyes.

I'm obviously desperate.

That explains what I'm doing here this afternoon, at

my sister's workplace, instead of at my studio developing the film I'm supposed to. I absolutely hate coming here, because I don't agree with my sister's lifestyle, but I have to face it—she gets laid and I don't, so there's clearly a thing or two I can learn from her.

Despite the eighty-five-degree weather, I'm wearing a scarf wrapped around my head, and the biggest, darkest sunglasses I own when I walk into the Pleasure Dome, the club where Samera works. When I called and didn't get her at home or on her cell, I figured she had to be working, because even if she's on a hot date, she always answers her cell.

The club is dark and smoky, just the way I'd expect a place like this to be. In the middle of the room, a large stage is illuminated with fluorescent blue lighting. For a Wednesday afternoon, I'm surprised that there's more than a handful of men in the place, and I have to look around to find a table that's unoccupied. It's to the very far right of the stage. I keep my eyes focused on the table as I head toward it.

Only when I'm safely seated do I check out the stripper onstage. The woman performing has long black hair and is wearing a garter belt with no panties. The garter is stuffed with cash. I suspect the long black hair that hangs to her ass is a wig. *Probably a French maid's outfit,* I think with chagrin, remembering my embarrassment over how Charles completely rejected me.

The woman does this lazy sexy-type walk to the pole onstage. She wraps a leg around it and does this gyrating thing against it, as if it's a huge penis. I watch her, both mortified and fascinated by the way she moves.

After swinging around the pole, she eases her body forward and presses the pole between her very large and obviously fake breasts.

Finally, I slip my sunglasses off, because they're straining my eyes in the dimly lit room. Surreptitiously, I watch the guys watching her. No man in the place can take his eyes off her. And I have to say, there's something about the way she's using the pole that is utterly erotic. Funny, I can see what she's doing as erotic today, as opposed to before, when I saw it all as filthy and sinful.

Gripping the pole with both hands, the stripper bends her body backward with the ease of a contortionist, giving the guys what must be a delicious view of her heavy breasts. Oh yeah, the men are mesmerized. I even see one of them lick his lips.

Maybe I need to get a pole like this in our bedroom. Surely Charles couldn't reject me if I were to do this sort of seductive dance. The idea seems absurd, but it's not half-bad. I could get Samera to teach me the basics…

Now the dancer slides all the way down the pole until she is on the floor. On all fours, she does this catlike crawl to the edge of the stage. It's all part of her routine, but I can't help chuckling at how she collects the pile of cash on the stage. A few more extended legs and back arching and gentle caresses of some men's faces, and then the stripper gets to her feet and makes her exit.

My eyes dart around the club. There are a few topless women working the floor, serving drinks, but my sister isn't one of them.

The slow music comes to an end, and the loud, pulsing beat of Christina Aguilera's "Dirrty" fills the club.

The next stripper, with wild blond hair and wearing a red leather minidress unzipped to her navel, hurries onto the stage brandishing a whip. It takes me only a moment to realize that it's my sister.

Her skirt is so short that as she passes me, I see more of her ass than of the red leather. She's also got these thigh-high shiny black boots on, the kind with spiked heels that must be at least four inches. How she even walks on those things let alone dances in them is beyond me.

The men hoot and howl in appreciation, and Samera slaps her whip against the stage. I glance away. *Oh, Sammie. Why do you do it? Why make yourself an object like this?*

When I look her way again, money is flying onto the stage. A lot of money. Which pretty much answers the question of why she does it—or at least that's what I like to tell myself.

Because I know Samera also loves her job. Long before she got paid to take off her clothes, she got off on wearing skimpy outfits and watching men's reactions to her. She especially had fun with our mother's second husband, teasing the poor guy until he broke down and screwed her. My mother kicked them both out, screaming about how they'd both burn in hell for what they'd done. I figure that Samera had heard so often that she was going to burn in hell, she figured she might as well enjoy the rest of her life in the most explicitly sexual way possible.

Doing a slow twirl, Samera completely unzips her dress. She teases the guys with views of her bountiful bosom—also enhanced by the help of surgery. Surgery I accompanied her to, and tried to talk her out of all the way to the clinic.

I turn my head. I'm not comfortable watching Samera like this. It's like my mother's internal dialogue is stuck in my head, and I can't get past thinking that what Samera's doing is completely sinful. I feel awful for her, so awful I'm almost tempted to pray for her soul.

Snap!

I jump at the sound of the whip, and my eyes fly to the stage. There's Samera, her breasts exposed, the dress gone, and only a black piece of leather covering her crotch.

Her eyes light up with recognition as our eyes connect. I give a small wave.

She heads off toward the front of the stage, her hips moving in an exaggerated sexual movement. She grabs the pole and twists around it, then bends onto her haunches, giving the men a view of the contrast of pale ass against black leather. When she goes onto all fours, I turn away again and pretend to be absorbed in a search for something that's inside my purse.

I know Samera's routine is over when I hear the round of applause. Now I look back to the stage. Except for the boots, Samera is completely naked. She winks at me as she exits.

How does she do it? Strut naked like that in front of strangers? I don't get it.

A few minutes later, Samera comes running out from the back area of the club and straight for me. I stand, and she throws herself at me, hugging me hard.

"Annie, what are you doing here?"

I'm not sure what to say. "We said we'd get together for lunch, remember?"

"And you want to do that here?"

As Samera and I pull apart, I take in what she's wearing. A white cutoff T-shirt that shows the bottom of her breasts. Instead of a skirt, she's wearing skintight leather pants and those spiked plastic-looking shoes I call hooker heels.

"Well…sure," I tell her. "Why not?"

Samera eyes me with suspicion. "You've either lost your mind or you've found your wild side. And why are you wearing a scarf on your head?"

"Oh, this. I…" I can't think of a decent thing to say, and pull the scarf off my head.

She takes my hand. "Come on. Let's sit down."

"Are you finished?" I ask her as we sit at the table I'd occupied a moment earlier.

"God, no. I've got four more sets to do. But I have around half an hour to spare. Now tell me, what's up? Because I know something must be up for you to be here right now."

I blow out a hard breath. "You're right."

"Charles?" she guesses, scowling as she does.

I'm not going to lie. "Yeah."

"What's the jerk done this time?"

"It's what he hasn't done. We're still not having sex." It's strange that I don't mind sharing this intimate detail with Samera when we're not very close.

Like I said, I'm desperate.

"What do you mean you're not having sex?" Samera asks in disbelief. "Didn't you buy all sorts of toys and stuff to use with him last week?"

"Not *all sorts,* but I did buy an outfit. Something I thought would turn him on, and it didn't. This really trampy French maid's out—"

"He's fucking someone else. You know that now, don't you?"

"No," I say adamantly. "I don't know that. What I know is that my husband is very busy, and somewhere along the way we've lost our connection. He's so busy, he's forgotten about sex. But it's not a reason to walk away from my marriage, even if right now it feels like we'll never make love again. I just need…help."

"What do you want me to do?"

What indeed? "I don't know."

"I'm sure you have something in mind. Or you wouldn't be here. You could have called me, asked for directions to more shops."

"Okay. I'm desperate. I guess I thought I'd come here and watch…and pick up some pointers." My admission surprises me as much as Samera. "And if you have any tips on how to turn things around with Charles and save my marriage, I'm all ears."

"I don't know what kind of tips I can give you. From everything I know, you get naked for a guy and he can't help but get hard for you."

"I think that works in a relationship when it's new, fresh. But Charles and I have been married for years. I guess…" It pains me to even think what I'm about to say, because I never thought it would happen to us. "I guess things have gotten stale."

"Which is exactly why I don't believe in marriage. Nor long-term relationships."

"Sammie." God, I sound whiny. I hate how pathetic I sound, but I can't help it. I'm as desperate as any of the women on *Desperate Housewives,* and I'm about to lose my mind.

"All right. Let me think. The toys didn't work."

"It was a French maid's outfit, and maybe it was too conservative. Maybe I have to go all out and become really skanky."

I stop talking when a topless waitress appears at our table. I feel so embarrassed for the woman, I want to use my scarf to cover her breasts. At least they look real, which is a plus. Why can't men like women the way they naturally are? We have to take *them* the way *they* are.

"Molly," Samera coos. "This is my sister, Annelise."

"Hi." Molly gives me a bright smile, as if I'm a long-lost friend or something.

"What do you want to drink?" Samera asks.

"Oh, I don't think—"

"Get her a sex on the beach," Samera tells her, then laughs. "I bet you'd like that right about now, wouldn't you?"

I grin—painfully—until Molly waltzes away. Then I say, "You don't have to announce to the world that I'm not getting laid."

"Relax. Molly doesn't know anything, and even if she did, she could care less."

I suppose Samera's right. "Can you teach me some of those slutty moves you girls do with the pole?"

"They're not slutty. They're artistic."

"That's what I meant," I say. I flash Samera a sugary smile, and then we both chuckle.

"Oh, Annie. I know we're not close, but I hate what Charles is doing to you. Making you doubt your sexual power. You're better off without him."

"Sammie, please." I know my sister feels this way. She made it clear how much she disliked Charles on our wedding day when she cornered me in the bathroom and told me that it wasn't too late to annul my marriage. Those were the days that Charles and I screwed like rabbits. "Will you teach me to use the pole or not?"

"I can teach you, but maybe what you need to do is make a big change—not just in the bedroom."

"Huh?"

"You know—change everything about yourself. Start wearing low-cut blouses and tight jeans and strappy sandals all the time." Samera's eyes slowly roam over me. "Let's face it—oversized T-shirts and baggy jeans don't exactly get most guys in the mood. Is this how you always dress?"

"No." *Yes.* "Well, some of the time." At Samera's doubtful scowl, I admit, "Okay, most of the time. But I want to be comfortable. When I'm at the studio, I get on the floor, on the grass, or climb a tree—whatever's necessary for the best shot. I need to be able to move."

"Do you want to get laid or don't you?"

"I want to get laid," I reply without hesitation.

"Then trust me. Make a change. A big one. Get some kick-ass skintight black leather pants. And a lot of tight, short skirts. Guys *love* that. It's easy access, and pretty much wherever you are, all you need to do is bend over for a quickie."

"Sammie!" I exclaim, mortified that she'd do such

things in public. But then I think about my dismal situation, and I can't deny that if I were out with Charles and he wanted me badly enough to sneak off into a bathroom and give it to me in a dingy stall, I would feel so loved.

Molly appears, breasts bouncing. She places my drink on the table. Then she heads off to deal with some guys at a nearby table who are calling out to her. Thankfully.

"You ought to try sex in public before you knock it," Samera comments.

"I'd have sex on national TV right now if it meant Charles could get it up."

"That'd send Mama right to her grave!" A sharp burst of laughter escapes Samera, but as her laughter dies, I see something in her eyes—something that says she misses our mother. "You talk to her lately?"

"Mama?"

She nods.

"About a week ago. She was heading off to some bible something or other in California."

"You mean they let her out of the compound in Alabama?"

"Sounded like it was a group trip."

"When is she gonna realize that those fucking assholes are cult leaders?" Samera shakes her head. "Religious freaks. I can't stand them."

"She seems happy." And that's the best I can hope for, really. I know she's had a hard life. Personally, I think she suffered some childhood trauma that's had her searching for peace ever since. I only talk to my mother once in a while, mostly when she has a moment to call me. She's thrown herself one hundred percent into this new church family of hers, and she doesn't have much time for me anymore. It's just as well. I can only take so much of her fire-and-brimstone talk.

Samera scowls. "Forget Mama. You came to talk about Charles."

Oh, Samera talks a good game, as if she doesn't care one bit about our mother, but I know she's does. And I know she was hurt when my mother cut her out of her life. Yet another person who rejected her the way our father rejected both of us when we were little kids.

But it's not a subject I want to discuss now, even if I think it'd do Samera good. Instead, I say, "Sexy clothes, huh? You think that will do the trick?"

"Not just sexy. Trampy. And don't just wear them around the house. Wear them when you leave to hang with your girlfriends. That'll make Charles wonder who you're going to meet. Seriously, give guys a little competition and you'll see how fast they try and get you in bed."

"You might just be right." When we were dating, if Charles noticed another guy looking at me, he always held me a little tighter.

"I am right. And you know it, or you wouldn't be here."

"I won't argue with that."

"Look, sweetie. Lana's just finished her routine, which means I have to go back and get ready. But you stay and finish your drink. It's on me."

We both stand and hug. "I love you, Sammie." And I do. With all my heart. Regardless of how little we see each other, she's always in my heart. As her older sister by four years, there's a part of me that's very protective of her, even though she's the one who could probably kick butt to save my ass.

"I love you, too. And one more piece of advice?"

We pull apart. "Sure."

"Start checking Charles's clothes. Check his wallet, his car. Everything."

"Sam—"

"I'm serious. See if that motherfucker's got phone numbers hidden and a secret stash of condoms. Because a guy's a guy. If he's not fucking his wife, then he's fucking someone else."

Chapter Six

Lishelle

When Rhonda peeks her head into the hair and makeup room, I immediately cut my eyes at her. I've been avoiding her all week. She, too, has been avoiding me, I'm sure. As well she should be.

But obviously she's decided that she'll make the first move and speak to me today. Her timing is perfect—Joanie, the hairstylist, stepped out to get coffee.

Coincidence?

Rhonda's eyes are downcast as she steps into the room and closes the door behind her. "Hey," she says softly.

"Hey, yourself."

"I just want to say—"

"Did you know?" I ask. "Did you know that your cousin is gay, or bisexual or whatever the hell he is?"

She doesn't meet my eyes.

"You knew?" I stare at Rhonda in horror. "Rhonda, why?"

She finally looks directly at me. "Trevor said he feels bad about what happened. That he was having a great time with you before—"

"Before his boyfriend decided that he wanted him back?"

"Trevor really likes you."

My eyes widen as I stare at her. "You're kidding me, right?"

"I think you could be the one for him. I really do."

"He's gay, Rhonda. Or at least sexually confused."

"Bisexual. Or so he says. But that relationship—it was just a phase."

"Ah, now I feel better."

"I'm serious. We had a heart-to-heart about it, and he said he'd gone straight, that he was looking to meet a nice woman and settle down."

"And you set him up with *me?*"

"He's really a nice guy. He was just confused for a while. You know."

Oh my God. I can't believe Rhonda. I can't believe she'd set me up with a guy she knew was into men.

"I'm sorry. I thought it would work out."

"Tell him I wish him luck working things out with his ex."

"No, that's over. Honestly. His ex is crazy, like some kind of stalker—"

I hold up a hand to stop Rhonda. "Rhonda, I don't

care if it's over or not. I'm not into bisexual men. Your cousin or not."

"I'm sorry."

"I don't really get why you wanted to set me up with him." It's not like I whine at the station every day about wanting a man in my life. "First of all, a bisexual man is really a gay man and trying to front. Why would you want to subject me to that?"

"I am sorry."

"No, really," I persist. "What were you thinking? That I'm dying for a man or something? Is that what people say behind my back? Do I come off as desperate?"

"No, no, of course you don't. This wasn't about you. It was about him." She blows out a frazzled breath. "I was kinda hoping…"

"Yes?" I prompt when she goes quiet.

"Well, hoping that by dating someone as fantastic as you, he'd realize that he's really straight once and for all."

Wow. Not at all the answer I expected.

Rhonda seems a bit upset over the whole thing, so I wrap an arm around her shoulder. "It's all right. I ain't mad atcha. Just please…no more trying to set me up."

She cracks a smile, just as Joanie opens the door. Rhonda takes that as her cue to leave.

"I'll talk to you later, okay?"

"Sure," I say. As soon as she's out the door, I shake my head.

"What was that about?" Joanie asks.

"Trust me, you don't want to know."

I'm back in my dressing room later, wiping the excess makeup off my face, when the phone rings. It's late, after midnight, so I assume it's got to be someone at the station when I pick it up.

"Hello?"

"You were great tonight."

I pause. Wait a few beats. "Do I know you?"

"You could say that. Yeah, you definitely could."

Great, not another stalker. "Thanks for the call—"

"Whoa, whoa. Lishelle."

Something hits me in the gut like a fastball, winding me. Excitement? No, not excitement. Well, maybe a little. But it's mixed with caution.

"Glenn?" I ask.

"Who else, baby?"

Oh, Lord help me, not Glenn. Glenn who used to make me orgasm for days when we dated ten years ago. Glenn, who brought out the best in me—and the worst. Glenn, who broke my heart when I found out he was screwing one of his teaching assistants at the University of Atlanta.

I should have hated him and pushed him completely out of my mind and my life. But how can you forget a guy you connected with so completely? No matter how badly he hurt you?

That's why, even though we'd broken up, we got together for a booty call a few times in the summer after I graduated from Spelman. Then, six years ago just before I met David, Glenn called me out of the blue because he was in town visiting a friend, and again we ended up in bed. He disappeared from my life the next day, I met David and moved on. But I never forgot Glenn.

"How are you?" I ask. I know, that's incredibly lame, but I can't think of anything better to say, considering I'm so stunned to be hearing his voice.

"I'm good. Better now that I'm talking to you."

"Why are you calling me? After what—six years?"

"Six years. Has it really been that long?"

"And counting."

"My bad. But hey, I'm glad to see how well you're doing. A big-shot news anchor. You always said you'd be some big shot. I see you on billboards all over town. Congratulations."

"Wait, wait, wait. Are you living here again? The last time I saw you, you were off in Los Angeles, trying to be the next Denzel Washington."

"And you know how that turned out."

"I do?"

"You haven't seen me at the box office, have you?"

"I haven't seen anyone at the box office. I've been way too busy."

"You must have at least one man taking you out and treating you right."

"Not that that's any of your business, but no."

"No, man. That ain't right. We have to fix that."

I inhale a deep breath. "Glenn, what is this—what's going on?" Not that I don't have a pretty good idea….

"I've missed you."

With those three simple words, heat spreads through my body. But I don't say anything. I don't dare.

"Did you hear me?" he asks.

"Um, yes."

"So when can we get together?" Glenn asks, using that

soft and seductive voice he always used to turn me on back when we were an item. Damn him.

"Who says I want to get together?" There is undoubtedly a coy quality to my voice though, and the thought of seeing Glenn is already turning me on. When we were together sexually, it was always explosive. That's the kind of thing a woman doesn't forget.

And considering I haven't been laid in so long...

How inappropriate is *that* thought?

"You don't want to see me?"

"Why would you want to see me?" *So we can have a one-night fling like we did six years ago?*

"I just do. You know."

"No, I don't know. I haven't seen or heard from you in so long."

"That's exactly why I'm calling. To rectify that. Because it *has* been too long."

"How long are you here for?"

"Till tomorrow afternoon."

Yeah, another one-night fling. "I can always call you in the morning. We can get together for coffee. What's a number I can reach you at?"

"Tomorrow?" he asks in that husky sexy voice again. "Why tomorrow? What are you doing now?"

"I'm going home and going to bed."

"Alone?"

My breath catches. I can't help thinking of my chat with Rhonda earlier, how I told her I wasn't desperate. Right now, the fact that Glenn's voice alone is turning me on, makes me think I'm a big fat liar.

"That's none of your business."

"Come see me. I've missed you," he says, his voice an octave lower. "I really have."

I don't say anything. I don't trust what might come out of my mouth. There's a huge part of me that's tempted to say yes—the part that wants to have sex with a man after such a long drought. But then there's the other part—the part that knows having sex with an ex is always a dangerous thing.

"I need to see you tonight."

My heart rate picks up speed. My body starts to tingle. Should I do this?

"Just come over. We'll…talk."

"Where exactly are you?" I ask.

"At the airport Marriott." He pauses. "How fast can you get here?"

"Thirty minutes."

"I'm in room 623."

"All right, I'll see you soon."

I hang up the phone and take a deep breath. Then I gather my things and head out of the room.

Thirty-five minutes later, my stomach flutters as I knock on the door to Glenn's hotel room. The entire drive here, I've debated what I'm doing. Because I know that walking into his hotel room at close to one in the morning means only one thing.

Sex.

And when it comes to Glenn—amazing sex. That's pretty damn hard to resist.

What does he look like? I wonder. The same, different? The same, I'm sure. He probably hasn't aged at—

The door swings open, and I reel backward in surprise. One look at Glenn and my heart stops. There he stands, six foot three inches of sinfully gorgeous man. Lean and muscular. He's dressed in a ribbed undershirt and black jeans.

Shit, I was right. He looks exactly the same. Which is to say he's still as scrumptious as he always was.

His eyes move over me as his lips pull in a grin. Those eyes. Those intense hazel eyes of his. The kind that with one sweeping look seem to undress you. They've always been my undoing.

And he smells so good. The light scent of his cologne drifts into my nose, and my body temperature starts to rise. Every amazing memory of Glenn floods my mind. He's the one man who knew how to totally satisfy me in the bedroom.

Yeah, I'm desperate for a man.

Fuck, I'm in trouble.

I clear my throat. "Glenn."

"Mmm mmm mmm, Lishelle."

I'm wearing an above-the-knee V-neck black dress—minus the tan jacket I wore on top of it when I was on camera. I know it's hot. Glenn knows it, too.

"So, what did you want to talk about?" I ask in a very straitlaced tone.

He holds the door open wide. "Come on in. Make yourself comfortable."

I slowly walk into the room. Behind me, I hear the door close, and the bolt click. I close my eyes, count to three, then turn to face Glenn.

He's walking toward me, and I can't help but take in

his incredibly sexy form. He heads straight toward me, and I tense, anticipating an embrace. But he stops before he reaches me and lifts two glasses of wine that have already been poured off the dresser.

He offers me a glass. I don't take it right away.

"Take it," he insists.

"Glenn, I came here to talk."

His lips form a lopsided grin. "Do you really want me to believe that you don't want to fuck me as badly as I want to fuck you?"

My pussy explodes with heat. Damn him. How dare he know me so well?

I finally take the glass from him and down a liberal gulp. The crisp Chardonnay hits the spot.

But not the spot I know Glenn can hit so well....

Given the satisfied smirk on Glenn's face, it's obvious he can see in my eyes what I'm thinking. "I remember what you liked," he tells me. "I remember *everything*."

"Do you?" My voice is husky, seductive.

"Oh, yeah."

He takes the wineglass from me and puts both down on the nearby dresser. He takes my hands and just holds them. Holds them and stares into my eyes.

"You look amazing," he tells me.

"You look the same."

"That good or bad?"

"You know it's good."

"Lishelle. Here we are, in the same room after all this time. It's hard to believe."

My nervous energy is killing me. I'd almost prefer that

he rip my clothes off and screw me than make any kind of small talk.

He presses his mouth to my forehead, and it's like I've been hit with an electrical charge. "I meant it when I said I've missed you," he whispers.

"Glenn…" My voice is shaky.

"I want to touch you so badly." His lips graze my cheeks.

"I don't know where you've been," I say. "It's been almost six years."

"I know, I know. You have nothing to worry about, but I've got condoms in any case."

Still holding my hands, he urges my body closer to his as his lips move to the side of my neck. "Ooh, Lishelle."

Fuck, fuck, fuck.

And then he's pulling me into an embrace. I don't resist, not one bit. I know why I came here, what he wants. What I want.

His lips come down on mine. I open my mouth to him for a deep and passionate kiss. Our tongues tangle while our hands desperately touch each other, like we've both been waiting for this moment for the past six years.

Maybe I have. Because Lord knows I haven't been able to forget the connection Glenn and I shared in the bedroom.

"Oh, baby." His hands cover my ass and squeeze. "Damn, you still feel so good."

I pull his vest out of his jeans. Slipping my hands beneath it, I sigh as I feel his warm skin.

"Feel me," Glenn says in a raspy voice. "Feel how much I want you."

I lower my hand to his crotch and stroke his erection

through his jeans. It's as hard as a slab of granite, and thick and long like I remember it.

"Damn you, Glenn. You know I can't resist *this*."

"I know something else you can't resist." He places a finger between my breasts and slowly trails it down my body. He keeps going, until he skims my vagina through my dress. His eyes are on me the entire time, even as he lowers himself onto his knees and pushes the dress up.

"Oh, yeah," he moans, fingering the edge of my thigh-high stockings. "This look is so hot."

He presses a kiss to my inner thigh, and I quiver. I grab his shoulders for balance as he kisses my other thigh, this time adding a flick of his tongue.

"Oh, shit," I mumble, closing my eyes.

His lips move higher, as do his fingers. My legs damn near collapse when he kisses me through my panties.

I've wanted this for so long. A man's hands on me. His fingers. His tongue. I want to stand here and spread my legs and be greedy. Let him feast on my nectar until I've come two or three times.

Glenn pushes the silk fabric of my panties aside and strokes my nub so gently, I ache from it. He strokes, looks. Strokes, looks again. But he doesn't touch me the way he knows I want to be touched.

"I've missed looking at you like this. Up close and personal."

"I forgot how much you like to tease."

"I'm teasing you?"

I meet his eyes. "Hell, yeah. If you only knew how much I wanted your cock inside me right now."

Now he slips a finger into me. "We'll get there."

I gasp as his finger enters me. Waves of pleasure overwhelm me.

"You're so tight," he says.

"It's been a long time for me."

He groans his pleasure at what I've said. Pushing his finger deeper inside me, he covers my nub with his tongue. It's heat on heat. I dig my fingers into his skin and moan.

"You…like…that?" he asks, licking me gently between words.

"Fuck yeah."

Still working his finger inside me, he takes my nub completely into his mouth and suckles. My legs tremble—I can barely stand.

Glenn pulls away from me to say, "Lie back on the bed."

I whimper softly, both wanting his tongue on me fiercely, and not knowing how much of it I can stand.

Glenn's hands guide me backward to the bed. As I lie down, he settles right between my thighs, burying his face in my pussy and inhaling. A grumbling sound escapes him. "You're amazing, Lishelle. Fucking amazing."

He spreads my folds for better access to my clitoris. And then he is licking and suckling and I think I am going to die from the pleasure. He eats me like he's waited his whole life to do this.

My body grows tense, like a string that's being pulled, and pulled, and is starting to fray at the edges and will pop any minute.

I raise my head to watch him. Watch as his tongue

works its magic. His moans turn me on as much as the sound of his suckling.

"I'm close. Oh, God." My breathing is faster now, frenzied. "Look at me."

Glenn lifts his gaze to mine, and our eyes connect. As I watch and feel his mouth on me in this very intimate way, every part of me starts to tremble. My orgasm erupts from my center and spreads over me like hot lava. I arch my back, calling out, "Oh, Glenn! Oh my God! Oh my God…"

I'm still moaning when I hear the tear of a condom package, and by the time I look up, Glenn is moving over me. I catch a glimpse of his impressive cock before he settles between my thighs and anchors his arms behind my knees.

He enters me with one hard, deep thrust, and I gasp from the pleasure and shock of it. It's been so long, I forgot how amazing that first moment is—the very first moment when a penis penetrates your vagina.

Glenn settles inside me—deep—and doesn't move. "Fuck, Lishelle, you feel so good."

"*You* feel amazing."

Finally, he starts to move, his strokes slow and deep and painfully pleasurable. Every one of them makes me quiver. Our momentum builds until Glenn is driving into me so hard and so fast that I get light-headed from this sensory overload.

"I can't take it, baby. Oh, Glenn…I'm coming…"

I arch my back and cry out as Glenn takes me over the edge one more time. I grip the bedspread with all my might.

And then he makes that familiar grunt-giggle sound he does when he's coming. I squeeze my inner walls around him.

A moment later, his body collapses onto mine. Our slick bodies rub against each other as our hot breath mingles. It's amazing how good I feel, how easily Glenn and I reconnected after all these years.

I trail the tip of my tongue along his jawline to his ear. "How do you always do this to me? Make me so damn hot? I swear, my pussy has your name on it."

He kisses me. A smoldering kiss that makes it clear just how much I do belong to him.

"I could stay like this all night, buried inside you. I really could."

"So could I," I answer honestly.

And it's not just about the sex with Glenn.

No matter how much time has passed, no matter how many other guys I might date, the moment I'm with Glenn again, I know where my heart is.

I'm in serious trouble.

Glenn and I fucked three more times during the night, each time as explosive and satisfying as the first. I'm not lying when I say no other man has ever loved me like Glenn has. His body speaks to mine on some primal level I can't understand, but I'm powerless to resist him anytime we get together.

He knows this, of course. Knows that he can call me a year from now and I'll be there for him. Knows that I'll get on my knees and let him ram me from behind. That I'll take him in my mouth and deep throat him the way he loves. That I'll cancel everything for a two-day fuck session.

Last night was incredible, but this morning I'm having regrets. And to be totally honest, I'm a little pissed off with myself. I needed to get laid. Needed it badly, so why am I letting emotion cloud the issue? Why not take Glenn for what he is—a great fuck partner who can always get me off in the most incredible way—and leave it at that?

Who am I trying to kid? I know it's not nearly that simple. Last night, getting caught up in a wave of heat and desire, I forgot how unsettling the morning after with Glenn can be. It was the same way six years ago. It was that way the few times we fell into bed in the months after our relationship ended. Because I've always cared deeply for Glenn, whether he's been in my life or not. And every time I have him for only a brief moment, I'm devastated when he's gone.

No matter how much I tell myself that I'll be fine without him, and move on after having amazing sex, that's just not true.

Beside me, he is silent and still. I snuggle my back against his front and sigh. Maybe I'm a hopeless romantic, but I wish this moment would last forever. Us lying together like this. That there didn't have to be a goodbye in the morning.

I'm surprised when Glenn links fingers with mine, because I thought he was sleeping. A moment later, he asks, "What are you thinking?"

"I thought you were asleep."

"I'm not. Tell me what's on your mind."

"I'm not sure you want to know," I answer honestly.

"Try me."

"You're leaving soon. Let's just…enjoy our last moments together."

He kisses my shoulder. "You never know. I might be thinking the same thing as you."

Now he's gotten my attention. I turn my body, positioning my breasts against the hard wall of his chest. I wonder if he's playing with my mind.

"You really want to know?" I ask.

"Uh-huh."

"And you want me to be completely honest?"

"Of course."

"Then I'm thinking that I don't know how I let myself go here again with you. Not that I don't enjoy fucking you, but what am I doing? We had our chance to make things work out, and it never did. Now I see you once in a blue moon, and my body craves yours like nothing else I've known, but what's the point? What's going to come of this?"

"A whole lot can come from this."

"Yeah, sure. More great sex." I roll my eyes. "Where have you been for the last six years, anyway?" Having tied the knot myself, I'd put Glenn out of my mind. "I thought I'd never see you again," I continue. "That you'd finally gotten married or something."

Glenn laughs heartily, amused by the idea. "No, not married. And why do you think I'm here with you now? It's because I can never quite get you out of my mind. How much you turn me on. How great we were together."

"Then why do you always call me when you're in town for just one night or two? It's obviously about the booty call. Not that I'm complaining, but it's getting harder for me to face you the morning after."

"Ouch."

"No, listen. You wanted honesty, and I'm giving it to you." I want to make Glenn see reason. "We can't do this anymore, no matter how much I might want to." Because you still have a part of my heart....

Maybe that's why the sex is so good, and that's why I haven't exactly moved on. That's why I always end up comparing other guys to you. Even the man I married.

"Lishelle—"

"I can't believe I'm admitting this to you, but it hurts when you leave me. There. I said it. And that's why we can't get together for these trysts once in a blue moon anymore," I say, unable to stop now. "I'll be thirty-one in August. I have to find my Mr. Right and settle down."

"Wow," Glenn says slowly. "You certainly got a lot off your chest."

"You wanted to know. And look, it's not like we're not friends, right? We can be honest with each other." Despite myself, I run a finger down the center of his chest. "I just don't want us to be friends who fuck each other anymore."

"No?"

"Well...after today, I mean." Shit, I'm already getting horny again.

Glenn moves his body so that he's now on top of me. He surprises me with a soft kiss on the forehead. I was sure he was going to lock lips with me and leave me begging for him to make me come again.

"What if I said I didn't want us to stop sleeping with each other?"

"Then I'd say you were being selfish and unfair to me. I don't even know what you're doing now. I know nothing about you."

"I'm a pilot."

Surprised at his announcement, my eyes meet his. "Really?"

"Uh-huh. All-American Air."

"How—when—"

"While I was in L.A. waiting for my big break, I was taking flying lessons. I started, oh, about seven years ago. Then the big break never came. And here I am."

I'm impressed. Really impressed. But I say, "A pilot. See—you could have a girlfriend in every city in the country. That's exactly why this has to end."

"I don't have a girlfriend in every city in the country, but yeah, maybe I am a bit selfish like you said. But there's a reason for that."

"I can guess what that is."

"Probably not." He pauses. "I'm in love with you, lady."

He's looking right into my eyes as he says the words, a steady gaze that doesn't waver.

I ask, "What did you say?" Can he be serious?

"It doesn't matter where I go, or where I've been. I always end up right back here with you. Why do you think that is?"

"Because I'm an easy lay?"

He chuckles, and the warmth of his laugh fills my body. "I'm easy, too. But only with you."

"Stop lying."

"I swear." His lips capture mine in a gentle, earnest kiss. "Honestly, Lishelle, why do you think I keep coming back to you? Six years have passed at this point. I could easily have moved on. I've met other women, sure, but no one can compare to you. I know now that I'll never be able to get you out of my heart."

Even though I don't want it to, my heart starts to fill with hope. "You mean that?"

"Hell, yeah. So why don't we stop playing around and get back together."

"Get back togeth—"

"Start dating again. But this time, knowing that we're headed on the path till death do us part."

I eye Glenn cautiously. "I don't understand."

"Are you listening to me? I'm telling you I love you. I've been in love with you the whole time we've been apart. And I'm ready, babe. Ready to make it work between us."

"Glenn." I frame his face and arch my hips against him. "Oh, Glenn." I kiss him deeply.

He breaks the kiss and asks, "Should I take that as a yes?"

"It took you long enough, you big jerk."

I can't believe the words that have come out of my mouth. I can't believe what's just happened. And so easily. But Glenn's warm smile makes me feel entirely comfortable. Makes me feel this is right. That it's finally our time.

"I know," he says. "I'm sorry."

"You're going to have to make it up to me," I tell him. "Right now."

"Oh?"

"Yeah."

"What did you have in mind?"

I spread my legs and wrap them around his waist. "There's only one punishment that's fitting," I tell him as his penis hardens against my stomach. "Do me, baby," I whisper hotly in his ear. "Do me good."

Chapter Seven

Claudia

I feel as if I'm going through hell with the wedding plans, and honestly, Adam isn't helping. Before, I thought his I'm-a-man-I'm-totally-clueless routine was kind of cute, but right now it's just plain aggravating. There's still so much to do, and I need a break from it.

That's why, as I approach the front door of Liaisons this Sunday morning, I feel a burst of happiness, knowing that I'm going to see my dearest friends.

Only Annelise is seated at our booth when I walk into the restaurant just before one o'clock. Every Sunday afternoon, Annelise, Lishelle and I have brunch at this restaurant in Buckhead, which serves the best brunch in the city as far as I'm concerned. We're so regular, the hostess saves our table for us.

It's a time for us to sit back, relax and catch up on each other's week while enjoying great food. Even though we talk quite a bit during the week with each other, during our brunches we really get to let loose.

"Hey," I say in a singsong voice as I reach the table. Annelise shoots to her feet, a wide smile on her face. She gives me a long hug.

"How are you, hon?" she asks.

"Ugh, stressed. This wedding's killing me."

"I know the feeling. I'm stressed, too."

"Oh?" I slink into the booth's soft leather. "Your wedding plans giving you grief?"

"No." She flashes a sugary smile. "But I've had a shitty week at work. Two customers canceled on me, and I was counting on that cash."

"Oh no."

"Lots to tell, but only after you get your first cup of coffee."

"I was thinking more like a mimosa today."

Annelise's eyes light up. "Thank God. I didn't want to be the only one."

She raises a hand to flag down the waitress, and moments later, Sierra, a petite Asian woman, comes to our table.

"Hello, Claudia," Sierra greets me. "How are you?"

"I'm great," I tell her. "You?"

"Busy. Taking a summer course in physics." She rolls her eyes. "What can I say?"

Despite the fact that Sierra has worked here as a waitress for the past two years, she's studying to be a doctor. I'm impressed. And a little envious. I've always wanted to go to med school. My father is a top neurosurgeon, and the profession fascinates me. But despite my schooling, I knew I'd never pursue a career. That's the way it is for a self-respecting society woman like myself. The average woman today doesn't understand that concept, that a woman in my position doesn't actually work outside the home. She supports her husband in his aspirations, does volunteer work for worthy causes, raises children, works the society circles. One day soon, Adam will be in the political arena, and I'll need to be by his side. He'll need a full-time wife to support him.

"Two mimosas," Annelise is saying to the waitress when I tune back in to the conversation.

"Lishelle's not coming?" Sierra asks.

"You're right, make it three," Annelise decides. "If she doesn't show up anytime soon, I can always drink hers." Annelise makes light of her statement with a smile, but I know she's serious. Which means she really must have had a shitty week.

"Help yourself to the buffet whenever you're ready," Sierra tells us. And then she's off to deal with more customers.

I glance at my watch. It's now one-ten. "Have you heard from Lishelle?"

Annelise shakes her head. "But I assume she's coming. I mean, she'd call if she weren't—right?"

"Right. It's just not like her. She's usually the first one here."

"She's probably stuck in traffic."

"Yeah, probably." Sierra suddenly appears with a tray

of drinks. "Wow, that was fast," I tell her. Both Annelise and I sip our drinks, then Annelise looks up.

"Speak of the devil…"

I turn. There's Lishelle, gliding toward the table.

"Hello, ladies," she practically sings.

If I'm not mistaken, Lishelle has extra pep in her step. And she's glowing. Yeah, she's definitely glowing. What the hell happened to make her so happy?

"That must be for me," Lishelle comments, reaching for the extra mimosa as she sits beside me in the booth. "Perfect." She takes a sip. She looks from me to Annelise. "Ooh, Annie. That's a really nice dress. You're showing a lot of cleavage. That's not like you."

"Yeah, well, I've got to do something."

"I don't follow you," Lishelle says.

"I've been having problems with Charles. In the bedroom. He won't…well, he won't touch me with a ten-foot pole, if you want to know the truth."

"At all?" Lishelle asks.

"At all."

"I'm so sorry to hear you're having trouble again."

"Again?" Annelise laughs without mirth. "It's been a constant for nearly fifteen months."

"Fifteen *months?*"

"Apparently," I chime, and Lishelle looks at me in surprise. "She only told me a few days ago," I point out.

"I know you were having trouble before," Lishelle says, "but I thought you got past that. You haven't said anything for what, a year?"

"I've been too embarrassed." Annelise then fills Lishelle in on all she told me earlier in the week.

"And Charles," Lishelle begins, "is he…reacting?"

"I spent five hundred dollars on new clothes, new bras, sexy shoes—and nothing."

"Wow." Lishelle reaches across the table and covers Annelise's hand. "I don't know what to say."

"What *can* you say? I'm starting to wonder if my marriage is in serious trouble."

"No," I assure her. "Charles loves you."

"Every time he rejects me, it chips away at my self-esteem. A little more here, a little more there."

"How can we help?" Lishelle asks.

"Just be there for me, I guess. Listen to me whine." She smiles, but it doesn't reach her eyes.

"Have you talked to Charles about this?" I ask.

"If I even try to talk about why we're not having sex, he gets upset. Defensive. Sometimes I'll ask if he's upset with me or what, and he tells me he's busy. Stressed. That my impatience is only making him more stressed."

"I'm sorry," Lishelle says. "But if he isn't having sex with you, don't you think he's fucking someone else? Let's face it—what guy doesn't want to have sex with his wife? You ask me, that's a neon sign that he's dipping his cock in another pussy."

Annelise reels backward, looking absolutely crushed. I shoot Lishelle a glare. She gives me an "I'm sorry" look.

I'll be honest—the same thought occurred to me regarding Charles screwing around—but I know Annelise isn't ready to hear that.

I try a more tactful approach. "What if Charles is having some sort of medical problem?" I offer. "That could explain why he's acting the way he is. Defensive. Stand-offish. Unwilling even to hear any talk about lovemaking. Maybe it's because he doesn't want to start something he can't finish with you."

"Oh my God." Annelise's eyes light up. "Do you think that could be it?"

"It's a possibility."

"It would explain a lot," Lishelle adds. "Let's face it, you and Charles were the type who couldn't keep your hands off each other."

"Which is what makes all of this even harder to deal with." Annelise sighs sadly.

"Maybe you should ask him about it," I suggest. "In a point-blank way. Tell him that you love him more than anything, that you're there for him, and that if he's having some sort of problem you'll still be by his side. You know how guys are—they don't want to admit that they're having sexual problems. But if you ask if he's having some sort of problem, and make sure to tell him you'll support him no matter what…"

"God, I think you're right," Annelise says. "It didn't even occur to me. I figured it was me who did something wrong, and he'd lost interest. My sister suggested I buy sex toys and sexy clothes—none of which has worked. How can it work if he's got some sort of medical problem?"

"You won't know for sure until you talk to him," I point out.

"I'm going to do that. I have to know. If he's got some sort of medical issue, I'll feel so relieved. You don't know how awful I've felt, being rejected by the man I love more than anything." Her eyes began to tear up.

"I can only imagine," Lishelle says. I catch the look that I hope Annelise missed—one that says Lishelle isn't convinced Charles's problems are medical.

"Enough about me and my problems in the bedroom." She's more composed now. "Tell us the latest with the wedding plans, Claudia. Four weeks away!"

I groan. "I'm so stressed."

"Honey, why? You've got that great wedding planner."

"But there are still a million things to be done. And Adam is seeming less and less interested."

"When I got married, David was the same way. Could care less about the plans. And the closer we got to the big day, the more he seemed disinterested. I think guys can only handle so much talk about cakes and dresses and food courses. They want to go on the honeymoon already."

"Charles was actually very helpful, and very interested in all the details—and even he freaked out once and told me he didn't want to hear another word about colors or food or anything more to do with wedding plans. You remember—that was the weekend he took off and went to Macon to go fishing with his brother."

I crack a smile. I do remember. And I remember how unhappy Annelise was at the time, how she seemed on the verge of having a breakdown.

Is that the kind of bride I've become? Uncool, uncalm and uncollected?

"In other words," I begin, "you both think I'm freaking out over nothing."

Annelise and Lishelle nod in unison.

"It's just the way guys are," Lishelle points out.

"Okay. I'll try not to lose my head over this stuff. I have to go to New York on Tuesday for another fitting, and after that, my gown should be ready." Nerves tickle my stomach. "Wow. I can't believe May twenty-seventh is coming so soon!"

"*And* your thirtieth birthday."

"I've all but forgotten about that."

"We were thinking to take you out that night," Annelise says. "Do a stagette-slash-birthday-party thing."

"Before you know it, you'll be a married woman, on a beach somewhere fucking your brains out."

I can't help but crack a smile at Lishelle's comment, however crude. "That's a nice thought."

"I might just have to tag along with you," Annelise jokes.

Little does she know, the way Adam's behaving now, he might just be down with that.

Lishelle sighs dreamily, and I can no longer wait for her to blurt out the secret she's hiding. Because I *know* she's hiding something. It's just like her to get all giddy and silent when there's something she's not telling.

"All right, Lishelle," I say. "What is it? Ever since you walked through that door, you've been trying to hide this huge grin."

"I do have something to share, but I'm not sure this is the right time," she says coyly.

"Of course it's the right time!" I exclaim. Now I'm dying to know what's going on with her.

"Not that I don't want to tell you, but after you've both

shared not-so-positive stuff, it'll seem like I'm gloating
to share my good news."

"Enough already," I tell her. "Spill the beans!"

"You're seeing someone, aren't you?" Annelise's eyes
light up. "Oh my God—you crawled out of bed with him
just before you came here!"

"Well…"

"Oh my God," I utter. "You *did*."

A guilty smile spreads across Lishelle's face. "Yeah, I
did."

I couldn't be more shocked—or more curious. "Last
week, you said you were swearing off dating."

"I know. Believe me, I'm more shocked than anyone
to be in a relationship right now."

"A *relationship?*" I ask. "What's going on?"

"Do you guys really want to hear this now?"

"Yes!" Annelise and I exclaim in unison.

"Okay." Lishelle is really beaming. I haven't seen her
this happy since—

"I'm seeing Glenn again."

My stomach sinks. "Glenn? As in Baxter?" *The guy
who only knows how to hurt you?*

"Yes," Lishelle gushes. "And I know what you might
think, but this is it, ladies. Finally it."

Annelise squeals with excitement. I reach for my mimosa and take a huge sip.

"How did this happen?" Annelise asks.

"He called me Friday night at the station. I didn't
want to, but I went to see him. And we clicked, like
we always do. Then, the next morning, I was upset
that I'd fallen into bed with him. We got to talking and

he said he's always loved me, that he wants us to be together."

"And you believe him?" I can't help asking.

"I do."

I finish the last of my mimosa. While I want to be thrilled for Lishelle, I can't help remembering how Glenn has hurt her in the past.

"I'm so happy for you," Annelise says. "I know how much you've always cared for him."

"That's the hell of it. I still love him. Isn't it insane? That's the real reason I can't resist him. It's not just the sex."

"You sure about that?" I ask.

She turns to me and nods. "The sex Friday night was off the hook. But Saturday morning, I couldn't detach my emotions from what had happened. I told Glenn we couldn't see each other like this whenever he got the itch. That's when he told me he's in love with me and wants our relationship to work. He was supposed to leave yesterday afternoon, but there was a last-minute change in his schedule. We hung out like friends the whole day. It wasn't about the sex at all. Until later, of course," she finishes with a sheepish grin.

"When it's time, it's time," Annelise comments.

"That's what I think."

"Look, it takes some guys a long time. Look at Big in *Sex and the City.*"

"*Exactly,*" Lishelle gushes. "I always wanted Carrie to end up with Big."

"Oh, me, too."

Maybe Lishelle notices that I'm not saying anything,

because she suddenly turns to me. "I know what you're thinking."

"Me? I'm not…I'm not thinking anything. Just enjoying…" I look at my empty glass. "I need another mimosa. Aren't they great?"

"Don't change the subject. You're thinking that I'm making a mistake. And I hear you. I know why you think that. But this time, it's different. This time, it's real."

I squirm in my seat, sip water and do my best to stay silent. I fail. "You know I love you, Lishelle, and I want what's best for you, but how can you forget how Glenn has hurt you in the past? I mean, you were dating the guy for two years in college, then you found out he'd been screwing other women. Not just one. Plural. How can you ever trust him?"

"For one thing, college was ten years ago. We were both young. Far too young to be involved in such a serious relationship. You have to admit that."

"But—" I interject.

"But…enough time has passed for us to mature and know what we really want. We're in our thirties now, for God's sake."

"Once a cheater, always a cheater," I mumble.

"Claudia," Annelise says in a tone that indicates I should chill. "Can't you try to be happy for Lishelle?"

"Yes, please." Surprisingly, Lishelle isn't annoyed as she looks at me. She's still beaming, like a girl in love for the first time. "Just trust me. I know this is right."

A ragged sigh escapes me. "Okay. I will." It's not like I can tell her what to do. "And if you're happy, that's what matters to me most. I just want you happy."

"I know that." Lishelle gives me a soft smile as she reaches for her drink.

"I guess we'll be seeing him again," I say, "if this is serious."

"Next weekend. I've invited him to the charity ball for the Wishes Come True Foundation."

"Ah." I wag a finger at Lishelle. "Now I get it. Getting back together with Glenn was all about having a date for the charity ball. Smart."

"I think she's onto something," Annelise agrees, laughing.

"Whatever!" Lishelle shakes her head. "Am I the only one who's starving here? We haven't even hit the buffet yet."

"Sure, change the subject," I tell her.

We all chuckle as we get up and head toward the buffet.

Chapter Eight

Annelise

As I sit at the desk in my office, I stare at the wall clock, watching the second hand tick by. It's five minutes after four, and I'm starting to feel like my next appointment isn't coming. I wouldn't be surprised. It's been that kind of day. Two other appointments were no-shows. Potential wedding gigs. The most lucrative of the work I do.

"I can't make a living like this," I mutter.

Maybe I need to be doing more advertising. This year, my income has been taking a steady nosedive. The one saving grace is that I'm doing Claudia's wedding, and her father is paying for a package that's over ten thousand dollars.

Tick, tock, tick, tock…

The door chimes sing, startling me out of my boredom.

Pushing my chair backward, I jump to my feet and force a smile on my face.

In walk a young man and woman, both dark-haired, holding hands and smiling from ear to ear. They can't be older than twenty-one, twenty-two.

"You must be…" My voice trails off as another man, a Greek God, really, enters behind them. His eyes meet mine, and I feel a zap of raw, sexual desire. It overwhelms me. Leaves me momentarily speechless.

"Sebastian and Helen," the first man says, moving toward me with his hand outstretched.

I step out from behind my desk. "Right." I pump the man's hand, then the woman's. "So good to meet you both."

My eyes wander to the man who suddenly has me remembering just how much of a woman I am. A woman with sexual needs not being met.

Earlier, Charles didn't even notice me in the tight leather pants I bought on Samera's advice. But this sexy stranger is noticing. And I tell you, it feels amazing.

I offer him a small smile as I say, "If you don't mind giving me a second to deal with this happy couple—"

"Actually, I'm with the happy couple."

"Oh." A nervous laugh escapes me. "I see."

"My older brother, Dominic," Sebastian informs me. "He wanted to tag along."

"No problem." I glance quickly at Dominic again, and a slow breath oozes out of me when I see that he's staring at me.

He looks sort of familiar, but from where?

I'm not exactly sure what I'm doing when I slip my left

hand behind my back. No, that's not true. I definitely know what I'm doing. I'm hiding my wedding ring. What I'm not sure of is why.

I clear my throat. "Please. Sit down."

Sebastian and Helen don't let go of each other, even as they sit side by side on separate chairs. Dominic stands, perusing the photos on the wall.

"When are you getting married?" I ask Sebastian and Helen.

"September twenty-third."

I sit behind my desk and jot that information down. Then I go into describing the various packages I offer, starting with the least expensive. "All of the packages are detailed in this brochure," I add when I'm finished, handing them a glossy full-color brochure that cost a small fortune to produce. "But don't feel that these are set in stone. I'm willing to tailor a package specifically to your needs. You can use this as a guide and tell me what changes you'd like to make, if any."

"You do all these photos?" Dominic asks, glancing at me over his shoulder.

Damn, he's got a nice ass. Honestly, I can't remember seeing a butt that looked so cute in a pair of Levi's.

"Yes," I answer. "I took all the photos."

"I love this one," Dominic goes on, fingering the silver frame of a black-and-white photo of a naked and sleeping baby.

"That's one of my favorites," I tell him, pleased.

A quick look at Sebastian and Helen and I see that they're still evaluating the various packages. So my gaze wanders back to Dominic. He grins at me.

Now I know I'm desperate, because that simple and sexy grin has my vulva pulsing. I'm actually shocked. I don't ever remember feeling this kind of immediate carnal attraction even in the early days with Charles.

And yes, he does look familiar. Where have I seen him before?

For the sake of my sanity, I have to look away from him. I shift uncomfortably in my seat as I face the young couple once again. "Do you have any questions?"

Helen shakes her head. "Not really. Obviously, you'll do both black and white and color."

"If you like."

"Oh, I know," Helen quickly says. "How much of a down payment do you need?"

"Depending on the package you choose—and you can change your mind anytime before the big day—I ask for twenty percent up front."

I watch Sebastian's and Helen's faces for a reaction. Helen worries her bottom lip.

"Or you can give me ten percent when you secure the booking, if it's easier, and the final ten percent thirty days before the wedding. Just let me know." I pause. I hate when the couple isn't saying much. I always feel as if I've lost them.

But, the last thing I want to do is pressure anyone. I don't believe in the hard sell, though Charles says I should. He tells me all the time that I'd make more money if I were a bit tougher.

But that's not me. "Take your time," I tell Helen and Sebastian. "Look around the studio if you want. I have sample albums you can go through, as well. No pressure."

"We'll take a look around, but we already know we want you," Helen says. "We've heard such great things about your work. And the photos you have displayed speak for themselves."

Yes! But I keep my cool and say calmly, "Why, thank you."

"We can't leave a deposit right now, though," she continues. "We'd like to figure out the package we'll go with, then come back and leave a deposit."

This is the point where some photographers get aggressive to try to secure the deal, by insisting that a client at least leave some money down. But I hate to scare anyone away, even though I know I might never see them again.

So I say, "Whenever's convenient. Just give me a call."

"Thanks so much," Sebastian says. "It'll be later this week, or early next week, when we can bring the deposit."

"There's always the chance that someone else might come in wanting me for the same date, so for now, I'll mark your wedding date down. I'll see you by next week?"

"Yes," Helen answers.

"I look forward to it. And congrats on your nuptials." Sebastian and Helen get up and start for the door. I get up, too. Dominic, who's still checking out my pictures, doesn't even realize that his brother is ready to leave.

"Yo, Dom," Sebastian calls out.

Dominic whirls around. "You ready?"

"Uh-huh."

It's like an invisible bat hits me hard when Dominic looks at me again. I can't help wondering why he bothered to tag along with his brother for this visit.

"Did you have any questions?" I ask him. There's a part of me—a big part—that doesn't want him to leave yet.

He shakes his head. "None."

"Okay." So he's Mr. Mysterious.

"I think Dom is bored and needs to get a life," Sebastian tells me. He turns to Dom. "When was the last time you were on a date?"

So he's single...

And you're married. Don't even let yourself go there.

Despite what I tell myself, I do my best to hide my ring as I see them all to the door. I know nothing will come of this, but at least I have someone to think about when I masturbate. Thinking about Charles usually doesn't work for me anymore, because it's hard to get off fantasizing about someone who doesn't fucking want you.

Sebastian and Helen are unable to let go of each other, as if the very act of releasing hands for even a moment would be physically painful. I watch them, feeling a lump form in my throat as I reminisce about my courtship with Charles, how he was the same way, always touching me, always giving me soft kisses on the cheek.

Always letting me know I was loved.

I can't stand thinking of Charles right now, so I let my gaze wander over Dominic's tall, muscular frame.

He's almost out the door when he turns back to smile at me. I smile, too, and wave.

And then he's gone. The door clicks shut.

"Fuck, fuck, fuck!" I whirl around, close my eyes. Dominic and I barely spoke, yet the way he looked at me has left me feeling like his hands have caressed every inch of my body. My vagina is still pulsing, and my panties are wet.

Is this what Samera meant when she said that dressing sexy makes you feel more sexually alive? If so, then I'm amazed.

The sound of door chimes has me whipping around. There he is again, smiling that charming smile that makes me so hot.

I swallow. "Hi. Did you forget something?"

Dominic walks the few steps toward me. "Actually, I realized I couldn't leave until I came back in to ask you something."

My heart slams against my rib cage. What could he possibly want to ask me? Something personal? Of course he won't ask something personal. He's thought of something he didn't ask about my services.

"I knew you'd think of something," I joke.

He withdraws his wallet, takes out a card. He extends his hand, like he's going to pass it to me, but instead asks, "Do you have a pen?"

"Yes." I head to my desk, aware that my walk is different. Sexier. Liberated.

Even the way I stretch forward to reach for the pen, lifting one foot that's in a cute sling-back as opposed to a comfortable flat shoe, is deliberately orchestrated to tease.

Really, what am I doing here?

I pass Dominic the pen.

"This is my card," he tells me as he scribbles something on the back. "My office and cell numbers are on the front. And on the back is my home number."

I scan the card as he passes it to me. "You're an architect."

"Yep."

"Impressive." Even more impressive, he's given me every possible way to reach him.

"It's all right. I work for myself. Have an office at my home. I'm not part of some big architectural firm. That way, I can set my own pace and do the projects I want."

"I completely get you on that one."

There's a glint in his eye, one I haven't seen in a long time but recognize immediately. It's hunger. Lust. Lust for me.

"You don't remember me, do you?"

I *knew* he looked familiar. "Should I? Have we met before?"

"Well, kind of. A couple of weeks ago. In a store not too far from here." He chuckles softly. "A Little Naughty?"

Oh my God, I could die! The hottie when I was checking out. My face flames.

"No, no," Dominic quickly says. "Don't be embarrassed."

"Too late."

"I only mentioned it because I thought you…thought you might have remembered seeing me."

I can't meet his eyes. "You did look familiar. I couldn't remember from where."

"Please don't feel bad. And I'd love it if you looked at me. You have the most incredible blue eyes."

My pulse is in overdrive as I lift my gaze to his. "There," he says. "I love those eyes."

Butterflies tickle my stomach. But I don't say anything. I don't know what to say.

Dominic is the first one to speak. "Let me ask this before I lose my nerve. I'm hoping we can get together for coffee sometime."

"Coffee?"

He nods. "Or dinner. Something else..."

Something else. I'd be a moron not to know what he's talking about.

Am I a moron for being attracted to him? Or worse, am I a dirty whore?

But how can I *not* be attracted to him? I'm so starved for sex from my husband that the first sexual interest in me from an attractive male has me turned on.

It's only natural.

But I can't cheat on Charles.

"I don't know..."

"Don't tell me no. Just think about it."

Seriously, Dominic has a voice that could probably leave me shuddering in the bedroom. And he's got such a warm smile. It's hard to resist him.

"Okay," I finally tell him. "I'll think about it."

"Thank you."

"I'm not making any promises." My left hand is still behind my back.

"That's fine."

Thankfully, Dominic turns and starts for the door. I don't deny myself the pleasure of checking out every inch of his magnificent body.

I'm gonna burn in hell...

It's incredible how you don't lose the internal dialogue you were raised with, and my mother was always preaching fire and brimstone. While other parents read to their kids at bedtime, my mother lectured us on all the sin in the world. She made sure to tell us that if we messed up in any way—from stealing candy at a store to engaging in premarital sex—we were going to hell.

I remember her saying all the time that just thinking something inappropriate is in fact a sin. I guess by that standard, I've already committed adultery. What's to stop me from doing the real deed?

At the door, Dominic looks at me over his shoulder. "You're really beautiful. Just thought I'd tell you that."

"Thank you." I swallow again. He has no clue how badly I'd like to rip his clothes off and have sex with him right here on my desk.

At least I can do that in my fantasies.

Who cares if I'll burn in hell?

I think about Dominic all the way home.

Mentally, I've already crossed the line with him, so I take it a step further. I imagine what it'd be like to have my soft breasts pressed against that hard chest of his. I think about what it'd be like to gaze into his eyes as I lay beneath him, his penis deep inside me. I dream of how he might taste, and how he'd moan with pleasure as I take him deep in my mouth.

The sexual images continue even as I pull into my driveway, and I don't want them to stop. The moment I step into my house, I know what I'm going to do. What I *have* to do.

I go to my closet and dig out the last-minute purchase I made after my day of shopping for new clothes. The vibrator. It's thick and long and lifelike, except that it's blue.

Before now, I've been embarrassed to try it, but I'm looking forward to it now.

I strip off my leather pants and blouse and lie down on the bed in my bra and thong.

I turn the penis on and close my eyes. The gentle vibrations stimulate my breasts, and I imagine that Dominic's hands are touching me. It's so easy to get hot thinking about this man, and when I touch myself, I'm already wet.

"Oh yes, Dom," I whisper, pretending it is his fingers stroking my nub, his fingers slipping into my folds. And then I imagine his tongue, hot and hungry, laving my pussy with such expert skill that I almost come from it.

But I don't want to feel his tongue. I want to feel his cock. So I move the vibrator lower, between my legs, where I rub it against my clit. Oh, that feels good. So good, I'm moaning as if it's really a man's penis.

Not just any man's. Right now, it's Dominic's. And he's hard for me and wants me more than he's ever wanted anyone else.

I spread my lips and insert the tip of the vibrator. Holy shit, I'm tight. It's like I'm a virgin again.

But I keep going, keep urging it inside. Finally, it's so deep inside me that the balls settle against my opening and the featherlike tentacles meant to massage me are rubbing against my clit.

"Oh, Dom…" My breathing shallows. "Hell yes…"

I tweak a nipple, picturing it in Dominic's mouth as he thrusts deep inside me. And those little tentacles work like magic, bringing me closer and closer to pure bliss.

"Ohh... Ohhhhh!" My moan is long and rapturous as the sweetest orgasm I've experienced takes its hold and doesn't let go for several seconds. Dominic has his penis nestled deep inside me, and he's watching me as I come. God, that smile of his. Right now, I am completely his.

The seconds pass. My breathing calms. Dominic fades away. I pull out the vibrator. I'm as satisfied as any woman could be, yet there's something hollow about it. Something that can't be completely fulfilled.

Because it's not the real thing.

After my orgasm, I rifle through every single pair of pants hanging in Charles's closet. And then I go through his drawers. And when I'm finished searching every spot in his dresser, I head back to the closet and even go through his shoes.

And find nothing. Not a single thing.

I slump onto the floor, exhausted both physically and mentally. And I'm disappointed.

Oh my God. I really am disappointed, when I should be elated.

"What am I doing?" I ask aloud. When Samera suggested I check Charles's clothes, I didn't. So why am I doing it now? Am I trying to find a reason to justify jumping Dominic's bones?

I groan softly, knowing that's the real reason for my disappointment. And God, how pathetic is that? I meet a guy who has my libido burning and suddenly I'm digging through my husband's stuff in a desperate attempt to find even one thread of evidence. It's like I *want* to find out that Charles is an unfaithful asshole who doesn't deserve my fidelity.

Lord but I want to get laid. This is what no sex does to you. It eats at the core of you, like a worm inside an apple. And slowly but surely it spoils you. It corrupts you.

I'm corrupted now. I don't care if I'm married to Charles. I want to have hot, wild sex with a man who finds me attractive.

I push myself up off the floor and walk out of the closet. I plop myself onto the bed. After a moment, I reach for the phone. I want to call Claudia, but then I remember she's in New York for her fitting. Lishelle's no doubt at the studio, so I don't want to bother her there.

Instead, I find myself calling Charles. The man I swore to be faithful to until death parts us.

"Charles Crawford's office," his receptionist says pleasantly.

"Emily, it's Annelise. Is Charles available?"

"Oh, sure. Hold on a sec."

A moment later, Charles comes onto the line.

"Annelise, hi."

"Hi, sweetheart."

"What's up?"

"Oh, nothing much. I was just thinking about you. I wanted to hear your voice."

"Everything all right?"

"Yeah," I lie. "I'm fine. Just…missing you." And feeling incredibly guilty for my mental infidelity!

"I'm sorry about last night," he says, surprising me. "Maybe you're right. Maybe what we need to do is plan some time away. I'm always so busy with work. Maybe if I get the hell away from this place…"

My heart fills with hope. All this time, I thought my suggestions were going in one ear and out the other. But Charles was listening. He really was.

"Oh, Charles. That would be fantastic. Do you really think you can get the time?"

"I'll see what I can do."

"Okay. That's all I can ask." I pause. "What about tonight? Do you want to go out for dinner?" I ask him. "It's a Tuesday, it shouldn't be hard to get reservations."

"Sure. We haven't done that in a while, have we?"

"No, we haven't."

"I can't believe how caught up with work I get. I'll have to make a better effort."

Charles is being so agreeable, I could cry.

"I'll call around and find someplace suitable. Is a reservation for seven o'clock okay?"

"Perfect. Now, I hate to cut this short—"

"Charles," I say quickly.

"Yes?"

"I love you."

There's a pause. I'm wondering if Charles is going to say anything when he finally speaks. "I know you do, sweetheart. And I love you, too."

When I hang up the phone, I immediately go to my purse and dig out the card Dominic gave me earlier. I rip it to shreds. Then I walk to the bathroom where I flush them down the toilet.

Chapter Nine

Lishelle

I'm gazing into Glenn's eyes. Yes, gazing. And holding his hand as we lie in my bed face-to-face, naked as the day we were born. One of Glenn's legs is slung over both of mine. This feels so natural—like he's been in my life and my bed forever.

I could stare into those mesmerizing hazel eyes all day. You'd think I've never been with a man before and Glenn's got some kind of spell on me.

But hey, I'm in love. And the truth is, I've never loved anyone like I love Glenn.

"Why are you looking at me like that?" I ask him.

"Like what?"

"Like you're trying to eat me up with your eyes."

"You want me to stop?" he asks.

"Not a chance. I want to stay here like this forever with you."

"I know what you mean."

A beat passes. I yawn. "I'm so exhausted. Thanks to you."

"You weren't complaining last night."

"I sure wasn't," I reply, chuckling softly. "What a start to my weekend!"

After speaking with Glenn during the week, I didn't expect him until today. But he surprised me by calling me at the studio last night and telling me he was in town.

We've been fucking ever since.

What can I say? I haven't had sex in two years. I'm going to take as much of it as I can get these days.

Glenn lifts my hand to his mouth and kisses it. "I aim to please."

"Did you ever!"

We both giggle, then gaze. Sheesh, you'd think we were fifteen and had just shared our first sexual experience together.

"You ready to get up?" Glenn asks me. Of course, he asks this as he tweaks one of my nipples.

"Oh, you don't play fair, do you?"

"Life ain't fair, sweetheart." Glenn lowers his head and his hot tongue covers my nipple. I close my eyes and moan. He takes my nipple deep in his mouth and suckles it slowly. Slowly, yet it nearly drives me out of my mind.

I run my hands over his closely cropped hair. "Damn you, Glenn."

"You want me to stop?"

"I thought…thought we were…" I can't finish my thought. Glenn is now massaging my clit, and oh, it feels so good. If I let myself, I could come. It's like my whole body is a giant nub, and the moment he touches me, I'm lost.

I'm his.

Glenn rolls onto his back and pulls me on top of him. His fingers dig into my ass, kneading my flesh. I quickly straddle him. Damn, his cock feels amazing pressed against my vagina like this.

But it feels much better inside me.

I ease my body up and stroke my finger over the length of his shaft—then guide his throbbing erection inside me. "Ooh, Glenn. Damn…"

He pulls my hips down so that he fills me with a hard thrust. We spent more than half the night screwing, so my inner walls are sore, but this pain is pleasure.

"You're so hot," Glenn whispers. He kneads my breasts, plays with my nipples. I ride him like he's a wild horse, hanging on to his solid legs for support. And I watch the expression on his face. It's a look of total ecstasy, the same one I know he must see on my face. I love how we stare into each other's eyes, like there's total openness and honesty between us.

"Come on, baby," Glenn moans. He grips my hips as he thrusts upward deep and hard, over and over again. I rub myself against him so that there's delicious friction against my clit.

A moment later, I close my eyes as a wave of orgasmic bliss washes over me. I arch my back and enjoy the ride.

Glenn's fingers dig into my butt. I'm still coming when I hear his grunt-giggle sound. I tighten my inner walls around him, knowing that will intensify his pleasure.

Slowly, his lips curl in a smile. He presses his palms against my shoulder blades, urging me forward. I collapse against his chest.

We're silent for a moment, our ragged breaths mingling. Then we start laughing.

"You do this to me every time, Baxter. Make me forget about everything but making love to you."

"I can't keep my hands off you."

I slide off his chest and onto my back. "I'd better take a shower. Alone. You're gonna have to keep that lethal weapon away from me if we're ever going to do anything else today."

"All right, all right," Glenn grudgingly agrees. Still, he reaches for my body as I move off the bed. He grins at me, then settles back on his pillow.

"I guess we should go out for breakfast," he says. "Eat something to build our strength up."

"For more sex?" I ask, twisting my lips in mock reproof.

"No, actually. There's something I want to show you."

My eyebrows shoot up. "Show me? What could you want to show me?"

"It's a surprise."

"A surprise?" I plop back down on the bed beside him. "Come on, Glenn. You know how I am with surprises. Just tell me what it is."

"You go get your shower. Or we'll never get out of here."

"Glenn…"

He pushes my leg. "Go."

I glare at him before scooting off the bed. I'm kidding, of course. I bluff a good game but I don't really want him to tell me what the surprise is. I *love* surprises.

"Hurry," he tells me. "Or it might not be today."

"All right, I'm going." I grin all the way to the bathroom.

"You can't possibly want more food?" I say to Glenn a couple hours later, when we're sipping coffees at a Denny's fifteen minutes from my house. I'm not a big fan of the Denny's chain, but most anyplace can do breakfast right.

Glenn peruses the plastic-encased lunch menu in the center of the table. "I don't know. I could have a burger."

"You could not, so let's just settle the bill and leave already."

"Impatient for that surprise, are you?"

I smile sweetly at him.

"Can I order dessert?"

"No dessert!" I laugh. "Boy, you know how to tease a girl."

"So I'm told."

Something catches in my chest. I know we're both joking here, but it hits me instantly that I've never asked Glenn about his past. We've been too busy getting reacquainted in bed, and the subject hasn't come up.

"I bet you have been, haven't you?" Before he can answer, I continue. "Tell me what your life has been like over the years. You said you've never been married, but there had to be someone serious. Maybe a few women you were serious with?"

Glenn sips his coffee. "You don't really want to talk about this, do you?"

"I do. At first I thought I didn't want to know, but I realize now that I was lying to myself."

"All right. There was someone serious. Only one since you and I have been apart. A couple quasi-serious relationships, but the last one was the most intense."

My gut tightens. Can you believe I'm jealous? "How long ago?" I ask. "And how serious?"

"How long ago?" He thinks for a moment. "I guess about fourteen months."

"Wow. That's pretty recent."

"I know."

"Don't leave me hanging. Tell me what happened."

"We dated for about two years. Yeah, two years," he says, seeing my surprised look. "I'd popped the question, and we were going to get married."

"Really?" I'm stunned. I know I didn't ask before now, but isn't this information Glenn should have volunteered? Or am I being too sensitive over the matter?

"Yeah." He rolls his eyes slightly. "But it didn't work out."

"Oh, no no no. You don't just tell me you asked a woman to marry you—barely over a year ago—then tell me it didn't work out. What happened—and do I have to worry that she's going to come back into your life at any moment?"

"No chance of that, since she decided to get back together with her ex-husband. She broke down and told me that my proposal made her realize she had unresolved issues with her ex—you really want to hear this?"

I nod.

"I proposed to her. She didn't answer, said she needed time. Three days later, she gave me some lame story about the sacredness of marital vows and how she shouldn't promise the same thing to another man that she'd promised to her husband. She said she wanted to give him another chance." Glenn shrugs. "As far as I know, they got back together, and they're married again."

I am feeling much, much better. Well, maybe not that much better. "So she broke your heart."

"I'm not still hung up on her, if that's what you're thinking."

"Are you sure? You *were* going to marry the woman."

"Yeah, I'm sure. Because I'm hung up on someone else." He gives me a pointed look. "Always was, if you want to know the truth, even though we'd gone our separate ways. Plus, I don't think things were really meant to be with Tess. She had a couple kids—"

"Tess?"

"—and she didn't want more. I'd be forcing it with her to make it work. I know that now. Believe me, everything's worked out for the best. Especially now that I have you back in my life."

I search Glenn's eyes. They seem sincere. Truthful. There's really no reason for me to be making an issue out of this.

But still I ask, "How did you two connect in bed?"

"Nowhere near the way we do," Glenn answers without hesitation. Then he reaches across the table and strokes his thumb across my palm.

"So I don't need to spend the rest of my life hating her?" I joke.

"It'd be a waste of energy."

"I know. You're right. What matters is here and now. Us."

"I couldn't agree more." Glenn reaches for his wallet in the back of his pants and pulls out some money. He drops it onto the table on top of the bill. Then he asks, "Ready for your surprise?"

"I can't wait."

My excitement mounts when Glenn and I arrive in Duluth, one of Atlanta's upscale and beautiful suburbs. The houses are large here, with sprawling, well-manicured lawns, neatly trimmed shrubs, colorful flowers and winding driveways that stretch for at least a couple hundred feet.

My heart is beating a mile a minute. What on earth could Glenn be doing taking me to a spot like this?

He's holding my hand, something that feels so comfortable. It makes me smile. It's nice to know that despite how well Glenn and I connect in the bedroom, there's more to our relationship than that.

"I'm dying here, babe. When are you going to tell me what's going on?"

"You'll see...."

I continue to survey the area as Glenn makes a series of turns. At last, we pull into the driveway of a gray stucco house with a For Sale sign on the lawn. The interlocking brick driveway veers to the right, where there's enough space for eight or so cars.

My eyes whip to Glenn's. He doesn't say a word. Simply grins at me like a fool as he pulls his cell phone out of the holder on his belt.

He dials a number. Then I hear him say, "Hey, Sandra. It's Glenn Baxter. I'm in front of the house. Great, see you shortly."

"Who was that?" I ask Glenn, although I know who it had to be. At least I think I know who it had to be.

"That was the real estate agent."

"Glenn! What are you doing? And when did you arrange to meet a real estate agent here? We've been together the whole time."

"I called her when you went to use the restroom. And don't get too excited. You don't know if you'll like it."

"Not like it? Glenn!" I look out at the line of trees dividing this property from the next one. In the distance, I can see the glistening waters of Lake Lanier. I want to throw my arms around him and squeeze the life out of him.

"I've always wanted a house on the water. And look at this place. I love the stucco. All the trees for privacy. The size of the land. What is it, an acre?"

"A little larger than that."

"Glenn!"

"Don't get excited..."

"How can I *not* get excited? It'll be a longer drive to get to work, yes, but this is the kind of house..." My voice trails off when I look at it.

"The kind of house you raise a family in," he supplies for me.

I could become an emotional mess right about now. I'm seeing my dreams come to fruition at a time I didn't expect it. When I'd convinced myself the dream no longer mattered to me.

"What are you doing, Glenn?"

"I want to see if you like the place. Then we'll go from there."

I throw my arms around his neck and kiss him. A deep kiss that goes on and on. It stokes the embers of my love for him.

We pull apart when we hear the sound of a car pulling up beside us. A pretty, dark-haired woman jumps out of a silver Lexus, smiling apologetically.

Glenn and I get out of my BMW.

"I'm so sorry I'm late," she says. "Got stuck in a bit of traffic."

"It's fine," Glenn assures her.

"Lishelle Jennings." Sandra offers me her hand, and I shake it. "I'd know you anywhere. I love you on Channel Four News."

"Oh, thank you."

"I'm Sandra Holloway."

"So nice to meet you."

Sandra turns and starts for the house. Glenn and I fall into step beside her. "I hope you like it as much as Glenn does," Sandra says to me.

"I'm sure I will," I reply. But I'm shocked to hear Glenn has already seen it. When? He just got back to the city last night.

I gasp my delight the moment Sandra opens the door. The massive foyer boasts cathedral ceilings and a double staircase heading upstairs. The entire area is covered in hardwood floors.

"There are six bedrooms, five bathrooms."

"Oh. My. God." I step into the house.

"Cherrywood floors," Sandra continues. "There's also a staircase at the back of the house that leads upstairs. Ten-foot ceilings throughout, except the foyer and family room, where there're cathedral ceilings."

"I love this place."

"I figured you'd like modern," Glenn tells me.

"I love the modern look. It's also got some classical touches," I comment as I look at the moldings in the nearby living room.

"It's a mix of styles," Sandra informs me. "European, traditional, colonial."

"Whatever it is, it's stunning."

"Do you like to cook?" Sandra asks.

"I love to cook. When I've got the time."

"You should see the kitchen."

Sandra leads us to the back of the house. I actually start to giggle, that's how giddy with excitement I am.

"All maple cabinets," Sandra says proudly. "And this breakfast bar could seat twenty."

I tune Sandra out as I make my way to the floor-to-ceiling glass windows at the back of the house. "Look at that pool!"

"It's an Olympic-size lap pool," she comments. "Heated. With a Jacuzzi."

"And that's the lake," Glenn tells me, pointing through the thicket of trees.

A house on the water. I could die.

The rest of the house only gets better. There are two master-bedroom suites, both with excessive closet space. There's a den, an office. Hardwood floors throughout.

Sandra's grinning as she faces me. "So, you like?"

"I love it. What's it selling for?"

"It's listed for eight ninety-nine, but I'm sure you can get it for eight twenty-five. It's vacant right now. You could move in anytime."

"It's a little pricey," Glenn comments.

"But such an incredible home," Sandra interjects. "An investment, really."

"The best kind of investment," I say. I don't just mean for real estate property. I'm thinking family here, and marriage.

Glenn must be thinking this, too.

When we arrive back in the foyer, Sandra says, "I'll let you two roam around without me as a third wheel."

I take Glenn's hand and head back up the stairs to the master bedroom that has a stunning view of the lake. I look out at it, shaking my head in disbelief.

"What?" Glenn asks.

"It's just…this has always been my dream. To have a place like this on the water…"

"Why do you think we're here?"

My heart stops beating as I face him.

"Don't you think I remember what you always used to say—that you wanted a place on the water one day? A great place to raise a family?"

For a moment, I can't speak. "You remember that?"

"When it comes to you, there's not much I forget."

I clearly have forgotten some things. I forgot how romantic Glenn can be, how he would surprise me on occasion.

"What about that view from the kitchen?" he asks.

"And we haven't even been outside yet. There's a tennis court."

"Why am I not surprised? I love it. The entire place is amazing." I glance around the master bedroom. Not only does it have a living-room area to the left offset by columns, it has a fireplace.

"Look." Glenn points out the window.

"What?" I ask.

"On the lake. Don't you see it?"

"See what?" My eyes search, but I see nothing out of the ordinary. And when Glenn doesn't respond, I turn around to face him.

He's on one knee, holding a ring box in his hand.

A tingling sensation runs along every inch of my skin. My hands begin to shake.

Glenn opens the burgundy-colored box, and I gasp. There's a three-diamond ring in there—a round diamond in the center, and two triangular-shaped diamonds at each side.

"That's got to be—"

"Two point two carats." Glenn beams. "I wanted to get something bigger, but—"

"Bigger? Don't be crazy. I love it." I start to reach for it, but pull my hand back. He hasn't offered it to me yet.

"I know this place is pricey, and maybe we won't be able to get it," Glenn begins. "Yet. But it's something to aspire to. Our dream, sweetheart. Yours and mine."

He takes the ring out of the box and then takes my hand. I realize I'm crying when a tear touches my lips.

Glenn slips the ring on my left hand. "Lishelle Amanda Jennings—will you marry me?"

I scream. Scream and throw myself onto him with so much excitement that I knock him off balance and he tumbles backward onto the hardwood floor. He puts one arm out to cushion his fall, while slipping the other arm around my waist. I land against the hard wall of his chest.

We erupt in a fit of giggles.

"Glenn Baxter, you little devil. I had *no* clue."

"That's the point of a surprise."

I'm planting kisses all over his face when I hear, "Oh, sorry."

My gaze flies to the door. Sandra is standing there, blushing.

"I heard a scream," she explains.

I heave myself off of Glenn and stand. "Guess I got a little excited." I thrust out my left hand and wriggle my fingers. "Glenn just proposed!"

"Oh, my." Sandra oohs and aahs as she inspects my ring. "How beautiful is that? Congratulations."

"Thank you."

"Thanks." Glenn speaks at the same time I do.

"With a wedding around the corner, it's the perfect time to get a new home."

"I *do* love it." I gesture around the extraordinary room. "How could I not? Of course, it's the first home we've seen—"

"I completely understand. And I wouldn't expect you to buy without looking around." Sandra reaches into the pocket of her blazer and produces two cards. "I know Glenn is out of town most of the week, but if you want me to show you some other options, just give me a call.

I'd happily do it today, but I have another appointment in half an hour."

"No problem," I tell Sandra. "We have a fund-raiser to go to this evening, and we'll have to go home to get ready."

"Call me anytime. We'll set something up."

We all walk downstairs. Outside, while Sandra locks up, I imagine two children chasing each other around the lawn.

A boy and a girl.

I can almost hear their happy laughter.

Glenn takes my hand, and I snap out of my reverie. I snuggle my face against his shoulder.

I've heard it said that it's usually when you're least expecting it that love comes into your life.

I can't believe it, but that's what's happened with me.

Chapter Ten

Claudia

I look amazing. If I do say so myself.

I've opted for color for this evening's charity ball, so I'm wearing a floor-length red Versace gown. It's an off-the-shoulder number that shows a good amount of cleavage. Quite frankly, it's stunning. And I stand out in a good way because many of the women here have opted to wear black and other dark colors.

Adam is resting his hand on the small of my back as we walk through the crowd. All around us, people smile. Other high-profile families we know, many of them who will support Adam's campaign for mayor when he announces his intention to run after our wedding.

Henry Dixon, an Atlanta judge, excuses himself from the small group of people he is talking with and approaches us. "Claudia," he says, taking both my hands in his and spreading them wide to get a good look at me. "You look fantastic."

"Thank you, Henry."

"And Adam." Henry pumps Adam's hand. "Great to see you, as always."

"Great to see you, as well."

"This evening looks like a roaring success. You're doing such wonderful work for children who so desperately need it."

I slip beside Adam and link arms with him. "I'm so proud of him," I say.

Adam, who has a law degree, gave up practicing a couple years ago to run the Wishes Come True Foundation, a charity to aid terminally ill children. He's president of the board—a volunteer position. I fully supported his decision, and every day I admire the work he does. It's such a great cause.

"It's all about the kids," Adam says. "What better cause is there than giving terminally ill children a chance to have their greatest wish come true?"

"I agree," Henry says. "You're doing great work. But I still think your talents are better suited to the legal arena."

Adam chuckles softly. "I know what you're getting at— and while I'm not ready to make any commitments *yet*, stay tuned after the wedding for a very special announcement."

Henry's lips spread in a wide and knowing grin. He clamps a hand on Adam's shoulder. "That's what I wanted to hear."

Adam Hart for mayor. I can't wait.

I'm gazing up at Adam lovingly when I feel a hand cup my ass so intimately that fingers graze the back of my vagina. I'm so startled that I gasp and nearly jump out of my skin. Adam quickly curls his fingers around my waist, and I don't even have to look at him to know he's the culprit.

"Are you all right?" Henry asks me with concern.

"Yes." I surreptitiously pinch Adam's arm. "I just had a…a chill."

"I hope you're not coming down with something," Adam says, and I want to smack that smirk off his face.

"With all the planning I still have to do for the wedding? Not a chance." I smile sweetly at him.

"Claudia!"

At the sound of my name, I turn, and there's Lishelle, hurrying toward me while holding Glenn's hand. She releases him only when she's close enough to throw her arms around me. No polite air kisses from Lishelle. She's my girl and shows me love no matter where we are.

"How you doing?" she asks, and I have to say, she's never sounded happier. "God, you look amazing. You said you were gonna look hot, but I didn't know this hot. Whoo!"

"Thanks. You look pretty hot yourself. That's the Kate Spade?"

"Mmm-hmm. Classic but sexy."

"That it is." I suddenly realize that I've totally ignored Glenn. I turn to him and take one of his hands into both of mine. "Glenn, hello. It's been a long time."

"That it has. It's good to see you."

"Good to see you, too. I hear I'll be seeing more of you."

"A lot more," Glenn agrees. Then he lifts Lishelle's left hand to show off a brilliant three-diamond ring.

"Whoa." My mouth hanging open, I reach for Lishelle's hand. "I know you said it was serious, but—"

"He proposed this afternoon."

"Lishelle!" Wow, she wasn't kidding when she said that Glenn had finally gotten his act together. "Congratulations!" I give her another hug, then hug Glenn, as well.

I whip around when I feel hands circle my waist. Adam is looking toward Glenn, waiting for an introduction.

"I don't think you've ever met Glenn, have you, Adam?"

"I haven't."

"Adam, this is Glenn Baxter. Lishelle's fiancé. Glenn, this is my fiancé, Adam Hart."

The two men shake hands.

"How are you, Adam?" Lishelle asks.

"Couldn't be better."

"Glenn and I just got engaged," Lishelle gushes. "Should I tell them about the house in Duluth?"

"What house in Duluth?" I ask.

"Well…" Glenn shrugs.

"I shouldn't say anything, because I don't know if we'll even get it, but Glenn took me to this fabulous house in Duluth, and that's where he proposed. It was so romantic."

I can't help being skeptical. "Didn't you just reconnect, like, last weekend?"

Glenn holds Lishelle close. "It's been in the making for over ten years."

"Congratulations," Adam tells them. "That's great news."

"Thanks."

"What do you do, Glenn?" Adam asks.

"I'm a pilot."

"Ah. Which airline?"

"All-American Air."

Adam nods politely, but I know what he's thinking. He's thinking the airline isn't big enough and prestigious enough.

"Now you'll be able to fly anywhere in the country," I tell Lishelle, hoping Glenn won't pick up on any of Adam's snootiness. Really, I love him, but I hate how elitist he can be sometimes.

"That's just one of the perks I'm looking forward to." Lishelle separates herself from Glenn to link arms with me. "Where's Annelise?"

"I haven't seen her yet."

"Then we should find her," Lishelle suggests. She turns to Glenn and offers him her free hand. He gazes deeply into her eyes as he takes it, like a man hopelessly in love.

"I'm going to circulate." Adam gives me a soft peck on the cheek.

"Oh, all right." I'm a little disappointed, even though I know Adam's going to want to make the rounds, thank people for coming out to support the event. "I'll see you later."

I force a smile as I turn to Lishelle and Glenn. "Come on. Let's go find Annelise."

When I spot Annelise, she's grabbing a champagne flute off of a sterling-silver tray. No sooner has she taken the drink than she downs it—every last drop.

Something's wrong.

As I get a little closer, I see that her eyes are red-rimmed. She's been crying.

Annelise's eyes light up as she sees us. Releasing Charles's arm, she floats toward me. We air-kiss, and then she does the same with Lishelle. "Glenn." Annelise takes his hands in hers. "How nice to see you again!"

She's a little too bubbly—like she's had too much to drink.

"We're engaged!" Lishelle flashes the ring.

"What? That's so great." When the tears flow from Annelise's eyes, I know they're not for Lishelle and Glenn. I wonder if Lishelle knows that, too.

Saying, "Excuse me," I link arms with Annelise and pull her aside to a spot where there aren't many people milling around. "Okay, Annie. What's going on?"

"I'm so happy for Lishelle—aren't you?"

"That has nothing to do with why you're crying. And how much have you had to drink?"

"Just one, I think. Maybe two."

"Stop lying. You can hardly stand straight. What's going on?"

Annelise starts to cry discreetly. I take her hand and cross the floor to the bathroom, which is thankfully not more than a hundred yards away.

"…fucking son of a bitch," a woman is saying as we enter. She's passing Kleenex to another well-dressed woman, who is also crying.

Drama. There's always drama in women's bathrooms.

I lead Annelise to a sofa on the opposite side of the bathroom's sitting area. "Tell me everything," I say in a hushed tone.

"I don't…" Her eyes sweep the bathroom. "I don't want to talk about it here."

"Is it serious?" I continue. I hate seeing my friend like this. "That's what I want to know."

"It's just…I was supposed to do a wedding in the morning. But the woman called and canceled when I was already at the church. Said she found her boyfriend making out with a stripper at the bachelor party and she ended things."

"And you're this upset about it several hours later?"

"No…I also had a fight with Charles. But I think we'll be okay," she adds bravely.

I wrap an arm around her as we sit. When the two other women in the lounge area get up and leave, I immediately ask, "What do you mean you think *we'll* be okay. You just had a fight, right? Nothing serious."

Fresh tears fill Annelise's eyes. For a moment, she can't even speak.

"Oh, no." I shake my head. "Annie, no."

"He said I'm driving a stake into our marriage, that I'm pushing him away."

"What?"

"Me—the one who's always there for him. Always washing his clothes, making sure even his briefs are neatly pressed."

"You've been nothing but a great wife to him."

"According to him, because I'm doing everything I can to get him in the mood, I'm putting too much pressure on him." Annelise pauses to blow her nose. Gone are the tears, replaced with a look of defiance. "You know what got him so pissed? That I booked a weekend away for us at that retreat in Arizona. Earlier this week, he told me he'd take some time off. Then I tell him I tentatively booked something for next weekend, and he got upset."

"Come on."

"I'm serious. I'm trying to save our marriage, and he got upset. Told me that he's knee deep in work with the lawsuit, and yeah, I know he is. But he's got to be able to book *some* time off, can't he? He's not the only one working on that case. Marsha Hindenberg can pick up the slack for one day, can't she?"

"I agree." I rub Annelise's back. "I don't know what's wrong with him."

"And it's not just that. On Tuesday, I made reservations for dinner at his favorite restaurant. I'd called him earlier and he sounded excited about going out. But you know what—he never even made it home. He called from the airport to say he had to go out of town for a couple days."

"Why didn't you call me?"

"I'm so embarrassed about all of this. Is this my husband or a stranger? I don't know anymore."

"You'll get past this. I know you will."

"What if we don't? What if he leaves me?"

"No. Oh my God, no. Listen, there were many times my father left my mother waiting after promising he'd be home at a certain time. Charles has a high-profile career. He's working on a high-profile case."

"Then why did he say I'm pushing him away?"

"Couples have arguments like that all the time. Say things they don't mean."

"I hope you're right."

"I am. Annie, you had an argument. That's all."

Annelise seems to consider my words but doesn't comment. Instead, she gets to her feet and straightens her buttercup-yellow gown. It looks fantastic on her, highlighting her blond hair.

"We'd better get back out there," she says.

"You're okay?"

"I'm fine," she assures me, and thankfully, she does seem fine. "Let me freshen up my makeup, and I'll be good to go."

We both spend a couple minutes retouching face powder and lipstick, then we head out the door.

I bump right into someone entering, and offer a quick apology before I see who it is. It's Arlene Nash, and unlike me, she doesn't offer an apology. Instead, she gives me the quick once-over, checking out my gown. Her lips turn ever so slightly in a barely noticeable frown.

"Arlene," I say. I have to admit she looks gorgeous in a formfitting black gown. I saw the same gown at Fendi and almost bought it myself.

She forces a smile. "How nice to see you, Claudia. How are the wedding plans going?"

"It's going to be *the* event of the season." I can't help boasting a little. I've often heard rumors that Arlene is interested in Adam. When I started dating him, she stopped inviting me to events.

"I can't wait," she says, but I don't believe her.

Arlene continues into the bathroom, followed by a woman I don't recognize.

"Whoa," Annelise comments. "She's a royal bitch, isn't she?"

"You've met her only once and you figured that out."

"I'm guessing there's a story there."

"Yeah, but I won't bore you with it. Let's find Charles."

There's something electric about Adam when he speaks. Something captivating. He has the power to mesmerize people, make them stop whatever they're doing and listen to him, just as they are now.

And he's so natural when he's speaking before a crowd. It's obvious to me and anyone who knows him that he should be in the public arena.

"The mother came to me in tears, and told me that the vacation to the Turks and Caicos brought a smile to her son's face that she hadn't seen since he'd first become ill. For the first time in a year and a half, he was able to be a child. To laugh and have fun without worry about treatments." Adam pauses as his eyes move over the crowd. "That, ladies and gentlemen, is why I do what I do. It's important work. The most important work." There are nods and hums of agreement. "I thank each and every one of you for coming out tonight to support this great cause. With your help, we'll make every child in need's dream come true in Georgia!"

The crowd erupts in applause. I smile at Adam with admiration. He raises a hand in a wave to everyone, then, as the applause dies, makes his way off the stage.

I wrap my arms around him. "That was a great speech, Adam. You knock 'em dead every time."

"Thank you, babe."

I'm by his side as he spends time shaking hands. He's already working the crowd like he's on the campaign trail.

After several minutes, he takes my hand. "I've got to escape for a minute."

He whisks me away. We hurry across the floor of Atlanta's prestigious Supper Club. It's a members-only type club, and you have to be invited to join. Of course, on a night like this, anyone able to pay the ticket price for dinner—the proceeds of which go to the Wishes Come True Foundation—is allowed entry.

I'm about to ask Adam where he's taking me when he opens the door to what looks like a utility room. He ushers me inside.

Before the door clicks shut, he's pushing my gown up to my waist. "Adam," I say cautiously.

"I've had enough of everyone out there. I want to eat your pussy."

I open my mouth to protest, but he's already pulling my panties down. When he flicks his tongue over me, he moans long and loud, like my nectar is the sweetest thing on earth.

"I've been wanting to do this all night."

I know there are five hundred guests just outside that door, but I can't resist my man. And I don't really want to. I doubt anyone else will venture into this utility closet, so I feel safe.

His hot tongue laves my clit, and now I'm the one who moans. I grip his shoulders to keep my balance.

I'm in the throes of passion when I hear the door creak open. I jump back so fast, I slip and nearly fall.

"Shit," I utter, trying to right my dress. It's then that I realize Adam isn't hurrying like I am. In fact, he's still on his knees, smiling as he swipes the back of his hand across his mouth.

"Adam!" I whisper sharply.

"Relax," he says, stroking my hand. "I'm expecting company."

"What?"

"Hello?" someone calls out. A man's voice.

Now Adam gets to his feet. "Around the corner," he answers.

My stomach takes a serious nosedive, and my breath leaves me in a rush. "Adam..."

"It's a surprise, babe."

Before I can say another word, an attractive white man rounds the corner. A moment later, I recognize him. Jason—the bartender who helped us create our own special drink for our wedding!

"What's going on here?" I ask. My voice is shaky, and I feel sick. And scared.

"You remember Jason," Adam answers.

"I remember him, but what's he doing here?"

Jason moves toward me slowly. His lustful gaze makes me feel dirty. "Think of it as a present."

My eyes fly to Adam's. "A present?"

Adam rubs the small of my back. "Uh-huh. It's okay. Jason enjoys...the lifestyle."

"The *lifestyle?*"

"Usually when you swing, you bring a partner, but I was working the bar here—"

"A swinger?" I hiss, glaring at Adam. I look at Jason and say, "Give us a moment, please."

I take Adam by the hand and pull him out of earshot from Jason. "What the fuck—"

He puts a finger on my lips to shush me. "I thought you wanted to try this."

"*Me?* When did I ever tell you that?"

"That night we were at the club. You said you were turned on."

"With you, yes. But it's not something I want to try with other people. You want me to be with another man?"

"I didn't think you were ready to be with another woman. I figured this was safer."

"Here's a news flash. I'll *never* be with another woman, okay? You've been watching too much porn."

Adam's gaze wanders beyond me, and his lips curl in a grin. I whip my head around. Jason has his cock out and is stroking himself.

"Oh my God, Adam. He's some kind of freak."

"No, he's just hot for you. He told me that the moment he saw you, he got a hard-on."

I glare at Adam. "You've been smoking up, haven't you?" Adam doesn't answer, but he doesn't have to. I can see it in his eyes. And in this absurd scenario he's suggested. I can hardly believe that just moments before he gave such an empowering speech.

He covers my breasts, then kisses me. "Relax, baby. You've got two guys here to fulfill your every fantasy."

I don't understand him. He wants to watch me fuck another guy in this utility room, when there are hundreds of well-dressed, influential people just outside the door?

He nibbles on my ear. "We get married in four weeks."

"And I don't want to be doing this kind of shit." I use a finger to angle his face so that he stares directly into my eyes. "Do you hear me? I am not into the 'lifestyle' or 'swapping' or whatever you want to call it. I am into you. But I'm not sure you're into me," I add, my voice cracking a little.

"Of course I'm into you. Why do you think I want to give you this gift?"

I inhale sharply when fingers skim my neck. I throw a gaze over my shoulder.

Jason smiles as he runs the tips of his fingers down my back. "I love your skin," he tells me. "It's so soft." His hands move lower. "And I love this ass. I wanted to touch you the first moment I saw you."

I quickly look at Adam. My eyes search his. For what—permission?

"It's okay." He plants a gentle kiss on my lips. "You'll like this."

Behind me, I feel Jason kiss my butt through my gown. A sexual charge shoots through me.

Oh, God help me.

"I'm not sure—"

"The moment you feel uncomfortable, we'll stop. Okay?"

My reply is a shaky breath. Then Adam is kissing me, and Jason's hands are trailing up my thigh…

I'm tense for a good ten seconds—Adam kissing me, Jason stroking my skin. I'm a little surprised that Jason's fingers feel so…so gentle. Like he's trying to savor every moment of this. Trying to seduce me.

But I jerk when his fingers graze my clit.

"Relax, baby," Adam whispers. "Close your eyes."

"I don't know, Adam…"

Jason pushes my dress up and kisses my ass. I shudder. Then stiffen. This is disgusting. It's wrong. Friggin' twisted. And yet…his touch is strangely erotic.

Electric.

Jason slowly turns me around, and though I can hardly breathe, I don't fight him. Fingering the lace of my thong, Jason groans with pleasure. "Oh my God, Claudia. What a beautiful pussy."

I feel a jolt of unexpected heat.

Behind me, Adam unzips my gown. Jason wets his fingers and massages my nub. Adam's warm lips kiss one of my shoulders as he pulls my dress straps down my arms. Now, my breasts are exposed. And to my shock, my body is thrumming with sexual energy. I'm feeling *turned on*. My body is excited and alive, reveling in the taboo of having a strange man's fingers on my pussy.

"Fuck, I want to eat you, Claudia," Jason rasps. "I want my tongue so far inside you…"

"You'll like that, baby," Adam says hotly against my ear as he tweaks my nipples. "You want that, don't you?"

"Yes." The word escapes on its own.

Jason pulls my clit into his mouth, and I gasp. And then I flinch. He's sucking me so fervently, it's too intense.

"Softer," I tell him. "Not so much."

Jason slows down, gently flicking his tongue now. "Like that?"

"Yes…"

Adam nibbles on my ear while playing with my nipples. "God, baby. You're so beautiful. So amazing…"

An electrical charge of pleasure zaps me when Jason inserts a finger inside me. And then he starts sucking my clit again, softly this time, and my legs weaken. My breathing grows shallow.

"Yes, baby," Adam whispers.

I explode, coming hard and panting fast. I close my eyes against the delicious sensations. Adam turns my face to his and kisses me while I ride the wave.

"I love you, baby," he says. "God, I love you."

"I love you, too." And for a moment, I'm in orgasm heaven. But as my carnal bliss subsides, I glance down at Jason, see his smiling face. I've just shared the most intimate part of me with a stranger.

Christ, I came in his mouth.

I'm disgusted with myself.

Chapter Eleven

Annelise

It's Sunday afternoon, the day after the charity fund-raiser, and I'm sitting with Lishelle and Claudia at our booth in Liaisons. I'm in a pissy mood and need to bitch.

"I mean, what is wrong with a sexual-wellness spa? Does something seedy happen there—something dirty? Because that's what Charles implied on the way home last night. Worried that he could tarnish his reputation if people found out we went there. Am I completely clueless? Everything I've read says that couples go there to reconnect sexually—and what's wrong with that?"

Lishelle swallows her mouthful of food, then answers. "Nothing. I would think Charles would jump at the chance to go."

My own plate of scrambled eggs and bacon is mostly

untouched. Instead, I'm sucking back mimosas like I didn't wake up with a hangover. "I'm beginning to think that even if Charles can get it up, he doesn't want to."

"Did you bring up the whole impotency thing?" Lishelle asks.

"I tried. Another brush-off." I can't help groaning. "What am I supposed to do—live without a man forever just because I'm married to a guy who doesn't want to make love to me? We got home last night and I hoped, I prayed he would make a decent effort to get it up. But he went right to bed. Leaving me there in a Dolce & Gabbana gown any other man would have wanted to rip off. I'm not sure I can take much more of this. I *need* to have sex."

"I understand your frus—"

"No, you don't," I say, cutting Claudia off. "I'm so desperate, I'm considering having an affair."

Claudia and Lishelle exchange a glance before looking at me again.

"I met someone," I continue. "He came into my studio. And the way he looked at me...I don't remember ever feeling so sexually charged just from a look. This guy made me remember that I'm a woman. He made me remember all the times I've been hit on in my life. Even by some of my clients' fiancés—you remember the stories. I used to look in the mirror and see a confident and beautiful woman, but somehow, Charles has taken that from me. I want that back."

"Wow." Lishelle pushes her plate of pastries to the side. Claudia suddenly stops chewing her bacon.

"After I met this guy, I went home and used a vibrator

for the first time, thinking of him through it all, and I had *the* best orgasm."

"Aren't vibrators fucking great?" Lishelle asks. "I've been telling you for years to buy one."

"I thought that would be enough," I say sadly, "but it wasn't."

"So now you want to have sex with him?" Claudia asks, sounding a little shocked.

A beat passes before I answer. "I'm not sure. I thought I wanted that, but then I ripped up his card, so I have no way to contact him. Unless…"

"Unless what?" Lishelle asks.

"He came in with his younger brother and the brother's fiancée. They said they want to hire me, but they haven't been back, so who knows?"

"Maybe that's a good thing," Claudia comments.

"You think I shouldn't have an affair?"

Claudia holds her forkful of eggs before her mouth. "If you want my honest opinion, no. But I'm about to get married."

"Yeah," Lishelle says. "You're still in that blissful stage. When everything about marriage seems wonderful and perfect."

"And what about you, Miss Suddenly Engaged to your first love."

"I'm just saying—I *was* married, and it wasn't always wonderful, and the sad reality is that yes, some people have affairs." Now Lishelle faces me. "I am in no way saying you should have an affair. But then, that's not my decision to make. If things are rough with Charles and you've tried all you can and you need to get some

sex on the side…" She shrugs. "I'll support you, whatever you decide."

"Wonders never cease," Claudia mutters.

"Annelise is a grown woman, and we're not her parents. We're her friends."

As Lishelle and Claudia banter back and forth about
what's morally right, my mind drifts to Dominic. I can't
stop thinking about him. Even last night, when I was so
pissed with Charles about Arizona, I began comforting
myself with thoughts of Dominic. I'll bet he wouldn't
balk at the idea of going to a sex spa. I'll bet he couldn't
pack his bags fast enough.

That's exactly what I imagined last night as Charles lay
with his back to me, snoring. I thought of me and Dominic walking into a magnificent room at a resort tucked
away in an Arizona desert, with a fire already going in
the living room's fireplace. Of course, there was a bottle
of champagne chilling, and excited, Dom took my hand
and hurried into the room with me. We both laughed like
teenagers. Then he scooped me in his arms and twirled
me around, and I clung to him, knowing that within
minutes we'd be naked and having the best sex of our
lives.

In my dream, once the twirling stopped, Dominic laid
a heavy kiss on me, his tongue twisting with mine. I
grabbed at his shirt, ripping it in my haste to get it off.
Then I went for his jeans, unzipping them and shimmy-
ing them down his hips with his briefs. I moaned in delight at the sight of his penis—large and solid and angling
to my right.

I took it in my hands, stroked him as I kissed the tip.

Stroked him as I added my tongue, tasting the flavor of salt. Then I ran my tongue in circles around the top of his cock.

"Christ, Annie…"

Pressing my fingers into his ass, I took him into my mouth as far as I could. In and out I moved around him the way my pussy would.

Dominic tangled his fingers in my hair. "I can't take this. I don't want to come yet."

He tugged me to my feet and pulled my simple black dress over my head. When he saw I was wearing nothing underneath, not even panties, his eyes roamed over me with heated appreciation. Then he kicked off his jeans and dropped to his knees, giving me not even a moment to catch my breath as he sucked my clit into his mouth and devoured it with his hot tongue.

With Charles beside me, it was too risky to get the vibrator, but I pushed two fingers as far as I could inside my body with one hand, while with the other I massaged my nub until I was panting.

"Oh, Dom…"

I stole a quick glance at Charles, wondering if my moans had wakened him. They hadn't.

I slipped another finger into my pussy, imagining Dominic pushing his tongue inside me as far as he could go. I imagined gripping his head, staring into his eyes as he twirled his hot tongue over my clit.

And, fuck, I started to come. I had to bite down on my bottom lip to quiet my moans, certain I'd wake Charles.

But Charles never stirred.

"Annelise!" I feel an urgent slap on my hand.

"Huh?" I say, confused for a moment as to where I am. And then I remember. I'm with my friends. In a restaurant. And I've just wet my panties remembering my hot fantasy of last night with Greek God, Dominic.

"You look totally flushed," Claudia says. "Are you all right?"

I shift uncomfortably in my seat. Holy shit, I can't believe I just zoned out like that. *Here!* And now I have to scramble to remember what we were talking about.

"You do look a little…something," Lishelle tells me.

I take a huge gulp of my drink. And then I remember. We were discussing the pros and cons of me cheating with Dominic. Of course, I already have—in my mind.

"I'm probably all talk, anyway," I assure Claudia. I drag a hand over my face in an attempt to regain my composure. I really am flushed. "There's a big part of me that believes I'll burn in hell for even *thinking* I might want to have an affair."

"Maybe you should try something else, but still drastic," Claudia counters.

I look at Claudia. "Like what?"

"I don't know. Like…like going to a swingers' club or something. That ought to get Charles's attention."

"A swingers' club?" Lishelle jerks her head in Claudia's direction so fast it's a wonder her neck doesn't break. "Where did that come from?"

"Yeah, where did that come from?" I echo, though I remember Claudia telling me about Adam's craving for weird sex these days.

Claudia gulps her mimosa before speaking. "It was

just…I saw something on HBO about swingers' clubs a while ago. Just an idea. Something different."

"I have a hard enough time trying to get Charles to have sex with *me*," I point out. "I don't want to watch him get hot and bothered for anyone else."

"Of course. Forget I even said it."

"Honestly, it's not like there's anything I haven't tried. I even rented porn in hopes that it would turn him on. He didn't even stay up to watch it with me."

"That would get Adam off," Claudia mutters.

"Do you think he's having an affair?" Lishelle asks me point blank. "Because when David stopped having sex with me—" Lishelle stops speaking, her eyes narrowing as she turns to Claudia. I look at her, too. She's quietly crying.

"Okay," Lishelle says. "What's going on, babe?"

"I'm being testy and miserable, and it has nothing to do with you, Annie."

"I'm not mad at you, honey," I tell her. "Please don't cry."

"That's not it."

"It's not about the dresses, is it?" Lishelle asks. "Because if you want violet—"

"It's not the dresses." Claudia blows her nose in her napkin.

"I'm starting to worry here, Claudia," I tell her.

"I did something last night," Claudia begins quietly. "And I feel so awful. So dirty. But Adam ambushed me with this. He told me how much it would turn him on if I did it." Claudia squeezes her eyes shut. "Oh, God…"

My heart is racing, that's how concerned I am for her. "What, hon? What did he make you do?"

Claudia inhales a deep breath, and glances around to make sure no one is within earshot. "After his speech, he took me to some utility room. He wanted to make out, like he always does. And that was fine. He gets off doing it in risqué places. But then…"

"What?" Lishelle asks.

Claudia sniffles. "Then some guy comes in. No, not just *some* guy—the bartender I told you about who helped us make our own personal drink for our wedding?"

I nod. "Right."

"Apparently this guy was working the party last night. And Adam arranged for him to meet us in the utility room so we could have a threesome."

I'm so stunned by Claudia's words, it's like there's no one else in the restaurant. All the noises I'd been aware of moments before—laughter and chatting and a baby crying—it doesn't exist anymore, I'm so focused on this situation with Claudia.

Lishelle is the first one to speak. "You had sex with a stranger?"

"I didn't let him…do that. He…he played with me. Fondled me. Ate my pussy in a serious way."

Lishelle gasps. "Some strange man went down on you?"

"Twice," Claudia admits shamefully. "The first time, I came quickly. You know—because Adam was touching my nipples. The guy—*Jason*—said he wanted to do it again, wanted me to really savor it."

"Holy shit," Lishelle exclaims.

"Believe me, Lishelle, I'm not proud of myself. It would have been one thing if I wanted to do it, but Adam was pressuring me, and then Jason started touching me…"

I have no clue what to say. The first thing that pops into my mouth is, "Did you enjoy it?"

Claudia's gaze bounces from Lishelle to me. "Not really, no. Well, I don't know. I guess…maybe. After he figured out how I liked it. At first he was chomping away on me and I kept telling him to slow down. It was like, 'Hello, I still need that in the future!'"

"I'm speechless," I say. "I really am."

"I didn't want to enjoy it, but it was a tongue on my clit and he was cute. I thought that the first time I saw him. There's no doubt I was physically attracted to him, but I don't go around fucking every guy I'm physically attracted to."

"Adam was excited?" I ask.

"I've never seen Adam so turned on in all my life. Jason's got his tongue so far inside me, and when I glance at Adam, he's jerking off."

Lishelle's eyes widen in surprise. "Holy. I can't believe Adam wanted to share you with some other guy."

Claudia downs the last of her mimosa. "Adam's sexual appetite lately is out of control. I don't know what's going on with him." She pauses. "Do you guys hate me?"

"Hate you? No," I assure her. "We don't hate you, and I certainly can't judge you. And hey, this is the new millennium. I know there are lots of people out there who swap partners, and they're happy."

"But I don't want that to be me. I told Adam that. I'm not into all that crazy stuff. I just want Adam. Please don't ask me any details about what I'm about to say, but he took me to a swingers' club a couple weeks back— shocked me with that, too. And no, we didn't swap partners. We watched, fooled around… But after last night, I had to put my foot down. Tell him this kind of thing is not okay with me. He swore last night was the last of it, that he wanted to live out some fantasies before we got married and he's satisfied now."

"And you believe him?" Lishelle asks.

"I have to. Beside, there's no way when we're married that I'm going to be saying okay to anything like this. I'm sick to my stomach admitting any of this to both of you."

"Maybe he's freaking over the wedding more than you realized," Lishelle says. "Some guys see marriage as the end of their sexual freedom. It doesn't make sense, I know."

"I give him everything he wants when it comes to sex. Everything. I should be enough, shouldn't I?"

"Of course you should," I agree.

"Should is one thing. Reality is another." Lishelle shakes her head. "Look at how David was screwing around on me. And that was a happy man when it came to our sex life. Sometimes, you just can't figure men out."

"And despite being burned, you're willing to get married again?" I ask.

Lishelle smiles, an ear-to-ear grin. "Fucking right I am. I have no doubts. Glenn's different, ya know? We go way back. Whether he's been in my life or not he's always been in my heart." She sighs happily. "What can I say— the man's my soul mate."

"I'm going to live vicariously through you," I announce. "You're totally in love, having great sex—right?"

"The best."

"It's a good thing I love you or I'd want to slap you right about now." I smile sweetly. "You're just so…happy."

"That's what love does to you. And Annie, if you get laid anytime soon, you'll be smiling like this, as well. It had been two years for me."

"I know. That's why I can't hate you."

"Well, *I* can," Claudia interjects. But a smile is tugging at her lips. "You're stealing my thunder, girl. It's *my* wedding that's four weeks away."

Lishelle mimes running a zipper across her lips. "No more about Glenn. For the next four weeks, it's all about you and all about that fabulous wedding that will be the talk of the town for years to come."

Finally, the smile reaches Claudia's eyes.

"And that dress." Lishelle lets out a low whistle. "I know it's going to be spectacular."

"For two hundred thousand, it's got to be." Claudia beams. "A one-of-a-kind Vera Wang."

"Fit for a princess," I tell her.

"Which she is," Lishelle adds. "A Black-American Princess."

"Enough already, guys. Stop."

"The point is," Lishelle begins, "you're going to have a fabulous wedding."

"I will, won't I?"

"Of course you will." I pat Claudia's hand. "And then you and Adam are going to have a wonderful life, with lots of babies."

"Ten," Lishelle interjects.

"Ten!" Claudia exclaims.

"How ever many you want," I say. "And you're going to be happy forever and ever. I promise."

THE GAMES BEGIN

Chapter Twelve

Lishelle

It's the weekend after the fund-raiser, and Glenn's here again, just as he promised he'd be. I stretch my neck to glance at the bedside clock beyond his shoulder. 7:14 a.m.

I'm amazed I'm even up, given how much of the night we spent making each other come. When we're together, we can't seem to keep our hands off each other.

"Why aren't you sleeping?" Glenn asks me.

"After last night, hell if I know."

Glenn sighs contentedly as he pulls me into his arms. We snuggle front to front. I close my eyes and try to sleep.

But several moments later, I find myself asking, "Are you sure you want to live in Atlanta?" We started discussing this a few hours ago, during a break between lovemaking. He said he had no problem relocating to Atlanta, but I want to be sure.

"All-American Air's hub is in Atlanta. It'll be a great move for me. Besides, this is where you're established. I wouldn't dream of taking you away from your career."

I kiss Glenn's chin. "You're so sweet. Have I told you that?"

"My goal in life is to make you happy."

I lift my hand and stare at my engagement ring. "I *am* happy. I have my career, and now I have my man."

"I'm really glad you're doing so well," he tells me. "You followed your dream and look where you are."

"You're following your dream, too. You're a pilot, Glenn. I never would have dreamed it."

"Yeah, but I'm working for a smaller airline, and I'm not making the kind of money I'd like. Six figures, but not high-enough six figures."

"As long as you're happy—"

"I am." But he doesn't sound convincing.

I ease my head back on the pillow to look at him. "What, baby? What is it?"

"Nothing."

"You're not happy, are you?" I place a hand on his face. "You never told me what happened to your dream of playing for the NFL. When we broke up, you said there were scouts interested."

"And I went to training camp for the Cowboys, but I wasn't good enough. I didn't make the cut."

"And you just gave up?"

"Naw, I didn't give up. My plan was to give it another

go the next year, and I would have—if I hadn't pulled out my shoulder."

"Glenn, no."

"Yeah, it was pretty bad for several months. Then it healed pretty much completely—but not good enough to play."

"Oh, baby." I stroke his face now, my fingertips moving over the stubble. "I'm so sorry."

"So am I. But I got over it. And went to L.A. Like every other hopeless fool." He chuckles. "But while I was there, a friend was taking flying lessons, so I took some, as well. I really did enjoy it. Next thing I know, I'm getting my commercial pilot's license, and the rest is history."

"That's good, isn't it? If you enjoy what you do? There's no point dwelling on the past."

"I'm not dwelling on the past. I guess…"

"What?"

"You want the truth?"

"Of course. You're going to be my husband."

"This might sound like a big dream, but I'd like to be my own boss. Instead of flying for someone else, I'd like to run my own charter-airline company."

"Glenn…"

"I know, it's crazy, right? The thing is, with some of the contacts I've made, I'm beginning to think it's a possibility."

"I don't think it's crazy. I think it's fabulous."

"I would base the company out of Atlanta, so I could be here most of the time. If all goes the way I'd like, I ultimately wouldn't have to do much flying—except to whisk you off to St. Barts or some other exotic place. And we'd have a lot of money, babe. We could have a second home in the Caymans, or in the south of France... And we'd be together more often than not."

I have to admit, though I trust Glenn, I'm not keen on him spending many nights away from home. Let's face it—where there's an opportunity, there's a well-meaning guy who'll fall into some slut's bed.

"It sounds like a great plan. And I can't deny I'd like to keep you closer to home."

"I feel the same way. Especially when our children come along... I'm going to want to be around to see them grow up."

Our children. The very suggestion fills me with such joy, I can hardly believe all this is really happening. I've never admitted this to anyone, but the sight of happy couples with babies tugs at me more and more these days. I'd always hoped to have at least one by thirty, but in the next couple years I won't be ancient.

"It sounds perfect, Glenn."

"It would be perfect—if I could afford it."

"You can get a loan. Banks would be happy to lend money to a guy like you."

"It would be a lot of money. I don't know if I can get that kind of loan based on my salary. I could try private investors. Of course, then the company wouldn't be mine the way I'd like it to be. Unless I had a significant amount to put down."

"Hmm. I see what you mean." And damn if I don't want that second home in the south of France! "Sweetheart, I've got a bit of savings."

"Not a chance."

"Hear me out."

"No way. I am not taking money from you."

"How much would you need?"

"Lishelle—"

I put a hand over Glenn's mouth to quiet him. "No, seriously. How much would it take to start the business? Tell me," I urge him when he doesn't say anything.

"All right. Here's what I'm thinking. Maybe five, ten million? I don't know for sure. I could start small, of course. I came up with a business plan—"

"You have a business plan?"

"Uh-huh."

"So you really are serious about this."

"I was playing around, running some numbers. But what does it matter, when I don't have the money? I'd want at least a million of my own cash if I was going to go to investors. Let's say I get five more people with a million—then I'd at least have a twenty percent share of the company. And who knows—maybe I can get it going for less, like maybe two mil. So if I find a business partner—maybe another pilot—we can start smaller and work our way up."

"To a Fortune 500 company."

"Ah. Wouldn't that be nice."

"It can happen, Glenn. And I can help you. I make an excellent salary."

"Lishelle, stop."

Once again, I cover Glenn's mouth. "I wouldn't have enough start-up capital, but I could cosign a loan."

He forces my hand off his mouth. "You heard what I said, right?"

We stare each other down. I'm the first to give. "Fine. But listen, we're going to be married. And that means we'll be a team. The one thing I hated with my ex is that he always thought of his money as his own money, and mine as mine. Of course, that's because when I married him, I wasn't making as much as he was. Then I got my big break in TV, and I thought he'd be happy. Instead, he was envious."

"Do you have to remind me you married someone else?" Glenn asks, but he's grinning softly.

"This time, I'll be marrying the *right* man," I point out. "But let me finish what I'm saying. We'll be partners one hundred percent. In the bedroom and out of it. So if you need me to cosign or whatever for this venture—which I think sounds like a fabulous idea—then know that I'm here for you and I'll do it."

"Good to know, but I'll do this on my own."

"Ugh!" I pinch him. "Why won't you let me help you?"

"Look, I love you for wanting to help. I really do."

"Then let me."

"I'll think about it."

"Will you?"

"Yes. I do love you, you know that? Because you're caring." He lifts my hand to his mouth and gives it a lingering kiss. "And sexy."

"Ooh, go on."

"And you have a delicious body that I just can't get enough of."

"Is that so?"

He nods. "I especially love it when you're sitting on

my face, and I've got my tongue deep inside you, and you just start to come…"

"Mmm." I writhe my body against his. "We'll never make it out of bed if you keep talking like that."

"Who says we have to get out of bed?"

This is the problem with Glenn. The moment he starts to turn me on, I lose all sense of reason. I think I could stay in bed with him and fuck him all day if I didn't have a life.

"Well, uh…I have to meet Claudia," I manage to say on a ragged breath, because Glenn's got my finger in his mouth. He's nipping and sucking it slowly, just like he loves to do to my clit. "Wedding stuff, you know. Dress fitting… Oh, shit…"

Glenn chuckles victoriously and covers my body with his.

A couple hours later, I'm sitting at a wrought-iron table with Claudia in her parents' backyard. We're sipping cranberry juice as we wait for the rest of the bridal party to arrive.

"I still can't believe you told me 10:00 a.m.," I whine.

"I totally meant to call you and tell you I'd changed the time to eleven. Sorry."

"It's okay. Since I'm here early, I have something to ask you. It's a favor, really."

"Anything. You know that."

"I'm wondering if you can talk to your uncle, the one who's a bank president, about getting me a loan."

"A loan? Why?"

"I'm trying to raise some capital for a business venture."

"What kind of venture?"

"Glenn. He's got this dream. He wants to open a charter-airline company—can you believe it—and I want to help him."

"Whoa." Claudia lifts her dark, designer sunglasses to look me in the eye. "You want to get a loan for a business Glenn wants to start?"

"Yes. We were discussing all the possibilities earlier today, and I think it's—"

"It's something you want to think long and carefully about. I know you love him."

"And that's why I want to do this for him. All he needs is a million. That's enough to attract other investors, or even get a business loan from a bank. And hey—" I reach for and squeeze Claudia's hand "—we could fly to the Caribbean anytime we want."

"You and me?"

"Yeah, sure. And Annelise, of course. Can you imagine it—having a private jet?"

Claudia doesn't say anything, but her eyes betray what she's thinking. She's thinking this is a bad idea.

"Claudia, please. Don't give me that look. You know how I couldn't stand it that David never supported my dreams. I don't want things to be like that with Glenn."

"I know, but—"

"And you also know I've been looking for some kind of business opportunity to invest in for some time now."

"Yes."

"Who better to invest in than my future husband?"

"Well—"

"Do not be the voice of negativity here. I know what I'm doing. Will you help me or not?"

Claudia lowers her shades and looks away. I almost want to smack her. After all, she's not my mother. And I'm not asking *her* for money.

"You're my friend," I tell her.

"And friends support each other. I know." She faces me again. "You know I'd do anything for you, even if I think you're making a mistake."

"So you'll help me?"

"I'll call you later with my uncle's number. He'll take care of you."

"I love you, girl." I feel guilty now for having wanted to smack her. It's just that she can be so stubborn at times. "And please don't worry. This will work out. I have a feeling about this. I know it will be great."

Chapter Thirteen

Claudia

When Adam's dick is in my mouth and it's not getting hard, that's a sure sign that something's wrong.

But I forge ahead, working my tongue in circles around the tip of his shaft while I gently massage his testicles.

"Mmm," I moan. "I *love* your cock." I take it completely in my mouth and try to coax it into erection. And I continue to moan. Adam loves it when I moan.

But he's not getting hard. Disappointment washing over me, I look up at him from the floor of his SUV's back seat. I'm cramped here, and one of my knees is at an awkward angle. Considering he's the one who wanted to pull off the road for a blow job, you'd think he could make an effort to enjoy this.

"Adam, sweetheart—what is it?" I ease my body onto the seat beside him.

Adam sighs long and hard and I can't help but look at him with concern. I've never seen him like this before. He's tense, on edge. And he won't meet my eyes.

"I'm hungry," he tells me as he does up his pants. "Let's head to the restaurant."

"That's it? You're hungry?"

"Starving."

"I don't think I can eat anything else. I'm still stuffed from lunch."

"Then you can watch me eat."

As I start to reach for Adam's face, he opens the car door. He heads out without so much as a backward glance at me.

I straighten my clothes and also get out of the back seat. A blast of hot air hits me. It's after six in the evening, and still the weather is like an oven. I hope the heat wave that's gripping Atlanta ends before the wedding.

Though Adam and I are parked near the very back of the parking lot outside of JCPenney, I do a sweep of the Cobb County Mall's parking lot nonetheless. I don't see any curious eyes looking our way, wondering why Adam and I are climbing out of the back seat.

I settle beside Adam. He's quiet all the way to the Cheesecake Factory. He does take my hand, though, which makes me feel marginally better.

Once we're seated at a booth in the restaurant, I scoot my butt closer to him and reach for his leg under the table. That's sure to warm his mood.

He studies the menu. "What are you gonna have?"

"I haven't even looked at the menu yet." I squeeze Adam's leg. "Sweetheart, are you sure you're okay?"

"Like I said, I'm hungry."

Maybe I should talk about the wedding. After all, there are only three more weeks until the big day. "The florist sent a video of the roses he'll be shipping from France. Adam, I've never seen such beautiful flowers." I admit, I've gone all out with the flower arrangements. The price tag is over thirty thousand dollars. "Hey, what are you doing on Thursday? I told my cousin that we'd do a conference call with him regarding the songs we'd like Babyface to sing. He can pretty much do what he wants, as far as I'm concerned, but if we have any favorites and a time we'd like to hear them—like the first dance, or whatever—"

Adam groans and puts the menu down. "Can't we spend some time hanging out and not talk about the wedding? It feels like that's all we ever do."

"It's in *three weeks*, Adam. Of course we have to talk about it."

He looks around anxiously, like he's hoping to see the waiter. "Why don't you talk to your cousin. Whatever songs you want will be fine with me."

"I'd like your input."

"Why? I'll have to go with what you want anyway."

That floors me—until I realize it's the stress talking. "Hey." I place my fingers on his chin and turn his face toward me. "I think I know what you're saying. Everything's about the wedding, it's like we've forgotten about us. But we're almost there, sweetie. We're so close. Our life will be normal again as soon as the wedding's over."

The waiter arrives. As he fills our water glasses he asks if we want to order drinks.

"I'd like—"

"Actually," Adam interjects. "Give us a few more minutes."

My stomach flutters. There's something wrong with Adam's tone. He sounds…I don't know. I can't quite put my finger on it.

"Is something going on, Adam? Something you're keeping from me?"

"Yeah," he answers softly, "I guess you could say that."

I reach for his hand, but he pulls it away.

"I just feel," he goes on, "like things aren't right."

"What's not right?"

But he doesn't say anything, and he won't look at me, either. I glance around the restaurant—and see nothing but happy people at the tables. Yet there's no joy at my table and I don't know why.

"If I did something, tell me."

"It's everything," he answers, still not looking at me. "The wedding. Us."

A weird chill brushes my nape. "Adam, look at me."

It takes a good few seconds, but he finally lifts his head and meets my eyes. "I'm sorry," he says.

Honest to God, I feel like I'm in the twilight zone. I reach for his hand. "Why are you sorry?"

"Because I can't marry you, Claudia."

My stomach lurches painfully and the next moment, my hands start to tremble. Not just my hands, but my whole body.

God help me, this can't be true.

I stare at Adam for what seems like an eternity, waiting for a grin to explode on his face so I can smack him and tell him he's a horrible jokester. But there's no grin. Nothing but a firm set of lips and undeniable regret in his eyes.

And now I understand why Adam wanted to come here even though I told him I wasn't hungry. He wants to end our engagement in a public place so that I won't lose my cool.

"Tell me you didn't say what it sounded like you said."

"I'm not ready," he continues.

"Not ready?" I repeat, flabbergasted. "We've been dating for four years."

"I know…and I'm sorry."

"You're sorry?" I sound like a pathetic broken record.

"I really am. I didn't mean to hurt you."

Something registers in my brain. The reality that this isn't a bad dream. "Are you saying you don't want to marry me in three weeks, or that you don't want to marry me at all?"

"I'm not ready to get married," is Adam's evasive answer.

Okay, now I start to panic. Thirty thousand dollars' worth of flowers are being shipped in from Europe for our wedding. Babyface is going to perform especially for us. Adam can't fall apart on me, not now.

"Adam, what you're going through is perfectly normal. It's called cold feet. This is going to be the biggest day of our lives. Of course you're nervous." I reach for his hand. "I am, too. But before we know it, all the craziness will be over."

"You don't understand."

There's a quiet strength to Adam's words, the kind that make me fear the absolute worst.

"Is this about last night? Because I didn't want to go back to that swingers' club?"

"It's about us. About the fact that we're not working."

"Since fucking when?" My voice rises with each word.

"Please calm down."

"You expect me to calm down!"

Adam's gaze flits around the restaurant. "I told you I didn't want to hurt you. But I had to say something… You don't feel the same way—like we're rushing things?"

"How on earth can you ask me that? One minute, I'm talking to you about the roses coming from France, and now you ask if I don't think we're rushing things?"

"Fine, maybe it's me. But I just feel… We're not always on the same page. Like last night."

"So this *is* about that swingers' club."

The waiter appears again. Adam impatiently waves him away.

"I'm trying to be fair to you. If we're incompatible now, getting married won't make things better."

Honestly, if you told me that Adam had suddenly morphed into Michael Jackson, I wouldn't be more surprised than I am right now. I feel like I'm on another planet, that Adam is talking to me in Chinese.

"You don't want to marry me?" I ask. I need a straight answer. I need to understand.

"No."

"Because we're not on the same page sexually?"

Adam shrugs, looks away.

"You've got to be fucking kidding me. When it comes

to sex, what *haven't* we done? And you think we're not *compatible?*"

A waitress's eyes bulge as she strolls by our table with food.

My anger starts to dissipate, and now sadness grips me. It's just cold feet. It's got to be cold feet. That's what Lishelle said. That's what makes sense. Because what Adam's saying right now makes no sense at all.

Adam and I barely argue. And for God's sake, I've done practically everything he's ever wanted me to do when it comes to sex. We are soul mates. He's told me so on more than one occasion.

I force myself to calm down. "I'm not sure why you're saying this—"

"Because I don't want to make a mistake."

"But how can you say that?" I retort, my cool veneer cracking. "We've been together for so long. We're in love."

Again, Adam looks away. My God, he can't even tell me he still loves me? My heart drops. I suddenly feel so unsure of myself, and it's an awful feeling.

"Adam?" I begin with hesitation. "We *are* in love, aren't we? You do love me, don't you?"

Adam swallows. "You know I love you."

I don't realize that I'm holding my breath until all my breath leaves me in a rush. "Thank God. That's all I wanted to hear."

When Adam meets my eyes, it's clear his expression is tortured. I want to wrap my arms around him and squeeze away all his insecurities.

"As long as you love me, we'll get through whatever you're going through."

"I love you, Claudia. But I'm not *in* love with you." A beat passes. "I'm sorry."

My breath nearly chokes me. A chill slithers down my spine. My hands start to shake.

"What did you say?" I ask, fully expecting him to verify for me that my hearing is suspect.

The waiter cautiously approaches the table. He's smiling way too brightly for me to handle, and I glare at him. He whirls right around on his heel and disappears.

"I love you, but I'm not in love with you. I don't know what else you want me to say."

"You're not in love with me?" I was confused before, but now anger is bubbling inside me.

Adam shakes his head.

"And you pick *now* to tell me. Three weeks before our wedding?"

"I'm sorry," Adam repeats.

Then I do something I have never done in my life. I take my glass of water and dump it into Adam's lap.

The next second, I burst into tears. I grab the Christian Dior purse he gave me as a present and I run for the door. My heart thunders so loudly, I can't hear any outside sound.

But I feel people's stares. I know they're all wondering what's going on.

They have no clue that what took four years to build, Adam has just destroyed.

Chapter Fourteen

Annelise

Hanging out with Claudia and the fourteen women in the
bridal party this afternoon definitely helped boost my spirits. I've been in a funk all week because Charles has been
acting even more distant than ever—if that's possible. He's
totally not interested in going to a couples' retreat at any
spa with me, no matter how many Web site brochures I
print for him showing that there are no raunchy pictures
of girls on their knees looking sex-starved.

He spent half the week out of town—another trip he
told me about last minute. And the days he was here, he
came home late from the office, ate his dinner quietly,
then went to bed.

I can take only so much of living with him as if I'm
his sister.

So today I resolved to put him and our problems out of my mind, hang out with the girls and have a good time. Trying to please him and get him in the mood is pointless.

And I did have a good time. In fact, I can't remember having this much fun in so long. Everyone had a great time—thanks in part to the pitchers of Island Love, the special drink Claudia and Adam personally created.

I still can't get over how great I looked in my dress! Forget all the magazines' advice about losing weight. There's nothing like the stress diet. I've lost probably seven pounds in the last few weeks.

By the time the afternoon fitting-slash-cocktail hour was over, I wasn't ready to head home. I approached Lishelle, hoping she'd be in the mood to hang out at the mall with me, something we haven't done together in a while. "Hey, Lishelle," I said, wrapping an arm around her waist. "Want to do something—maybe find a salon and get our toes painted?"

"Sorry, sweetie, but Glenn's still at my place and I've got to get back to him. He's not in town for much longer."

I then tried Claudia, who at the time was seeing the various women out. "Oh, I wish. But Adam has been so patient waiting for me to finish with this fitting, and he wants us to go for dinner or something. Not that I can eat any more—especially if I hope to fit in my dress!"

Screw it, I decided. I can go out by myself, can't I? So instead of heading home, I headed to the mall to shop. What's the point in spending another loveless evening with Charles?

"Find everything you were looking for today?" a

young salesclerk asks me as I place an assortment of bras and panties on the countertop.

"Oh, I'd say so." I've picked up lacy bras and push-up bras as if I'm a lingerie model. Not to mention all the thongs I never thought I'd like wearing. But I do feel sexier in sexy clothes, even if I'm not getting laid.

"Do you have our Victoria's Secret credit card?"

"No, I don't."

"Would you like to apply for one?"

I consider it. "No, not today." My gaze wanders to the display of nail polish on the counter. "Oh, look at all these fabulous colors."

I reach for a muted tan color—the typical color I like to wear, but I stop myself before picking it up. I don't want Plain Jane tan today. I want something vibrant. Something sexy to match all the stuff I'm buying. The kind of polish that makes a man notice your feet.

Red.

I pick up a bottle that looks like the shade of a fire engine, and I add it to my pile.

And then something makes me turn.

I glance over my shoulder. There's a line of women behind me, some looking impatient. Nothing out of the ordinary. So why do I feel...what, exactly?

Like someone is watching me.

Shaking my head, I turn back to the clerk. Beside her, another woman opens up a cash register, and I hear audible relief as women behind me change lines.

"That comes to four hundred and sixty-three dollars and twenty-eight cents," the clerk announces.

I pass her my Platinum American Express card, the

one Charles opened for me under his account, and settle the bill.

As I head out of the store, I feel that weird sensation again, like eyes are on me. But once again, I see nothing out of the ordinary.

Maybe I'm suffering from a bad case of wishful thinking.

Wishing I'd bump into Dominic.

"Wow," Charles says when I walk into the house with my four Victoria's Secret bags. "You've been busy."

"I decided to do a little shopping," I say proudly.

"I can see that."

"And sorry—I didn't get to make any dinner. I wasn't sure you'd be around anyway, and I knew I was going to eat at Claudia's."

"That's fine," Charles tells me. He's lounging on the sofa this evening, like he's actually got free time. "I'll find something to eat. Or order a pizza."

"Great."

I take my bags and head up the stairs. I'm going for the I-could-care-less-if-you're-not-fucking-me tone. No matter how much it hurts, begging him to touch me and being rejected hurts more.

There's still a sway to my hips as I make my way up the stairs, though—just in case Charles is looking.

In the bedroom, I'm putting the contents of my bags on the bed when the phone rings. I snatch up the receiver.

"Hello?"

There's a brief pause before I hear, "Annelise, hello. It's Marsha. Marsha Hindenberg. How are you?"

"I'm good, thanks."

I hear a click on the line, then, "Hello?"

"Oh, Charles. It's Marsha."

"I got it, Annelise."

"Sure. Take care, Marsha."

I replace the receiver and go back to sorting my lingerie.

A minute later, Charles appears in our bedroom doorway. "I've got to head out," he tells me.

Now? is the first thing that comes to my mind, but somehow I curtail that response and simply say, "Oh?"

"Yeah. Marsha and I have to be in court in the morning. There're a few things she has to go over with me."

"Will you be long?" I ask simply. And it's strange, but I almost want Charles to be gone for a while. I can watch a movie, paint my toenails and generally have an evening of peace as opposed to anxiety. I'm not sure what's come over me.

"I don't know. But probably. Yeah."

I don't look up from sorting lingerie. "Okay, then."

I don't even break my rhythm as Charles disappears from the room. Instead, I concentrate on sorting my lingerie into colors. I bought a lot of pink and white but not enough red.

Red… I fish the nail polish out from the bottom of one of the bags. I'm almost ready to do my toes when I decide instead to try on all the stuff I bought. I only tried a few of the bras, but none of the panties.

I strip out of my floral skirt and cotton underwear and slip into a lacy white thong. I didn't try these on at the store, just scooped them up hoping they'd fit.

This one does. I examine my body in the mirror on my

dresser. I like what I see. The high cut of the thong outlines the shape of my hips, and damn if I don't look sexy.

I turn so I can see the view of my butt. From this angle, all I can see are my pale cheeks and the wisp of material at the top of my ass. There's a tiny bow there, a cute touch.

I really love this. And I love the fact that while I'm wearing underwear, in a way it seems like I'm wearing nothing at all.

I get it now. I totally get why women wear these.

I try on a few more bra-and-panty sets, liking each more and more. But when I try on the red set, I can't help inhaling sharply at the image I see in the mirror.

I'm beautiful. I am. My body's still slim and firm, and I have an hourglass figure. I've got the kind of body I see men admiring in pinups. How did I ever feel I wasn't attractive?

Glancing down, I catch sight of my toes. The dainty French manicure is chipping away.

Forget dainty. It's time for bold. Red toes to match this stunning red push-up bra and matching hipsters.

I waltz into the bathroom, where I take my nail polish remover from the cupboard and wads of cotton balls. Then I sit on the toilet and place one foot on the edge of the tub to start removing the old polish.

I'm just about finished cleaning the polish off my second foot when I hear, "Wow."

Gasping softly, I spin around. Charles is standing in our bedroom, watching me.

"How long have you been standing there?" I ask him.

"Long enough."

"I thought you were meeting Marsha."

"I was. But on the drive to the office I called her and told her that whatever had to be done could be handled in the morning."

"Oh. Okay." I reach for the bottle of red polish.

"You know, you really look amazing."

When I turn, Charles is strolling toward the bathroom door. Something about the way he's looking at me makes my heart stumble.

Do not get your hopes up. Do not...

"Victoria's Secret lingerie can make anyone look amazing."

"That's not true. It's you. Your body." His eyes move over me. "Red's a great color on you."

Is this all I needed to do for the past year and three months—wear the color red?

Charles steps into the bathroom. He leans his butt against the edge of the sink. "I know you tried to talk to me once about us not having sex. I'm sorry I wasn't responsive. It's just..."

I swivel my butt on the toilet seat and look up at Charles, waiting.

"I've been having a...problem. Erectile dysfunction."

"I see."

"And that's made it incredibly hard to look at you, knowing I can't touch you and get it up, much less talk to you about what I'm going through. So I've thrown myself into work. I've tried to ignore the issue."

You've more than tried...

"But today—I don't know." He shrugs. "I guess I'm ready to talk to you about everything. That's why I told Marsha she'll have to deal with this case without me for tonight."

I'm really not sure what I should say. Charles hasn't had a heart-to-heart with me in so long, this moment seems surreal.

I finally say, "Erectile dysfunction."

"In my case, it's a fancy term for impotence."

"Why didn't you tell me? All you had to do was tell—"

"I kept hoping it would pass. And then it didn't, and I couldn't face you about it."

I'm still sitting on my spot on the toilet. Charles is still resting his butt on the sink. Neither of us makes a move to get closer.

"You've pushed me away so often."

"I know, and I feel shitty about that."

"I don't think you understand how that's made me feel. Like I'm not desirable. Do you know what it does when your husband won't look at you, won't touch you?" I hesitate before adding this part. "I gave some thought to having an affair."

"Oh, God."

"I didn't, and I wouldn't. But a part of me wanted to." Charles needs to know this. To know how serious this is for our marriage. "When I saw how other guys looked at me—the way I needed you to look at me..."

"Oh, Ann." Charles shakes his head ruefully. "I'm so sorry. I never meant to make you feel undesirable. You've got to know that's not true. You're a beautiful woman. Any man would be proud to call you his."

"Just not you."

Now Charles kneels before me. "That's not true." He places both hands on my legs and strums my inner thighs with his fingers. Like he hasn't missed a day doing this during our marriage.

And it feels odd, even if desire begins to take its grip. I've had to repress my desire for so long, its awakening is like a slow ache.

"You are beautiful." He plants a lingering kiss on my thigh, and I gasp softly. God, it's been so long. To feel a real man's touch, his kiss… I'm at the edge of heaven.

"I've been selfish," Charles continues. "Thinking only of my pain. But I don't need a penis to please you. There are other ways."

One hand crawls up my thigh. The other urges my legs apart. When Charles's fingers reach my vagina, he moans in delight.

I close my eyes because tears fill them. "Oh, Charles…"

He pushes my panties aside and oh my God, his touch is so sweet. I'm like a woman dying of hunger offered a morsel of bread.

"You're as wet as a river." Charles licks at his fingers, tasting me. "I love it when you're so wet. And I love how you taste, how you smell…"

The phone rings as Charles puts a finger deep inside me. I groan in disappointment, expecting him to get up, but he doesn't. Instead, he pushes his finger deep, then slowly pulls it out. He thrusts it in again, and I throw my head back and moan.

"Charles, if you're there, pick up." It's Marsha's voice.

"Fucking Marsha," Charles utters.

"Charles, I need you to call me. As soon as you get this message."

"Do you have to get that?" I ask.

"Hell, no."

And the next thing I know, Charles is scooping me into his arms. He carries me out of the bathroom and lies me on the bed. Our eyes connect as he takes each of my feet into his hands and spreads me as wide as my legs will allow. I could die of the pleasure when his tongue heats a path all the way down one of my legs and stops at my center.

The phone rings again, and we both go still. I silently curse. Charles's lips hover over my vagina, and every one of his heated breaths makes my body tremble.

The answering machine picks up, but no one leaves a message this time.

"Should I unplug it?" Charles asks.

"Please don't move. Don't…" My voice trails off, ending on a sigh, when Charles's tongue strokes my nub. A million delicious sensations shoot through me. He licks again, pulls back, and I'm certain I'll go crazy.

"Please…it's been so long…don't tease me…"

"You want me to do this?" Charles covers my clit with his mouth and suckles me hard.

I scream. Grip the bedspread. "Charles…oh, baby…" It's too intense. I'll shatter any moment. And I want to savor this.

I pull my hips back a little, try to close my legs, but Charles doesn't let me. But he does pull his head back and massages me with his fingers.

"You're so beautiful, Ann. Look at you."

He slips a finger inside me, thrusting it hard and deep. I arch my back and moan.

His tongue replaces his finger. He licks at me, pushes it inside me. Runs his tongue along my opening back up to my nub.

Then he suckles me again, gently this time. The heat within me rises. My breathing shallows. I start to move my hips, and he splays one hand across my stomach and grips my butt with the other to keep me in place.

And then I explode. Explode into a million pieces of pleasure. My body quivers, shakes, bucks against Charles's mouth, and still he suckles me, never letting me go.

My passionate moans become soft, shaky sobs. Tears pour down my cheeks.

I reach for him. "Charles. Oh, sweetheart."

The fucking phone rings again.

"Goddammit!" Charles exclaims, jumping off the bed.

"Ignore it. It's my turn to please you." I get onto my knees. "I want to taste you, Charles. Please…"

He stands at the foot of the bed, his eyes flitting from me to the phone. Finally, the machine picks up.

"Charles, it's Marsha. Are you there? I really need to talk to you." Her voice is a little high-strung. "I can't proceed with this brief until you get back to me."

My eyes wander to Charles's pants. Sweet Jesus, he's erect.

I crawl toward him. Reach for him. Stroke him.

"Fuck," he mutters.

"Call her later." I start to undo his pants. "You're hard, baby. We can make love."

"I…" He moves away from me. "I don't want to disappoint you."

"You won't disappoint me. I promise you."

He groans loudly as he plops onto the bed and buries his face in his hands. "You don't understand. Sometimes, I can get hard, but I can't…can't keep it up."

I wrap my arms around him from behind. Lord, but it feels good to have my husband back. "It's okay, honey. Lie with me. Let me hold you."

I urge him backward, and he doesn't resist. Charles stretches his body out beside mine and we hold each other.

The simple act of lying in bed holding my husband, but oh it feels so good.

I don't ever want to let him go.

Chapter Fifteen

Lishelle

I groan softly when I hear the phone ring. Stretching across the bed, I glance at the phone's call display.

"It's Claudia," I say, and I debate whether or not I should answer it. Glenn's leaving in a couple hours.

"You think it's important?" Glenn asks. He's lying beside me, running a fingertip over the palm of my hand. We just finished eating Chinese takeout, since we couldn't bring ourselves to leave the house. Elmore Leonard's *Be Cool* is playing on the DVD.

The phone stops ringing. "I guess not," I answer.

But no sooner does the phone stop ringing than it starts again. Again, I see Claudia's number on the caller ID.

"I'd better get this." Glenn sinks his teeth into my ass as I grab the receiver. "Glenn, stop it," I giggle, angling my head over my shoulder to face him. He uses his tongue instead, running the tip of it over my skin, and I do my best to tune him out. "Hey, you."

For a moment, I hear nothing. Then I hear some ghastly choking sort of sound, and panic grips my heart like icy tentacles. "Claudia?"

"H-h-he…he…he…"

If this is Claudia, she sounds nothing like herself, which has me even more concerned. "Honey, are you okay?"

"Come…over… Please."

I hang up the receiver, already jumping from the bed. Glenn's hands slide down my body, but I move away from him before he can grab me.

"Babe?" His tone is worried.

"That was Claudia. She sounds…she sounds friggin' awful."

"What happened?"

"I don't know, but I have to go there right away. Damn, I wonder if she called Annelise." I snap on my bra, then reach for the phone again. I quickly call Annelise. The machine picks up. "Hey, Annie. It's Lishelle. When you get this message, call me right away. I'm heading out now so—"

There's the sound of the receiver being picked up. "Hello?" Annelise says.

"Did Claudia call you?" I ask.

"No. Well, maybe. The phone rang a couple times, but—"

"I just got a call from her. I'm not sure what's going on, but she sounded fucking awful, and I'm heading over there right now. Maybe you should, too."

"Oh my God, of course. What did she say?"

"She couldn't even tell me. She sounded that bad."

"But things were great just this afternoon."

"They're obviously not great now. I'll see you there, okay?"

I replace the receiver and spin around to face Glenn. "I'm sorry," I tell him.

"Want me to go with you?"

"You have to get ready to leave. Don't you have to be at the airport in a few hours?"

"Yeah, but…"

I shimmy into my jeans. "I think this is one for the girls. But thanks for the offer."

Glenn sits up in bed, his gaze landing on my chaise and his clothes that are stacked there. "All right."

"You don't have to leave right now," I tell him as I slip into a T-shirt. "I'll give you a key, in case I don't get back before you have to go. Which I'm pretty sure I won't." I'm already walking toward my purse, which is on the floor beside my bed. I hurriedly pull out my key ring, where I have a second key.

I pass Glenn the key. "Here—" I yelp when he pulls me onto the bed and on top of him.

"Glenn," I admonish. "I really have to go."

"I know." He surprises me with a soft kiss, the kind that lifts you up when you're feeling down. "But I wanted to give you a kiss before you run out. I won't see you until next weekend."

In my haste to leave my house, I've forgotten this fact. "I'm not sure I can get used to this—you leaving all the time. I like having you around."

"I'm working on that," he tells me. "Meeting a couple investors in Phoenix this week, actually."

"Really?"

"Uh-huh."

His fingers press into the small of my back, a subtle sign that he wants me to stay. I pull away from him, moaning softly. "You know I want to stay here, but Claudia needs me."

"Go be with your girl. I love you," he adds in a soft whisper.

"I love you, too."

A pang of regret stings me as I slide my body off Glenn's. He holds my gaze.

I blow him a kiss, then turn and walk out of the room. Somehow, it seems right—leaving the man who's always had my heart lying naked in my bed.

Claudia is a complete mess. When she opens her door to me, she looks as if she's had a date with a makeup artist for corpses. She's pale, sickly so. Her normally perfect hair is flat on one side and spiky on the other. Her eyes and lips are red, and tear-streaks stain her foundation.

Her entire face looks swollen, like she's been crying since last week.

I draw her into my arms. "Oh, baby. Baby, what happened?"

Gasping sounds escape her, as though she's trying to speak but there's a hole in her vocal cords.

I squeeze her, rub her back in support, my own eyes filling with tears. I've seen this kind of grief before. Saw it in my mother's eyes when she stood over her mother's casket at her funeral.

"Okay, Claudia." I exhale nervously. "You're scaring me here."

"A...Adam..."

My pulse quickens with dread. "He's not hurt, is he?" The tragic possibilities fill my mind. A car accident. A mugging. God, no. "Claudia?"

"H-h-he...h-he..."

Icy fear shoots through me. I pull back and look into Claudia's eyes. "No, honey." I shake my head, but I'm fearing the worst. "Tell me nothing awful happened to him. *Please.*"

Now she shakes her head, wiping her eyes as she does. "Not hurt." She takes a deep breath. "He..." Her face crumbles, but she forces herself to go on. "Doesn't want t-to get m-married."

The first thing I feel is a wave of relief. Then profound shock. In fact, it takes several seconds for me to find my voice.

"Adam doesn't want to get married?" I ask, praying I've misunderstood.

Fresh tears fill Claudia's eyes. All she can do is shake her head.

"But the wedding's in a few weeks! What do you mean he doesn't want to get married?"

Claudia is crying. Deep, racking sobs that break my heart.

I step into her place and close the door behind me. Then I take her by the shoulders and lead her into the living room. This has got to be the absolute worst thing that could happen to her. Worse, even, than Adam dying in some tragic way.

She slumps into the soft leather sofa, looking more defeated than I've ever seen her.

"Did he really tell you he doesn't want to get married?"

She nods.

"How long ago?"

"Couple hours ago."

I reach for the box of Kleenex, pull several out and pass the wad to Claudia. "Tell me what happened. Exactly."

"We were out. For dinner. Didn't get t-to eat. Said he's not in love with m-me."

"Okay, now I know I'm not hearing you right. How could he say he's not in love with you? You've been together for what, four years?"

"Loves me...not *in* love with me."

Claudia buries her face in her hands.

I do the only thing I can. I sit beside her and rub my hand over her back.

The sound of pounding on the door startles us both. At first I think it must be Adam, and Claudia must draw the same conclusion based on how her eyes light up. But then I remember that I called Annelise.

"That's probably Annelise," I say. "I called her after you called me."

I hope I'm wrong, though. I hope that it *is* Adam, so the shit head can tell Claudia that he momentarily lost his mind.

Not getting married... I shake my head with disgust as I open the door.

As I figured, it's Annelise. Her blue eyes meet mine with concern.

"What's going on?" she asks.

"It's Adam," I whisper. "He broke off the engagement a couple hours ago."

"What?" Annelise gasps.

"I can't believe it, either."

Annelise's expression hardens as she steps into the house. She looks all around as if she expects to see Adam and slap him upside the head. Of course, Claudia is the only one inside, and she looks inconsolable as she sits hunched over on her sofa, quietly crying. Annelise rushes to her and wraps her in a hug.

I take a seat on the opposite side of Claudia. "Did you and Adam have a fight?"

"No."

"Nothing? No disagreement, even over something small?"

"No," Claudia stresses. "And that's the thing. I don't get why he did this all of a sudden."

"Tell us exactly what happened," I instruct her.

Claudia inhales a deep breath and lets it out slowly. Somehow, she's keeping it together. I know when David and I split, I was like a walking zombie. For the first few days after I learned of his affair, I couldn't even put my clothes on straight.

"After the bridal fitting, Adam wanted to get something to eat. I told him I wasn't hungry, but he was. We went to the Cheesecake Factory. Then he was acting all strange, didn't want to order any food. I asked him what was wrong, and the next thing I know…"

Claudia can't finish her statement, so I fill Annelise in. "She said Adam told her he loves her but isn't *in* love with her."

Annelise's pretty blue eyes widen in shock. "He did not say that."

"Uh-huh," Claudia confirms between tears. "One minute we were in his back seat and I was giving him a blow job, the next he's dumping me. I do everything to please him. Everything! How could he just blurt out that he doesn't want to get married?"

"You mean he wants to postpone it," Annelise says. "Right?"

Claudia shakes her head. "It's over, Annie."

"No," Annelise says in a horror-filled voice.

"I don't understand. We were so happy."

For a long moment we're all silent.

I think long and hard about the situation as Claudia pulls herself together. And surprisingly, I don't want to kick the shit out of Adam. Because this makes no sense, he's obviously got a serious case of pre-wedding jitters. "Listen," I say. "He can't mean that. It's not like you were dating only a few weeks before planning a wedding. You were together for four years. Long enough to know if you're ready to walk down the aisle. He's got to have cold feet. Hon, I think he freaked out. Nothing else makes sense."

"Of course." Annelise sounds relieved. "He got cold feet. Sweetie, that happens all the time. Sometimes, a couple can be together for ten years, and as soon as they're about to get married, one or both has some sort of panic attack."

Claudia's eyes light up with hope. "You think so?"

"Definitely," I tell her. "No one waits until a few weeks before the wedding to tell you he isn't in love with you. Come on."

"The whole time he was telling me this, he couldn't even look at me."

"And what does that tell you?" I ask.

"Yeah, what does that tell you?" Annelise echoes.

"The guy's confused," I insist. "And if he isn't, I'll kick his fucking ass. Honestly, if he isn't in love with you, Claudia, then what the fuck's he been doing all these years?"

"I want to believe that."

"Have you talked to your parents yet?" I ask.

"No. I couldn't. I only called you two. What do I do? Cancel the wedding?"

"No," I exclaim. "Don't you dare. You've got three weeks until your wedding day. I bet that by the end of the week—maybe even sooner—Adam will be singing a different tune."

Claudia nods. "Okay. I—I won't."

God, poor Claudia. She sounds so scared.

"Oh, hon." Annelise gives Claudia another hug. "I don't know what's going on with Adam, but whatever you need, we're here for you."

"That's right," I concur. "Whatever you need."

Claudia reaches for both of us, taking one of our hands. "I know. And thank you for coming. I feel better. You always make me feel better. That's why I love you so much."

At least Claudia seems hopeful again, and for that I'm

glad. I want this to work out for her. I really do. But I'll tell you one thing—if Adam is fucking her over, the little shit is gonna have to answer to me.

Chapter Sixteen

Claudia

Monday and Tuesday passed and no word from Adam. I can't lie. I spent those two days in a deep depression. I couldn't have been more devastated. But this morning, a new emotion began to brew inside me.

Anger.

How dare he? How dare he dump me, and not even treat me with the respect I deserve? We've been dating *four* years. Friends for at least ten. If he's gotten cold feet, I can understand that, but to not talk to me at all—that's pretty damn low.

I wish I could say I've been strong, but I haven't. I've been weak and pathetic. I called him at least three times on Monday, and yesterday, as my panic intensified, I called him twice that amount. I've left him breathless, sobbing messages begging him to call me back. But still I haven't heard from him.

It's entirely possible he's scared to face me. But what the fuck does he think I'm going through after his bombshell?

Groaning, I roll over onto my back. I try my best to muster the strength to get out of bed, but I can't. I haven't eaten in two days. I've got the air-conditioning cranked on high and spend most of my time under my duvet. When I wake up, I have a glass of wine and two sleeping pills, debate calling Adam, then count the moments until I fall asleep again.

I haven't even answered the door for my mother. When she called, I told her I had the flu and was resting up for a couple days.

Honestly, should I even care if I hear from Adam again? Oh, but I do. Every moment, I wait for the phone to ring, hoping it'll be him.

My eyes wander to the phone. I consider calling him again. But if he's got cold feet and needs some time, any more of my blubbering messages are sure to push him away even further.

God, I can't take this any longer. I plop one of my pillows down on the phone so I don't have to see it.

"I can't do this," I utter. I can't stay here in my bed all day like I'm waiting to die.

I've got to go away. A ray of hope shines on me when the idea comes to me. Yes, I'll go away for the weekend. Somewhere close and drivable, but far enough away that it'll feel like an escape.

Pensacola. It's perfect.

I've been there before, and really enjoyed it. It's quiet, has a great beach, some nice shops. It'll be like I'm a million miles away from here—which is exactly what I need right now.

My limbs feel like lead as I make a concerted effort to sit up. That accomplished, I swing my feet out from under the covers and off the bed. Then I reach for the phone and dial Lishelle's number.

"Lishelle," I say when I get her answering service. "Sorry I haven't called you since Sunday. I've been…well, I've been avoiding the world. I haven't gotten out of bed. I haven't even checked my messages. The plus—I've probably lost ten pounds. I'll look really great in my dress now." I chuckle, but the hollow sound morphs into a cry. "I'm sorry." I fight the tears and pull myself together. "I'm trying here. I really am. But Adam hasn't even called me… Oh, forget Adam. That's why I'm calling. I'm ready to say 'fuck Adam' and show my face again. Get out of here before the walls close in on me. Let's go to Pensacola this weekend. Leave Friday afternoon, get there by evening. I'll rent a suite. We'll have so much fun. Please say yes. I need you and Annelise to go with me." My voice cracks a little. "I'm sorry. But call me back, okay? As soon as you can."

I wait a few minutes to call Annelise. She doesn't answer her home phone or her office phone, so I leave her a similar message. Minus the tears.

I get off the bed and drag my feet until I reach the kitchen. I open my fridge and scowl. Nothing decent there. I definitely don't want to call for Mae, my parents' housekeeper, who could make me something wonderful in a snap. I'm not that ready to face the world.

At least the freezer has a package of waffles. I take it out and pop two of them into the toaster.

I hope my girls will call me soon. I do need to get out of here, and I don't want to go to Pensacola alone. If I stay here, I'll sink further into depression. And I'll continue to be tempted to pick up the phone and call Adam again.

I will *not* call Adam again. He has to call me. When he's ready.

And in the meantime, I'll be drinking margaritas on the beach. In Pensacola. With my girlfriends.

Adam wants space, I'll give him space. So much space it'll damn well suffocate him.

Yeah, I need to go away. And I hope to God he calls me when I'm gone. Finds that I'm not here and I'm not available to take his calls.

Let him wonder where the fuck I am and what the fuck I'm doing. Let him experience the panic—the sick, overwhelming feeling deep inside that you feel when you're disconnected from your soul mate.

The toaster pops.

I burst into tears.

Chapter Seventeen

Lishelle

I kick my sandals off and revel in the blast of cool air the moment I step into my brownstone. Seven-thirty at night and it's still so damn hot outside. To make matters worse, the air-conditioning at the station was on the fritz, and I had to pretend to be cool on camera, even though my armpits were sweating.

I head straight for my kitchen, where I see my phone's red light is blinking. My lips curl in a smile.

Glenn.

My phone display says there are five new calls. I check the numbers. Four from Glenn, one from Claudia. I lift the phone to my ear and dial the code to check my voice mail.

"Lishelle, babe," the first message begins. "The meeting I had with the possible investor went better than I expected. I showed the guy the business proposal, and he was totally impressed. He thinks it can fly—no pun intended." Glenn exhales hurriedly. "Now, I have to see about raising my own capital. I'll find a way, though. Call me later. I miss you."

I don't listen to the rest of the messages. Instead, I dial Glenn's home number. It's Wednesday, and he's home in Phoenix on Wednesdays.

He answers the phone on the first ring. "Hello?"

"That was quick. Were you expecting a call?"

"Hey, babe." I hear a smile in his voice. "I was hoping it would be you."

"I got your message. The meeting with the investor went well?"

"Amazingly well. But I already have better news."

"You do?"

"Remember I told you there was another pilot friend I'd discussed this idea with—we'd talked off and on about possibly doing a joint venture?"

"Yeah."

"Keith Hatcher, my pilot friend, talked to me on Monday. Turns out he's already started the ball rolling on this business and wants me to join in. He's got a definite investor lined up, and wants us to be partners."

"Oh my God. But what about doing it on your own?"

"I've always known that I'd probably have to have a partner, and Keith Hatcher's a great guy. I had a phone conference with him and his investor today and things are serious. Very serious."

"Wow. That's fantastic."

"It is, but there's only one sticking point."

"Oh?"

"The money. My share of the money. Keith's got a million of his own to put in, and he wants me to contribute the same. That way, we'd have a majority of the business, rather than the outside investor controlling a majority share."

"Right. Of course."

"It's all happening really fast. Like the next few weeks fast. What I need to do now is find a way to come up with my share of the money. I've already put in a call to my bank."

"No need," I announce.

"Why not?"

"I have a surprise of my own, Glenn."

"You do?"

"Uh-huh. One of Claudia's uncles is a president of a bank here in Atlanta, and she pulled some strings to get me an appointment yesterday. He's putting through the paperwork for a million-dollar line of credit for me to use for the business!"

"Lishelle." Glenn's tone sounds full of reproof. "I told you not to do that."

"I've been looking for a business opportunity for a long time. Glenn, you're going to be my husband. Why shouldn't I invest in your company?"

He sighs. "I could definitely use the money, but I don't feel right about this."

"I get the checkbook tomorrow. I was going to surprise you with the news this weekend."

"You really want to do this?"

"I do. Wait a second. This Hatcher guy—he's okay with basing the business out of Atlanta?"

"He's single, unattached and thinks Atlanta is a great location."

"Then there's no reason not to move forward with this."

"Hey—maybe I can set up some sort of meeting with Keith this weekend, if he can arrange to be in town. You can meet him, he can tell you his vision."

"That'd be great," I reply. Then I remember the chat I had with Claudia at the station and the fact that we're heading out of town this weekend. "Oh, wait, I can't do it this weekend. I'm heading to Pensacola with Claudia and Annelise."

"You're going out of town? You never mentioned—"

"It came up suddenly."

"Hmm," Glenn says.

"What do you mean by 'hmm'?"

"Just wondering."

His tone is…odd. "Wondering what?"

"Well…things happened between us pretty fast. Maybe there's another guy you were seeing…"

"You are kidding, right?"

"Hey, it's possible. And here I am on the other side of the country. You could have a guy with you right now, slipping your panties off as we speak."

"Glenn—"

"You can tell me, you know. If there is someone else. Even someone casual. Better now, if you're not sure about us. I'm too old to play games."

My mouth drops open. Why on earth is Glenn talking like this?

"Glenn," I finally say. "I'm wearing your ring. You know there's no one else."

"You're stunning. Successful. You could have a man on each street if you wanted."

I laugh without mirth. "If you only knew."

"You could."

"But I don't want just anybody."

"So you're not trying to avoid me this weekend?"

"No. You brought up this absurd accusation before I could tell you the whole story. Claudia needs to get away because Adam broke up with her."

"What?"

"Yeah, I know."

"But they're getting married in—"

"I don't think that's gonna happen. And as you can imagine, she's totally devastated. She begged me and Annelise to go away with her this weekend, and I can't say no to her. Not with what she's going through."

"Wow. That's got to be rough."

"I don't even want to imagine what that feels like."

"Neither do I, babe." Glenn pauses. "Look, I'm sorry for suggesting there was someone else."

"The important thing is that you believe me."

"I do." He sighs softly. "So I won't see you at all this weekend?"

"I just asked for Friday off. I won't be back until late Sunday night."

"You know I want to see you. Need to see you…"

"Believe me, so do I. But I can't. I have to be there for Claudia."

"Hey, I got ya. I'll see what I can do about hanging around Sunday night."

"Just see about this business venture," I tell him excitedly. "Making it happen. Because as soon as it does, you'll be here most of the time. Baby, I can hardly wait."

"It's happening faster than we thought," Glenn says, and I can hear the smile in his voice.

I squeal, giddy. "I love you so much, baby."

"I love you, too." Glenn pauses, and I think he's going to tell me that he has to run. But instead he asks, "What are you wearing?"

"Oh, you don't want to know. I'm hot and sticky—"

"Mmm. Just the way I like you."

"Glenn…"

"Touch yourself. Tell me how it feels. How it smells."

"Glenn, I have to take a shower."

"I'm hard, baby. I'm lying on my bed, I'm holding my cock and I'm thinking of how much I love it when you've got me deep in your mouth."

My skin flushes as the visual image hits me.

"Tell me, baby. Tell me how you feel."

I slip my hand beneath my skirt. "I'm wet," I answer, moaning softly. "Sloppy wet. And my clit is swollen."

"I wish I was there right now. I'd lick you like you were a Popsicle."

Closing my eyes, I stagger backward until I hit the counter. "You know how much I love it when you do that."

"I know."

"You know what else drives me crazy? I love it when

you're on your back on my bed, and we're in the sixty-nine position, eating each other at the same time."

Glenn's moan is long and loud. "Fuck, I could come right now, thinking of how sweet your pussy looks when you're straddling my face."

A jolt of sensation hits my nub. I move my fingers over my vagina faster, imaging Glenn's here and stroking me.

"Are you touching yourself?"

"Yes…"

"Put your fingers inside you."

I push three fingers into my vagina, as deep as they'll go.

"That's my tongue," he rasps. "My tongue, deep inside you. I want you to come. Come in my mouth. Please…"

Glenn's erotic words are my undoing, taking me to the edge and pushing me over. I cry out his name as I ride the wave of my orgasm.

"God, yes. Yes!" Through the phone, I hear the sound of him stroking his shaft. Wildly, the way he thrusts inside me when he starts to come.

"Holy shit, Lishelle. Holy shit."

"I know." I'm breathless. "You do it to me, too."

"I wish you were here. Fuck, I need you in my bed."

"Soon," I tell him.

"You better believe it, babe."

We both grow quiet as we catch our breath. I'm the first to speak. "As much as I'd love to stay on the phone with you, now I really need to go and get that shower."

"Yeah, me, too, at this point."

I chuckle, imagining his hand covered in semen. Then I get serious. "I do love you."

"I know. I'll see you this weekend."

"Remember—"

"I know what you said, but I have to find a way to be with you. Even if it's only for a few hours."

"If you can make it happen—"

"I will. Trust me, I will."

And that gives me something to look forward to. My weekly sexual healing I suddenly can't live without.

Chapter Eighteen

Annelise

I am a changed woman.

Rejuvenated.

Revitalized.

My husband craves my physical love as much as I crave his.

I can smile now. Lord, it's been so long since I smiled in a room with Charles. But that's what I'm doing now. Smiling as I lie in bed early this Friday morning, listening to the sound of running water in the bathroom.

Since last weekend when Charles and I were finally intimate after our horrendously long dry spell, I haven't tried in any way to seduce him. He took a big step telling me about his erectile dysfunction, and an even bigger step in trying to reconnect with me in a sexual way.

Believe me, that alone speaks volumes. To know that my husband desires me is incredibly satisfying, even if all we do at night is cuddle.

There's no awkwardness between us anymore. Isn't it amazing what a dose of the truth can do for you? And while I'd be happy to swing from the chandelier in the sixty-nine position, right now I'm happy to settle for reconnecting our souls.

And let's face it. I got married for the long haul. For good or for bad. Sex is only one part of a relationship, and if Charles and I go through a periodic dry spell here or there, that's only a small amount of time in the scheme of fifty or sixty years together.

I angle one leg over the other in a sexy pose when I hear the water stop running. Moments later, Charles exits the bathroom. He's got a towel wrapped around his waist, and I take in his form like it's water quenching my thirst. My husband still has it going on. His abs are softer than they were ten years ago, but still flat. I miss the ponytail he used to wear when I first met him at a Bible retreat (one I went to at my mother's urging!), but there's enough kissing the nape of his neck for me to run my fingers through.

Charles sits on the edge of the bed and lifts his watch from his night table. I lean forward and run my fingers down his back. He doesn't pull away, and Lord, that makes me feel good. It's been nearly a full week since our sexual encounter, and he's not rejecting me, even if we can't make love.

"What time are you leaving?" Charles asks me.

"About eleven." I glance at the bedside clock. It's just after seven, so that'll give me about four hours to get ready. "Maybe sooner. I'll talk to Claudia around nine." The girls and I are heading to Pensacola for a little holiday. Claudia hasn't heard from Adam yet, and she's naturally in the dumps over him ending their relationship. She's really looking forward to this getaway.

Charles turns his body to face me. "Three days in Florida, hmm?"

"Yep." I pause. "Are you gonna miss me?"

"I will." He gazes deeply into my eyes. "Definitely." He pauses briefly. "Maybe when you get back, we should plan a weekend away for ourselves. Like you suggested before. That place in Arizona for couples?"

"Really?" I can't help feeling a rush of excitement.

"Yeah." He nods. "I'm feeling better about us, aren't you? Like we're back on course again."

"Oh, Charles. I feel the same way."

He gives me a kiss on the lips, soft and full of promise. "But you enjoy your time with the girls. I know how much Claudia needs you right now."

"I know. Can you believe that Adam turned out to be such an asshole?"

Charles simply shrugs.

"Did he ever tell you that he was planning to dump her?"

"He didn't tell me anything."

The very mention of Adam has me tasting something bitter in my mouth, and I don't want my last thoughts with my husband to be of him. So I lean forward and kiss him again.

"Are you trying to tempt me to stay?" he asks me.

"You know I'm trying."

"One day at a time," he tells me. "One day at a time and we'll get there."

"Okay, Annie," Lishelle says not long after we hit the road. "You've been smiling like a fool for half an hour straight. Tell us what's going on."

From the back seat of the Lexus SUV, I glance at Lishelle, who's driving. She's right—I've got a permanent smile on my face. It almost hurts from all the grinning I've been doing.

Claudia cranes her neck around to look at me. "You have some gossip? Something scandalous to tell us? Oh my God—you had an affair, didn't you?"

"No gossip, and no, I didn't have an affair."

"Lishelle, turn down that radio," Claudia instructs her. When the music is lowered, she faces me again. "I didn't hear you. Did you just say you had an affair?"

"No, I did not say that, so don't give me that look. But I guess I do have sex on the brain. Charles and I, we've reconnected."

Lishelle whips her head around to look at me. "Girl, did you get laid?"

"Not quite, but it was just as satisfying. And you know what? It happened the moment I decided I didn't care if Charles ever touched me again. So Claudia, maybe it's a good thing that you haven't called Adam in two days. Let him start to wonder what's happening with you."

"Tell us the story!" Lishelle demands, giggling.

"It was last weekend, right after the bridal fitting." If

not for Claudia's crisis with Adam, I would have mentioned this before. "I decided not to go home right away, so I went shopping, bought some great lingerie. Came home and within minutes, Charles got a call and had to leave. I was like, whatever, no big deal. Then there I was, trying on lingerie, and he comes back. Suddenly says he's ready to talk to me."

"And?" Claudia asks.

"And he finally told me that for the past fifteen months he's been suffering from erectile dysfunction."

"No…" Claudia shakes her head in disbelief. "All this time? Why didn't he just tell you?"

"Yeah, what'd he say about that?"

"He said he was embarrassed. That he thought it would go away. That the more I wanted sex, the worse he felt because he knew he couldn't stay erect."

"So he made a big deal out of nothing," Claudia comments. "Well, not nothing, but certainly nothing he should have kept from you."

"I guess men don't like to admit that sort of thing," I comment.

"Ain't that the truth," Lishelle says. "Men act like everything that's important about them can be found between their legs."

"Can't it?" Claudia asks, cracking a real grin for the first time since we got in the car.

"That's what it all boils down to," I agree.

"So did you get laid or not?" Lishelle asks.

"No." A smile erupts on my face as I remember last weekend with my husband. "But he did go down on me. Ate my pussy till I was speaking in tongues."

"Ah!" Lishelle screams with delight.

"A real live man-induced orgasm for the first time in nearly a year and a half. I tell you, I thought I wouldn't be able to get up for days."

"Maybe by the time you get back, he'll be missing you so much he'll have a hard-on when you walk through the door," Lishelle says.

"God, I hope so. But for now, I'm happy knowing we're getting there."

On Friday night, we ate loads of popcorn and watched *The Best Man, Brown Sugar* and *How Stella Got Her Groove Back* into the wee hours of Saturday morning. Claudia wanted a Taye Diggs marathon night, and who can blame her? Taye Diggs has a smile that could melt any woman—and make her forget about the asshole in her life.

But while lusting after Taye probably helped Claudia put Adam out of her mind, watching all those romantic movies made me miss my husband more. That's why the moment I woke up this morning, I reached for the phone and called him.

"How's the hotel?" he asks.

I play with the phone cord as I lie on my back. "It's gorgeous. Did I mention we're in Alabama, not Pensacola?"

"Alabama?"

"Well, at first the plan was Pensacola, but Claudia found out about this amazing spa the Marriott has in Point Clear, Alabama," I finish with an exaggerated southern drawl. "And it's really nice. You should see this suite. And the pictures I've seen of the spa are incredible. We all head down there for a day of pampering in a little over an hour."

"Sounds like you're having a great time."

"So far. It's the kind of place that helps you forget, you know? And Claudia needs to forget right now."

"I miss you," Charles says softly.

I close my eyes and savor the words. "I miss you, too."

I think about Charles all day long, even as we get our feet scrubbed and our nails painted and talk about which movie we like Taye Diggs best in. I think about him as I do laps in the spectacular pool and as I dine on lobster in one of the resort's restaurants.

And by the time we finish our early dinner, I know what I have to do. I have to go home. I have to surprise my husband. My God, we're reconnecting—this simply isn't the time for me to be away from him.

I've had a great getaway with my friends so far, but now it's time to get back to my husband. I have this feeling that he needs me. And I need him.

We take a leisurely stroll of the grounds after dinner before we head back upstairs. The resort is on Mobile Bay, so it's got a view of the water—something I always find calming. It's surrounded by aged oaks and magnolia trees and there's a hint of jasmine in the air. It's exactly the kind of place I'd love to come with Charles.

"What are you in the mood for?" Claudia asks when we get back to the suite. "More Taye Diggs or *Sex and the City?*"

"*Sex and the City,*" Lishelle responds immediately. "You

have the season when Carrie fell for Aidan? That's the one I want to see."

"I've got it all with me," Claudia responds.

As Lishelle settles onto the sofa and Claudia rifles through a suitcases checking out DVD cases, I stand back. I hate to leave them, but it's already four o'clock and if I'm going to make good time, I'll have to go now.

Lishelle glances over her shoulder at me. "Annie, you're standing up. Wanna get the wine?"

"Here it is," Claudia announces. She holds up the DVD like it's a prize.

"Ladies," I say, and they both look at me. I stroll into the living room. "I hate to do this to you both, but I have to go home."

"Why?" Lishelle asks. "Is something wrong?"

"No, no." I shake my head. "Nothing's wrong. In fact, for the first time in a long time I think that things are really, really great. On Monday, Charles will be back at work and we won't have any time to spend together. I want at least one day with him this weekend. One day when we can relax in bed and hopefully have the best sex of our lives."

Claudia frowns as she slumps onto the floor. Lishelle simply shrugs.

"I know, I'm ruining our girls' weekend, but we've had a great day and last night was lots of fun. Oh, and don't get me wrong—I'm not asking you both to leave with me. Stay and enjoy the rest of your time here. I can get a rental car and make my way home."

Claudia moans her disappointment. "Annie…"

"I'm sorry. Really I am. But you know all I've been

through with Charles." I swallow, gathering courage. "I have to do this."

"You gotta do what you gotta do," Lishelle comments.

"She's right," Claudia agrees, albeit reluctantly. "If your instinct is telling you to go home and be with your man, then go. In fact, we can all go. Like you said, we had a good time while it lasted."

"Claudia, no. Honestly. You and Lishelle hang out. I'll rent a car and drive back."

"You shouldn't go alone," Claudia says. "That's nearly a six-hour drive."

"I'll be fine. The long drive will probably do me good anyway."

Claudia and Lishelle look at each other, as though silently trying to figure out what they'll do.

"I insist," I tell them. "I'll feel awful if I ruin your vacation."

"Okay," Claudia finally says, nodding. "We'll stay. If that's all right with you, Lishelle."

"It's fine. As long as you're fine, Annie."

"I'm totally fine. And thank you guys for understanding. You're the best."

I hug them both. I love them so much. I have for years. They mean the world to me.

But so does my marriage. And right now, that has to be priority number one.

"I guess I'll call Enterprise," I announce. I scoop up the Yellow Pages and head into my bedroom.

God, I can't stop smiling. It's like I've reverted to my early twenties when I first met Charles at that Bible retreat. I'd been bored out of my mind that hot Sunday afternoon—until I'd turned and seen Charles standing there.

I'd gone to please my mother. He'd gone to accompany a friend. We were both bored and hot in that oversized tent crammed with people and needed a break.

I joked later that God had a hand in our meeting, because Charles and I clicked instantly. In fact, by the end of that afternoon, I knew he would be my husband.

Tonight feels like the early days, the days full of hope and promise and spontaneity. As I near the Atlanta city limits, I'm tempted to call Charles and let him know I'm on my way. But I don't, because I want to surprise him. Hopefully surprise him right into an erect state when he sees me walk through the door.

It's minutes to midnight when I pull into the driveway of our home. It's been a long drive, and I should be exhausted, but instead I'm excited. I listened to sappy love songs most of the way home, and I'm definitely in the mood for romance.

Please, Charles. Please be able to get it up. I need to make love to you. I want hot, sweaty, mind-numbing sex.

I'm a woman on a mission as I slip the key in the door, and that mission is to get laid. I want it so badly that the raunchiest thought comes into my mind. If Charles can't get it up for me, I won't settle for a night of cuddling. I'll take out my new vibrator and have him watch me get off. Watch me stroke my breasts and tweak my nipples while I finger my clit. I've never done this in front of anyone before, but the thought alone is getting me hot. How erotic would that be for Charles to watch me—how naughty? If Charles doesn't have a rock-hard boner after I'm finished with myself, I'll have to check if he has a pulse.

I don't hear anything as I creep into the house. I don't expect to. Knowing Charles and the hours he keeps at the office, he's got to be zonked out.

Nonetheless, I tiptoe up the stairs to the bedroom, where I slowly turn the doorknob. I'll sneak in quietly, strip off my clothes and lie next to—

I reel backward when I open the door, my gasp getting caught in my throat. At first I'm stunned—too stunned to move. Too stunned to breathe.

Oh my God…

My fantasy of the night Charles and I would share is shattered.

Everything is shattered.

My whole life.

I can't breathe….

Somehow, I suck in some air. I want to run away. Run back to the car and start this part over again.

"Fuck, your pussy feels so good," Charles moans. He's ramming some woman from behind—giving it to her hard.

Oh. My. God.

The room's spinning. I stand there and watch. Watch as he moans and groans in ecstasy, oblivious to my presence.

I'm not sure where I get the courage, but I take a step into the room. I know why. It's because I want to see the woman. The vixen. The striking bombshell for whom Charles can't help but get it up. Can't help but screw like he's a nineteen-year-old.

In our fucking bed.

"You asshole!" I scream.

Charles's eyes whip in my direction a fraction of a moment before he pushes the bitch forward onto the bed. I see her face then, the vampy temptress who has led my husband astray.

Confusion hits me like a slug in the chest. Because it's Marsha. His partner at the firm—his significantly older partner.

She flies off the bed with the agility of a ten-year-old and cowers behind the nearby chaise as though she expects me to pull out a gun. Charles, on the other hand, stays on the bed, staring at me for several long moments. I see shock in his eyes. It even looks as if he's shaking.

I'm shaking. Both my hands are trembling. And I'm making some sort of wheezing sound I can't control. I don't take my eyes off Charles.

He gets up and takes baby step after baby step toward me. His penis is now limp, and his palms are outstretched in a sign of surrender.

"Ann, don't freak out."

More wheezing. I hear the thunder of my pulse in my ears.

"I didn't want you to find out like this. Oh, fuck."

Some sort of primal cry escapes my lips. I drag my arm across the top of Charles's dresser, knocking everything to the floor.

"For God's sake, Ann—don't freak out!"

"Don't freak out?" I repeat. "Don't *freak out?*" I snatch up a bottle of cologne off the floor and whip it at

Charles's head. He ducks. The bottle lands on the bed behind him.

"Let me explain."

"Explain that you *lied to me for the past fucking year?*"

"We've drifted apart. I knew this was wrong, but—"

I shoot a venomous gaze at Marsha. Something is wrong with this picture. I can't wrap my brain around this one. "You can get it up for Marsha, but you can't get it up for *me?* How old are you anyway, you fucking skank?" The words come from a place deep inside me; a place where understanding sees the face of deception. I remember her calling my house last weekend nonstop. Those pathetic, whiny calls. "My God, Charles. This is *our* bed. The bed you haven't fucked me in in how long—" I have to stop. Have to take a breath. "What was last Sunday about, then? Finally, we get close again. Charles, we almost made love…and now this?"

This is all so surreal. I don't get it.

"What does she mean you two almost made love, Charles?" Marsha demands. "You said you told her it was over!"

"Marsha, let me handle this."

"Handle what?" I snap.

"The truth, Annelise," Marsha responds in the smuggest way possible.

I know I will lose it if she stays in this room. "You get out of here. Now."

Marsha's eyes bounce from me to Charles. He meets her gaze. "It's okay," he tells her. "Just stay there a minute."

"Stay there a minute?" I shout, staring Charles down.

Seriously, there's something weird brewing inside me. I could snap at any moment.

"Let's…" Charles's chest rises and falls with a deep breath. "Let's go downstairs and talk about this, Ann. Me and you."

"While Marsha stays here in our bedroom?"

"It's a complicated situation."

"Let me uncomplicate it. Get the fuck out of here."

"Let's just go downstairs," Charles pleads.

"No." This again from Marsha, who is slipping into a shirt. Charles's shirt, the bitch. "You tell her, Charles. And tell her now. Damn you, we have plans."

With those words, I feel the raging locomotive inside me start to slow down. I'm confused again.

What the fuck is going on? And why am I the only one who doesn't know?

"If you don't tell her, I will."

"Marsha, just wait a second, will you?"

"Tell me what?" I demand.

"You tell her right now, or I swear I'll walk out that door and that'll be it. I am through waiting on you to deal with this."

"All right, all right." Defeat streaks across Charles's face.

"*Now,* Charles."

My eyes volley back and forth between the two of them, and quite frankly, I'm getting dizzy. A mix of emotions are fighting for control of me right now. I could either collapse into a quivering heap on the floor, or I could snap someone's neck.

"Yes, Charles." Somehow I speak calmly. "Tell me what's going on."

He doesn't look at me. Instead, he looks at the bitch in my bedroom. "I'm in love with Marsha."

My knees threaten to give way. "You-y-you…"

"We're not working out. You know that."

"I…I…do?"

"Yes, you do. How long has it been since we've made love?"

"B-but last weekend…"

"Last weekend…" Charles throws another glance at Marsha, who's standing with her hands akimbo. "I wasn't sure I should be doing what I've been doing with Marsha. I was torn. Feeling guilty for lying to you. I thought I could make things work with you…." Charles looks at Marsha again. She's now marching toward him. "But now I want a divorce," he hurriedly adds.

"You want a *what?*" Honestly, I feel like someone zapped me onto another planet, that's how bizarre this is. I'm completely lost.

"It's no secret you two haven't been getting along. Why don't you just let him go?" Marsha, who has barely said two words to me in six years, sure is full of hot air now.

"You know what?" I glare at her. "You need to shut your mouth and get out of my house. Before I make you get out. And if you think I'm lying, just try me." If she pushes me, I *know* I'll hurt her.

Marsha looks to Charles, her eyes frantically searching his for an answer.

"Look at my husband a second longer, bitch, and it'll be the last thing you ever do."

Charles nods. "Go. I'll call you later."

Marsha doesn't even have the decency to change into

her own clothes. She breezes by me in Charles's shirt and nothing else. My eyes follow her to the bedroom door. As soon as she's gone, I rush to the door and slam it. Then I whirl around and face my husband.

"You want a divorce?"

"This isn't how I planned for you to find out."

"How long has this been going on? And with *Marsha?*" That's the most puzzling part of all. If he had cheated with Pamela Anderson, I could understand. But Marsha? She's almost fifty, and looks it as far as I'm concerned.

"You can't help who you love."

My hands fly to my hips. "Oh, so now you're in love with her?"

"About two years now," he admits, again not looking me in the eye. "Look, I thought it would just be an affair, but our feelings grew deeper."

"But you're married to me."

"I'm sorry," he says lamely. "This isn't easy for me. For any of us. Marsha wanted me to leave you a year and a half ago, but I stayed, still hoping for the best."

I slap Charles across the face. "Are you kidding me? You're treating me like I'm the freaking other woman?"

"I've made my decision," Charles says calmly. More calmly than he should, considering he's just pulled my whole life out from under me.

"You're supposed to tell me this was a fling—that it was sex and nothing more. Then you're supposed to beg me for forgiveness, and hope to hell I don't kick you out. I'm your *wife*, Charles. That's the way it works."

"Maybe in a fucking romance novel," Charles barks

back. "But this is real life. I fell in love with someone else."

"Don't you dare yell at me. Not under these circumstances!"

"Sorry," he mumbles. "Look, I'm stressed out here. I'm trying to make this as easy as possible."

I snort. "Like that's not a fantasy."

Charles shakes his head ruefully. "Ann—"

"You want to be with her?" I ask, dumbfounded. "You really want to leave me and be with *her?*"

"Life's too short. I have to be true to my feelings."

OhmyGodohmyGod! Panic slams me in the gut like a sledgehammer. He's really saying this. He really wants to leave me. "What about your vows? What about being true to them? I know we're not regular churchgoers, but we both believe in God. We were raised in Christian homes. I thought you took your vows before God seriously."

"Let's not start that religion shit. I'm not going to stay married to you just because—"

I lose it then. I charge toward Charles, shoving hard against his chest. He stumbles backward but doesn't fall.

His eyes flash fire at me.

"Don't you dare! Don't you dare look at me like that, you lying, cheating son of a bitch!" My voice trips over the last few words and tears cloud my eyes.

Devastation is suddenly taking control of the anger, and I fear I'll fall apart.

I can't do this. I can't be here in the same room with Charles.

So I turn around and flee. I pound down the stairs like

a rapist is on my tail. I snatch my keys off the hall table and burst through the front door and don't stop running until I reach my car. I jam the key into the lock, but it doesn't work.

"Damn!"

It takes me a moment to realize I'm at my Jetta, not the Grand Am I rented. I run around the back of my car to the rental car. It takes me two tries to get the key in before I remember it has a remote control. I pop open the door and jump behind the wheel.

Now I look to my front door. No Charles.

And that's when I break down. I cry, and cry, not sure I'll ever stop.

Chapter Nineteen

Claudia

By Sunday morning, I was itching to leave the piece of paradise in Alabama and hit the road for home. I told Lishelle that a girlfriend weekend wasn't the same without Annelise, but the truth is, I'm desperate to hear from Adam. Last night, I had a nightmare. In the nightmare, I gave him all the time in the world, and when we spoke again, he had moved on.

I woke up with a feeling of terror. I thought giving Adam some time to think was a good idea, but what if it's not? What if the longer I stay away, the more comfortable he becomes without me in his life? The less chance we have of getting back together?

With Lishelle's blessing, we packed up and left the resort right after brunch, which was shortly before noon.

"Girl, what are you doing?" Lishelle asks, casting me a sideways glance as she drives. We've finally merged onto I-10.

"I'm just…" I am almost tempted to slip the cell phone back in my purse, feeling like I've been caught shoplifting. But I pull the phone onto my lap. "I figured I'd check my messages."

She tsks softly. "And if he called, you're gonna call him right back?"

"I didn't say that."

"You didn't have to. But quite frankly, I'd advise against it. He's hurt you in the worst possible way. The last thing you need to make him believe is that your arms are wide open for him."

"I want him back," I admit. "What's the point in playing games?"

"Because you don't want him to walk all over you at any point in the future. If he comes back to you, you have to make it seem like you gave serious thought to being without him. That's the only thing that will keep him in line. Trust me—that's what I should have done with David the first time he stepped out on me. But I was so hurt, then so relieved that it was only a fling that I took him back with open arms, as if I deserved substandard treatment for the privilege of being with him."

I'm not in the mood for a lecture right now. "If it's all the same, I'm still gonna check my messages."

"Suit yourself."

My voice mail tells me that I have four messages, and my splintered heart fills with hope. The first message, however, isn't from Adam. It's from my mother. She wants to know where I am and how I'm doing. She's worried I ended up in emergency with a flu that got much worse.

But it's the second message that causes my breath to snag in my throat. It's Annelise, and she sounds like I must have last week when Adam said he didn't want to marry me.

"Oh my God," I utter.

"What?" Lishelle whips her gaze at me.

"It's Annelise," I explain. Then I try to listen to the remainder of her message. I hear only something about her needing to talk to me, and that she's staying at an airport hotel.

I replay the message.

"Claudia, it's Annelise. I don't know what I'm going to do. I really need to talk to you, okay?" She sniffles, takes a loud breath. "And Lishelle. You're the only people I trust in the world. If you get this on your way home, please call me." More sniffling. "I'm at a Red Roof Inn near the airport. I really need to talk to you both."

"Okay," I say to Lishelle. "Now *that* was weird. Annelise is staying at some airport hotel and wants us to call her there."

"She's at a hotel? She didn't say why?"

"Just that she needs to talk to me. And to you. Something about us being the only two people in the world she trusts. And she was crying."

"Oh, God. What kind of drama is she going through? When she left she was so full of hope."

"What is going on with everyone?" I ask. "Is May fucked-up-relationship month?"

I check the rest of my messages, and there's one from my sister, and one of my bridesmaids, but nothing from Adam. Asshole.

I hate to even think it, but I'm almost glad that Annelise is going through some drama. It'll give me a reason to forget about my own problems.

At least for a while.

We pull into Atlanta proper around 6:00 p.m. I call Annelise's cell phone. There's no answer, so I dial directory and then call the Red Roof Inn.

Minutes later, I'm connected to her room. "Hello?" Annelise answers, sounding as if someone's died.

"Annie, it's Claudia."

"Oh, God." Her voice crumbles. "Claudia."

"Shh, honey. It's okay. What's going on?"

"The absolute worst thing."

"Lishelle and I are just getting back into Atlanta. We're on our way to see you."

"Okay."

Obviously something serious is going on, something that's probably better said in person. "Sweetie, we're on our way right now, okay?"

"I'm in room 410."

"See you in about fifteen."

"Thank you. I love you guys."

"Do you think he kicked her out?" Lishelle asks as we walk briskly through the hotel lobby. "Because if he did…"

"Maybe she left," I suggest. "You and I know there's

been a serious lack of passion in that marriage. Maybe she went home and he rejected her again and she had enough of it and decided to move on."

"Lord, I hope Charles didn't turn into a fucking dog. That's the last thing she needs."

We stop talking as we near the bank of elevators, as there's a family of four waiting there. The elevator doors open and we all step on. Something tugs at my heart as I listen to the kids, a boy and a girl, argue over who'll get to press the button. I can't help thinking about Adam, how we're supposed to have children together. I have to look away, or I might start to cry.

When the elevator stops, Lishelle heads out, and I follow her.

My thoughts return to Annelise and her crisis when we reach her door. Lishelle knocks. She's about to knock a second time when the door swings open.

"Oh, Annie." I float into the room and gather her in my arms. "What the hell?"

She pulls apart from me. "I moved out. I went home to surprise Charles with amazing sex but I'm the one who was surprised. I caught him in our bed fucking his law partner!"

"Oh my God," Lishelle exclaims. "No, honey. Not Charles."

"Oh yeah."

I stare at Annelise in complete shock. "But you just told us he's suffering from erectile dysfunction."

"So I thought." She brushes away her tears, and anger fills her face. "That was only one of his surprises for me. Trust me, they get better."

"Not Stephanie Morton," I ask in a horrified tone. I've met the woman, and I know she'd be happy to flirt her way up the corporate ladder. "She can't be more than twenty-two."

"She's not a partner and believe me I *wish* it was Stephanie. Thin as a rake, fake breasts and legs that go on forever. I wouldn't be happy, but at least I'd understand how he could be so weak."

Annelise strolls into her hotel room and lifts a bottle of wine. She puts it to her mouth and gulps down the Chardonnay like it's water. She's not a huge drinker to begin with, so I know how badly she must be hurting. I'm in an incredible amount of pain—and Adam and I weren't married. Plus, I didn't catch him screwing some other woman.

"Who's the bitch?" Lishelle asks.

"Marsha Hindenberg."

Marsha Hindenberg Marsha Hindenberg Marsha Hindenberg. "Marsha *Hindenberg!* She's—"

"Old enough to be his mother."

Lishelle gasps. "You're shitting me."

"Well, not really, but she looks it," Annelise says, looking to Lishelle. "She's around thirteen or fourteen years older than him, which makes her forty-nine or so. And you should see how she dresses. Shirts up to her nose, skirts down to the floor."

"She's not an attractive woman," I tell Lishelle. "Every time I look at her, I see this odd resemblance to a turkey."

"How could he get it up for her?" Annelise asks, though the question is rhetorical. "He can't get it up for me, and I'm his wife. I'm at least moderately attractive, aren't I?"

"You're fucking gorgeous," Lishelle tells her.

"I don't understand it." Annelise drinks more wine.

"Maybe he was...drunk." It's the only thing I can think of. "Or high. Or temporarily insane. You know there's no way he would sleep with Marsha otherwise."

Annelise plops onto the bed. The tears return. "He said he's in love with her. That he's been in love with her for a while and that it's not fair to *her* if he stays married to me."

"Okay, hold up." Lishelle sits on the second bed in the room and stares at Annelise in shock. "He's in love with her?"

I sit beside Lishelle. "He can't mean that. How can he mean that?"

"I don't know. But Marsha was in our bedroom, damn near getting in my face. Telling Charles that he had to make his choice right there, or it'd be over with them. And Charles...Charles...he..."

Lishelle reaches across the bed and takes Annelise's hand in hers. "Oh, Annie. I don't know what to say."

"I keep hoping to wake up. Realize this is the worst nightmare of my life." She hastily wipes away her tears. "I don't want to cry over him. If he could treat me so badly, he doesn't deserve my tears."

"Men," I say. "I swear, you just can't trust most of them. First Adam, now Charles." I don't say what pops into my mind—*How long before Glenn shows his true colors?*

"You shouldn't be staying here," Lishelle tells Annelise. "I don't like the idea of you being here alone."

"Come to my place," I offer. "I could certainly use the

company. I don't want to sit around crying over Adam anymore."

"No, I'm fine." Annelise waves off the suggestion. "I don't want to burden you."

"If I were you, I'd go back to that house. Kick Charles the fuck out."

"I know, Lishelle. But I'm not ready to go back. I keep seeing Charles screwing Marsha from behind... Hearing how much he enjoyed it... If I go back there..." She closes her eyes tightly and shakes her head.

"I've got space for you, too," Lishelle says. "Glenn should be moving in shortly, but hey, I'll always be here for you. If you need anything. Anything at all."

"And if I need you to beat the shit out of Charles?" Annelise cracks a small smile.

"Tell me the time and place," I say without hesitation. "As long as you beat down Adam for me, as well."

"No word from him?" Annelise asks.

I shake my head. "Nothing. I guess he needs more time."

Annelise sighs. The sound is full of regret and disappointment. "You think you know a guy, and you give him your heart, you give him the best part of yourself for years. You lie with him night after night. You listen to his problems, his hopes and dreams. You take care of him, because you want more than anything for him to be happy. You give him more of yourself than you've ever given anyone. And still, you can never be sure that one day he won't fuck you over in the worst possible way."

"You know that's right," Lishelle says.

"But your girlfriends," Annelise continues, "they're

the ones you can really count on. The ones who will be there with you through thick and thin."

I don't say a word. I can't, because my throat is clogging with emotion. What Annelise said was so poignant and so true, and it strikes a chord deep in my soul. I wonder, despite everything Adam and I have meant to each other over the years, if he's really capable of walking away from me without a backward glance.

I wonder if he ever loved me at all.

Chapter Twenty

Lishelle

I'd be lying if I said that Annelise's words didn't affect me in any way. That and what Adam did to Claudia after how long they'd been together. Both scenarios have been playing themselves over in my mind since I got back to my place, and here I am in the middle of the night, staring at the ceiling in my room, unable to sleep.

I'm not thinking too highly of men right now.

Of course, this extends to Glenn. I'm remembering how he broke my heart in college. At first, there were the rumors of his cheating that I always ignored. Then there were the slips of paper I found with phone numbers on them. I let him explain those away, too. I knew he was fine, and unavailable—a combination that to many women is irresistible.

I remember how, after we had a tryst during the summer after our breakup, I reflected on how the true attraction between me and Glenn was purely physical.

But do people make a sexual connection last over two years? And why am I even thinking of the past? Glenn broke my heart, yes, but that was ten years ago. What's a twenty-two-year-old guy to do when there's constant pussy in his face? Now in his thirties, I don't expect the same kind of behavior from him.

I glance at the clock: 3:33 a.m. Damn, I have got to shut my brain down. In less than four hours, I have to be up and looking my best. I'm one of four media personalities from Channel Four who will be heading to a McDonald's in downtown Atlanta for a fund-raiser.

I'll be donning a McDonald's uniform and serving up burgers and fries. Fifty percent of today's proceeds will be donated to a children's ward at a local hospital.

It's the kind of day where I'll be facing fans for hours on end. I'm going to need to be able to smile.

If I'm going to smile, I need to get some sleep.

I close my eyes and start counting sheep.

The first half of my day was brutal. My face actually hurts from smiling so much.

And it's not over yet. I still have to do the six o'clock broadcast.

"How great was that?" Randy Harmon, a fellow on-air broadcaster asks me when I pass him in the hallway en route to my office. His voice is dripping with sarcasm.

"Gaawd. If I never do another one of those fund-raisers, it'll be too soon."

Randy chuckles. "Come on—you don't like smelling like lard?"

I try to think of a humorous comeback but can't. "Ah, no."

"See you after you shower."

"Later." I continue past Randy to my office. But no sooner than I'm there, Linda Tennant, the station manager, peeks her head in.

"I heard you were back," she says.

"Barely." I smile sweetly.

Linda sits down on the sofa, clearly not taking the hint that I'm not ready to chat. "There's a story breaking in Macon."

I pull my blouse out of my skirt. "What kind of story?"

"Connor House. The—"

"Haven for children suffering from terminal cancer," I finish for her. "What about it?"

"Twelve children and their families were supposed to be leaving for Orlando this morning. But when they went to the airport, they found their reservations had been canceled."

"What?"

"Uh-huh. The money for the trip came from the Wishes Come True Foundation right here in Atlanta. Well, it was supposed to."

"I know that foundation very well. My best friend's fiancé is the president." *Ex-fiancé.*

"I know. That's why I'm talking to you about this."

I take a seat beside Linda. "What exactly happened?"

"The Wishes Come True Foundation wrote the check, but apparently it bounced."

"Wow."

"From what I understand, the foundation is supposed to be financially sound."

"It is. They had a fund-raiser about a week ago that brought in over a hundred thousand dollars. Are you sure about this?"

"I'm sure. I was hoping you could fill in a few more blanks."

I shrug. "I can't."

"I know Adam Hart is a good friend of yours, and I didn't want to run this story before talking to you about it. In case there's something going on here that our researchers haven't found out."

"Let me talk to Adam. I'll see what he says. But I'm sure there must be some mistake somewhere."

Linda pushes herself off the sofa. "All right."

When she leaves the room, I head for the phone. I dial both Claudia's numbers, but she doesn't pick up. I'm worried about her. I wonder if she's back to moping and hiding from the world.

I do the six o'clock broadcast, and finally I step into my house after 8:00 p.m. I head straight to my kitchen and check my phone.

The red light isn't blinking, which means there are no messages.

With all the drama over the past two days, I've all but forgotten about Glenn. But it finally hits me that he didn't show up last night as he said he'd try to do. Not only that, he didn't call.

Chapter Twenty-One

Annelise

"I told you that son of a bitch was boning someone else," Samera says, her lips twisted in a scowl. She's dressed in short-shorts and a bra, and is sitting in front of the window AC unit in her apartment with one leg pulled up onto her chair. She's busy painting her toenails a shade of ocean blue.

Across from her, I'm sprawled out on her sofa, where I slept last night at my sister's insistence, but already I'm regretting that I did. I was hoping against hope that she'd spare me the Charles-is-a-cheating-asshole lectures and simply offer me comfort.

No such luck.

"I hope you sue his ass for everything he's got." She takes a drag off the cigarette in the ashtray on the windowsill. I don't know how she can smoke and paint her nails at the same time. "Men. I fucking hate them."

"Amazing—considering what you do for a living."

"And the longer I do it, the more I see that men are such pathetic pigs I can hardly stand looking at them." She closes the nail-polish bottle. "Do you know how many married guys come into the club for business lunches and end up in private rooms with the girls who are willing to put out? And you wonder why I vow to be single for life? If only I didn't like the feel of a big cock deep inside me so much…"

I put my hands over my ears. "Too much information."

"Oh, you don't like a big cock?"

"I don't remember what one feels like!"

Samera's eyes light up as she grounds out the remains of her cigarette. "Hey, if you want, I can hook you up with someone. I've got a few friends who can blow your back out, that's how great they are in bed."

"Sam!" I protest in disgust. We don't really talk about our sex lives, except that she knows I'm not getting any from Charles. But the last thing I want to know is how many "friends" she's slept with. Or, God forbid, sleep with one of them. That's a very scary thought.

"That's exactly what you need. Instead of moping around here on my sofa. Ooh, there's Lorenzo. He's a bouncer at the club, and if you want an Italian Stallion—"

"Please, Sam. Let's just drop this, okay?" But the mention of an Italian Stallion has me thinking of Dominic. His brother hasn't been back to the studio, so I'm sure they're hiring another photographer. Damn, Sebastian and Helen had seemed so eager.

They're not the first ones to seem eager and then not hire me.

Why did I throw away Dominic's number?

"There's always Tyrell. He's another bouncer. Kinda looks like Will Smith. The man is *hot,* and I swear, his tongue is as big as his—"

"Samera!"

"I'm just trying to help," she tells me. "And honestly, I think it's the best thing for you. Jump right into the next relationship to forget about Charles."

"Maybe that works when you date a guy for a few months, but Charles and I were together for years." Just saying the words, and the reality that he told me he's in love with another woman, has my stomach twisting in a painful knot. God help me, what am I going to do?

Samera gets to her feet and walks toward the kitchen. "I wish I didn't have to work tonight. We could go clubbing or something. Take your mind off of the shit head."

"I'm not in the mood for clubbing."

"Which is exactly why you need to go out."

I love her, but my sister and I are never on the same page. What I need is to have a bitch session with *Sex and the City* playing in the background. I need to be able to cry my eyes out on a caring shoulder.

But Lishelle is busy with work, and Claudia has her own problems.

"I've got to get ready," Samera tells me. "But before I go, can I get you anything? Some wine, vodka, beer? I'm all out of Ecstasy pills, but I've got some weed in my bed-room."

"I'm fine," I reply, unnerved. "Sam, you keep weed in the apartment?"

"Sure," she says, as though it's the most natural thing in the world. Then her eyes widen and she gapes at me. "Don't tell me you still don't get high."

"You know I'm not a fan of marijuana."

"Mom may be in Alabama, but it's like she's still right here, in this room. Tell me you at least believe in oral sex."

"What does getting high have to do with oral sex?"

"Guys don't like their women to be boring in the bed-room. I'm just wondering…"

I can't help glaring at her. "Charles was very well sat-isfied, thank you very much." And now I have a worse headache than I did when I came here last night. Why did I think this would be the answer?

Samera walks toward me and draws me into a hug. "I'm sorry. You know all I care about is your happiness."

"Yeah," I answer softly.

"And I say fuck Charles. Just make sure you get your half and move on. Don't beg or do any crazy shit like that. It's over, Annie. And I for one think it's about time."

"Gee, thanks. I feel so much better." Thank God Sam-era is leaving. I don't think I could take a night of her "support."

She pulls away from me and glances at the clock. "Oh, fuck. I've got to run."

"Shall I wait up? The club isn't open that late on a Tues-day night, is it? Maybe we can watch a movie when you get back."

"I won't be home until after three."

"Amazing. The weekend I can understand, but Tuesday?"

"Actually, weekdays can be very lucrative. All those businessmen in town." She smiles. "But I'll see...I'll see what I can do."

"Well, if you can, that'd be great. If you can't, I'll understand." Samera starts for the bedroom. "And Sam?" I quickly call out.

She stops and looks over her shoulder. "Uh-huh?"

"I think I do need something. Wine'll be great."

"Red's under the sink and the white's in the fridge. Drink all you want."

At nine o'clock, there's a knock on the door. I raise my head from the sofa with caution. Should I answer it? I know it's got to be someone for Samera, so what's the point? Besides, I feel like shit. The cheap red wine Samera had isn't doing much for my headache, and I've been intermittently crying over Charles and cursing him.

There's another knock. It sounds more insistent. Moaning softly, I lower the volume on the reality dating show I'm watching and pull myself up off the couch.

I drag my feet all the way to the door and peer through the peephole. I jerk my head backward when I see the face of an attractive man with olive-toned skin.

"Annie?" I hear him say through the door.

"Who are you?" And how does he know my name?

"Sam asked me to come."

Great, I think. What's this about? Nonetheless, I swing the door open.

The mystery man grins at me as his eyes drink in every part of my body. "Sam was right. You're really hot."

Please don't tell me this man will be hanging around until Samera shows up. "Is there something you're supposed to pick up for her?"

He gives me that look again, like he's trying to undress me with his gaze. I don't like it. I cross my arms over my chest.

"You could say so," he answers.

"What does that mean?" I think I sound a bit testy, but I can't help it. I'm not in the mood for games. I want to go back to wallowing in my misery.

He steps over the door's threshold. "Hey, Annie. I don't bite. Unless you want me to." He winks.

"Please just tell me what Sam wants you to pick up. I've got a migraine, and I'm not in the mood to be friendly right now."

"I thought Sam told you. She said she was sending me over to cheer you up. She kind of hinted that you might need…" His voice trails off, but his eyebrows move up and down suggestively.

It takes another second for me to realize what he's getting at. And then my jaw hits the floor. "Oh my God. Now I get it. You're the Italian Stallion." Holy shit—did I just say that?

"So I'm told." He grins proudly.

"I'm sorry. I don't know what my sister made you think about what…what to *expect,* but I certainly didn't tell her that I wanted…you know."

"She said it's been more than a year for you."

Oh, lovely. Thanks, Samera. Why not take out a billboard? And while you're at it, let the whole world know that my husband has dumped me for a woman thirteen years older than him whose ass is the size of a horse's!

"My sister shouldn't have discussed my sex life with you." To my surprise, Lorenzo seems disappointed. "No offense, Lorenzo, but I'm not in the mood. For sex with anyone right now. But if I *were* in the mood, I'd be seriously tempted to…you know. Because a guy women call the Italian Stallion's got to be—" I take a deep breath, wondering when I had this much wine to make my tongue so loose. "I just want to be alone."

"You sure?"

"Yes," I insist.

He nods. "All right."

"But thank you, anyway." Was that the right thing to say? Was it totally stupid? I don't know. I have no clue what's appropriate in these situations.

I close the door and lock it, but look through the peephole once more. Lorenzo stands there for a moment, like he's dumbfounded, before heading off down the hallway.

"Damn you, Sam."

In the morning, when I'm sober and rested, I'm out of here.

The question, of course, is where do I go?

Chapter Twenty-Two

Claudia

"Is it true?" my mother asks.

I sigh softly. "Yes, it's true."

Her glossy red lips part in surprise. But there's also anger and disappointment in her expression. And how can she not be upset with Adam after the lowdown dirty thing he's done?

"How could you not tell me about this?" she demands.

Wait a minute—is she upset with *me*?

"Every day, I'm on the phone finalizing plans. I've been dealing with Diana while you've been sick. This event is less than two weeks away!"

This *event* is my life! I want to scream. Instead, I look at the pot of tea on the kitchen table in front of us that neither of us has touched. I don't even want to meet her eyes, I'm so ashamed.

"Do you know what it was like to hear this while I was at the spa getting a pedicure?" She paces the floor in front of me, staring down at me—something that's always made me feel one inch tall. "Monica Williams was there with her daughter and they asked me how you were holding up, so full of fake concern. I thought they were referring to the fact that you'd had the flu. I looked like a fool, Claudia."

"I'm sorry." *And this is exactly why I didn't tell you. Because I knew I'd get some kind of lecture, not support.*

Her face suddenly softens. "You haven't heard from him at all?"

"He won't return my calls. It's like he doesn't even exist anymore."

My mother tightens her lips together as she shakes her head in disbelief. "How could he do this to you just days before the wedding?"

Finally, some concern for me! "I don't know."

"You must know something," my mother insists, her expression going hard again. "A man doesn't simply up and cancel a wedding without a reason."

I swallow. Bite my lip to keep from blurting out something nasty. Then say, "Everything was fine between us. I have no clue why he did this. That's also part of the reason I didn't say anything. Because his decision was so…irrational. I kept expecting to hear from him, thinking he'd tell me he had cold feet. But I was planning to talk to you about it today because I think…I think it's time to cancel the wedding," I finish with difficulty. I can't believe I'm actually saying this. "Or postpone it. We've got to tell people something, because right now I'm not sure it's gonna happen."

"I'm going to have a talk with Avery Hart," my mother says sternly. "There's a lot of money invested in this wedding. If Adam thinks he can cancel like this, he's going to have a very big bill to pay. Whatever your problems, there's no reason you can't work them out."

I want to tell my mother that she shouldn't bother calling Adam's mother, to let me deal with this—but maybe that's what Adam needs. A firm talk from his mother or father could have him seeing the error of his ways.

I know—that's a pathetic thought. But I love that man. And I'm hurting here.

"And in the meantime, I'll start making calls." My mother wanders to the sliding doors off the dinette and looks out at the sprawling backyard. "The day was supposed to be perfect. Look at what Dick did with the garden. The flowers are spectacular." She sighs with chagrin. "I hope you two work this out, or this will be such an embarrassment."

Thanks, Mother, for always making me feel so much better....

"No one wants this wedding to take place more than I do," I point out.

My mother whirls around to face me, her eyes narrowed with suspicion. "And you're sure you didn't have an argument? No sort of fight that led up to this?"

"I'm sure, Mother."

"Have you tried going to see him?"

"Um, no. I figured he wanted space, and I didn't want to pressure—"

"Pressure is exactly what he needs to see reason. You go to him. You talk to him. Tell him how much you love him. Don't let Adam slip through your fingers."

"I will, Mother." I have to get away from her, or I'll be popping cyanide pills before I know it. "And I guess there's no time like the present."

Her mouth curls in an ear-to-ear grin. "Maybe I should hold off making those calls."

"I'll talk to him and let you know how it goes, okay? I'll see you later."

"Oh," my mother begins, forcing me to halt. "Dinner will be at five sharp, in the formal dining room. I hope you have good news by then. I certainly don't want to have to tell your sister about this." She sighs wearily. "First her marriage fell apart, now you might not even make it down the aisle…"

I start walking backward. "Later, Mother."

I'm rolling my eyes the moment I start to turn around. Sometimes, I just need my mother to be a mother. Hold me against her chest and let me cry. This is one of those times.

Apparently, that's too much to ask for.

When I reach the door to my adjoining apartment suite a few moments later, I hear the phone ringing. I throw open the door and charge inside. I snatch up the receiver without looking at the call display. "Hello?"

"Claudia, it's Lishelle. I'm glad I caught you."

"Hi, you." It's so nice to hear her voice after dealing

with my mother. I lean my butt against the kitchen counter. "What's up?"

"Did you get my message yesterday?"

"No. I...I was depressed. I haven't checked my messages since we got back Sunday night." Only my caller ID, and with no calls from Adam, I figured what was the point?

"I'm not sure if you know this already, but the latest story in the newsroom has to do with Adam."

"My Adam?"

"Uh-huh. Apparently a check to some charity in Macon bounced. Some kids were supposed to go to Disney with their families and got quite the surprise at the airport."

"What?"

"That was my first reaction, and I thought for sure there was some mistake, but the story's true."

"How could it have bounced?" I ask. "The charity is very healthy. The last fund-raiser brought in close to two hundred thousand dollars."

"I don't know how it happened but it did. I tried to reach you, and I even called Adam, but he hasn't gotten back to me. We're running the story at six o'clock."

"Oh my God." How can this be happening? And despite the fact that Adam hasn't been in touch with me since his bombshell, the first thing I think is that he must need me now. "There's no mistake?"

"Afraid not," Lishelle tells me. "I was kinda hoping you'd know what was going on."

"I have no clue. Like I said, I can't imagine how this story could be true."

"I did reach the charity's spokesperson, and she says there was some kind of clerical error. But it doesn't look good that Adam isn't speaking, and the children's families in Macon are very upset. I think the media is going to have a field day with this one."

Why didn't he call me? I wonder.

"Hon, I've got to run right now, but if you find out anything, please call me at the station."

"Thanks, Lishelle, for letting me know." God knows I didn't want to hear about this by watching the evening news.

As soon as I hang up with Lishelle, I call Adam's home number. He doesn't answer. I block my number and then call his cell.

"Hello?" He answers almost right away, and sounds impatient.

Oh my God—he picked up! "Hey," I say softly. "It's me."

"Oh. Hi."

"Baby, I just heard about the kids in Macon. What is going on?"

"I don't know, Claudia. It's messed up. There's obviously been some mistake, but the media is acting like we deliberately set out to screw these kids over."

"Where's Charles?" I ask. Annelise's husband is the charity's secretary, and in charge of the books.

"Out of town on business, I guess. He hasn't gotten back to me." Adam groans. "Look, Claudia. I have to go."

"Oh. Uh—"

"We'll talk later, okay."

"You'll call me?"

"Yeah."

And then he hangs up, and I know he has no intention of calling me back.

The next morning, I know I have to see Adam. I watched the various news shows last night, and every one of them featured the story. Some made it sound suspicious that Adam had been unreachable, but apparently around ten last night, he finally made a public statement.

"Our charity made a promise to those children, and we will honor that promise," Adam said in a clip that's been replayed over and over. "Unfortunately, we depend on donations from the good people of Atlanta, and even when money is pledged to us, it's not always delivered when we expect it. I'm sure that's what happened here."

"What do you mean you're sure?" one reporter asked, and then there were a barrage of other questions.

Looking distressed, Adam held up both hands to quiet the questions. "I'll have more answers for you in a couple of days, but I assure you that we're working as hard as possible to get the money for these children. We will not let them down." He cracked a smile at the end of his statement, the kind of warm smile he uses to charm people.

It worked on at least some of the newscasters, because they made comments like, "There's no doubt that Adam Hart is an upstanding citizen. He gave up his career in law to run this charity," and, "I've met him, and he's definitely a nice guy." One newscaster went on to comment, "Maybe it's time for the people of Atlanta to open their hearts and their wallets and give more money."

The media certainly could have been harder on Adam, given the circumstances. Regardless, he's got to be stressed. Maybe there have been problems with the charity he didn't want to share with me, and he's been preoccupied.

Is this why he dropped that bombshell about canceling the wedding?

I drive from my parents' home in Duluth to Adam's place in Buckhead in record time. Before I turn off my ignition, I'm halfway out of the car.

My mother's words about talking to Adam and making him see reason sound in my head. But this visit isn't just about trying to win him back. It's about letting him know I'm there for him through thick and thin.

In sickness and in health.

In good times and in bad.

Till death do us part.

Adam's Mercedes is parked in the driveway, so I know he's there. I half expected to see a throng of media people here, too, but there was breaking news about a fire at some huge factory not too long ago. Maybe that's why Adam's been spared.

I inhale a deep breath, surprised at how nervous I am about seeing my man. And then I dig the key to the front door out of my purse.

But before I can find it, the door opens. All the air in my lungs rushes out of me when I see Adam with his arms wrapped around Arlene Nash's waist.

Arlene Nash!

Seeing me, his eyes bulge. Arlene quickly throws a surprised gaze over her shoulder and looks me dead in the eye.

And then her lips curl in a slow, victorious smile.

"Adam?" I manage to say.

He slams the door shut. I hear the bolt lock.

OhmyGodohmyGod!

I stand there like a fool for a long moment. And then I turn and run back to my car.

Chapter Twenty-Three

Annelise

"I'm sorry, Mrs. Crawford. This credit card has been declined, also."

My stomach sinks as I stare at the hotel clerk. "There's got to be some mistake."

"I've tried both twice," she tells me in a voice that barely hides her impatience.

I glance behind me. Three people stand in line, waiting for me to be done already. One man checks his watch in an obvious gesture of his annoyance. The woman clutching a baby looks as if she'll lose it if she has to spend another moment waiting in line.

"Since there's only one person working right now, I don't want to hold up the line." I force a smile. It's the middle of the day, for God's sake. One clerk! "I'll just, uh, get some cash and come back."

I don't meet anyone's eyes as I walk away from the front counter. I head to the right and the ATM. But then I change my mind and slip outside the door instead.

Screw it. I'll call Claudia and see if I can stay with her.

I ended up staying with my sister until this morning, but when she didn't come home last night, I decided this was my chance to escape. Between her sex stories and her bashing me for staying with Charles so long, I can't take much more of her.

I get in my car and drive out of the hotel's parking lot. A couple blocks later, I see a bank and quickly swerve to the right so I can turn into it. Considering something screwy is going on with my credit cards, I'll take out a hefty amount of cash to have on hand.

I opt for the ATM inside the bank, where it's cooler. I put my card in and input the figure of one thousand dollars, which I suspect is the daily withdrawal limit.

The machine spits my card out.

INSUFFICIENT FUNDS flashes on the screen.

Maybe I was wrong. Maybe this bank has a lower withdrawal limit. I insert my card again, punch in my PIN, and this time try to withdraw five hundred. But once again, the machine spits my card out.

INSUFFICIENT FUNDS.

"How can this be?" I ask aloud. This is the joint account I share with Charles, and the last time I checked there was over thirty thousand dollars in there.

I go over the whole process again, this time hoping to get the modest amount of one hundred dollars.

INSUFFICIENT FUNDS.

A prickly feeling sweeps over me.

Oh my God.

My knees give way and I falter backward. I land against the glass window and slump onto the ledge.

No, God. Noooooooo!

An older woman enters the bank, sees me and draws up short. She stares at me, clearly wondering what my problem is. If I'm a psycho, or distressed. I guess she decides I'm not a threat because she continues to the ATM.

When she finishes her interaction, she heads to the door. But she stops there and turns. "Is there something I can help you with, dear?"

I shake my head. I can't find my voice.

I sit there for only God knows how much longer. Three more people use the ATM, but none of those people utter a word to me.

If I weren't so completely shell-shocked, I would have had the good sense to get myself out of here instead of looking like some crazy person. But the reality of what Charles has done has left a hole inside me. I feel like my very life is ebbing away.

Charles denied me sex and intimacy for a year and a half. He made me feel as if there was something wrong with me. And then I caught him in bed with his law partner and he didn't even have the decency to apologize. Instead, he told me he loved another woman and that he wants out of our marriage.

Now he's withdrawn money from *our* account, leaving me *penniless?*

How dare he?

Shooting to my feet, I brush away my tears. No more feeling sorry for myself. I'm mad. Madder than hell.

Fuck Charles. Fuck the fact that I ever loved this man with all my heart. If he can do this to me, he doesn't deserve even one of my tears.

I stomp out of the bank and curse Charles all the way to my car.

I'll confront the slimeball at his office, where he can't avoid me.

I march into Hindenberg, Hoffman and Crawford, heading straight for Charles's office. Emily, the receptionist, smiles brightly when she sees me. "Hello, Annelise."

I don't say a word, but instead breeze by her to Charles's door. "Annelise," I hear her call out, "Charles asked not to be disturbed."

"I don't give a shit what Charles told you."

I pick up my pace, feeling like I'm some escaped convict in the law firm where my husband is a partner, instead of his wife. That's messed up.

A moment later, I throw open Charles's door. It bangs against the doorstop. As it starts to bounce back, I quickly slip inside and allow myself the pleasure of slamming it shut. I guess I expect to see Charles and Marsha going at it again, but instead I see him with three other well-dressed men.

Charles's stunned eyes meet my cold ones.

"Annelise—"

"I'm sure you're in the middle of a very important

meeting," I say, "but right now, I don't give a shit. And you shouldn't, either, if you know what's good for you."

The men exchange glances with each other, then look at Charles. I can see on his face he's weighing the pros and cons of what to do.

"If you want me to get into this right here…" I let my statement hang in the air like a dark storm cloud.

Charles pushes his chair back and stands. "Gentlemen, I'm sorry about this. But if you'll excuse me for a moment?"

When he reaches me, he takes me firmly by the arm and ushers me outside. "What the hell do you think you're doing?"

"Oh, you don't even want to ask me that," I shoot back. "You son of a bitch. You took all the money out of *our* bank account?"

He pauses only briefly before saying, "That's money *I* earned."

"You?"

"Well, let's see. Your little photography hobby doesn't pay squat. So yeah. It's my money that was in that account. Not yours."

"What are you doing?" I ask. "Hiding all your assets or something so you don't have to give me any money? What the hell has happened to you?"

Charles doesn't answer.

"You know what? I don't care about the money. You want a divorce so badly, give me my half of the house and let's be done with this already."

Dennis Hoffman exits the men's washroom and eyes us suspiciously. The moment he passes us, Charles lets out a loud groan. Then he takes me by the arm again and drags me down the hall. He ushers me into the men's bathroom and locks the door behind him.

"What are you thinking? You can't just come to my office like this."

"And you can't treat me as if we were never married."

"Can you keep your voice down? This isn't the time or the place. You need to let me contact you. You can't disrupt the office like this."

"Like I'm supposed to sit back and wait for you to call me?"

"Exactly."

I can't believe he has the nerve to expect me to be docile and conciliatory in this situation. "Have you called a Realtor, or shall I? Because if you're cleaning out our account, I'd say it's pretty obvious there's no reconciling our marriage!"

"You can call someone if you like. I'm not sure what you expect to get out of it."

"I'm going to get my half. That's our matrimonial house, you fucking cheating bastard!"

"A home you abandoned," he answers calmly. "Now, if you'll excuse me."

Now I'm the one to grip his arm. "Excuse me?"

"You heard me. You abandoned our home. It'll be a cold day in hell before you force me to sell it and give you half."

"You don't have a choice," I shoot back, but my voice wavers a little.

"Really? I wouldn't be too sure about that."

Charles is entirely too smug. Can he do this? Because

I left the house, can he really rob me of what's mine? Or is the bastard trying to scare me into submission?

"Fine—you want to be an asshole, I'll get myself a lawyer."

"Better be a damn good one," Charles shouts as I storm out of the bathroom.

I called an emergency meeting with Claudia and Lishelle tonight, so here I am, heading into Liaisons to meet them both just after nine o'clock. I'm glad they could meet me, because I've been driving around aimlessly half the day, not knowing where to go or what to do. I'm afraid to go back to my house in case Charles has changed the alarm code. Given what he's done already, I fear what he's capable of.

Claudia doesn't look much better than I feel when the host leads me to our table. She's nursing a Cosmopolitan. Lishelle has a glass of wine in front of her and besides appearing tired, concern clouds her beautiful face.

"Annie," Lishelle says. "Your message sounded so—"

"That fucking son of a bitch!" I exclaim before I plop myself down on the plush seat.

"Angry," Lishelle finishes.

"If I could smash his face into a bloody pulp with a baseball bat and get away with it, I promise you I would."

"Uh-oh," Claudia says. "Tell me you've turned into a psychotic maniac because you're taking drugs to make it through the day."

"I've turned into a psychotic maniac because Charles has turned into a motherfucking bastard!"

"Wow." Claudia gulps at her Cosmo. "He must have done something really shitty for you to be cursing like a trucker."

"I thought I was the one with the foul mouth," Lishelle comments. "Annie, you hardly cuss."

"I've been cussing something awful today." Something I didn't think I was capable of, given the way I was raised. But hellfires or not, I've discovered what a stress reliever it is to curse a blue streak.

"You sound madder than when you found out Charles was fucking his law partner," Lishelle comments.

"Because I *am* madder. I am pissed the fuck off."

"Let's get you a drink." Claudia gets the waitress's attention, someone I haven't seen before. I order a Cosmopolitan. It's a nice strong drink.

"Now," Lishelle says when the waitress is gone. "What the hell is going on?"

"Do you believe that scum-sucking pig cleaned out our account? Leaving me exactly zero?"

Lishelle gasps. Claudia giggles.

I stare at Claudia.

"Sorry. I don't mean to laugh. But I've been popping antidepressants since noon. I know you're not supposed to drink when you take them, but when you've had the day I've had..." She finishes her Cosmo and starts laughing again.

"Ignore her," Lishelle tells me.

"What's going on?" I ask.

"She's got some news of her own. Maybe it's something in the water. The men drink it and it turns them into world-class assholes."

"She talked to Adam?"

"I'll save that story for dessert," Claudia announces.

The waitress arrives with my drink, and before she walks away, I tell her that I need another one. Then I down the contents of the glass, wincing the entire time.

"Charles really cleaned out your joint account?" Lishelle asks. "I can't believe he'd stoop so low."

"He's a man," Claudia chimes. "They're hard-wired to stoop low."

"Tell me about it," I comment. "And it gets better. He pretty much implied that I screwed myself out of my half of the house."

Claudia's eyes bulge. "Okay, now that's low."

"Oh, yeah. You'd never think I was married to the guy. He wants to cut me out of his life like I never existed."

"Well, he can't do that. He's going to owe you big-time. He's the breadwinner in the family, and you're not in a position to support yourself."

"He says that because I abandoned our home, I'm no longer entitled to any money from it."

"That's fucking absurd," Lishelle blurts out. "It's got to be—right?"

The reality of all that's happened today hits me anew. "Oh, God. I can't believe this is my life. I need another drink."

The Cosmo I downed is warming my entire body, and I already feel the slightest bit light-headed. But the one Cosmo isn't enough.

It's not nearly enough.

"Where's that waitress?" Claudia asks, glancing all around.

"You have definitely had enough," Lishelle tells her.

"What happened?" I ask Claudia, who now has her tongue extended into her glass in hopes of catching the last dregs of Cosmo.

She looks beyond me. "Thank God."

It's the waitress. She's got two more Cosmos on her tray.

I sip my drink this time, knowing I'll need to go slowly with this one. Claudia sniffs at hers, then makes a face.

Lishelle drags the drink across the table. "I told you— you need to stop drinking."

Claudia drops her head onto the table and softly sobs.

I look at Claudia, who might just be out cold, then at Lishelle. "Someone needs to tell me what happened."

"Claudia saw Adam with Arlene Nash today. She was at his house, and they looked pretty cozy."

"And she's a rival socialite," Claudia chimes without lifting her head.

"So it appears the wedding is definitely off," Lishelle concludes.

"Oh, God. I'm so sorry, Claudia. Then again, maybe I'm not—if Adam's that kind of pig, you're better off without him."

"All that money, wasted. My parents won't be happy." Claudia lifts her head. "And you know what's really messed up? I went to his place to offer *him* a shoulder to cry on, after that story broke about the charity."

"What story?"

While Claudia lowers her head again, Lishelle fills me in on the story about the children in Macon who won't have their wish come true because the Wishes Come True Foundation screwed them over.

"How can that be possible?"

"According to Adam's brief statement, some kind of clerical error," Lishelle answers.

"Clerical error? That doesn't make any sense."

Lishelle shrugs, but her expression says she's skeptical of the story.

"I'd ask Charles about it—if he weren't being such a fucking prick."

Claudia whips her head up. Surprisingly, she reaches for her Cosmo and sips it. "I won't let him screw you over. I've got lawyers in my family. If you can't afford one, I'll help you out. You know I'll help you in whatever way you need to get what you deserve."

At Claudia's words, my anger turns to a deep, hollow sadness. I think back to the weeks before my wedding, and I want to cry at how stupid I was. "It won't work," I say, fighting my own tears now. "I won't get anything."

"Of course it will work," Lishelle assures me. "What you need is a man-hating lawyer who knows how to go for the jugular."

"You don't understand." And of course they won't. I'm overwhelmed with shame over what I'm about to admit to them, something I couldn't admit five years ago when I was getting married.

"Oh, Annie." Lishelle squeezes my hand.

"Damn him. I swore I wasn't going to cry anymore."

"Cry now—but get even financially," Lishelle tells me. "That's what you do."

"I can't!" Two women at a nearby table shoot a curious glance at me. I face my two friends and whisper, "I signed a prenup with Charles."

My confession leaves both Lishelle and Claudia dumbfounded.

"You signed a *prenup?*" Lishelle asks.

"He said he didn't want me marrying him for his money."

"But the firm's only started to do really well since you got married."

"He said he *might* be worth millions one day." Now I gulp my Cosmo, needing something to numb the pain.

"I'm lost," Claudia admits. "What prenup?"

"About five days before we got married, he produced this prenup agreement. I was shocked. We'd never even talked about one. He basically said he wanted to know that I loved him for who he was, and not his potential income. We were so in love, about to get married...I didn't even think of a possibility of getting divorced."

"He obviously did," Lishelle comments. "Or he wouldn't have made you sign a prenup just days before your wedding."

"Yeah, that sucks," Claudia agrees.

"I wish you'd told us," Lishelle goes on.

"What good would it have done?"

"We'd have made sure you didn't sign anything so ridiculous. Let's face it—you've been with him from the time his business started doing really well. Whatever he's earned, you deserve half of."

I shake my head with regret, wishing I could turn back the clock. "I won't get a penny. Unless..." My brain, despite being clogged with alcohol, starts to work. I remember something I'd long ago forgotten.

"Unless what?" Claudia asks.

"Unless Charles is making seven figures. I think there's some kind of provision in the prenup that states if he's making over seven figures, I'll get a six-figure settlement should we divorce."

"Then you have nothing to worry about," Lishelle tells me. "As a partner, isn't he making that much?"

I shake my head. "I'm not sure. I...I would think so. But even if he is, how can I fight him? It's going to take money—money I don't have. You'd think that because he was screwing around on me, he'd at least want to do right by me in the divorce."

"Honey, it doesn't work that way," Lishelle says. "Remember how David tried to go after me for support? The slimeball."

Anger brews inside me again. Never in a million years did I expect Charles to treat me this way, even if we were to split. But how good was he to me during the marriage? He rarely brought me flowers, rarely took me out for dinner, rarely spent time with me even when we were both home together. And it's not just that. Charles has got to be making big bucks, yet I'm suffering to keep my business above water. It's not that I haven't asked my husband for help. Every time I've broached the subject, he reminds me how much he has to pay the nursing home monthly to take care of his mother.

How hard off can a man be who drives a top-of-the-line Mercedes and wears expensive clothes? According to him, he's stretched to the limit financially, and I never questioned that.

But now...

"Something's not right," I say.

"Exactly," Claudia chimes in, sounding as if she's high. "You let me see that prenup. I'll have my uncle look at it, tell you if it's on the up-and-up."

I nod. But that's not what I'm thinking about. I'm thinking about the fact that Charles has cut off my credit cards and cleaned out our account. Lishelle's right. He's got to be worth oodles of money. Our house alone is over five hundred thousand.

So why leave me penniless? Out of spite?

Or, I wonder, is there something Charles is trying to hide?

Chapter Twenty-Four

Lishelle

I've had a fucking shitty week.

If all the drama my friends have been going through weren't enough, I've been having my own issues—with Glenn. The biggest problem—he hasn't called. *All week*. And he hasn't returned my calls. Until last night, that is.

Last night, before I got home, Glenn called and left a message. He apologized for being out of touch and said that he's been really busy with work, and that the company had him working the West Coast this week. But at least he promised he'd be in town tonight so we could have at least one night together this weekend.

That's why, despite the fact that I'm fighting a killer migraine, I'm lying on my bed, wearing the raunchiest black negligee I could find at Frederick's. I'm waiting. Have been for hours now.

Glenn's message said he'd be in town around seven. I rushed home, expecting to greet him. When I didn't find him here, I assumed he would arrive shortly. But it's now close to midnight and he's not here yet.

Another half hour passes, and I only barely sip on my wine. I haven't called him yet because I don't want to seem like the pathetic overly anxious girlfriend who doesn't have a life. But now, I can't wait another moment. I need to know if Glenn will be showing up, or if I should get some sleep.

I position myself on the edge of the bed and lift the receiver. I punch in his cell number. It rings and rings. Not even his voice mail picks up.

So I try his home number.

The number you have reached is not in service.

Odd. I thought I dialed correctly. But obviously, I misdialed. I punch in the number again.

The number you have—

My pulse quickens. I'm starting to feel uneasy here. I slam the phone down, then stare at it for a very long time. What the heck is going on?

I try Glenn's cell again. It rings and rings.

"Where the hell are you, Glenn?"

I call his cell one more time. One more time, it just rings.

My phone finally rings a little after six the next morning, and I snatch it up immediately. I pray it's the call I've been waiting for.

"Hello?"

"Baby, hi."

My eyes flutter shut as a slow breath oozes out of me. *Thank God.* "Glenn."

"I'm sorry, sweetheart."

"You were supposed to be here last night."

"I know. I'm so sorry."

"Please tell me you're on your way."

"Aw, baby. I wish I was."

"Glenn." My voice comes dangerously close to whining. "What's going on?"

"My schedule was changed, and I had to fly to Montana. The weather here has been awful. Part of the airport's flooded, and all the flights have been canceled."

"Then why didn't you call last night?" I'd almost forgotten what it's like to be in a relationship. There's not just the sex and the laughter. There's the worry and the fights.

"I didn't want to call until I knew what the deal was. Then it got too late."

"So you won't be in Atlanta today?"

"Afraid not. I really am sorry. If you only knew how much I wanted to see you last night. I whacked off at least three times."

That gets a smile out of me. "Where are you now?"

"Some shit hotel near the airport."

I nod. Then I frown. "Are you sharing a room with someone?"

"No."

"Then why are you whispering?"

"Am I whispering?" His voice rises marginally. "Habit, I guess. That and the fact that it's early."

"I guess."

"I didn't ask how your week was. Is everything okay? How's Claudia?"

"I've had a crazy week. Both Claudia and Annelise have drama with their men now. I feel like I just need to see you and hug you. Ya know?"

"I hear you." He pauses. "That's it—nothing else bothering you?"

"That's more than enough."

"True, true." He blows out a soft breath. "Listen, I've got to go."

"Hey, wait."

"I know—you love me. I love you, too."

"That's not what I was going to say. I was going to ask why your home phone is cut off."

"Huh?"

"Your home phone. I called and the number's out of service."

"Christ, you're kidding me."

"No."

"Must be one of the bills I didn't pay. I'm really bad that way. I travel so much, I often set my bills aside and forget them. I can't believe they cut off my phone though."

I shake my head. This is the same Glenn I knew ten years ago. "You've got to get organized."

"I know, I know. Things will be better when we're married. You'll see."

When we're married... Glenn's words should comfort me, make me feel blissfully happy like when he first proposed.

But they don't. I'm not sure why, but I can't quite shake the nagging feeling in my gut that something is wrong.

* * *

Hours later, I still can't shake the feeling. I find myself sitting before my computer instead of getting ready for brunch with my girlfriends. They're not expecting me, since Glenn's supposed to be in town, but considering he didn't show I plan to surprise them.

At my computer, I type in the search words "Montana weather."

Several Web site options pop up, and I click on the first one. According to this Web site, the weather in Montana is sunny. In fact, this Web site says Billings has been suffering a drought.

"Okay, so Glenn didn't say he was in Billings," I find myself saying out loud. "But does All-American Air fly to other spots in the state?"

I ponder the other cities to check, but after a moment I place my hands on the edge of the desk and heave myself away from it. My chair rolls backward on the hardwood floor. Damn it, I don't like what I've been reduced to. This is exactly the way I became with David, searching his e-mails and documents on the computer to see if I could find proof of his cheating.

I don't want to be that person again. I hated that person.

Go to the brunch. I force myself to my walk-in closet. The first thing that jumps out at me is a black Ann Taylor suit.

Black, like my mood. It'll do just fine.

I don't make it to the brunch. Instead I drive to Duluth and cruise through the Thornhill neighborhood, searching for the house where Glenn brought me to propose.

I pass lush green lawn after lush green lawn until I finally reach the house. I slow down in front of it, but don't turn into the driveway.

The For Sale sign is still up.

Inhaling a deep breath, I get out of the car. I make my way up the cobblestone walkway to the front of the house. The house is close to five thousand square feet, but despite its large size, it still has a homey feel. Making a funnel around my eyes, I peer inside. That grand staircase. The gleaming hardwood floors. I try to see the back of the house and the kitchen, but my sight is obscured by the staircase. I do, however, catch a glimpse of the floor-to-ceiling windows facing the impressive view of the lake.

"I want this house," I whisper. "I want this life. I want it with you, Glenn."

I call his cell number. No answer.

And then I dial another number, one that is also committed to memory. It's the number to Channel Four News, where I work.

A minute later, I've got Juan Cortez on the line. He works in the weather department on the weekend.

"Juan, hi. It's Lishelle."

"Hey, Lishelle. Why are you calling here on a weekend?" he asks in that sexy Spanish accent of his.

"I'm curious about something. The weather in Montana."

"Montana! Trust me, darling, you don't want to go to Montana. I went there once when I first came here from

Colombia, and there's nothing but cows and corn over there."

"Thanks for the warning, but I'm not planning a get-away. I just want to know about the weather. Across the entire state."

"Give me a moment."

Less than a minute later, Juan comes back on the line. "Well, Montana's hot right now. Brutally hot. It's been over one hundred degrees across the entire state. They're in the middle of a drought."

"A drought. You're sure about that? Because I heard something about some flooding—"

"Not a chance," Juan assures me.

"Thanks, Juan."

"No problem, darling."

I end the call and once again stare into the window of this gorgeous house I hoped would be mine. The house I hoped to fill with children with the man I love.

I wanted the fairy tale. But fairy tales don't exist.

You'd think that at my age, I would know that by now.

My years as a field reporter taught me to trust my gut. And my gut, on my drive back home, tells me there's something drastically wrong with this picture.

"Please, God," I pray, fearing the worst. I don't know why I didn't think of this before, but it's all I can think of now after seeing my dream house again.

Money.

Was I totally duped? Did I miss the signs?

Please, God. No.

It seems like days later when I finally pull up to my

brownstone. I charge inside and head straight for my office.

I open the drawer where I placed the checks for the line of credit.

The checkbook is gone.

HELL HATH NO FURY

Chapter Twenty-Five

Claudia

"Are you sure you don't want to go with me?" I ask Annelise. She's staying at my place for the time being, in one of my two spare bedrooms. I'm glad she's here. She's helping to keep me sane, given all I'm dealing with concerning Adam.

"I can't," she tells me. She's in the bathroom, slipping silver hoop earrings into her ears. "I *have* to go to the studio today. I'm broke as a joke and have to find a way to get more business."

"I hear you. Look, if you need some money—"

"You're already giving me a place to live."

"I know, but—"

"If I need anything, I'll let you know."

"All right." Annelise breezes out of the bathroom, and

I follow her to the living room. "I wish you could come. I'm not looking forward to one-on-one time with Chantelle."

"She was one of your bridesmaids. Aren't you two close?"

"You know how you have some friends you can't totally trust? That's Chantelle. She smiles to my face, and she's always polite, but I'd never share my deep dark secrets with her."

"Ah. One of those." Annelise heads to the door and slips into her sandals.

"You're off right now?"

"Yep. I can only imagine all the calls I'll have to return. At least, I can hope. God knows I need all the gigs I can get."

"Have a good day, sweetie."

"You, too."

I give Annelise a quick hug, then she's out the door.

I trudge into my bedroom to get ready for my trip to the gym. There's a huge part of me that doesn't want to go, because I don't want to face anyone who'll talk to me about Adam. But what can I do? Hide out at home for the rest of my life?

Forty-five minutes later, I enter the upscale gym in Buckhead, determined to show Chantelle and anyone else that I'm doing fine despite what Adam has done to me.

"Chantelle," I practically sing as I float toward her in the gym's massive foyer. We greet by air-kissing both cheeks. As usual, Chantelle looks stunning in her dark Gucci sunglasses and pink Baby Phat sweats. A multicolored Coach bag rests in the crook of her arm. Her long black hair is pulled back in a ponytail.

"How *are* you?" she asks, full of fake concern.

"I'm great," I lie.

"I almost thought I wouldn't see you today. Given everything." She pats my hand and whispers, "You know."

I straighten my spine. "Yes, Adam did me wrong, but life goes on."

"Wow. You're a better woman than I am. If John did that to me, I'd cut his balls off and shove them down his throat."

"Are we going in?" I ask her. I'm not in the mood to talk about Adam.

"Sure."

I start walking, and Chantelle falls into step beside me. "I have to warn you, I saw Arlene here," she says.

Now I stop dead in my tracks. How the hell does she know about Arlene?

"Uh-huh." Chantelle nods. "And I have to tell you, she's flashing this rock that's got to be four carats like she's the first woman to get engaged."

"What are you talking about?" I ask.

Chantelle finally takes off her sunglasses and meets my gaze head-on. "You *have* heard the news, haven't you? Of course you would. You wouldn't be the last to know."

"I have no clue what you're talking about," I tell her.

"Oh, God. Oh, no." She shakes her head ruefully.

"Chantelle?"

"I don't know how to tell you this. I only heard it last night myself, then about ten minutes before you got here

Risha called to tell me about some press conference that was on the noon news."

Do I have to shake the news out of her?

She links arms with me and walks me to the corner of the gym's juice bar, far from where the patrons sit. "Claudia, Arlene and Adam got engaged."

"What?" I shout the question, and everyone in the immediate area whips their heads in my direction. But I can't be cool at a moment like this, not with this kind of news.

"Risha told me just this morning. One of her friends saw Adam and Arlene out last night. It was a big deal because there were news cameras there and everything. I guess with that whole scandal about the charity and those poor, terminally ill kids!"

I want to ask "What scandal?" because the last I'd heard the situation was under control, but I'm more concerned about myself right now. I know, that's selfish of me, but this news is such a bombshell, I'm surprised I'm still standing as it is.

"Adam and Arlene are engaged? Are you sure?"

"I wish I weren't so sure. But Risha just watched the noon news and there was footage of a mini press conference right outside the restaurant last night. Adam and Arlene were glued at the hip as he announced their engagement. He also said that Arlene's father, the Right Honorable Arthur Nash, had come to the rescue of those kids in Macon. He's donated the money to send them to Disney."

The room is spinning.

"Claudia, are you okay?"

It spins faster and faster. I'm getting dizzy.

"Claudia?"

The next moment, my world goes black.

Chapter Twenty-Six

Annelise

It figures.

If I were in my office the last few days, I would get three or four serious calls. But because I was away, my answering machine is flooded with messages from people who are desperately looking for a photographer.

One of them needed a photographer for today, and was willing to pay double the price.

Of course.

"Hi, this is a message for Jessie Whitfield," I say when an answering machine picks up. "This is Annelise Crawford from Memories for a Lifetime. I'm returning your call about needing a photographer for a fall wedding. I'm back in the office today, so please give me a call at 555-3600. Thank you."

I drop my head onto the desk and groan. I can't believe I have twenty-two calls to return. I wonder how many of them have already found other photographers?

I clench my fists and bang them on my desk. "Damn you, you worthless piece of shit!" I scream at the top of my lungs. "You've ruined my entire life!"

I continue to pound my fists. Hoarse, angry breaths wheeze out of me.

"All I did was ask you out for coffee."

My head whips up so fast, it's a wonder I don't break my neck. Standing not more than ten feet from my desk is Dominic. Looking as gorgeous and coolly put together as ever.

And he's carrying two cups of Starbucks coffee.

"Oh fuck," I mutter. I brush away my tears and tuck my hair behind my ears. "How long have you been standing there?"

"Long enough to know you're having a really bad day. I figured since I hadn't heard from you, I'd come to you. With the coffee. Cappuccinos. Sweetened. I hope that's good."

"Um, sure." I make a show of straightening papers on my desk. "I'm sorry I didn't call you. I wanted to, but I, uh, lost your number." That's not exactly a lie.

"Ah," he comments, slowly walking toward my desk. "That happens to me a lot."

Oh, shit. He's looking at my ring. Now I feel really stupid. I might as well fess up.

"Okay, so I lied. I didn't really lose your number. I threw it away." I wiggle my left hand. "I'm married."

"I have a confession to make, as well."

"You're married, too? Is no man faithful anymore?"

Dominic keeps walking until he reaches the edge of my desk, where he rests his butt. He places a cup before me. "No, I'm not married, but I haven't been exactly truthful with you."

"Meaning?"

He lifts a card off my desk and examines it, though I'm not sure why.

"I'm interested in you, Annelise. And your husband. In your lifestyle."

Instantly, I'm on edge. I stiffen in my seat.

"I've watched you shop. You spent quite a bit at Victoria's Secret recently."

"What woman doesn't?"

"True, but here's the thing that doesn't quite jibe. This business isn't making all that much money. Yes, your husband's a successful attorney, but even with his salary, I'm not sure how you both manage to spend so much."

"I spent four hundred dollars on lingerie. Big deal. And who the hell are you? And what do you mean you've been watching me?"

He holds up a hand to pacify me. "I'm going to get to all that. And for the record, I asked you that question about spending money so I could gauge your reaction. From what I can tell, you don't know anything about your husband's side ventures."

"Please tell me who you are or I'm going to have to ask you to leave."

"I'm Dominic Bertucci. An auditor."

I stare at him, still not understanding.

"Right now, I'm investigating charity fraud. I've been watching your husband for a few months now."

"Lovely." Could my life get any worse? "So Sebastian probably isn't really your brother, and that's why he and his *fiancée* haven't been back to confirm me for their wedding?"

"No, Sebastian's really my brother. And he and Helen are getting married. And they do want to hire you. I asked them to hold off booking you until I'd finished my investigation."

Now my heart pounds feverishly. "You think—you think I'm funding this business with *stolen money?* Stolen *charity* money?" All at once, Dominic's words hit me. *Charity fraud.* Those children in Macon who didn't get their wish.

Is my husband really responsible for that?

"My belief is no. I think your husband has hidden the money elsewhere."

"Let me get this straight, because right now I'm really confused. You think my husband has been stealing money from the Wishes Come True Foundation."

"Yes."

"Oh my God."

"I'm probably crossing the line talking to you about this." He gives me a heated glance. "But my gut says I can trust you. That you'd never want to cheat children."

"Never!" I exclaim. "If Charles has done this, I had no knowledge of it."

"He's fixed the books, too. On paper, it looks like the money is going out to worthwhile causes, but when I dug a little deeper, I saw that there were two recipients that kept getting donations. They were dummy organizations. I got a tip saying the money really went to a bank out of the country. I'm trying to determine where."

"You're going to arrest my husband."

"I'm very close to doing that, yes."

"What does that mean?"

"I can't reveal the specifics of my investigation. But I am trying to determine how far-reaching this fraud is. Is there more than one person at the charity dipping their hand in the pot? Is the entire charity a fraud?"

"Of course it isn't. I've been to the fund-raisers. I've seen the children who have been helped by the charity. And are you *sure* about my husband? He's a very wealthy man, even if he *is* being an ass to me right now."

"Pardon?"

"Nothing." I sip the cappuccino, which is delicious. My brain is working again, and I can't help remembering that just a short while ago I suspected that maybe Charles was up to something. That he's always been evasive when it comes to the topic of money.

"Your husband might have been wealthy a couple years ago, but the firm has taken a substantial financial hit with that class-action lawsuit."

"Which should bring in a pretty penny any day now." And the firm will take its huge cut, leaving the rest to be spread among a large number of victims. I've never really liked that reality of Charles's job. He said he didn't, either, and that's why he felt it was important to give back to those less fortunate by way of volunteering on the charity's board.

"…husband hasn't told you?"

My head snaps up at Dominic's words. "I'm sorry. I zoned out for a moment. What'd you say?"

"I asked if your husband hasn't told you."

"Told me what?"

"The class-action lawsuit was settled about, oh, four months ago."

"What?"

"For far less than your husband's firm anticipated. Only eight hundred thousand dollars."

"*What?*"

"There were allegations of misuse, and fraudulent injuries—"

"But Charles didn't say a word. He said he's still working on the case."

"He's not."

"I don't believe it." But there's a lot about Charles that I would never have believed. He has cheated, he has lied. How far a stretch is it that he'd embezzle money, maybe because the class-action lawsuit was a bust?

"Oh my God," I suddenly say. "Marsha Hindenberg. She's the charity's treasurer, and one of the partners at the firm." Now my eyes fly to Dominic's. "They're having an affair. They could be in this together. She writes the checks to the dummy organizations, and he fixes the books."

"That's exactly my guess. Especially because of the affair."

"You knew about that?"

He nods.

"I wish you'd told me about it. I wish *someone* had told me." Is this why Charles and Marsha are together? Because of the money? Or does he really love her?

"For what it's worth, I'm sorry," Dominic says truthfully.

I meet his eyes. His gaze is steadfast on mine. An electrical charge shoots through me.

Disgusted with myself, I grab the coffee cup and down a gulp of the cappuccino like it's a shot of tequila. How on earth can I be feeling a sexual attraction for the man at a moment like this?

"Now that I've told you this," Dominic continues, "I'm hoping you'll be willing to help me."

"How exactly can I help you? And why on earth should I?"

"I know you're not living at your house anymore, and any man who could screw children out of charity money has got to be a son of a bitch. Sorry."

"No, don't be sorry. You've nailed his character dead-on."

"I'm hoping you'll help me because your conscience tells you you should."

"My conscience is telling me a lot of things right now." One of Dominic's thick, dark eyebrows raises at my comment. "I mean, with respect to my life. Not you." My face flushes. "What do you need me to do?"

"The true books have got to be somewhere. I'm guessing at your house."

"And you want me to search my place and find them for you."

"That'd be ideal, yes. And this time, we could meet somewhere decent. Maybe have lunch. And talk."

I eye Dominic warily. And, Lord help me, he's staring at me with that honest and heated look that has my vulva pulsing.

"Do you like me?" I hear myself asking. "Or are you simply using me to get close to my husband?"

Holy, where do those words come from? I don't recognize myself these days.

Dominic chuckles softly. "The truth? I like you. I liked you the first moment I saw you. Even if you are a married woman."

Not for long…

Clearing my throat, I push my chair back and stand. "I'm going to have to think about it."

Dominic rises, too. "I understand." He slips a hand into his blazer and pulls out a card. "Here, again, is my card. Try not to lose this one."

Chapter Twenty-Seven

Lishelle

The moment the phone rings in my office, I snatch it up. "Lishelle Jennings."

"Lishelle, it's Harlan Fisher. Claudia's uncle from Bank of Atlanta."

"Yes, hello." I've been waiting for this call.

"I'm afraid I have bad news."

Oh, God.

"Four checks were written from the line-of-credit account, each in the amount of two hundred thousand. Unfortunately, the checks have cleared. There's no way to put a stop payment on them."

"God have mercy."

"At this point, I'm afraid, the only recourse to get your

money back is civilly. Because you had his name on the account, you can't make the claim for fraud."

And the courts will think I'm a scorned lover out for revenge. I sigh wearily. "Thank you, Harlan. I'll take it from here."

The moment I hang up from him, I call Claudia's number. She doesn't pick up so I leave a message.

"Claudia, I'm coming over after work. Probably around eight. Since Annelise is staying with you, that's the best place to meet. If you guys have plans, cancel them. I need you both to be there. Something really awful has happened, I'm talking really serious here, and I need you two like I've never needed you before."

I replace the receiver and reach for my bottle of Motrin. I can't lose it. Not yet. I still have the six o'clock news to do.

At eight-ten, I pull into Claudia's driveway beside Annelise's car. Seconds later, I'm knocking on Claudia's side door. Just seeing the look of concern on her face as she opens it is my undoing. Emotion overwhelms me, and I'm normally so good at keeping my feelings in check.

"Oh, God." The tears fall freely as I walk right into Claudia's open arms. "I trusted him. I loved him. And he screwed me over. In the worst possible way."

"Shh," she coos softly. "It's okay."

"No," I tell her. "It's not okay. This is so not okay."

Annelise is suddenly there, reaching for my hand and giving it a supportive squeeze. "I'm so sorry. I hate seeing you like this."

"I hate seeing any of us like this," Claudia says. "And all because of the men in our lives. This is what we get for loving them." She pats my back, then pulls away from me. "Come in. Let's have a talk."

"Yes, let's," Annelise echoes. "But first, what would you like to drink? Claudia made some great margaritas."

"If it's got alcohol, I'll drink it."

I follow them into the house. Annelise heads to the kitchen, while Claudia walks into the living room. She drops onto the leather sofa, and I plop down beside her. I bury my face in my hands, thinking of the awful truth I must face.

Eight hundred thousand dollars.

Lord help me, I'm screwed.

"Here you go, sweetie." I look up at the sound of Annelise's voice. She's holding an extra-large tumbler filled with green-colored margarita.

"Thank you." I guzzle the drink, finishing off half of it.

"Tell us what's going on," Claudia says.

"You were right, Claudia," I admit sadly. "I should have been wary of Glenn coming back into my life. But I thought…he was older, more mature. Not out to play games."

"You still haven't heard from him?" Annelise asks.

I shake my head. I'm here because I need my two best friends, but I can't look either of them in the eye right now. I didn't want to tell them about my suspicions when I discovered the line-of-credit checks missing because I couldn't admit to myself that Glenn was only using me. But now…

"I haven't heard from him. And this is the worst, worst part of all. Remember I told you that I opened a line of credit to get money to invest in his business? You advised me against that, Claudia, and you were so right. Glenn wrote himself some checks. Eight hundred thousand dollars."

"Holy Jesus!" Claudia exclaims.

"I know. I didn't even know he'd taken the checks. I had no reason to suspect he had. But when he wasn't getting back to me, I just had this feeling. I looked in my desk, and the checks were gone."

Claudia shakes her head. "The pig."

"On the way here, I racked my brain trying to figure out how he got a hold of them. I haven't seen him since I went to the bank. And then it hit me. The weekend we went to Alabama."

I fill them in on the absolute worst part of my news—that I'll have to sue Glenn civilly because I had his name put on the account. And it's too late to put a stop payment on the checks.

"I can't believe he'd do that to you." Annelise's lips twist in distaste. "Then again, I can't believe Charles would lie to me the way he did. Or that Adam would fuck Claudia over in such an embarrassingly public way."

Last night, Claudia and Annelise filled me in on the latest. That Charles has most likely been embezzling money from the Wishes Come True charity along with his law partner, Marsha. And Adam... What a scum-sucking bastard he turned out to be.

"Honestly," I begin. "I think Adam proposed to Arlene to save his ass. You said Arlene has always been after him.

Saving his image in the media with that huge donation to his charity—wouldn't you propose to her?"

"That's what I said to Annelise. It's the only thing that makes sense."

"*Not* that you should take him back," I stress. "Hurting you the way he did, even if it was to save face, is the lowest thing he could have done."

"Believe me, I wouldn't take Adam back now if you paid me. What I want, though, is for him to realize that I was the best thing that ever happened to him and come crying back to me. That would make me feel...a helluva lot better."

"Like that's gonna happen," Annelise comments sourly. "Do you think Charles gives a shit about what he did to me, how he destroyed my life? And who knows—maybe before he'll even see justice, he'll be off somewhere in the sunny Caribbean, sipping margaritas with his whore and living off stolen money." She looks at her own drink and frowns, then places it on the coffee table in front of her.

"I, for one, want my money back. I don't want it—I need it. I put my house up as collateral for that line of credit, and I'll probably lose it."

We sit in silence for a while, each of us ruminating over our dismal situations.

"That auditor—he's convinced that Charles has the real books for the charity hidden somewhere. Maybe even in the house." Annelise snatches up her drink again and downs the last of it. "I can just imagine the look on Charles's face if I were to announce to him that *I* found them. The asshole probably thinks I'm too stupid, but boy, it'd be amazing to show him exactly who the stupid one is."

"You think the books are there?" Claudia asks.

"Who knows? But I can have a look."

"And give Charles his rot-in-jail card." My lips curl as my mind churns. "You know, that's not a bad idea. Heck, I work at a news station. It's not like I can't blow this story wide open if you find some evidence."

"And let Adam try and play innocent," Claudia adds. "Who cares if he knew nothing about the embezzlement. The motherfucker should have. He runs the damn charity." Claudia's eyes widen with delight. "Oh my God. Annelise—I think you're onto something here."

"You mean I should look for the evidence and throw Charles to the wolves?"

"No." Claudia shakes her head slowly. "Not just Charles. Charles and Adam."

Annelise bites down on her bottom lip, but it's not enough to hide her excited gasp. "You're really serious, aren't you?"

"You're damn right I am. Why should we be sitting here, drowning our sorrows in alcohol while Charles plans some exotic new life, and Adam smoothes over his image so he looks like he's nothing but upstanding? I could share a few shocking stories, let me tell you. From his interest in swingers' clubs to his dabbling in drugs, if people were to find out about the real Adam, there's no way he'd win a mayoral campaign. Hell, he'd probably have to hightail it out of Atlanta." Claudia claps her hands together and laughs. "Oh my God. It'd be perfect,

Annie. We *have* to do this. And when the shit hits the fan, Charles and Adam will know that payback is a bitch."

Claudia high-fives Annelise.

"I think it's doable." I can see Annelise's brain churning. "And we'll be doing the people of Atlanta—*and* the children—a service. Outing two slimeballs."

I watch Claudia and Annelise, all animated as they discuss this plan to get even. I feel their excitement. How nice it must be to have an avenue to get vengeance. I have no clue where Glenn is, and I can just imagine the long, ugly legal battle once I find him.

"What if people don't believe the stories about Adam?" Claudia suddenly asks. "What if they dismiss them as conjecture?"

"Hmm." Annelise looks pensive. "I hear you. Let me think." After a moment, she says, "Then we catch him in the act. Get him on film."

"How?"

"Uh uh uh." Annelise wags a finger. "Let me finish." She really is adorable when she's drunk. "My sister's a stripper, remember. And if Adam's as sexually motivated as you say, he probably won't be able to resist her. You find out where he'll be, we'll send her over there dressed like a slut…"

"Bingo, baby!" A burst of laughter escapes Claudia. "Oh, yeah. That'll work. If Adam paints himself out as Mr. Innocent, then the media—" Claudia looks to me "—can expose the pictures… Lishelle, what is it? You don't think we should do this?"

"No." I exhale harshly. "I'm just thinking about Glenn. Wondering if I'll ever track him down."

"You will," Claudia stresses. "We will. Whatever it takes, we'll find that asshole, and he *will* pay you back. If we have to beat his ass to make him do it, then that's what we'll do. Right, Annelise?"

"Absolutely," she agrees.

And I know they'd do it. There's no doubt my friends would do anything for me.

But I'm wondering now if there's hope of me ever finding Glenn. Or if he, like Charles, is planning an exotic new life far, far from Atlanta.

With my fucking money.

Chapter Twenty-Eight

Claudia

All night, I can hardly sleep for how excited I am.

I am going to do this.

Really do this.

A smile spreads on my face and I stretch my body, luxuriating in the eight-hundred thread count of the Egyptian-cotton sheets. Yeah, I'm going to do what Adam asked me to—put on a strap-on and fuck the shit out of him.

I'm so high, I practically float out of bed. In my en suite bathroom, I look at my reflection in the mirror. Thank God, the bags under my eyes are fading because I finally got a decent night's sleep. And the dull ache in my head that's been there for days is gone.

I have a purpose. A positive way to expend my energy so that I don't go slowly mad.

There's no time like the present to put my plan into action.

A short while later, I'm showered and dressed in an outfit deliberately chosen to reflect an upbeat mood. I'm wearing a cute white leather skirt I picked up at Fendi, a silky black top and flip-flops adorned with a crystal-studded flower. I look good, and I look happy. And I am happy. So happy that I'm humming (yes, humming!) as I exit my bedroom.

"Annelise?" I glance around, but I don't see her. I hope she hasn't left already. I want to talk her. Maybe even get some breakfast before we head off on our respective quests.

"Annelise?"

I walk across the living room and knock on her bedroom door. "Annelise?"

"Come in," she calls out.

"You haven't changed your mind, have you?" I ask as I open the door.

She's brushing her long mane of blond hair. "Are you kidding? I haven't slept this well since all this crap happened with Charles. I *have* to find those documents. And it's not just about getting even—it's about doing the right thing for the charity."

"Well, for me, it's all about getting even!" I exclaim, laughing.

Annelise laughs, too. "Trust me, revenge will definitely be sweet."

"You want to get some breakfast? We could go to Li-aisons. Or somewhere else. I don't have to be at the spa until—"

"Actually, I'm not sure I can eat anything. I'm excited and nervous and I don't think I can put anything in my stomach until after I go to the house."

"I got you." I pause. "You want to come to the spa with me? For some moral support while I spill the beans to Risha and Chantelle?"

Annelise strolls toward me. "I was kinda thinking I'd head to the house now. Get it over with. But if you want me to go with you—"

"Naw." I wave off the suggestion. "I'm just—"

"Having second thoughts?"

"God, no." I take a deep breath. "I'm nervous, I guess. Like Risha and Chantelle will figure out that I *want* them to spread the word about Adam. But I don't think I have to worry about that. They love gossip. And, sad to say, but you've got to have that catty edge when you're gonna spread gossip, and Risha and Chantelle fit the bill."

"Things will be fine," Annelise assures me. "Plant the seed, and watch the flower grow. If you can call what's gonna grow from this a flower."

"All right." I hug her. "Before I meet Chantelle and Risha, I'm heading to the bank to talk to my uncle. See if there's not something he can do for Lishelle. Wish me luck—with everything on my plate."

Annelise hugs me. "Good luck."

"And good luck finding the charity's books," I tell her. "Hopefully by the end of the day, we'll both have good news to share."

* * *

When I meet Risha and Chantelle in the lobby of the spa, they're also decked out in hip designer fashions and look as cute as I do. Three Black-American Princesses dressed for the spa.

"Oh, Risha. Love the shoes," I say of her gold-colored strappy sandals. "Jimmy Choo, right? Their new summer collection is to die for."

"Yes, darling. And look at you. All cute and perky."

"Thanks." I do a quick twirl, taking a little pleasure in the fact that I look the coolest today. "Shall we head in, ladies?"

I lead the way to the receptionist and tell her that we have an appointment for three for pedicures and manicures.

"And it's my treat today," Chantelle tells me as we take a seat in the waiting area. "After all, tomorrow's your birthday."

My birthday. I'd almost forgotten all about it, with everything that's going on in my life.

"The big three-oh," Risha chimes. "It's all downhill from here, baby." She laughs.

"No, don't say that. I'm actually looking forward to being thirty. I'm healthy, happy and have a lot to be grateful for."

"Amazing," Risha comments.

"What—that I'm still counting my blessings after all I've been through?"

Risha nods. "Yeah, I guess." She looks around, then adds in a hushed tone, "I hear Arlene's planning a wedding for the fall."

I shrug nonchalantly as a hostess comes to take us into the spa. We get to our feet and follow her.

"Sometimes, things happen so you can be free," I say as we walk. "You don't know it at the time, but you can look back and see where you're much better off than you were before."

"I know you're trying to be strong," Chantelle says, "but you don't have to be. We're your friends. You can tell us how you really feel." Her voice, I think, rises on a hopeful note.

"How I really feel?" I repeat.

Risha nods. "Mmm-hmm."

Before I can answer, we are each ushered into our seats at tables side by side, and introduced to our manicurists. But the moment the women start to work on us, I feel Risha's and Chantelle's eyes from both sides of me.

"If you want the truth," I begin, "I'm kinda relieved."

"How can you say you're relieved?" Risha asks. "You were supposed to be getting married this Saturday!"

"I know that. But…"

"But what?" they both ask in unison.

How easily they take the bait.

"If I tell you something, do you promise not to repeat this to anyone? Not one soul?"

"Of course," they assure me.

"Adam…as much as I loved him, there were some things I found out about him that I knew I'd never be able to deal with."

"Like?" Chantelle asks.

"Like…he was into some freaky stuff."

"What kind of freaky stuff?"

I turn to Risha. "Freaky sex stuff."

Her eyes widen. I nod.

"How freaky?"

"Like sex-club freaky," I answer in a hushed voice. "Not that I ever went with him to one of those places, of course, but he asked me to. About a month or so before our wedding date. He asked me if I'd go there and have sex with another couple with him!"

"No!" Both my friends gasp. I notice that Jolly, my manicurist, eyes me curiously.

"I told him no, absolutely not. I'm not into that! Then, one night when I was waiting up for him, he came home smelling like he'd just come from a club. He was high—something else he's been doing a lot lately—and I got pissed. I asked him where he was. He'd missed a meeting with our wedding planner. You won't believe what he told me."

"What?"

"He told me that he went to a swingers' club. You know, the kind of place where people have group sex." Again, I lower my voice, but not low enough that nosy ears can't hear. "That that's where he'd spent the evening. I got angry, threatened to call off the wedding right then and there. But he swore to me a friend brought him there as a surprise, as a sort of pre-bachelor party stunt, and that he just watched. He told me all kinds of freaky stuff he saw. Like guys kissing other guys. Group sex. Women giving guys blow jobs in plain view of everyone." I shudder. "I was disgusted—and even more disgusted when he told me that it turned him on! That he wished I was there so we could have had sex in front of all those people!"

Risha snorts, then rolls her eyes. "That's so gross."

"I know. And I told him that. But he said he thought it could be…exciting. Liberating."

"And what did you say?" Chantelle asks.

"That I never wanted to hear him suggest anything so vile ever again. He apologized and swore he wouldn't give it another thought. But…"

"But what?" both my friends demand at the same time.

I sigh, as though it's really hurting me to tell this part. "I've already heard from someone close to me that Adam was spotted at this seedy strip club where the dancers are known for having sex with the patrons. This was just a few days ago! When I heard that, I thought 'Good riddance. Arlene can have him!'"

"Wow." Chantelle shakes her head. "I had no clue he was like that."

"Neither did I," I say sadly. "Just goes to show, you can be with someone for years and not really know them. I'm so glad I found out about him *before* the wedding."

"I think you're right to write him off," Risha tells me.

Chantelle says, "And quite frankly, I've never liked Arlene. If she suffers through a few years of hell with him, it will serve her right for all the stuff she's done to hurt people over the years."

I chuckle at that. I can't say I disagree. "After everything that's happened with Adam, I can't believe I was ever going to marry him! What kind of man proposes to another woman after barely ending one engagement?"

"That speaks to his character, that's for sure," Risha comments.

"Exactly," I respond. "I mean, don't you wonder now

what's really happening with the charity? If there's not something fishy going on? With everything I've learned about Adam's character…"

I know that the manicurists and the other patrons in the salon are getting an earful today—just as I'd hoped. In fact, things are going according to plan so well, I have to try not to smile.

There's no doubt that the moment Risha and Chantelle get into their cars, they'll be calling friends, who will then call more friends, and so on.

But my work isn't done yet. I'm meeting two other friends who were bridesmaids for lunch, and after that, I'm off to the gym.

I give it until eight o'clock tonight before the word about Adam's dirty secrets spreads through our community of friends.

Chapter Twenty-Nine

Annelise

Once a week, a professional cleaner comes into our home to give it a thorough cleaning. It's always on a Wednesday, and always during the hours when Charles is at work. To make it simpler for her, we gave her a key, and she knows the security code for our home.

Katya is my key to getting into my house today.

Even if I'm nervous as hell at the prospect of doing it.

My Jetta parked in the driveway, I grip the steering wheel and count to ten. Katya's Sunfire is here, so I know I can get in.

"Just do it," I whisper. "Get out, walk to the door."

I open my car door. A shaky breath oozes out of me. God, why am I so nervous? I'm still married to Charles. This is still my house.

My legs wobble as I walk to the door. I turn the handle.

It's locked. And I'd bet my last dollar that Charles changed the locks.

I reach for the doorbell but think better of that. Katya's going to wonder why I don't just use my key.

I quickly scan our front porch. There's a huge potted plant. Not the greatest choice, but I heave it into my arms nonetheless and bring it to the door. Then I use my nose to ring the doorbell.

It takes Katya a good minute to get to the door, at which point I'm sweating from holding this freaking plant so long.

"Annelise!" she exclaims. "My goodness. Let me help you with that."

"No, I got it." I huff and groan as I stumble across the threshold. But once inside the house, I can no longer hold the plant. Katya helps me ease it onto the floor.

"You should have put it down until I got to the door. You're going to break your back."

"I know… I wasn't thinking." I take deep breaths and look around. "Wow, the place looks great. Smells great, too."

"Thank you."

"Are you almost finished?"

"Upstairs, yes. Downstairs, no."

"Ah, I see. Well, don't let me keep you. I'm gonna try and figure out where I should put this plant. Maybe right here in the foyer, for now," I add with a laugh.

Katya shrugs. But thankfully, she heads off in the direction of the kitchen.

I run in the opposite direction, to Charles's home office. I disappear into the room and close the door.

I waste no time going to work. I open desk drawer after desk drawer and rifle through papers. My eyes frantically scan to see something out of the ordinary. Not just the charity books, but something I can use to help my cause. Like a bank account number, because I'm sure Charles is hiding money from me and will try to screw me in the divorce.

I search for anything but find nothing.

I pause to look around the room. There's a sixteen-by-twenty-inch photo of Charles on the west wall, framed in beveled glass. I always thought it was tacky.

But tacky or not, there's a safe behind that framed photo.

I carefully take the picture down from the wall, hoping to hell I don't break it. As I stare at the wall safe, I think. Think about what the combination could possibly be.

I try his birth date. Doesn't work.

I try our wedding date. Doesn't work.

I try my birthday. Again, that doesn't work.

I bang on the safe. "Open, damn it." I know Charles keeps cash in there. But short of going at it with a power saw, it's unlikely I'll get it open now.

I head back to the desk. This time, I go through it more carefully. And this time, I notice something *beneath* the hanging folders.

It's another folder. The tab reads, "Mortgage."

Bingo.

I flip open the folder. Inside is the deed to our house. I quickly scan it. Only Charles's name is on it.

Jerk, I think, remembering how he told me that with my financial history, it would be better to have just his name on the deed. I have no doubt that even then, he was thinking about the day he would screw me over.

I don't know if it's going to help me to have this, but I'll take it anyway. On second thought, I decide to make a copy of it on the office color copier.

The copy in the folder, I fold and stuff the original into the back of my jeans, beneath my shirt.

Satisfied that I've found all I'll find in the office, I replace the picture, head out of the room and up the stairs. The deed is helpful, but I need to find the books for the charity, and hopefully information about an offshore bank account.

The more I thought about Dominic's bombshell, the more I realized that Charles probably is hiding money out of the country somewhere. I remember the sudden business trips where he came back with a tan. I'll bet the asshole is hiding money in the Caymans.

Once inside our bedroom, I close the door. My heart is still beating out of control. Charles shouldn't show up at this hour—but what if he decides to come home on his lunch break?

I quickly rummage through his night table. Nothing out of the ordinary. I go through the closet, searching for secret papers hidden in pockets, shoe boxes. Anywhere.

Damn. I see nothing.

Where can the papers be?

I search his drawers, look at every scrap of paper. Why is there nothing here?

Defeated, I sit on the edge of the bed and bury my face in my hands. What am I doing wrong?

The bed, a voice says. *Look under the bed.*

I drop to my knees and lift the skirt on Charles's side of the bed. I sigh with relief when I see a shoe box.

I pull it out and flip through the contents. I don't see anything incriminating, but I do see something that piques my curiosity. It's a brochure with a picture of several boats moored in a bay framed by picturesque mountains. Big, cursive letters boast the name LOS SUEÑOS. Beneath that reads, Resort and Marina.

I flip open the brochure. "The Bay Residences are an exclusive enclave of thirty waterfront condominiums," I read aloud. The night shot of an illuminated infinity pool is to die for. I scan the rest of the text and see the words *Costa Rica's Central Pacific Coast.*

Costa Rica!

All of a sudden, I remember a few months back, walking in on Charles in his office practicing Spanish from a cassette. He'd said he was simply broadening his horizons by learning a second language.

Son of a bitch. It all makes sense now.

I had heard that Costa Rica was a new hot spot for Americans. Apparently, it's the new hot spot Charles is interested in.

"Got you, asshole."

Still on the floor, I slip my hand between the mattress and the box spring. I don't feel anything, but maybe there's something beyond my reach.

I shove the mattress off the bed. It bangs into the night table and sends my lamp crashing to the floor.

"Shit," I mutter. I do a quick sweep of the box spring and don't see anything.

"Mrs. Crawford?"

Katya's voice nearly scares me out of my skin. I whirl around to see her standing in the doorway. Then I glance at the mattress half pushed off the bed, and the drawers in disarray.

I can't imagine what she's thinking.

"What's going on in here?" she asks.

I have no clue what I'm doing when I march toward her. "I found a box of condoms in Charles's drawer," I find myself saying. "Are you having an affair with my husband?"

"W-what?" she sputters.

"Are you?" I demand.

"Of course not! I would never!"

"You're fired, Katya. Right now."

"But Mrs. Crawford—"

"Leave right now, Katya. I'll see to it that Charles sends you your final check."

Katya starts to sob. "Please, Mrs. Crawford. I need this job."

My heart is ramming hard against my chest wall. "Fine. I'll leave. But make no mistake, I'm going to talk to Charles about this—tonight!"

I leave a stunned and distraught Katya standing outside my bedroom door as I charge down the stairs. When I sail through the door, a smile erupts on my face.

"Costa Rica, here I come."

I'm driving along I-285 when my cell phone rings. I dig it out of my purse.

"Hello?"

"Annie! Where the hell did you disappear to?"

It takes me a moment to realize who it is. "Sam?"

"Yes, it's me! One minute you were staying with me, the next you were just gone."

"Sam, that was a week ago. You only now noticed that I left?"

"Ugh," she groans. "Last week was insane. I was seeing this guy, and staying at his place. For the first time in a long time, I actually thought I was in love. But he was screwing another dancer behind my back. Do you believe it? One minute he was in love with me, and a week later, he was cheating on me. That's why I don't trust men. I dumped his ass this morning." She finally takes a breath for air. "But what is going on with Charles?"

"A lot," I tell her. "He's not just cheating on me, he's cheating the charity he volunteers for. And I'm pretty sure he's got property out of the country. In fact, I have to go to Costa Rica as soon as possible."

"Costa Rica?"

"Yeah. But the bastard's left me penniless." I groaned. How the hell could I afford to leave the country? "I'll call one of my friends, see if I can borrow some money to get a flight tomorrow."

"Uh, hello? What about me? I've been wanting a reason to go to Costa Rica for a long time. You know I love me a hot Hispanic man."

"I thought you just had your heart broken."

"What better time to take a trip?"

"Sam, you're not serious."

"Of course I am. And don't worry about the money. One of the perks of my job is that I've always got lots of cash on hand."

"Well," I began, "maybe you can just float me some cash—"

"Uh-uh. I want to go."

"Sam, you are not going to Costa Rica with me."

"Why not? It'd be fun. We hardly spend any time together. It'd be nice to do a sister trip."

"But this trip isn't about hanging out. I've got business to do."

"I'll help you."

"Charles might be there. I called the office and they said he's out of town. Again. And his slut, too." I shake my head, thinking of how long he's been planning this behind my back.

"Then you're gonna need me. For support."

Samera might just be onto something. Maybe I will need her. What if I get into trouble and Charles tries to hurt me? Being in Costa Rica alone, no one would ever know what happened to me.

"You really want to come with me?"

"I want us to be closer," she says softly. "We don't hang out the way sisters should. This trip…it could be good for us."

Her words touch me, more than I expect.

"And I speak some Spanish. One of my boyfriends, Paco, taught me some stuff."

"I can only imagine what he taught you!"

"There's this thing guys do in Cuba, with a papaya. They teach the young men how to perform oral sex on a woman. Apparently, the shape and feel of a sliced papaya—"

"Okay," I say, stopping her. "Too much information." But I'm laughing. A papaya as a tool for teaching oral sex. Who knew?

"Can I come with you?" my sister pleads.

"Are you near a computer?"

"Yeah."

"Then start looking for flights to San José, Costa Rica. Even tonight, if there is one."

Samera squeals, excited. "We're going to Costa Rica! We're going to Costa Rica!"

"Stop singing and check the computer. Then call me back."

"You got it."

Chapter Thirty

Lishelle

I spend a miserable few days moping around not only my home but the office. It's so bad that before I go on the news at noon on Wednesday, my station manager has to pull me aside and ask if everything's all right with me.

It isn't, of course, but I don't tell Linda that. "I'm fine," I lie.

Linda closes the door to my office behind her. "I know you're not fine. And I'm not stupid. I've noticed that you're not wearing that huge rock anymore."

"I'm sure everyone's noticed."

"Glenn, right?"

I nod.

"It's pretty obvious to me that he's broken your heart.

But you can't let him get to you, Lishelle. You're beautiful. Intelligent. You have a lot going for you. You'll meet
a decent guy."

"That's the last thing I want to hear."

"I know. But remember when Martin broke my heart?
Announced after five years of marriage that he wanted a
divorce? I let it eat away at me for months, not knowing
he was doing me a favor."

"I'm not sure what you're getting at."

"I don't want you to spend months letting this suck the
life out of you. Just be happy things ended now if they
weren't going to work out. Trust me, you're far better off."
Linda shrugs. "And if you need to make a voodoo doll
and stick it full of pins, go ahead. But please, remember
you have a life outside of this guy. I'm only saying that
because I know what I went through, and I know how
much it hurts."

Surprisingly, Linda's words make me feel better.
"Thank you," I say.

"You're welcome. Now get to makeup. You go on air
in thirty minutes!"

A couple hours later, Linda's words are still with me.
And I realize how right she is. Glenn took a lot from me,
more than he ever should have, but I can't let him take
any more.

If he'd just broken my heart, that'd be one thing. But
he had to take my money, too.

After leading me on in the worst possible way.

I shouldn't be moping—I should be pissed. Pissed
enough to take action.

Hell hath no fury like a woman scorned.

Glenn's about to find out just how pissed off I am.

A short while later, I walk purposefully into Ruben Santiago's office. Ruben is known at our station as "The Man." You need someone found, and Ruben can find him. Provided the person isn't hiding in a monastery in Tibet under an alias—although Ruben did track an AWOL slumlord down in Mexico City once. That feat won him a broadcaster award for excellence in investigative journalism.

Needless to say, I trust that if anyone can find Glenn, Ruben can.

Ruben's face lights up as he sees me. He's a mix of black, Irish and Spanish. His skin looks like he has a permanent tan, but the long, kinky hair he always wears in a ponytail shows his African-American heritage.

"Lishelle, sweetheart," he says as he rises from his desk. "You're looking fabulous, as usual."

"Thank you, Ruben." He never fails to make me feel special. But his flirting is always harmless. A good thing, since he's only about five foot four and I'm not physically attracted to him. He's married though, something else I'm happy about, because I believe Ruben's one of the good guys. He deserves a decent woman.

"What's happening, Ruben?"

"Nothing much. What's happening with you?"

"I need a favor, babe. And you're the man for the job."

"All righty, then." Linking his fingers, he stretches his arms, then moves his head from side to side. "I always knew one day you'd be ready for me."

I laugh. "Oh, I'm ready all right. Ready for you to find someone."

"What you got?"

I hand Ruben a piece of paper on which I've written Glenn's full name, plus his birth date. I also list the phone numbers he gave me, even though they're both disconnected now.

"This is a Phoenix number," Ruben comments.

"Right."

He nods. "Piece of cake."

"How long, do you think?"

"Probably by the end of the day."

Excitement fills me. "Really?"

"If not, then I'm slipping. But if not today, then early tomorrow. You sure this is his real name?"

"Yeah, and I don't expect that wherever he is he's using an alias. He's just trying to hide from me." I smile sweetly.

"I pity the fool."

"Oh, you should."

Ruben winks at me. "I'll get right on this."

Nearly four and a half hours later, when I've just finished the six o'clock news and I'm back in my dressing room, there's a knock on my door.

"Come in," I call.

Ruben opens the door and peers his head inside. "I wanted to catch you before you got out of here."

"You found him?" I ask excitedly, sitting straight up in my chair.

He kisses me on the cheek as he hands me an envelope. "Everything you need to know is in there, babe."

"Oh, Ruben." I throw an arm around his neck. "You're the best."

"So my wife keeps telling me."

"You hang on to her. And don't do anything stupid to mess that up."

"Honey, please," he says in a tone that implies he knows he'd be a fool to screw up a good thing.

When Ruben's gone, I open the envelope. There are five printed pages in there. The first one lists Glenn's name, date of birth and social security number. It goes on to list his current address and contact information, as well as his employer.

The second sheet has DMV information, and I see that Glenn was charged once with DUI as a minor in Indiana. Beside that information, Ruben has written, *Charge was expunged.*

But it's the next page that catches me off guard. Winds me as surely as if I've been kicked in the stomach.

It's a marriage certificate.

I don't even look at the woman's name. I quickly scan the next page to see if it's a record of divorce. Instead, it's a record of where he went to school.

But the page after that delivers the knockout blow. Children. Glenn has two of them. According to this printout, two boys ages three and five.

Oh. My. God.

"He's married! The son of a bitch is *married!*"

Why on earth would he propose to me if he's already married to someone else?

But I don't even have to think about this one. As painful as it is to admit, Glenn was using me. Traveling to Atlanta as often as he did, he clearly knew I'd made something of myself. He wanted to get his hands on some cash and saw me as a way to do it. I wonder if he really wants to open a charter-plane business, or if that was a lie, as well.

I'll bet it was a lie. I can't believe a friggin' word he said to me.

The jackass probably faked his orgasms.

I flip back to the marriage-certificate page. Glenn apparently got married six years ago in the state of Arizona.

Son of a bitch!

Maybe Glenn and his wife have separated, I think. *Maybe he didn't want to tell me he was married because of how it would look...*

No sooner does that thought come to me than I want to shoot myself. Why am I even trying to make excuses for him? If he were separated, he could tell me that. He wouldn't have had to come up with some whole other scenario to pretend he was free and available.

I scan the marriage certificate. The woman's name is Tess Baxter. Tess...Tess... Why does that sound familiar?

And then it hits me. The woman Glenn told me he'd been engaged to. Her name was Tess. Tess, who had a couple of kids and was married.

I have to laugh, it's so pathetic.

Fucking prick.

I debate what to do as I drive home.

I could get on a plane and head right to Phoenix— confront Glenn, and even his wife.

Oh, I could give Tess an earful. Tell her exactly what

her husband has been up to. How he ate my pussy and made me come nonstop. How he proposed to me like I was the only woman in the world for him. How it was all a ploy to get at my cash.

Surely if I tell the wife all of this, Glenn will be throwing my money at me faster than I can blink.

But what if Glenn is married to the type of woman who will allow him indiscretions—as long as he always goes home to her? That's entirely possible. What if she knows about the scam and encouraged it? With some women, you just don't know what they're capable of doing to keep a man in their lives. Women who become partners in crime when otherwise they would never have done anything against the law.

And what if she's nothing like that? What if she's sweet and caring and I'll devastate her world by showing up on her doorstep? Quite frankly, she deserves to know—but should I be the one to break it to her?

At home, I go over the possibilities in my mind the entire night. I'm still torn in the morning when I'm driving to work. I think about Annelise and Claudia and how they're planning some delicious revenge. They deserve no less. Let's face it—they were both screwed royally. Above and beyond the typical breakup.

Glenn has done the same to me. And while I'd love to get my money back, I'd also love some serious payback. To make that motherfucker fear *his* world is falling apart.

I'm almost at work when an idea hits me. Oh, God. It's perfect.

Glenn's a greedy bastard. And I know exactly where to

find him. If I dangle some bait for him, he's as sure to gobble it up as a fish going after a worm.

But is it ethical?

Not entirely, but neither is what Glenn did to me. And maybe it'll be exactly what I need to do to get him to give me back the money he's stolen from me.

Yeah, I think, smiling for the first time in a long time. *This could be perfect.*

Chapter Thirty-One

Claudia

I throw my head back and laugh at the wicked idea Lishelle has just shared with me. "Lishelle, that's *perfect*."

"You don't think it's a little…unorthodox?"

"And stiffing you for nearly a million-dollar loan *is* orthodox? I say hit Glenn where it hurts. And the harder the better."

Lishelle and I are at my place, this time sipping apple martinis and watching season one of *Sex and the City*. It's just me and her, because Annelise is apparently in Costa Rica. I came home yesterday to find a note from her saying she was catching a red-eye there with her sister. Which means she's missing my thirtieth-birthday celebration and the new recipe for Cosmos I decided to try.

I have to say, I'm really getting good at mixing drinks.

I guess that's what you do when your love life falls apart—find another passion.

My passion, right now, is getting revenge. One month ago, I didn't think I'd be capable of doing anything to destroy Adam's life, let alone anyone else's. But I'm a different person now. My pure and endless love for him has been tainted. It's a different beast now, one I can't control.

Adam has stolen a part of me. A part I won't get back by just walking away and hopefully finding love again.

Fuck love. I don't want love. I want revenge.

"You think it will work?" Lishelle asks.

"Glenn will fall for that as easily as he falls for pussy."

"That's what I think. But how do we do it?"

"How do you get Glenn to dirty his hands with charity money? Oh, Lishelle. That's so fucking perfect, really. And maybe easier than you think."

"How so?"

"You don't need to get someone to meet Glenn and dangle a carrot in front of his face. We can take care of the dirty details with a little creative bookkeeping."

Lishelle gasps as her eyes light up with excitement. "Oh, you might be right. Make it *look* like he took charity money."

"Exactly. When Annelise comes back from Costa Rica, hopefully she'll have the charity's books. Maybe you could say the line of credit was a donation for the charity? That'd get *lots* of attention."

Lishelle slowly shakes her head. "Everyone will wonder why a newscaster took out that kind of loan to give to a charitable cause. Yeah, I inherited some money when my father died, but not enough that I'd be that generous."

I sip my apple martini. Damn, it's good. This might be my new drink of choice.

"Okay, so we don't even mention the money he took from you. We stick to saying that Glenn's taken charity money. Whether or not Annie finds the books, that's the story we can leak."

"Without proof?" I ask. "What if my station manager wants proper documentation?"

"You're right," I say after a moment. "That could be a little suspect. Can you get his signature on some papers?"

"He's hiding from me, remember."

My head spins a little. I've had too much to drink. I'm not even sure what I'm saying anymore.

"I don't think we need his signature, and I don't even think we need the books. Glenn had his picture taken at that fund-raiser, remember?"

Lishelle eyes me skeptically. "Yeah."

"Bear with me. This will all make sense in a second." I drink the last of my martini, and have to pause a moment to collect my wits. "Photo op. Okay. We get the pictures from the event, leak those to the media, point out that Adam was my man, Charles is Annie's husband, and Glenn was your fiancé. Not only did they screw us over, they screwed over the charity. They were all in cahoots. Get it?"

"Maybe," Lishelle says, but doesn't sound convinced.

"In reality, it's not *if* you're guilty—it's if you *look* guilty. I say we fix the books, roll with the story and give Glenn the chance to come clean by returning his share before he's brought up on charges. This isn't the time to worry about being ethical. Glenn sure as hell didn't give ethics a second thought."

"You're right about that."

"The moment the scandal breaks, just mention Glenn's name. Then call him up privately with the chance to save his ass by returning your money. If not, tell him he'll face jail time. Two can play his bullshit game. But you'll be better at it."

Lishelle laughs and stomps her feet, she's so excited with the idea. "I *love* that. Blackmail his ass. That's fucking amazing. Remind me never to cross you."

My laughter dies as I get wistful. "Girl, I love you with all my heart and soul. There's no way in hell I'd ever do anything to hurt you. Just as I know you'd never do anything to hurt me."

"You can say that again."

"I just don't get men. You give them the best of you. Give them your very essence, and they abuse that. Screw you over like they didn't care one bit how much you loved them. Honestly, I don't get it."

"Fuck them. I for one am through looking for love. I'm successful. I have a life. I don't need a man."

"Don't need one, but it'd be nice to have one."

Lishelle nods. "That's true. But what if we never have the kind of love we want—deserve? Are we supposed to settle? I'd rather grow old and gray sipping Cosmos with my girlfriends than settle for some lame-ass man who's going to put me through the ringer again. Aren't we having a great time here, me and you, sipping these fabulous apple martinis for your birthday?"

"And plotting revenge."

"And plotting revenge. We're having a great time."

"We are...but to never be with a man again? What about sex? Let's face it, a vibrator will only go so far."

"Women can get sex anywhere, anytime they want it."

"Meaningful sex?"

"Did you really have meaningful sex with Adam? Did I have it with Glenn? They lied to us. Nothing was real about what we shared with them."

That's a hard pill to swallow, but I know she's right.

"And I know women want kids, but single moms exist, and they survive, and they probably have a hell of a lot less headache because they don't have men in their lives."

"That's a scary thought. But God, I think you might be right."

Lishelle downs the last of her apple martini and reaches for the pitcher to pour another one. Her eyes are a little red and her speech is slurred. She's clearly tipsy. She always has these philosophical conversations when she's tipsy.

"Wanna watch *How Stella Got Her Groove Back?*" she asks.

"After this whole anti-men talk?"

A mischievous smile plays on her lips. "What can I say? If Taye Diggs were to walk through that door right now, you'd have to fight me for that pretty ass of his."

"So you still do believe in love," I say.

"Hell yeah, I believe in love. Glenn may have stolen my heart and my money, but I'm not gonna let him steal that from me, as well."

"I couldn't have said it better myself." I force my butt off the sofa and to the pitcher of apple martini. I refill my glass, then clink it against Lishelle's. "Here's to imagining that both of us—and Annelise, too—find a man as hot and sweet as Taye Diggs in this movie."

"Screw that." Lishelle clinks her glass against mine. "Here's to getting your birthday wish. Revenge. Sweet revenge."

I smile. "I'll definitely drink to that."

Chapter Thirty-Two

Annelise

My life feels like a whirlwind of action right now, and I suppose it is. Last night, only hours after finding the Costa Rica brochure in Charles's belongings, Samera and I took a red-eye flight directly from Atlanta to the San José airport. God bless her, she charged the outrageous last-minute fee to her credit card and said I don't have to pay her back. She said she was looking for adventure. I will, of course, pay her back. As soon as I get my share of the house in our divorce settlement.

Provided all the proceeds don't have to go toward repaying the money Charles stole from the Wishes Come True Foundation.

The early-morning sun has fully risen now. I glance at my watch. Two minutes after eight. Our plane landed at quarter to six, an ungodly hour. I should be sleeping but I'm not. I guess adrenaline and caffeine are keeping me going.

Samera and I are in the back seat of a taxi. We've been driving through winding, mountainous roads that will take us from the center of the country to the Pacific shore. We have a room booked at the Marriott resort in Los Sueños, which we learned is right beside the real-estate property featured in the brochure I found.

Beside me in the back seat, Samera's eyes are closed and she's snoring lightly. I've been too wired to sleep, though I did snooze a bit on the plane.

It's amazing what five and a half hours on a plane can do for a relationship, because mine and Samera's has improved dramatically. I can't believe how much we laughed! I can't believe how much *I* laughed at her scandalous stripper stories! Before, we used to spend so much time disagreeing over each other's lifestyles that we didn't spend much time being friends. But all of that is so unimportant in the grand scheme of life. If stripping makes Samera happy, so be it. I just don't want her hurt.

Just as she doesn't want me hurt.

Which is why she's here with me on this trip. And I love her for that.

I gaze out at the landscape. Lush is the only way to describe it. The mountainside is a sea of green leafy trees. It's stunningly beautiful. And terrifying. The sudden need to swerve on this narrow road could send us careening down the mountainous slope. A slope that, from where I sit, is very steep.

And lethal.

Don't think about that. Think about your mission. Think about finding the charity's books, exposing Charles and getting on with your life.

God, I'm so tired.

Despite all the excitement of the day, my eyes flutter shut, and sleep finally claims me.

"Okay, now *this* is a piece of paradise," Samera exclaims an hour and a half later when our taxi pulls up in front of a stunning and posh-looking hotel. It's painted a vibrant orange and has lots of archways. It's like a grand Mediterranean villa. Already, I wish I were here on vacation and staying a while. With a man who is so hot for me, he can hardly keep his hands off me.

"I'll check in," Samera announces. "You get the luggage." A bellhop heads toward us, smiling widely, and Samera lets out a low whistle. "On the other hand, why don't you check in, and I'll stay right here."

I open my wallet and peel out some bills. "You have to ask the taxi driver how much we owe. You're the one who speaks some Spanish, remember?"

"Oh. Right."

"Help with your luggage, ma'am?"

"I'm no ma'am," Samera replies, smiling coyly at him. I shove a hundred dollars into her palm. "The driver." Samera scurries off to deal with the driver.

To the bellhop I say, "We don't have much. Just these two small suitcases."

"I will help you."

"Thank you."

"Is this your first time in Costa Rica?"

"Yes."

"*Bienvenido.*" He grins.

"*Bienvenido,*" Samera replies as she stands beside me. "That means 'welcome.'"

"That much I do know."

We follow the bellhop through the main archway into the hotel. I glimpse the ocean through the archway on the opposite side of the building. It glitters beneath the sunlight. To the right, there's a massive, elegantly decorated lobby with comfy sofas in different sections. I expect that the bellhop will lead us through this lobby to the front desk, but we stop at a desk between the bank of elevators and the sofas.

"Name on the reservation?" the bellhop asks.

"Peyton, Samera. *Miss.*"

A moment later, the bellhop passes us an envelope, in which there are two keys to our room. Talk about a speedy check-in. Our room is on the third floor, with an ocean view.

"I could move here," Samera announces as we head to the elevators.

"How do you know that? You've hardly seen any of the place."

"Are you kidding me? Look at the mountains. Smell that ocean air. And the brochures I picked up mention waterfalls and zip lines and all this great outdoor stuff. So much more exhilarating than the boring crap in Atlanta. And there's surfing. I can just imagine all the hot bodies riding those waves…"

The first thing I think is that Samera has a one-track

mind. But then I think, so what? Maybe I need a bit more of her spunk and spontaneity in my life.

"Well, we can come back one day," I tell her. "After all, I'm pretty sure my husband owns property here. Maybe I'll get it in the divorce settlement," I add, smiling sweetly.

The elevator doors open, and we get on. Samera yawns. "I'm definitely ready to zonk out."

"Me, too. What a long flight."

"But we're here now, and soon we'll get the info you need to nail Charles."

I look at her and smile softly. "Thank you. For being here with me. It means a lot."

She squeezes my hand. "I know."

I wake up to the smell of eggs and bacon.

"Rise and shine, sugar," Samera sings.

I open my eyes. She's wearing a white robe from the hotel and her damp hair is hanging around her shoulders.

"Am I dreaming, or is that really breakfast?"

"It's breakfast. And it's delicious."

Though my head feels like I've got cotton balls for brains, I force myself to a sitting position. "A plate of turd would be delicious right now, that's how hungry I am."

I yawn, stretch, then climb off the bed. In a flash, I'm at the table where the tray of food is.

"I've already been downstairs," Samera tells me while chomping on crispy bacon. "Honestly, this place is incredible. You should see the pool! There are five different sections to it, and they all connect, even though they look separate. You can swim under walkways, there's a waterfall…"

"You've been swimming already?"

She shakes her head. "No, I just did a walk-around while you were sleeping."

"You got more rest than I did, that's for sure. How do you sleep so well on a plane?"

She doesn't answer. She's eating. I pick up a fork and wolf down some eggs. No taking my time. I'm starving.

"I can't wait to check out the pool," I tell Samera. "After I go to the condos. I'm not sure how I'll find out which one is Charles's."

"More good news. Downstairs, just outside the main entrance, there's a bunch of shops. There's a neat little coffee shop—apparently, the coffee of choice here is Café Britt."

"And?" I prompt.

"And, there's also a real-estate agency beside the coffee shop. It's specifically for the Los Sueños condo properties. I'm betting that if Charles bought something here, the people in that office will know about it."

"Sam!" I throw my arms around her.

"It's a small office, too. There was only one person there when I went in. I can't imagine more than three people working there, period. So the agents will have to know who Charles is, or can at least look up his purchase."

"I can't believe it. We're so close."

"We sure are."

We eat for a while in silence. I swear, these hash browns have got to be the best I've ever tasted. I wash them down with some freshly squeezed orange juice.

"Hopefully, we'll find the file by this afternoon, then we have some time to explore. Head to Playa Jaco," Samera says, feigning a Spanish accent.

"Where's that?"

"Just down the road. The concierge said there are lots of great restaurants there, and great shopping. Hot men."

"The concierge told you there are hot men there?"

"No," Samera replies slowly. "But I figure there's got to be. We're in Costa Rica, baby."

I playfully roll my eyes. "It's always about the men with you, isn't it?"

"Is there anything else?"

"You should ditch the wig," Samera tells me an hour later as we're heading to the real-estate agency.

"I like the wig."

"It's tacky."

"I feel better in it."

"In case, what—you run into Charles? If you do, he's gonna know it's you. No one else here knows you."

I sigh wearily and turn to face her. "Why do you get dressed up as a dominatrix instead of just walking on-stage naked? Because you're playing a role. That's what I'm doing—playing a role. Okay?"

"Ah. Okay."

I pause to get up my nerve to go inside the office, but Samera forges ahead, opening the door. She's already greeting the man inside when I step across the threshold.

"Hello, again," the man says. He takes Samera's hand in his and kisses it.

"This is the woman I was talking about," Samera tells him. "My sister."

What? You told this man about me?

"Oh, hello." The man smiles brightly as he offers me his hand. "It's nice to meet you, Mrs. Crawford."

"Likewise." *Samera, what did you do?*

"My name is Miguel Santos, and I've been expecting you."

"You…you have?"

"Yes. Your husband called."

I swallow. "H-he did?"

"Of course, it was when I stepped out of the office for coffee." Miguel rolls his eyes. "When I returned, there was a message from your husband. He mentioned you would be arriving later this week, and he wanted me to give you a key in case he was off golfing. Or fishing. I have to say, he's really enjoying the community here."

"I'll bet," I mumble.

"I got the impression, from his message, that you were arriving tomorrow."

"Ah, right. Um—"

"We decided to come a day early," Samera interjects. "My sister and her husband are such lovebirds, they can hardly stand to be away from each other."

"Ah, I see."

I chuckle awkwardly.

Samera snatches my purse from my hand. I shoot her a look that screams, "What are you doing?"

"Your husband did not tell me how beautiful you are," Miguel comments.

"Why, thank you." I blush as Miguel holds my gaze. The flirt. "You're too kind."

"Here they are," Samera coos, showing Miguel my

wedding picture. "When she was a blonde," she adds, chuckling, and I nervously finger my wig. "So in love. And this place is so romantic. I can only imagine what they'll be doing together later."

I clear my throat.

Miguel crosses the room to a large desk, and behind his back, Samera flashes me a victorious smile. I give her a two-thumbs up.

Miguel turns. I whip my hands behind my back.

"You are going to love the unit. Three bedrooms, two bathrooms. Whirlpool tub. A Jacuzzi on the balcony. A beautiful view of the ocean. And of course, there's the marina where you can moor your boat."

"I'm so excited." I'm all bubbly and animated, sickeningly so, but I have to sell this. "So you have the key?"

He lifts a key ring off the desk from which dangles a single key. "Right here."

"Do you know how to get there?" Miguel asks.

"Not really," I admit, hoping he doesn't realize I'm not who he thinks I'm supposed to be.

"I would take you there, but I have to stay in the office. Let me give you a map and show you the route."

"Is it far?"

"It'll take only a minute to get there if you're driving. Maybe five if you're walking."

"Wonderful."

"But your husband is not there now. His message said he was off for lunch with a friend."

"Oh, great." I clap my hands together. "I'll get to surprise him! I just love when I get to surprise him."

"What did I tell you—they're *so* in love."

A minute later, I have a key and directions to the condo that Charles purchased.

Easy as pie.

"You didn't tell me you spoke to Miguel about me!" I say to Samera when we leave the office.

"I wanted to surprise you."

"You could have at least prepared me."

"Relax. It all turned out okay. You've got the key."

I inhale sharply. "You're right. You're totally right." I pause. "What'd you do when you went in there? How'd you get the info?"

"Miguel's a man. I simply worked my charm. By the way, I have a date with him later."

"What?"

"Don't look at me like that. He's totally hot."

I shake my head. "I thought *we* were going to spend time together once I find the file."

"We will. We're all going dancing at a club in Jaco. He's going to teach me how to salsa. I told him Charles will come, too, but obviously he won't be there. I couldn't blow your cover."

"Great, a third wheel."

Samera suddenly looks around. "Do you hear that? Is someone calling your name?"

"Charles!" Panic washes over me.

And then I hear it. My name. But it doesn't sound like Charles's voice.

Miguel?

I turn. And oh my Lord, my heart stops.

Dominic!

He's jogging toward me from the direction of the hotel lobby.

"Dominic?" I say lamely. Of course it's him.

"Hey." He breathes in and out heavily, slightly winded. "I saw you from the lobby, and was pretty sure that was you." His eyes sweep over me. "The wig's a nice touch."

Feeling a tad self-conscious, I run my fingers through my faux-black strands. Dominic seems slightly amused as he looks at me—or is that lust I see in his eyes? Or maybe it's me who's feeling lustful.

I can't help eyeing him from head to toe. He's dressed in khaki shorts that reveal his muscular legs, and a white polo shirt. And man, he looks sexy.

Do not get distracted! My eyes fly to his. "What are you doing here?" I demand.

"Saving your ass," he responds.

"My God, you're determined. You actually followed me here? To Costa Rica?"

"Hi, I'm Samera." Samera offers Dominic her hand.

"I got here on my own," he answers while shaking Samera's hand.

"I don't believe that. This is too much of a coincidence."

"I found out through my sources that Charles had left town. I confirmed with his secretary that she booked a ticket for him to Costa Rica. Then, I learned that Marsha is planning to come here on the weekend, and I knew this was it. I had to make a move before I lost them forever."

"When did you get here?"

"Yesterday," he tells me.

"How do you know this guy?" Samera asks.

"He's the investigator I told you about."

"Ahh. You're right. He's a hottie."

One of Dominic's eyebrows shoot up.

"Sam, please—"

Now Dominic faces Samera. "She said I'm hot?"

"Oh, yeah. She said you were the hottest guy she'd seen in a *long* time. That she—"

"Sam, *shut up!*"

"Interesting," Dominic comments.

"Why is that interesting? Ugh, why do I care? It's obvious your only interest in me is my husband."

"Is that what you think?"

"Uh, yeah."

"Well, you're wrong. I want to find him, naturally, but that's not my only interest in you."

"Should I give you both a moment?" Samera asks.

"No."

"Yes."

Dominic's gaze locks on mine. We stare at each other for a long while.

"Is that the key?" he asks me. "The key to the condo?"

I shove it in my purse. "That's none of your business."

"Don't be rude, Annie. The guy's not being an asshole or anything. And he's cute."

I shoot Samera a gaze to silence her.

"Listen, about saving your ass," Dominic begins. "I wasn't kidding. Charles is in the hotel."

I dart behind a palm tree. "What?"

"He's eating lunch. And he's with a woman."

"A woman?"

"Young. Pretty. I figure he'll be occupied for a while."

"A prostitute," Samera supplies. "I saw this documentary once, about how rich white Americans love to come here for the underage prostitutes."

Just last week, the mere thought that Charles could do anything like that would have made me cry. Now I can't help but laugh. "Not my problem anymore. It's Marsha's." And boy, does the bitch deserve it.

My stomach lurches as I feel a sudden sense of urgency. "Hey, if we're going to do this, we need to do it now. While he's occupied. Before he decides to be occupied in his new condo."

"You're not doing this without me," Dominic announces.

"Why not?" I ask.

"For one—an extra person to help out in a situation like this is critical. Two, I have a car. And three, you owe me."

"Oh, I owe you? How do you figure that?"

"Because the woman your husband is with—she *is* a prostitute. One I hired. She's slipping Charles sleeping pills as we speak."

A burst of hard laughter escapes Samera. "I love this guy."

Dominic stares at me, waiting for my word.

I frown at him, even though inside I'm feeling relieved, and happy that he's here. "All right," I say. "Let's go."

Chapter Thirty-Three

Lishelle

I've decided there's only one way to deal with Glenn, and that's to force him outside of his comfort zone. That comfort zone being the bed he shares with his wife at five in the morning. My hands sweat as the phone on the other end of the line rings. On the third ring, someone picks up.

"Hello?" a woman says, her voice groggy.

"You must be Tess."

A pause. "Who is this?"

"Oh, I'm Lishelle. A friend of Glenn's. Actually, an old ex. We go way back. In fact, we got reacquainted recently when he called me up in Atlanta. Is he there?" I finish in a sugary tone.

There's the sound of a hand covering the phone's

mouthpiece. I hear, "…for you…Lishelle…calling here at this hour?"

Glenn comes to the phone. "Lishelle, hi." Then, "She's from the office in Atlanta."

"…said she was an ex-girlfriend."

Glenn clears his throat. "Has there been a change with the schedule? Because I've taken the week off."

"Yeah, I know. That's why I'm calling you at home."

"Mmm-hmm."

"I know, you're wondering how I found you. But you're forgetting that I work for one of the biggest networks in the country. Our researchers can find anyone."

"Uh-huh."

"I'll make this easy for you. My money—you need to return it. Immediately. Because if you don't, there's a story here that's going to break on the weekend about the theft of funds from the Wishes Come True Foundation, and thanks to a little creative bookkeeping, the money you stole from me looks like money you took from the foundation."

"Oh."

"Yeah." I can't help sounding smug. "Of course, if by the end of the day all the money you stole from me is deposited back in my account, I'll do my part and keep your name from the story. If not…"

"I won't be back until next week."

"Not my problem. Get your ass out of bed with your wife and go to the bank. Immediately. Because Glenn? I not only have your phone number. I have your address. And your cell number. And your wife's cell." I pause to let the reality sink in. He must feel as awful as I did when

I realized my checkbook was missing. "Now, I know you could try and take off, but you wouldn't get far. You'd have to explain to your wife about me, and you don't want to uproot the kids."

I hear something like a gasp from Glenn.

"Yeah, I know about the boys. I can just imagine what a beautiful family you have. You do your part, and you won't fuck it all up." I sigh happily. "Now, shall I say goodbye to Tess?"

"I'll take care of it right away," Glenn says hurriedly and hangs up the phone.

Oh, to be a fly on the wall as he explains who I am to his wife.

Smiling, I replace the receiver on my night table, link my hands behind my head and plop backward onto my bed.

Even if Glenn does get my money to me today—which I have doubts he'll be able to do—his name will still be linked to the scandal. He deserves no less for everything he did to hurt me. The I-love-you-so-much lie. The I-want-to-spend-the-rest-of-my-life-with-you lie. The elaborate proposal in a house he knew he'd never share with me.

Oh yeah. I'm going to get the jerk, and good.

"Yes!" I punch a fist in the air. And then I laugh my head off.

Chapter Thirty-Four

Claudia

When I hear the incessant pounding on my door, a smile creeps onto my face. I'm pretty damn sure I know who it is.

I glance at the clock. Nearly 4:00 p.m.

A little later than I expected, given the rumors I heard at the gym earlier today.

Everywhere, everyone was talking about Adam and his appetite for raunchy sex. That and the fact that Arlene's already called their engagement off.

Oh, payback's a bitch, isn't it?

I place the bowl of popcorn on the coffee table and pause the DVD on the shot of Will Smith naked in the shower in *I, Robot*.

There's more pounding. I leisurely stroll toward my

foyer. I smooth out my skirt—one that makes my legs and ass look fabulous—and then swing open the door.

"Oh," I say, feigning surprise. "Hi."

Adam charges into my house. "What the fuck did you do?"

"Excuse me?"

"I'm getting calls. From everywhere. People who are saying they saw me with a *stripper?* And there are rumors flying all over the place about me going to swingers' clubs—"

"Someone must have seen you there. You really should be more careful."

"You couldn't just let me go, could you? You had to get vindictive."

"Letting you go would be one thing. Letting you humiliate me—" I wag a finger in front of his face. "Uh-uh."

Adam groans and he sinks onto my sofa. "Fuck. Now I'm hearing rumors that the Wishes Come True charity is corrupt. Money's missing. I don't know where the hell Charles is. Marsha won't return my calls. My life is falling apart. There's no way I can run for mayor now."

"And you're telling me this why?"

Adam rises from the sofa and walks toward me. "Because whatever you did, you need to undo it. You've got to fix this."

"I thought that's why you got with Arlene. To fix your tarnished image."

Adam doesn't say anything.

"How could you treat me the way you did, after I loved you so much?" Regret passes over me, but it's the only weakness I allow myself. Because I don't want Adam back, no matter how much I loved him. "And now you have the nerve to blame me for your problems?"

"I know you're the one behind this! You've been filling people's heads with lies!"

"Adam, your own actions are coming back to haunt you. Some things you just can't hide, no matter how hard you try."

He grabs me by the shoulders, gripping me hard.

"You're hurting me, Adam," I say coolly. "You don't want me screaming. My parents will hear me. And they'll call the police. And how will that look for your precious image if the police come here to arrest you?"

Adam stares me down, breathing in and out heavily. Angrily. Then he releases me as if he's been shocked by a live wire.

"Fuck you, Claudia!"

"Fuck *me?*" I glare at him. "No, fuck you, Adam! You brought all this on yourself. And I, for one, am going to enjoy watching you crash and burn. Now, get the hell out of my house."

Chapter Thirty-Five

Annelise

The moment that Dominic, Samera and I enter Charles's condo, we get to work. Samera heads for the living room, where she pulls out the cushions on the sofa. I make my way to the bedroom, where I start rifling through drawers. I work one side of the room while Dominic works the other.

Ten minutes later, we've found nothing. And I've checked under the bed and between the mattresses.

"The bathroom?" Dominic asks.

"May as well."

"I see nothing out here," Samera says.

"I know it's here," I say when I leave the bathroom.

"I checked the kitchen. The top of the fridge."

I shake my head. "Fuck."

"Maybe he destroyed them," Dominic says. "If he's not planning on returning to the States, maybe he figures he doesn't need them anymore."

"Charles doesn't throw anything away. He'll keep it, just hide it." I open the fridge. There's white wine, and orange juice, but nothing else.

No documents.

"You don't think Charles would hide them in the fridge?" Samera asks.

I ignore her and this time open the stove. And voilà— there's a file folder. I snatch it up.

I open it. "Yes, yes, this is it!"

"That's it?" Samera asks excitedly.

I scan the contents. I see numbers and figures and the title Wishes Come True Foundation. I flip through more pages and see the deal for the purchase of this condo.

Five hundred and twenty-five thousand dollars! Wow. I can't believe Charles's nerve.

When I flip to the back of the contract, my breath catches in my throat. There's a photocopy of the check Charles used to pay for this place. It has a numbered corporation listed in the top left-hand corner. And I know that the charity uses such a number.

"Oh, you son of a bitch! You are so fried."

Dominic reaches for the folder. "Let me see that."

"Not so fast."

"All right." Dominic backs off. "But you know I'm going to need that. Because he's out of the country, I'll need cooperation from the authorities here, and I'm going to need proof—"

"Everything you want is here—every piece of incriminating evidence. And I'll give it to you. Later. But right now, we need to get out of here. Wherever Charles is passed out, he could wake up at any moment."

I stuff the dirty evidence into an oversize tote I brought with me. And I have a photocopy of the certified check Charles paid to the Realtor that came from the charity's account.

As we head for the door, I do a quick sweep of the place, checking to make sure there's nothing out of place. Nothing that would put Charles off guard when he finally walks in.

Satisfied, I reach for the door handle. But before I can touch it, it starts to open.

It's too late for any of us to hide.

The door opens fully, and I gasp in alarm.

It's Charles.

My stomach drops as an intense feeling of dread spreads right through me. Oh my God...

Behind me, I hear Samera say, "Oh fuck." I don't hear a peep out of Dominic, but I don't dare to turn and look at him.

"Ann?" Charles asks.

What do I do, what do I do?

I square my shoulders and prepare to confront him. I'm not afraid of this prick anymore. Besides, I have backup.

But before I can say anything, Charles speaks. "Whatareyoudoing..."

He sounds weird. His voice is slurred, and he narrows his eyes like he's trying to concentrate.

"I'm leaving, Charles. And you're not going to stop me. You won't get in my w—"

Charles starts to move, coming at me, and all I can think is that he wants to squash me with his whole body for how fast he's moving. I scream and jump backward. Charles tumbles forward and grips the nearby column for support.

"I don't feel so good," he mutters.

"He's out of it," Samera says just as I realize what's going on. "Let's get the fuck out of here."

I don't hesitate a second. I dash through the door. Samera and Dominic follow closely behind me. We don't stop running until we're downstairs in the parking lot. I keep looking over my shoulder, expecting to see Charles sprinting after us, but there's no one.

"Start the car," I command. "We've got to get out of here before he realizes what's going on."

Dominic jumps behind the wheel of the Jeep while Samera and I hop into the back. The SUV jerks forward as Dominic tries for a hasty getaway. Soon, we're speeding off from the condos and toward the Marriott hotel.

Satisfied that Charles is nowhere in sight, I say, "Man, that was a close call."

Samera's nervous look morphs into a smile. "Holy shit, could it have been closer?"

"With the sleeping pills that prostitute gave him, I'm surprised he could even open his eyes before morning," Dominic comments from the front seat.

"All that doesn't matter now." I allow myself a victorious smile. "It's over. And we've got the goods. Yes!"

"Charles is going to wish he never messed with a Peyton," Samera chimes. "Oh, is he ever."

"I prayed I'd find this," I admit to Samera. "All the way here on the plane. And in the condo just now, when it seemed we were going to come up empty. I hope you don't think that sounds stupid. I guess old habits die hard."

"I don't think that's stupid. I'm not a religious freak, but I still believe in God."

"I'm Catholic," Dominic announces, clearly wanting to be part of the conversation.

I crack a smile as I look at Samera. "High five, sis?"

Samera squeals happily as we high-five each other.

"I'm going to want a copy of everything in that folder, for my own purposes—like my divorce—but otherwise, you can have it."

Dominic is flipping through page after page while nibbling on lukewarm fries. We're all gathered in my room. "This is damning stuff. Exactly what I was after."

"You could sell this story to Hollywood, it's so juicy," Samera says.

Dominic lets out a loud sigh as he closes the file. "I'll see if the hotel has a place to photocopy these pages. If not, I'm sure there'll be a place in town."

"Certainly," I agree. As I pull the wig off my head, my gaze wanders to the view below. Everywhere, there are people enjoying the spectacular-looking pool. They have no clue of the scandal that's about to break.

"What are you planning to do next?" Dominic asks me.

I turn to him and shrug. "Now that we have that file, I don't think there's any reason to stick around. In fact, I'd prefer to get out of here fairly quickly—in case Charles figures out sooner rather than later what we did."

"And when he does," Dominic begins, "he won't be happy. He'll also probably try to disappear. Which is why I'll have to stay and keep an eye on him. Until I get the cooperation of the authorities to detain him."

I shudder. "I still can't believe this."

"So much drama! But it's exciting, isn't it? Certainly better than hanging around Atlanta." Samera, who is sitting cross-legged on the bed, gets up. She wanders to the table and snags one of the fries. "I'm going out."

My gaze whips to hers. "What? You—you're leaving me?"

"I told you I had a date, remember?"

I heave myself off the windowsill and hurry toward her. "Yeah, but—"

"Stay here with him!" she mouths urgently.

"You said—"

"I lied. Miguel wants it to be just the two of us. Dominic, I'll see you later. *Much* later."

Now I push her to the door. "Don't give him any ideas," I whisper.

"Oh, I don't think I have to help him out in that department. And what's wrong with you? You're about to divorce your asshole husband and Dominic's totally hot! Go get lucky!"

My heart pounds hard at the mention of how hot Dominic is—and at the thought of being alone in this room with him.

"When will you be back?" I ask Samera.

"Don't worry—you've got plenty of time." She winks at me, then takes off.

I close the door and gradually turn around. I flash a

sheepish smile at Dominic, who looks entirely too comfortable lounging in the armchair. Kind of like a lover who's waiting for you to slowly walk toward him, loosening your clothing with every step.

"My sister. She knows how to find a party wherever she goes."

"It kinda seems like she wants us to spend some time together."

My face flames. "I'm so sorry about that. For a woman who's anti-relationships, sometimes I don't understand her."

"I like her."

My eyes widen in alarm.

"I mean, she's nice. Fun. But I don't like her as much as I like you."

The air in my lungs leaves my body in a rush. "Oh, I don't think you should tell me that."

Dominic slowly gets to his feet. "Why not?"

"Because…because…" He's walking toward me now, and I can't think.

When he slips his arms around my waist, I can't stifle a moan of delight. My God, it's been so long since a man has touched me like this. Sincerely touched me. He presses his lips to my forehead in a gentle kiss.

"I need to know," I say softly, "if this…" He kisses my chin. "*That*. If it's real. Or because of Charles."

"Are you kidding me?"

"I just need to know." If I'm going to do what I think I'm going to do, then I need to know if he's attracted to *me*. "Would you have been interested in me if I didn't hold the key to you solving your case?"

He pulls his head back to stare at me. His expression seems to say, "What do you think, doofus?"

But the words that come out of his mouth are: "I would totally be attracted to you. If I met you in the grocery store or at the post office or at a restaurant or at a car wash. Or—"

"I think I get it."

"—walking through the park. Or—"

"I get it."

"—at a sex shop."

My eyes bulge as my mouth falls open. "I can't believe you just said that."

He kisses my forehead again. "You know I'm teasing you. But it was so cute, the expression on your face when you saw me checking you out."

I cover my face with both hands. "I'm going to die of shame."

Dominic chuckles. God, it's such a sexy sound. Such a manly sound.

"Oooh," I moan when his lips skim my neck. I dig my nails into his shoulders. "You're making me very, very weak."

"You're making me very, very hard."

I chuckle at that and hide my face against Dominic's shoulder. He smells incredible.

"What are you thinking?" he asks me.

"Honestly? There's a part of me that doesn't think I should be doing this. I'm married. Officially, even if not emotionally. I know I'm getting a divorce—there's no doubt about that. And yet I can almost hear my mother's voice telling me I'll burn in hell for even thinking of doing this."

"But?"

"But I haven't been laid in a *very* long time."

A smile pulls at Dominic's lips. "Now that's a shame. I think I need to rectify that."

I suck in a shaky breath. "Oh, please do. *Please* do."

Dominic's mouth comes down on mine. I expect him to kiss me senseless, but his lips barely brush against mine. Then he kisses one corner of my mouth, and the other. His fingers tease the back of my leg as they make their way up my thigh.

A rumble sounds deep in his chest as his hand roams over my ass. *Thank God I'm wearing a thong!* And then he's kissing me, heatedly. Our tongues tangle as an inferno of passion swallows us. I run my hands through his hair. I nip at his tongue. He grips my ass with both hands and pulls me against his hard and throbbing erection.

"Oh, God." I grab at Dominic's shirt, urging it free from his shorts. "Don't make me wait, Dominic." I press my hands against his chest as I nibble on his jaw. "Don't make me b—"

He unzips my shirt and covers my breasts with his hands. Through my bra, he runs his thumbs over my nipples. They harden instantly.

I hurriedly unhook my bra at the back, and it loosens. I push it upward, exposing my breasts to him. "Touch them, kiss them… Taste them. *Please*."

He takes one nipple into his mouth and suckles me. I cry out from the rush of delicious sensations.

"Oh, baby. You are…" He suckles my other nipple until I moan. "Perfect."

Dominic drops himself onto his knees before me. He runs his hands downward from my breasts to my hips.

"The way you touch me, Dominic… Oh my God."

Dominic's lips skim my belly. Then he kisses my skin. Dips his tongue into my belly button. Runs a hand along my inner thigh.

My eyelids flutter shut as his hand reaches my vagina. He plays with my folds, slips a finger inside me. Then two. I grip his head, holding it close to my belly as my legs tremble.

"Dominic, baby…"

His fingers are moving in and out of me faster now, making my breath come in ragged spurts.

He pushes my skirt up. "I want to kiss you here. I want to taste you."

"I want you to fuck me."

I pull at his shirt, urging him to his feet. Dominic inhales my essence from his fingers, then puts one in his mouth and sucks on it. Slowly. His eyes never leave mine as he does this, and my God, it's utterly erotic.

I wrap my arms around his neck and kiss him deeply. I press my body against his rock-hard erection.

A moment of sanity makes me pause. Pulling apart from him, I ask, "Do you have a condom?"

"No."

I groan my disappointment. And then I remember my sister, and that she's *got* to have a condom in her luggage somewhere.

I tear myself away from Dominic, saying, "My sister. I'll bet she has one in her suitcase. Or twenty, knowing her."

Dominic holds my hand, not wanting to let me go even as I walk toward the small burgundy suitcase on the other side of the room. Finally, he's forced to release my hand.

I do a quick search of my sister's luggage. I find a package of condoms in seconds.

Smiling victoriously, I turn around. Dominic has taken his shirt off and is slipping out of his shorts. Wow, what a chest. What legs. What a body. I toss my own shirt and bra to the floor in haste.

Dominic sits on the edge of the bed and reaches for me.

I ease my body on top of his. "It's only a three-pack," I tell him, taking one out.

"Enough to start."

"But not nearly enough for what we're going to do together."

"No?" Dominic asks, the question hopeful. He takes my breasts into his hands and plays with my nipples.

I straddle him, feeling like a new woman. "Not a chance," I tell him. I reach for his penis and wrap my hand around it. A sexual charge surges through me. He's large and thick and am I ever going to enjoy this.

I lower my lips to his ear and whisper hotly, "I want you to ram your cock in me so hard that I'm screaming like a virgin. I don't care who hears us."

"Fuck, baby…"

I silence Dominic with a deep kiss, one that has me tingling all over. His penis throbs against my nub, and that's all I can handle of him *not* being inside me.

He must feel the same way, because he moans and reaches for the condom.

"No." I take it from his hands. "Let me do it."

I slither down his body, kissing his belly. When I reach his groin, I inhale deeply, loving his musky scent. Then I rip the condom package open and pull out the rubber. My eyes on Dominic, I roll the condom down his throbbing shaft.

Hurriedly, I straddle him, taking his cock in my hand and guiding it to my opening. A deep moan rumbles in my chest at the feel of his tip against me. I'm wet and hot for this.

Dominic plants his hands on my hips and urges me down while he pushes upward. The pleasure and pain make me scream in ecstasy.

"Shit, you're as tight as a virgin. Fuck, Annie…"

"You're amazing, Dom," I utter. "Friggin'…ama…" My word morphs into a rapturous moan. Nothing has ever felt better than Dominic inside me. He fills me completely, seeming to reach my broken soul. With each stroke, he heals me, makes me whole again.

He plays with my nipples, increasing my level of sensual bliss. I arch my back, whimpering as my head gets light.

Together, we move faster. Dominic's strokes are harder and deeper, and deeper and my God, he's hitting my spot. I'm going to die, this is so freakin' delicious. I can feel my body winding up like a coil, tighter and tighter…

An orgasm rocks my body like a volcanic eruption. I scream, loud and long, unashamed as I convulse and tremble. My scream becomes a sobbing moan and tears actually fill my eyes. I can't help myself. I've been craving this release for so damn long.

Dominic pulls my face down to meet his, and he kisses me hard, his tongue moving as zealously in my mouth as his cock did inside me.

"Don't stop," I murmur. I want him to come. I want to make him come.

Easing backward, I gyrate my hips over him, picking up the pace as I move back and forth. Lifting one of his hands, I take one of his fingers into my mouth. I flick my tongue over it, suckle it, take it deep in my mouth. "This is what I want to do to you next," I tell him, thinking of my fantasy. "Make you come in my mouth."

And then he grips my hips hard as he cries out. His body shakes as he groans and still he pushes his shaft deep inside me. My pleasure builds and soon I am coming again, riding the orgasmic wave with him.

Spent, I collapse on his chest. Our ragged breaths fill the room.

"Baby," he rasps, "I swear—"

"I know," I tell him. "Oh, Dom, I know."

That's all I say, because I don't want to get all emotional. But I think, *Thank you. Thank you, Dom, for making me whole.*

Chapter Thirty-Six

Lishelle

"And some shocking news now. It is with sadness that I report what's unfolding with the Wishes Come True Foundation, a charity that grants wishes to terminally ill children in and around the Atlanta area. Charles Crawford, the charity's secretary, and Marsha Hindenberg, the charity's treasurer, have both been charged with embezzling over 1.8 million dollars from the foundation. Adam Hart, whom we all got to know very well in Atlanta after he began his philanthropic work with the charity, is being investigated for his role in the scandal. Some say the charity began to suffer after Adam's reported marijuana and cocaine use. Glenn Baxter, a pilot with All-American Air, is also under investigation after it was learned that he recently deposited eight hundred thousand dollars into an account in Arizona. Sadly, the entire legitimacy of the charity has been called into question." I pause for effect as I look into the camera. "I, for one, am deeply saddened at these stunning turn of events. The Wishes Come True Foundation is near and dear to my heart, as I know it is for many of you. I've been to many fund-raisers in support of its efforts. I can only hope that the charity doesn't suffer too greatly because of this, as the cause is such a worthy one."

I watch the entire report with my hands on my cheeks, and my legs curled on the sofa beneath me at Claudia's place. Claudia hits the pause button on the VCR, and neither she, I nor Annelise speak for a moment.

Annelise is the first to break the silence. "Wow."

My heart is pounding in my chest. "I know."

"We really did it," Claudia comments.

More silence. I'm not sure what my friends are thinking.

Regret, perhaps?

Annelise starts to laugh, completely giddy with excitement. "Did you see the look on Charles's face? Oh my God, I thought he was going to pass out before they put him in the police cruiser. And Marsha—she looks like she's aged fifty years overnight!"

"And Adam." Claudia stifles a laugh. "Seeing the footage of him trying to run from reporters like the coward he is. Priceless."

"And the look of pure horror on Glenn's face when he's exiting the plane and sees all the cameras." I clamp a hand on my mouth to stop my hysterical laughter. "I can just imagine what his wife's gonna say when this news gets back to her."

"I feel relieved," Annelise says. "And I couldn't be happier—even if I'm going to be totally broke."

I face her. "I have to thank you for planting that seed in Dominic's head about Glenn. I'm sure it won't take long for him to realize that Glenn wasn't really part of the embezzlement scheme, but at least to have his name linked to the scandal, and that footage of him—it's the best revenge. And oh, how shocked he must have been. But, I did tell him I wanted the money transferred to my account by Friday, and the money wasn't there until Saturday."

"Hey," Claudia begins nonchalantly. "He was warned."

"I can't believe I was just in Costa Rica a few days ago. It's only Tuesday, and already this story's broken wide open. Charles is back in the U.S., and he's going to jail."

"Sweetie, I'm going to hook you up with my uncle who's the divorce lawyer. There's probably a way for you to get *something* out of the house, even if it has to be sold because of this whole fiasco. I don't know if it does or not, especially given that the house was purchased before Charles ever stole a dime from the charity."

"It'll all work out," I assure Annelise. "I believe that."

She smiles softly. "I think so, too."

"Ooh, I don't think she's talking about the house anymore—what about you, Lishelle?"

"With that smile, I'll bet she's thinking about Dominic." I sing his name like a fifth-grade schoolgirl.

"He called me today. Just like he did yesterday. Like he did while he was still in Costa Rica. I think he really likes me."

"Uh, yeah." Claudia rolls her eyes jokingly.

"I never thought I could feel like this. So…"

"Sexually invigorated?" I suggest.

Annelise's smile widens. "That, too. But I was going to say, so happy. I didn't realize how miserable I was all these years with Charles until I spent time with Dominic."

"That means he's well hung."

"Claudia!"

"Are you denying it?" Claudia asks.

Annelise giggles. "I have *no* complaints at all about Dominic's anatomy. He's…"

"Well hung," I say.

"Yeah, that," Annelise admits. "And incredible over-all. Even if things don't work out with us, I'm so totally grateful for that night in Costa Rica."

"You got your groove back," Claudia chimes.

"Did I ever!"

"And your sister?" I ask. "Have you heard from her?"

Annelise shakes her head, though she's grinning. "I can't believe her. Says she's in love with Miguel. That now she knows what all the fuss is about." She shrugs. "I give her seven, ten days tops before she's back in Atlanta. But, you never know."

"Yeah, you never know," I agree. "There *are* some good guys out there. And I can't believe I'm saying that, given what Glenn did to me, and Charles to you and Adam to you."

"Because you don't want Glenn or anyone else to take away your hope," Claudia tells me. "That'd be the worst thing of all."

I finally reach for my glass of apple martini, knowing

that Claudia is right. Who knows if I'll ever meet a man that's right for me, but I can't give up hope.

"We always have to have hope," Annelise says. "Look at how much my relationship with my sister improved in just two days? We're closer than I ever thought we would be. And who thought I'd meet someone as great as Dominic already?"

"Rub it in," Claudia whines. "Rub it in."

"You enjoy it," I tell Annelise. "I ain't mad atcha. You deserve to be happy."

Silence settles over us as we all sip our drinks.

"You know what's weird?" Claudia asks after a moment.

"What?" I ask.

"I've gotten my revenge and thought for sure I'd feel so much better. Instead, I feel sort of empty inside. Yes, I've outed Adam, and I'm glad to know he can't hurt me anymore, but I feel like something's missing. Know what I mean?"

Annelise looks thoughtful. "What, you want to go on *Oprah* or something?"

"No, not like that." She pauses, and her eyes light up. "Oh, I know. We have to do something for the kids!"

A warm feeling starts to spread inside of me. "You must be psychic. I was thinking the same thing."

"Something good has to come from all this," Claudia says. "Revenge is sweet, but—"

"Helping out the kids who so desperately need it is even better." Annelise's face fills with happiness. "Oh, guys. That's such a great idea."

"How can we do it?" Claudia asks.

"Some sort of pledging drive," I answer. "I can get the station to back it. Maybe it can be nationwide through the network."

"Yes, yes," Annelise agrees, waving a hand excitedly. "All those children we can help... And to think it's because we were hurt so badly. You'd never imagine it."

"I know," I say wistfully. The prospect of giving such positive meaning to the negative we experienced makes all we suffered worth it.

"This is perfect," Claudia says. "I'm getting teary-eyed just thinking about how many kids we'll help because of this."

I raise my martini glass. "A toast. To us. To the kind of friendship that will never die. The kind of friendship that lifts you up when you so desperately need it. The kind of friends you know you can count on, without ever having to ask. The kind of friends who know that even better than getting revenge is doing something to give back." I pause. And smile, even though emotion is causing tears to fill my eyes. "And to saying goodbye to the schmucks in our lives. To moving onward and upward. And to never giving up the faith that we deserve, and will find, the kind of love that's real." I inhale a deep breath. "There. I think that's all."

"It couldn't be better," Claudia says.

"No," Annelise agrees. "It's absolutely perfect."

"I think so," I say.

And then we all clink glasses, toasting friendship and a fabulous tomorrow.

Kayla Perrin

Author Kayla Perrin has been writing since the age of thirteen when she submitted her first story to Scholastic Books. Since then she has become the *USA TODAY* bestselling author of several mainstream and romance novels with St. Martin's Press, BET Books and HarperCollins, and has been nominated for many industry awards. Kayla lives with her daughter in Ontario, Canada.

Spice

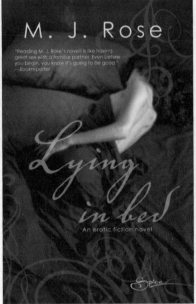

SPICE & BootyParlor.com
live your fantasy CONTEST

**For the launch of our Spice line of books, we've teamed up
with our friends at BootyParlor.com™ to offer you a chance
to win an irresistibly sexy contest. Why not enter today?**

Live Your Fantasy Romantic Island Getaway Contest

You could win a trip for two to the beautiful Jalousie Plantation Hotel™ on the gorgeous island of St. Lucia! Nothing is sexier than spending a full week at this tropical all-inclusive resort. All accommodations, airfares and meals are included! Even spa treatments— nothing's more sensuous.

Simply tell us about your most romantic fantasy—in 100 words or less— and you could win!